WINTER'S END

CASCADE OF LIES
BOOK 3

Cora Flynn

Content Notice

This book is intended for mature audiences, recommended for readers 18+ years only. It features scenes of recreational and addictive drug use, drugging, attempted sexual assault, and graphic depictions of violence. It contains profanities, sexual innuendo, and detailed sexual scenes, including group scenes with anal play, double penetration, double vaginal penetration, frotting, snowballing, and light breath play. The epilogue features Winter and her harem six years into the future, where an unexpected pregnancy occurs.

Winter's End is a direct continuation of the Cascade of Lies Series, and it is highly recommended that you read *Days of Winter* and *Nights of Winter*, books 1 & 2, before reading this one.

If you have read the first two books (and please, PLEASE do!), you know that this is a reverse harem/why choose story, where the FMC does not have to choose between her love interests. The development of an MM relationship within the harem is a focal part of the storyline.

This novel is written in American English by a Canadian author, and the spelling, terminology and grammar have been edited accordingly.

Winter's End has been edited multiple times by multiple people, both personally and professionally, but the imperfection of human beings is a beautiful and inevitable thing. If you notice a typo in any form, please contact me at coraflynnauthor@gmail.com with the subject "Typo Found."

Thank you!

xo Cora Flynn

Acknowledgments

Thank you for loving the world of Cascade Falls so much that you're ready to dive into this final leg of their story like they're your own friends. Winter has become my best friend, on the page and in my mind. She reminds me to be strong, to release the judgments and expectations of others, and to just 'do the damn thing.'

I've fallen in love with every one of her book boyfriends; Drew, Shane, Travis, Cam, and Logan—each man carries a piece of my husband in him, so they were really written to honor the real lover of my life.

This book did not get written without the help and support of so very many people; and truly, without them, this book wouldn't have been written at all.

I suffered a mental break during this part of my writing journey. I was put off work and medicated. It was only my closest friends and my dearest loved ones who knew that part of the story, and they encouraged me to write, checked in on me daily, and supported me in the truest way. Without them, I might have ended up in a puddle somewhere in Thailand.

To my husband—this last stretch has been one tough ride, and you've never wavered. Thank you for believing in me and for believing in this book, even if you never shipped Drew and Shane.

Megan Butchard, for your social media content, time and energy, but most of all, your friendship; it is what made this book possible for an impossible deadline. I am forever indebted to your kindness.

Jen Larkin, you were the friend I never knew I needed, and now that I have you, I am never letting you go. You are my absolute favorite and best accounta-buddy.

Carrie and Emily, my biggest champions and unpaid therapists. I would be undoubtedly lost without you.

A special shout-out to Elle Sparrow and Rebecca Quinn for your unquestionable advice and support whenever I needed it.

To my reading team: Shelby, Paula, Brianne, and for this book, Brandi and Megan. Your insight and input made this book what it is; thus far, my greatest creative creation. Thank you for loving this world and these characters as much as I do. You mean the world to me.

To my editor, Lara. You are amazing at what you do, and your thoughtful comments and ability to understand me at a fundamental level have made this book the best it can be.

To Artscandare Book Cover Designs, for your breathtaking cover. This series is going to look so incredibly pretty on a bookshelf.

To this fantastic, wonderful community. Every single author I have reached out to has willingly shared their knowledge and encouragement. It is the most positive, creative environment I have ever known.

And to YOU, my lovely reader. Thank you for supporting these make-believe worlds that are living rent free in my head, and the characters that have become my real-world best friends. I hope their lives touch yours as much as they've touched mine.

XO,

Cora

To all you one-handed warriors
Who fall in love over and over
Between the pages and between the sheets

Sending you good vibes
And good vibrations

...

CHAPTER 1

You've got to be fucking kidding me.

My brain had to be misfiring; surely a result of my panic attack and the fact I had been arrested for something as ludicrous as prostitution.

There was no possible way Kellan Carlos was standing in front of me. The hulking, beautiful, majestic and raw face of the blond Viking God himself, the man who had taken pleasure in giving me three body-bending orgasms in twenty minutes, was here.

In this room. With me.

He hadn't aged a day in the two years since I'd seen him last. Two and a half? Could someone really age in two and a half years?

Why was my brain even thinking of that right now?

My processing center was a melted mess of confusion and ire as I now questioned whether this was my actual reality.

Quick must have micro-dosed my tea earlier. It was the only logical explanation. And not the first time.

"Are you going to speak, little songbird, or just stare at me?"

His voice was the same familiar rumble, its resonance sinking through me and into my bones. I didn't have a single feeling for him. Nothing more than an obvious attraction to a man who might as well be a god, but that voice could still give me incredible tingles down in my belly.

Still, I wasn't a dainty wallflower. I was my namesake; fierce, frigid, and stormy. I had been snapped up from my friend's wedding like I was a thief with leprosy on a clearly bullshit charge, and pretty or not, Viking Man was going to have to explain himself.

"I'm trying to figure my shit out, Viking," I spat out, unable to smother the irritation that threatened to encase me in a protective shield. "What are you doing here?"

An average-looking man with brown hair and darker eyes smirked in the background—Logan's handler?—I didn't know what they were called outside of the movies— but I ignored him. He wasn't my problem; he was Logan's. Kellan, on the other hand …

The big man's ice-blue eyes crinkled with unabashed amusement, curving his luscious pouty lips into the most satisfied smile.

"I'm glad you haven't lost your fire. I loved that about you."

"We hooked up on one night, Viking. I don't see how that warrants continued thoughts on the subject."

The other man choked awkwardly on air in the background behind me, while Logan seemed to get closer to me on the bench.

For a moment, I had forgotten he was there.

"I guess you made a lasting impression."

Kellan shifted his considerable weight to kneel next to me on the concrete, producing a key from his pocket. He unlocked the handcuffs still holding my wrists. I desperately shook my arms to regain feeling, and the harsh, painful heat of blood flow back to my limbs spread through me. He moved beside me to do the same for Logan.

He stepped back and leaned against the bars of our cage on the other side of the room. I shakily pushed myself up from the floor onto the wooden bench behind me. Logan reached out to help, guiding my elbow when I collapsed on the hard surface.

My body felt like heavy-leaded balloons in need of mooring. Despite my hesitance to use Logan, of all people, as a crutch, I needed someone to lean on right now. I rested my head on the sleeve of his once pristine and dashing suit jacket and drew in a deep, soul-cleansing breath.

A shiver wracked my body as I settled into the inevitably all-consuming cool-down from my panic attack. I needed to start meditating again because my treasonous brain was getting ridiculous to manage. I couldn't continue to drop and freeze anytime something unexpected happened in my life.

I mean, being arrested at your friend's wedding by the FBI was probably a little *more* than 'unexpected', but still. Enough was enough.

Logan shifted, pushing me upright as he shrugged the expensive jacket off of his shoulders. Then he draped it over me, tucking me back into his side and holding me tight to him.

I startled at the kindness, but only for a micro-second as his scent of frankincense and aftershave enveloped me.

He was offering me a peace treaty while we figured out how the hell we were going to get out of this situation. His touch was oddly comforting.

I wouldn't overthink it. I would let Logan offer me some comfort in this clusterfuck of all clusterfucks. Right now, I needed comforting, or I was going to discover what my inner She-Hulk looked like.

Even if, from the sounds of things, his informant status may have gotten us into this situation.

No, I corrected myself. *Dad got you into this situation.* You're being used as a pawn right now because of *his* crimes.

That sobering thought didn't make me feel any better.

I closed my eyes and allowed myself one peaceful second in the silent air to collect my thoughts.

A shuffle of feet made me crack open one eye, only to stare into the bemused cool eyes of Kellan Carlos. *The* Kellan Carlos—a baddy.

He was eyeing me carefully, assessing me. His gaze kept hovering over the point where Logan held me close to him. Instinctively, I gently pulled myself out of Logan's arms and tugged his jacket tighter over me, squared my shoulders, and stared straight into the soul of the lesser-known Carlos brother.

"You never told me you were a criminal," I stated sarcastically, cutting through the thick loaf of quiet.

"As I remember it, you didn't ask for my name until you were about to walk out on me." He cocked one bushy blond eyebrow in challenge, folding his enormous arms across his barrel chest. "And I wasn't a criminal. I'm *not* a criminal."

Logan muttered something indecipherable but equally belligerent under his breath.

Kellan swiped a meaty palm down his jaw and sighed, moving to kneel on the concrete in front of me.

"I'm sorry, little song-Winter," he corrected with a rueful smile. "I didn't want to have to push Darren to this point, but it was the best opportunity to get the evidence we need to take my brother down once and for all. I've been working on all the brothers, but Georgio—Georgio's a slippery snake that needs to be shot in the grass."

"So, you're not ... the Columbian Commando?" I practically whispered the title. Icicles steadily crept up my spine at the memory of reading the news article Logan had thrown in my face after I had spent one incredibly blissful night with Kellan.

It was one of my deepest secrets, one Quick didn't even know. The only people who knew were Raven and Logan. And to this day, I never revealed to Raven who he really was.

Kellan's booming laughter echoed off the playground of metal bars and empty concrete rooms. "Yes, I am," he admitted with a wink, his thick fingers curling through his beard. "But I've been with the FBI for a very long time. A dual player, you might say."

"Great," Logan stated flatly, shifting away from me and glaring at Kellan with undisguised hate. "Then get us the fuck out of here, and clear us of these *bullshit* charges."

Kellan's warm gaze snapped to Logan, instantly freezing into frosty appraisal.

"Logan," he barked in an authoritative tone. "You are not in a position to make demands here."

"I am tired of this *shit!*" Logan stood with an aggressive flourish, wrathful hate exploding from his irises.

"I've been working with you for over a fucking year. A fucking *year.* I've brought you everything you've asked for. Everything,"—he turned to the other man in the room with the contemptuous sneer—"that I *could* get, and here we are, being used again because you guys are *shit* at doing your fucking jobs."

He stalked over to Kellan in such a vicious rage, it took me by complete surprise. Over many years, I had witnessed Logan be cruel, entitled, and arrogant, but I had never actually seen him this angry. Fury consumed his features, and I could see in that moment fury had embedded in his heart.

"So, I'm an addict, so fucking what? You used that over me instead of doing anything for me to fucking *help.* Fuck you. I'm done with this game. I'm lawyering up when we get out of here, and we'll see what the Confidential Informant Act has to say when we rake you over the coals for fucking exploitation."

He ended his diatribe with a satisfied smirk—*that* look sure was familiar—but my heart ached for him. It was a bad day when I was empathizing with the devil, but I had been used for a total sum of an hour to assist with their end game. Logan had been used for a year? Because of drug charges?

So many things were wrong with this scenario.

Kellan let out an aggravated sigh while mystery FBI guy stepped in with equal irritation.

"It's fucking trash like you–"

"Stop." Kellan's voice boomed through the cell and his partner—employee—minion?—fell quiet.

"He's not wrong, Maverick." He turned to face Logan and me, cocking his head in perceived thought.

"I want to partner with you, Logan. You and Winter, and your gang of friends. You're all involved at this point; money laundering, money-running, illegal fighting, withholding embezzling information ... We've known about much of your involvement for some time.

"We've been biding our time because this construction deal will actually open up a window of opportunity for Georgio and my brothers that could take them all down. We know they're silent partners. We know that this would be the gateway to an enormous amount of unwittingly government-funded crime, and we're going to use it to remove them from the picture, once and for all."

Okay—that's not what I was expecting.

"How?" I asked, my voice coming out more timidly than I had hoped. "I'm not interested in being anyone's chess piece, Kellan."

I gulped hard, truly acknowledging Dad had been involved in this far more deeply than my heart wanted to admit. "It's bad enough the people we love are involved."

"By going about your business. Doing what you're doing now, except the amateur sleuthing part—leave the police work to us. Act normal. Keep your eyes and ears open. Report what you see."

I let out a bitter laugh at the notion of normal. "Do you think either of us is going to go back to 'normal' after that little display? Prostitution and bribery, Kellan? The whole town is going to be talking—hard to blend into the background after *that.*"

"A statement will be issued that you're cleared of all charges. It's the best I can do. You were the right pressure point for your father, Winter. It was a statement, and I don't think we'll have any issues with him complying in the future. And you—"

His stare turned glare when he set his sights on Logan. "You were a red herring. Georgio's getting suspicious and harder to read. He knew I was traveling up here, but not why—I've been keeping close tabs on him through someone in his organization. I needed to throw him off the trail, and with your history as an FBI informant—it was a good opportunity to do so."

He grinned smugly, his perfect white teeth at odds with his ruddy Viking face. "And I did you a favor. I made sure the paperwork was signed before storming in, so your wife can get her inheritance. I'm a good guy, eh?"

"I guess you know everyone's secrets," Logan muttered darkly, his gaze murderous as he sat defiantly back down on the hard bench and crossed his arms.

"No," Kellan murmured slowly, a teasing smile tracing his lips. He waved his hand between the two of us. "I didn't know you two were a thing."

"We're not," I snapped.

At the same time, Logan piped in with, "She has other dicks to keep her happy."

So help me, I was going to sucker punch him in the throat.

"How are we getting out of here?" I asked, needing a distraction and an actual answer to the question.

"We've posted your bail at the sheriff's office. You'll be transported back to Cascade Falls, and once it's paid, you'll be released. I've informed the right people, so with the rumor mill, Hillary or your friends should pay it any moment now. It's nice to have friends in high places, no?"

Great. Now Hillary would need to be brought up to speed, because there's no way I was going to keep any of this from her. I sighed inwardly, knowing I was in for a very long night of explanations and serious side-eye.

"Alright." I pushed over to the other side of the bench, leaving a good two feet between me and Two-Face. "I guess we have no choice. We'll wait for the cavalry."

"We'll need to have a group 'chat'," Kellan mused as he gave us one last once-over. "I'll be reaching out via my inside source in the next week." His eyes hardened, and I immediately saw how he had earned the title of Commando.

"Lives are at stake here, Winter. I need to trust that you and your friends are on the right side of this."

He held out a calloused palm for a handshake. I quirked a brow at him at the offer, but reluctantly shook it, sealing the deal between rough skin and a secret history. Logan refused the offered hand, and Maverick and Kellan left us to our brooding silence.

I shook my head at our predicament. We were another fifty feet deeper into the bowels of deceit.

The burden was crushing.

CHAPTER 2

WINTER

"I guess it's a race to see who will bail us out first." Logan shrugged flippantly. "My new wife, or your gaggle of boyfriends? I'll bet it'll be the one you haven't slept with yet … so, that lost little puppy you call a best friend."

The last was said with a sneer; the blatant mask of jealousy and judgment crazy-glued to his features.

Where was the man comforting me minutes ago, who actually tried to protect me from my blind panic?

Logan was the best millennial representation of Jekyll and Hyde.

I sighed, an aggressive burst of air escaping my lips in irritation.

"Are you slut-shaming me, Logan?" I crossed my arms defiantly and stared at him across the cold stone cage. He glared right back, unblinking under the harsh fluorescent lights.

We were transported back to the sheriff's office and led to one of the rear jail cells through a back entry. No one from the department had come to see us, but a sole FBI agent stood posted down the hall. I could only assume Kellan was keeping his distance from the sheriff's office, given that our current sheriff, Ralph Sutton, was one of the dirtiest men in town.

All the other cells were empty; other than our own shitshow, not much else happened in Cascade Falls to warrant a night in jail.

I was reeling from Kellan's news, although the truth of it was he had barely told us anything. How was he an FBI agent with a known crime-lord family? How was he in his brother's territory without Georgio even knowing he was here?

His presence brought far more questions than answers, and I couldn't help but shake the deep-seated uneasiness that plagued my insides. Everyone I cared about was about to become even larger game pieces on a board we never had wanted to play on. We'd just traded one game master for another; I wasn't feeling any safer under the younger Carlos' brothers' oversight.

Logan hadn't breathed another word to me, nor I to him. We had settled on opposite sides of the jail cell, on opposing sagging cots shoved up against barren metal bars, avoiding each other's presence as much as possible in an eight-by-eight cell.

Certainly, we were both reeling from the events of the day, and I appreciated the quiet.

When I said nothing, too tired to spar with him, he continued, apparently spoiling to fight.

"I just don't understand how you can get caught up with all of them."

He made a disgusted face and waved his left hand in the air at the word "them", as in "my relationships" like they were something dirty, and it repulsed him.

"What does that even mean? Polyamory? Seeing more than one person at one time? Orgy parties you'll never be invited to?"

OK. Game on. I smirked and let the venom in my blood come to the surface, just enough to poison, but not enough to kill. This was a hot topic for me.

"Monogamy is a social construct, just like the ridiculous notion of virginity. Sex is a completely natural act, and at some point in our history, men made it a commodity to symbolize a woman's value."

The *Bridgerton* series came to mind in that moment, of all things. The women didn't learn what sex was until their literal *wedding night*, while the men were having sex with 'loose and immoral' women in brothels to scratch the itch. If a woman decided to *also* scratch the itch, if she even held hands with a man in an unsupervised setting, she would have to marry the guy or risk ruining her entire reputation because she was now 'tainted.'

I had to stop watching after that episode. Not that it was a terrible show, but it was an accurate reflection of our history as property, and it made me too mad to keep up with the storyline.

Misogynistic society was my ultimate trigger, apparently.

Logan was, too. At some moments, I caught glimpses of goodness—real snapshots of a caring heart; the man he could become if he allowed himself the pleasure. He was as damaged and broken as I was, and wore a shield as protection—not to hold things in, but to keep people *out*. I could understand that motivation far more than I'd care to admit.

But there were more moments like this—irritating, arrogant moments—where I could wholeheartedly stab him in the kidney with a rusty knife without a drop of remorse.

Well, maybe a speck of remorse. One micro atom-sized speck.

"Did the poor Billionaire Boys Club just come straight out of the fifties?" I continued, using Cam's favorite nickname for Logan and pouting my lips in fake sadness. "If the world hadn't told you that you were only meant for that one special someone, would you still believe that? Or maybe it's just that you couldn't get two women to sleep with you, so you're a one-woman man out of necessity."

I tapped my finger to my chin in mock thought. His honey-brown eyes flashed darkly. I was walking on dangerous ground.

Fuck it. I had already been arrested today. Might as well go for a death wish, too. A good spar with Logan would burn off all of my frustrated tension and kill some time while we waited.

Win-Win.

"Or maybe you're a straight-up missionary man, alllll vanilla." I sing-songed the words with an obnoxious wink. "If you want a nice, simple, sex-in-the-dark relationship with a special someone, that's fine. No shame." I held up my hands in mock placation. "But don't shame me for the orgasms *I'm* getting."

I smiled sweetly and batted my eyelashes. A royally smug sense of accomplishment flooded through me when his jaw ticked in anger.

I understood people had sexual hangups. I also understood how they happened. But no one, man or woman, was going to shame me for *my* choices with the men I cared for.

A guttural growl escaped the confines of Logan's chest. His hand snapped out like a viper's open jaw, and he grabbed the nape of my neck, pinning me to him.

My scalp stung at his aggression; tears pricked my eyes as he tugged further down and pulled my head up to meet his burning eyes.

He took two long strides, keeping one arm banded around my waist. With the other still latched on my hair, he dragged me over to the wall and pressed my breasts up against the cold cinder blocks.

"You're a brat, Winter Wallace. Brats need to be put in their place."

The words held no malice, they held a promise. I was going to pay for my insolence. The taste of forbidden excitement hit my tongue.

Drew liked it when I dominated the bedroom. Travis was my feral equal, and Cam—that dynamic was still being sorted, but I was eager to find out. Logan—it would seem that Logan wanted to own me.

A hot thigh wedged between my legs and held me in place; his warmth and my arousal were a sharp contrast to the sting of the frigid, unyielding wall.

My body lit up in one thousand different places; Las Vegas at night when viewed from a satellite.

I shouldn't like this. I shouldn't *want* this, but—

"I'm all flavors of the ice cream cone, Princess. Every. Single. Flavor." Logan leaned forward, lacing one hand leisurely up my torso from behind. When he landed on my chest, nimble fingers swirled gentle, circular patterns over my nipple, hardening it to a sharp point.

He traced his nose across my cheek in a surprisingly intimate gesture given the way he was currently walking the line of dub-con in a police cell.

His lips brushed over my cheekbone in the tiniest semblance of a kiss, then slowly trailed to the tender spot of flesh just beneath my earlobe. The softness of his dark eyelashes painted across my skin. Each touch was erotically intoxicating.

"But what I really want to know is how *you* taste. Are *you* all vanilla, Princess?"

Panties. Gushing.

His trailing fingers stroked down my abdomen to squeeze my hip, teasingly pushing farther down to the hemline of Hillary's ruined dress. His thumb danced beneath the fabric and swept my inner thigh, getting far too close to where I wanted him.

"How will you taste when you come all over my fingers? When you soak my face?" He nibbled the shell of my ear while I could barely contain my wanton want. "My guess is sweet and tangy, like strawberries."

His hand reached the apex of my thighs and his thick thumb brushed the wet fabric of my panties, making me jump at the shock of electricity the slight touch shot through me.

A low rumble from his chest vibrated through our bodies as he grazed the soft fabric over my clit, rubbing in leisurely, torturous circles.

I should have been pushing him away. I shouldn't have been frozen in place by my need and forbidden lust for a man that for years, I loved to hate.

Two fingers slipped beneath my panties and pushed into me without warning; my greedy pussy sucked up the hot delicious intrusion. I bit my lip hard enough to bleed to stop a satisfied moan from escaping, but the full-body shudder and arch into his body from behind was a dead giveaway.

His hand hooked inside me, stroking my sensitive walls until they landed on that oh-so-body-shaking spot.

"That's it, Princess. Take my fingers like you're going to take my cock. Fuck my hand like you own me. I want to feel your cum dripping off of me while you scream my name."

This was wrong. He was wrong. Then why did this feel so. Damn. Good?

Travis had made a joke last week that Logan would be the misfit annoying brother of our harem; I had given him the finger and muttered, "Never."

Never say never, they say.

Logan continued his movements; one hand pressed across my ribcage, holding me tightly to him with no escape, the other working hard and fast to pull an orgasm out of me.

The practiced, *perfected* strokes of his fingers on my G spot became unbearable. Tingling warmth expanded from my lower belly into all of my extremities as I writhed against him, chasing the release I was so desperate for.

The tension was going to break me, the need to come bordering on painful, and I soon felt the uncomfortable urge to pee.

His teeth grazed over the exposed flushed skin at the crook of my neck. Then he bit down on my favorite erogenous zone of them all—hard.

I let out a yip of surprise, and a delicious heat spread across my abdomen. I came so hard the sound of my own harsh breathing became muffled and my vision went hazy. My pussy gushed its release all over his hand like he'd asked for. The flood of liquid drenched my underwear. And splashed onto the hard floor.

My first time truly squirting had been brought on by my former enemy in a shared jail cell.

My head fell back, and my body sagged against his hard, warm chest as every cell in my body flooded with post-orgasm endorphins.

I would be lying if I said it didn't feel incredible. Impossibly incredible. Sanity-melting incredible to let Logan finger fuck me on the same day as his sham of a wedding.

He released me and pushed away from the wall, leaving me breathlessly spinning. I yanked down my dress. A satisfied smile mirroring the Chesire Cat crossed his face.

He refused to blink as he stared through me and brought his hand to his lips, sucking each finger clean. His nostrils flared and eyes fluttered with each taste.

"I was wrong, Princess. You taste like peaches."

He licked his lips, sucking the bottom puffy flesh between his teeth, and threw me a knowing, conceited smirk.

Hot blood rushed to the surface of my skin despite the chill in the stale air, my panties so soaked I was going to have to take them off.

My body was a despicable traitor.

I summoned my darkest glare and catapulted it into Logan's smug, handsome face.

I was about to rail him out for that disgustingly delicious display of dominance when his softer words stopped me.

"I wasn't calling you a slut, for the record. Sleep with whoever you want. Ride that double-triple dick train. I just think your choice in dick could be improved. I can help you with that."

His eyes betrayed him, the fleeting wisp of longing and jealousy so potent I could practically taste it on the air between us. In a blink, it was gone, and his signature arrogance returned.

He winked knowingly and adjusted the cuffs of his shirt. "When the fortunate Mrs. Eccles does show up, the *real* one, she'll be all I need. You would be so lucky."

I scoffed, my eyes rolling back into my head at the notion. "You wish."

"In all of my favorite daydreams, Princess." His eyes turned molten, and he didn't disguise the sheer need in them. My eyes flickered down to the bulge in his pants. The proud outline of a very thick cock caused my treasonous mouth to water.

What the fuck was *wrong* with me?

Sharing this moment with Logan was uncomfortable. And amazing. And bad. So very bad.

Time to take back my power.

A sultry smile crossed my lips as I slid up my dress, hooked two fingers into my panties and pulled them down my thighs and off. Balling the wet fabric up in my fist, I sauntered over to him with an exaggerated sway to my hips. Then I leaned over and tucked the panties into his pants pocket, intentionally brushing my fingers over his erection as he shuddered beneath my touch.

I stood on tiptoe and breathily whispered in his ear. "A memento." Dropping back to my heels, I finished, "For the one and only time I'll let you touch me."

I nipped the bottom of his earlobe, felt him grow impossibly harder against me, and trailed a line of kisses down his smooth jaw. Stopping at his lips and hovering in a tease, I challenged him.

"You can't control this brat, Pretty Boy."

Going in for the kill, I pressed my lips to his in hunger, tasting my flavor on his tongue. He wrapped his arms around my body, releasing an untamed groan against my teeth. He kissed me like a starving man, and his tongue explored with surprisingly tender torture.

I was enjoying this too much.

When he was perfectly vulnerable and relaxed into the kiss, I sucked his bottom lip between my teeth and bit down until I tasted the coppery tang of blood.

"Fuck!" Logan pushed me off. I let out a satisfied giggle, mentally scoring myself a point.

Before he could exact his revenge, footsteps echoed in a symphony, coming closer down the dark hallway. A uniformed officer I didn't know led the beautiful sight of Hillary in all her glory, storming through the maze. Still in her wedding dress and four-inch heels, she looked a Valkyrie-in-training, a warrior in battle-mode etched into her expression.

If I didn't know her, I'd be terrified.

Okay, I was still a little terrified. But mostly, I was relieved. This beautiful boss of a woman would get us out of here and protect me while she interrogated me for the rest of the night.

And she was the cock-block I desperately needed. I'd be keeping that to myself, though.

"Logan!" she barked, her normally angelic features molded into a severe frown. "How dare you ruin our wedding like that!"

The austere woman waited until the guard opened the cell door before she rushed inside, throwing her arms around me in a crushing hug. She smelled of champagne and rose water.

Hillary pulled back from me, cupping her hands on my cheeks, gaze searching mine as if probing for dark secrets. She'd get them, all right.

Logan stepped closer, managing a rueful look of apology. It was a foreign look for him, but made him incredibly hands-

Stop it.

"Look, Hill—"

Hillary's face broke into a grin so wide her cheeks were going to burst. "It was genius! You embarrassed our fathers so badly; I thought Stanley was going to have a heart attack right at the altar. Daddy was beside himself, profusely apologizing to the leaving guests and offering them takeout containers for their meal. You would have died!"

She cackled with glee and moved away from me, wrapping her arms around his waist before squeezing the shit out of him, too.

"I can't figure out why you roped Winter into it, though. Prostitution? Really?" She stepped back from him and wrinkled her nose. "We need to get you out of here. This place smells like sex and your jock strap."

I wasn't Christian Grey, so instead I just turned 50 shades of red at *that* observation. Trust Hillary to casually bring up my ultimate moment of weakness, none the wiser to my throbbing cunt and sopping panties in Logan's pocket.

"It wasn't a joke, Hill," Logan murmured softly. His gaze flickered to the officer, desperately appearing to not be listening on the other side of the bars. "We're going to need to talk. But not here."

Her delicate, perfectly shaped brows frowned in confusion, but she didn't question him further. Instead, she transformed from her vivacious self to the cool, collected image she so carefully curated for the public eye.

"Of course," she agreed smoothly, her tone now one of professional grace.

She looped one arm through mine and squeezed. "Come on," she mock-whispered. "We can go back to the suite we booked for the night. The lodge is in shambles anyway, after Daddy threw his tantrum."

We walked down the hall arm in arm, with Logan and the officer trailing behind. Her voice bounced around the deserted space.

"And," she continued, with a wink, "you can invite your harem. I have a feeling they'll need an explanation, too."

Yes, yes, they did. I snuck a glance at Logan as we got into Hillary's car. As if he could sense my eyes on him, he stared through me as if in challenge, but without his usual cocky broodiness. He looked contemplative, maybe even as confused as I was.

Me and the guys had lots of confessions to make.

CHAPTER 3

SHANE

My knee wouldn't stop bouncing as I drove back to Spruce Acres Mountain Chalet, the original scene of the crime.

Well, today's crime.

Winter's text had done nothing to calm me; her cryptic message had only riled me up even more.

Snow: *We're released. Can you and the guys meet us at the lodge? We're going to need a group chat.*

The guys and I had been waiting for six hours, not having a sweet fucking clue what was going on. I'd expected the Lane-Eccles wedding to be the spectacle of the century in Cascade Falls, but an FBI showdown where my best friend was hauled off to a secret jail cell was not what I'd bargained for.

Secret, because the first place we'd gone once we finally could make it out of the chaos of the wedding hall, was the sheriff's office, where no one had a remote idea of what we were talking about. I couldn't even lean on Aunt Donna, who was just as baffled as the front clerk.

If there hadn't been over 300 witnesses and Winter and Logan hadn't disappeared, I'd swear we'd all shared a lucid dream. Or the same acid trip.

I had been out of my freaking mind with worry, and I wasn't faring much better now. Watching her barely concealed panic attack as the Rambo lookalike agent forced her out of the room in cuffs had been enough to break me. The agonizing terror at the thought of anything happening to her felt all too familiar.

Drew sat beside me in the passenger seat, equally silent and concerned, watching the dark trees fly by as I sped up the mountain road. Cam and Travis sat in the back seat; Cam, his usually stoic self, and Travis uncharacteristically still.

It was like we were all headed to our mother's funeral.

I parked at the lodge, and we rushed into the building, now in shambles. All that money flushed down the toilet bowl like it might as well have been shitty ass-paper.

Oh, well, not my money. When I got married, it'd be at the base of Mt. Everest or on the crest of a waterfall. Something epic.

I snuck a look at Drew when his hand accidentally brushed mine as we walked side-by-side down the corridor to the bridal suite. We'd had no time to really talk about what happened between us at Haven's Head, but I wanted to. I also wanted to do it again. With my Snow between us in our hot-man sandwich.

Since that hotter than hell moment, I couldn't stop visualizing the look on Winter's face when she came. How she bit her lip and thrust against her fingers, watching me hold Drew's cock in my palm. My heart was literally dissolving at the thought of losing her.

I would not deny my feelings for her any longer.

I pounded my fists on the large door at the end of the hall, surprised when it swung inward immediately.

Winter's tired face broke into a wide smile, and she let out a shriek when I pulled her into my arms, squeezing her as tight as I could without crushing her, and spun her around in the move that was solely ours.

She wore an unfamiliar teal green velvet sweat suit—Hillary's, I'd bet—with her hair in a messy bun and looked more beautiful than earlier in the day. More beautiful than I'd ever seen her.

Or maybe it was just me really seeing her for the first time.

"You've got to stop hogging, man." Drew gently but firmly tugged on my elbow, then held her tight in his own arms before handing her off to Travis, who had his own snuggle before giving Cam a chance at a hug.

Right. Cam was now in on the party, too. I would not let the slight sting of jealousy ruin the moment. Winter's eyes had shone when she told me they'd connected, and I couldn't shit on that parade.

"Alright, harem." Hillary came to the door, quirking an amused brow at the—well—harem of men in her doorway, and beckoned us inside. "Winter and Logan have some explaining to do."

When we piled into the large open room, I took a split second to admire the ornate wooden beams and luxurious fur rugs. Then my eyes settled on Logan, seated on the far end of the large sectional centered in the room, his usually cocky gaze staring forlornly into the half-filled crystal whiskey glass in his hand.

I dropped into the seat next to him as the rest of our motley crew settled into the surrounding seats. As much as

I wanted Winter nestled in beside me, I was grateful she had snuggled in between Drew and Travis on the shorter end of the couch. Cam sat down on the other side of Travis, his arm across the back of the couch, with his hand cupping the back of Winter's neck.

My Snow was being taken care of; if it couldn't be from me, I wanted it to be from them.

My attention turned back to the man beside me.

"Should you be drinking that, man?" I asked hesitantly, unsure of the protocol here. We weren't friends, but he was part of the crew now. I didn't want him falling off the wagon.

He looked up at me in startled surprise.

"It's Pepsi," he muttered, before taking another long draw of the liquid and setting the glass down hard on the coffee table beside him. "I can't even take the edge off of this clusterfuck of a day."

Hillary shot a sharp look in his direction as she sat across from us in an oversized arm-chair, not looking one bit like a Bridezilla. "You've sanded enough edges for a lifetime, Logan. Maybe you just need to get laid."

Winter choked on apparently nothing and attempted to cover it up with an exaggerated cough.

"Okay, gaaang," Hillary drawled the word as if it amused her. She looked around the room with raised eyebrows and a haughty tilt to her lips. "Spill."

She shifted her pointed gaze to Winter.

"You've been keeping secrets, sweets. It's time to share with the class."

"I want to get to today, but sure, whatever," Travis mumbled under his breath in an uncharacteristically snippy tone.

Winter brushed a kiss across his cheek. "I promise we'll get there. Hillary's going to be an ally here. And it isn't just my story to tell."

I felt an enormous sense of déjà vu as our story was shared with yet another person. First it was Travis, then Cam, then Logan, and now Hillary. I really hoped we wouldn't have to tell it again.

Layer by layer, the short version of our story came out; each interconnected piece of Lego locking into place through a series of coincidences, and what seemed like fate.

I longed for the days of lighthearted road trips with Snow and boarding my troubles away. Our lives were getting too heavy to carry.

To her credit, Hillary didn't interrupt once. I watched her facial expressions closely, not exactly sure how I felt about her being privy to all of our dark secrets.

But after her wedding was ruined because of our issues, I guess I couldn't fault Winter for wanting to bring her up to speed.

"So, what happened today?" Hillary prompted once Winter had finished with the flash drive information. "Why did the FBI show up?"

Winter drew in a breath, and her gaze caught on Logan. I swung around to glimpse him myself, caught off-guard by the apprehension that smothered his face.

"Well, I think it's fair to tell you all that Logan's been an FBI informant for the past year. And"—her gaze landed on me—"he delivered your flash drive right to his handler. Today was a power show to remind us who's in charge."

I froze for a split second, my mind racing with all the evidence on that tiny piece of metal—evidence that could bury my father and ruin his life.

"The fuck, man?" I leaped up, feeling betrayed and now straight-up stupid for trusting Logan in the first place.

"Isn't that what you wanted?" His previous vulnerability was gone and replaced by the familiar cocky as fuck sneer. "Didn't you say you didn't know how to deliver this information? Problem solved."

I glared daggers at the infuriating fucker, clenching my fists as an abnormal bite of anger burned through me.

"I knew you couldn't be trusted, you preppy asshat." Cam slowly rose from his seat, his body shaking in a silent rage I had only witnessed in the boxing ring. "You suckling tit of a—"

Winter wriggled free from Drew and Travis' grasp and stood in front of the bristling boxer, placing two hands against Cam's chest.

"Cam," she spoke softly, imploring him with her eyes. "They had him on drug charges and used his addiction against him. What did you say to me once? Desperate people do desperate things? Does that only apply to your best friend or to all human beings in shitty situations?"

My brows furrowed at that admission while I gave Logan another once-over. I didn't like to admit it, but I'd be an absolute hypocrite if I chose not to see Logan as human, too. Even if he was a suckling tit of a preppy asshat.

I lowered myself back down in the seat beside him and fought every urge to elbow him in the spleen. I could grant him some grace, but I didn't have to like it.

"He put all of us in danger," Cam growled, not backing down an inch. "He put *you* in danger. If I have to see you take another fucking panic attack again, I'll ..."

Winter reached up and cupped Cam's cheeks, bringing his face down to kiss him gently on the lips. "I'm okay, Big Guy. *We're* okay. And it turns out, Dad is mostly to blame."

She pulled him back down to the couch and shared how she was being used as bait. Cam's face turned into a stony mask at that revelation, and nothing Winter was doing was calming him down.

"I think Dad's study was—is bugged," she admitted, scrunching her nose up at the thought. "It's the only way I can gather they knew about all of us."

Huh. I didn't see that coming. All of my happy memories of Darren and Dad were melting away as anxiety gnawed away at my stomach lining. If Darren was this deep, Dad couldn't be far behind. I couldn't disillusion myself into thinking Dad had any chance of being innocent with Darren as the mastermind any longer.

"By the way," she added, her lips curling into an unnatural sneer. "I actually was reported for prostitution. Obviously, it's not true and there's no evidence for it to stick, but keep an eye out for the Karen who has it out for us. Someone doesn't like the fact that I'm sleeping with multiple men."

Hillary laughed out loud at this. I'd chuckle, too, if it wasn't a pretty serious accusation. Another instance of societal misogyny. Karen would choke on *my* body count.

Winter drew in a deep breath and looked like she was steeling herself for … something. I was about to ask what was wrong when she spoke again.

"I have two confessions to make tonight." Her eyes landed on mine in apology. I shook my head in confusion. What could she possibly tell me I didn't already know?

She visibly gulped and looked down at her hands.

Drew's knuckles gripped his knees so tightly they were turning white, and Travis blankly stared straight ahead, as if preparing himself for a firing squad.

We were a bunch of party animals tonight. Real rager over here.

"The FBI agent in charge is Kellan Carlos—Georgio's half-brother. I have no idea how or why he's involved, but he knows about all of us and wants to us to work with him to take Georgio down once and for all. It looks like we're all going to be desperate now."

My brows hit my hairline. Georgio's brother in the FBI? A leader in the FBI? I didn't know what that title was. Wasn't he the Columbia King or something? I made eye contact with Travis, who looked visibly disturbed; that would make Kellan his uncle, too.

What a tangled web of fuckery. This town couldn't possibly get more fucked.

She took a breath and continued. "And I had a one-night stand with him a few years ago, not realizing who he was, so there's that."

Hillary snorted behind her hand while the rest of us blinked, dumbfounded. I didn't know the details of all of Winter's conquests, and she didn't know mine, but *this* was news.

"Okay." Travis shook his head slowly, as if clearing it of cobwebs. Right—that meant Winter had slept with his uncle.

That was a weird twist.

"Okay." Travis tried again. "Well, hard to fault you for that when it was so long ago. Other than also sleeping with his nephew"—he cringed at that statement—"is that going to complicate things?"

Winter winced and bit her lip. "I don't think so. I don't have feelings for him or anything, if that's what you mean. I'm more concerned that we're about to become someone else's pawn, and I don't think there's any way out of it. And I don't know if he knows you're his nephew. It didn't come up."

She smiled weakly and shrugged.

"He has someone on the inside and wants us to meet sometime this week. So, for now, we sit tight, I guess."

Logan was uncharacteristically silent.

"I'm sorry this shitshow ruined your wedding, Hill. I know it was a fake wedding, but you put so much time and effort into it, and now the whole town will talk about this for the next ten years." Winter rolled her eyes and grimaced. "Sorry for being my friend, yet?"

"Hell, no," Hillary declared with a grin. "That spectacle will be a pinnacle moment of my life. With any luck, our fathers will suffer aneurysms tonight and put us out of our misery."

She leaned forward in her seat, making eye contact with every one of us. "The question is, how can I help? Other than my money?"

"I think we'll have to cross that bridge when it comes, Hill. But knowing you're on our side is a huge help," Winter said. "We need all the resources we can get. We're running out of people to trust in this town."

"What's the other confession?" Drew spoke up. "You said you had two confessions?"

His tone was uneasy and my heart ached for my friend who'd had to deal with too much change this year. Straitlaced Drew was getting his ass kicked; I didn't know how much more the man could take.

I cursed myself for not sitting beside him. I wanted to rest his head on my shoulder and wrap my arms around him in a big bro hug. Then kiss the ever-loving shit out of him.

My cock stirred to life in my jeans, the very definition of wrong-time, wrong-place.

"Umm…" Winter fidgeted in her stance, and her eyes flicked nervously to Logan's; they stared at each other for an agonizing second. "Logan and I had an—intimate moment—and it's only appropriate that you all know."

Talk about a climactic finish. I didn't intend the pun, but now that it was out there, I was proud of it.

I mean … I wasn't surprised, necessarily. I had watched the change between them over the past few weeks. I don't think any of us *should* be surprised if we were paying proper attention. Despite that insider's intuition, another sting of jealousy shot through my guts.

By the look on Cam's face, *he* was surprised. And downright disgusted.

"I'm going to give you guys some privacy." Hillary abruptly left the living area and headed down some hallway, closing a door behind her.

Cam stood from the couch, too. He didn't say a word, choosing instead to head over to the patio doors, opening them up and stepping out onto the deck. Through the large windows, I watched him light up a cigarette as he leaned over the wooden railing on his forearms, looking up at the mountain in the distance.

Winter stared after him, apprehension etched into her features.

A heavy hush hung in the air as we all looked back and forth between Logan, whose smile rivaled a smug cat, and Winter, who stopped staring after Cam and somehow managed to look both defiant and apologetic.

"So, is this a thing now?" Travis asked, pointing between the two of them before wiping his palms over his face.

Logan opened his mouth, but Winter beat him to it. "No. It was one time, and won't be happening again."

"Don't make promises you can't keep, Princess." Logan folded his arms over his chest and winked at her; the look she shot him could kill a man.

A man with lesser resilience, maybe. Logan apparently had the resilience of a cockroach.

"I can't say I'm shocked, but I've got to ask, Winter; how many guys are we going to share your time with?"

Travis peered intensely at her before his gaze flicked to his best friend outside; Cam hadn't moved a muscle from his perch on the deck.

"I'd like to know that too, Winter." Drew said quietly beside her. "I love you, and I want this. I'm not comfortable with outsiders coming into our family, though. That's what this is, isn't it? Our family?"

He pursed his lips and stood, reaching over to grab her hand and tugging her tightly into his lap on the couch between him and Travis once again.

"My turn to speak," Logan interrupted before she could respond.

He stood from his seat beside me and circled around to the front of the couch, a casual hand in his sweatpants pocket while rubbing his other hand over the stubble on his jaw.

"I don't want to be a part of this family. I don't like half of you and I only tolerate the other half. I care about *her.*" He pointed at Winter. "Yes, Princess, whether you want it or not."

He smirked again, but it was softer somehow.

"And," he continued, stuffing both hands in his pockets and slumping his shoulders in an unexpectedly humble pose, "I'm as fucked as all of you. All of my cards are on the table. I was on a bender. They threatened me with trumped-up drug charges, or I could comply and be a good little bitch boy."

"Now, I know I was being watched and cornered; they probably pegged me as an 'in' a long time ago. Just like they used us as bait today. I was fucked up and willing to do whatever it took to keep my reputation intact. I'm not that man anymore."

He rubbed his neck absently as he spoke, the whole truth finally spilling out of his mouth. I wanted to hate the man who had been a Grade-A asshole from the first day we met, but I somehow couldn't. Winter obviously couldn't if she finally succumbed to his—whatever his appeal was.

"The money I owe Georgio is due a month from today." He laughed caustically. "I won't get a cent of Hillary's inheritance, and Carson was my insurance policy, but now I'm taking him down too, which means I'm still fucked."

"So, no, I don't want to be a part of your made-up gang-bang family. But the FBI is going to make sure we're all in this together and frankly, I don't trust any of you to keep her safe. Especially now that Kellan Carlos, the Columbian Commando, has his eyes on her."

Commando! That was his nickname. Nice ring to it. Catchy.

Not the focus of that diatribe, though. Logan, as arrogant as ever, was at least opening up; no more lies to put barriers between us. That guy needed a hug; one day I might give it to him.

"But make no mistake, Princess. That was *not* the last time between you and me. I don't give two shits about these guys, but I want *you*, and I'm going to have you."

"Bullshit." My usually calm-and-collected Drew stood from the couch and folded his arms across his chest; the out-of-character, aggressive display caused another hit of arousal to spiral down my spine.

He stood toe-to-toe with Logan, an inch taller and markedly larger when they were standing side-by-side. Or in this case, front-to-front.

"I call bullshit," he repeated, his hazel eyes flashing in challenge. "Travis' quick thinking has saved your life twice now; in the basement and from your overdose. Shane trusted you and handed you the evidence to get yourself a nice 'get-out-of-jail-free' card for when this hell is all over. Winter's given you the benefit of the doubt far more times than you deserve."

He released a finger from a clenched fist and poked a viciously glaring Logan in the ribs.

"Who else do you have in your life, Logan? A fake wife? An asshole friend who tries to date-rape women? Don't pretend that you don't need people who give a shit about you."

Fuck me and this man. Fuck us together. I liked this side of Winter's Hardy Boy. Maybe my Hardy Boy now, too?

Travis made his way over beside Drew, the two of them a united front.

"You think you're going to maintain your sobriety without people to help you?" Travis said. "How many times can you call Hillary in a day, Logan?" Travis's voice had gone quiet. My heart squeezed, knowing it would secretly kill him if Logan fell off the wagon, too.

Oh, hell, I should say something too, if we were officially inviting Logan into our Buried Alive clusterfuck family of love.

"I'm not even mad at you, man." I leaned over and rested my elbows on my knees, seeking his eye contact and holding him there.

"I get you were trapped. We're all trapped now. You want her?" I nodded my head toward a very concerned-looking Winter, still seated on the couch across from me. "It's obvious she wants you, and we're a package deal. This is our family. If you plan on being in Winter's life, you're going to have to count on us being there, too."

"So, what? We get matching tattoos and sing kumbaya?" Logan broke out his trademark douchebag sneer and pushed Drew back a step.

"Maybe." I matched his sneer with a smirk of my own. "Put your shield away, Captain America. We're all friends here."

So enthralled by the display in front of me, I didn't hear Cam come back in. He was suddenly in view out of nowhere, his hand wrapping around Logan's throat in a tight grip. Logan spluttered beneath his hold, but refused to back down. His eyes darkened into defiant slits as Cam loomed over him.

"Are you gonna make good on your promise and take Carson down?"

His fingers twitched against Logan's reddening skin and the smaller man spluttered for air. I wasn't sure if Cam was capable of committing murder tonight, but I didn't want to take the chance. I was about to leap off the couch to Logan's rescue when Cam abruptly let go. Logan slumped on the floor, wheezing on his knees.

"Fuck you, Chase." Logan rubbed at his throat as he let out choked coughs. "I told you I would take him down, and I meant it."

"Then I—we," he corrected, "will help you." The large boxer turned on his heel and faced a shocked Winter.

"I'm going to need more time, little violet. I didn't ..." His piercing blue eyes crinkled in pain. "If I'm going to share the woman I love, especially with someone like *him*, I'm going to need more time."

She drew in a sharp intake of air at that confession, tears brimming on her eyelids. In commiserating silence, we all watched Cam walk out of the room, his footsteps fading drumbeats down the hall.

Internally, I sighed and moved to pick up the pieces of my Snow's crestfallen face.

So, we were a full-fledged family now. A dysfunctional family of misfits, with massive baggage and a potential prison sentence.

Sign me up.

CHAPTER 4

DREW

I stared out the window of Shane's truck as we made the drive into the mountains. I needed to stare out the window, or I would continue to stare at the man's sexy hand lazily resting on the stick shift between us.

He had finally gone back to work at WAQ for the last few days of his co-op. Emmett had tasked him with checking on the survey markings for the proposed bridge project. The tender release had been delayed three times, but the final go-ahead was expected this week, so they were dotting their i's and crossing their t's.

Since I was now a jobless bum living on my parent's property, my gracious friend invited me to tag along. It was that, or contemplate my lack of a future for the billionth time, so here I was, sneaking glances at the Native American hottie in the driver's seat, wondering if he daydreamed about me as much as I had been daydreaming, night dreaming, and fucking my hand in the shower to thoughts of him and Winter.

As if reading my mind, Shane reached out and playfully stroked my knuckles on the hand that had slowly inched closer to his in the past half hour.

I looked over to see an amused twinkle lighting up his gray eyes as he turned my hand over and interlaced our fingers. I enjoyed the feel of his warm, calloused palm against mine. Winter's hands were delicate and smooth. Shane's were strong and rough.

I loved the feel of them both.

"Sorry." He squeezed my fingers lightly and smiled with a wink. "I've been wanting to hold your hand since we got in the truck. Is this okay?"

I couldn't help the dopey grin spreading across my face. "Yeah, this is okay." I squeezed his hand back, the fresh memories of him stroking my dick overwhelming my senses and causing an immediate hard-on.

"Are you alright if we take a detour before heading home?"

He eyed my growing erection with a smirk and pulled over to the first arrow of paint on the side of the road.

"We've got ten markers to check over the next ten miles or so. Then I want to show you something."

"Okay." I smiled curiously, missing his hand already when he pulled it out of mine to get out of the truck. "How can I help?"

He and I unloaded the gear, set it up, and tore it down at all ten stops. It took nearly four hours to finish the task, but the weather was on our side. Early April was a crap-shoot in the mountains, but the spring sunshine lifted my spirits and got me out of my head.

It helped that Shane cracked a joke every few minutes and took the time to explain the project to me as we confirmed each marker and double-checked the measurements on his GPS.

An old abandoned mine from gold rushes of eons past would act as the central tunnel for the proposed record-breaking bridge on the other side. We never went inside the tunnel entrance, but we marked out the distance from the current road into the ominous opening, and that had been far enough for my liking. Caves and mines and dark, dusty spaces were not for me.

Cascade Falls was a tiny town, but this project was a much bigger deal than I realized. Shane's face lit up when he spoke about concepts I didn't understand and acronyms that went over my head.

Still, he was so damn cute I didn't stop him. I didn't *want* to stop him; there was nothing in my life that brought the same enthusiasm Shane had with engineering. I could only hope I would find something to give me that same spark one day.

We packed up the truck and Shane grabbed my hand again once we were back on the road. Then he took a turn down an unfamiliar dirt path into the deeply wooded side of the mountain.

"Where is this detour?" I mused as I squinted to see into the thick of the treeline. The forest in here was so dense, the sunlight only dappled the tree trunks through the spruce boughs. I had no idea where we were going.

He painted circles on the back of my hand with his thumb, the gentle touch shooting currents of electricity through me.

"We're checking out the Quicksilver family cabin."

He pulled off onto another road; this one muddier and harder to get through. Flecks of dirt splashed the windows as he drove through the patches of soggy ground. Finally, he stopped in a clearing.

A simple log cabin sat in the middle of it, the chimney stack of an enormous stone fireplace taking up most of one side. It didn't look abandoned per se, but it definitely hadn't been tended for a long time.

Shane bounded out of the truck with a 'whoop' and barreled towards the front door. "Come on!" he hollered back to me, a wide grin lighting up his features. "This is my happy place!"

I followed him, unable to contain the grin filling my face, too. His energy was infectious, and I couldn't stop the butterfly flutters in my stomach, like I was a lovesick 14-year-old.

We were out in the woods, alone. We'd been alone a hundred times before now, sure, but that was before we kissed.

That was before Shane had jacked me off in a public pool, and before I fully understood I was into this man.

And fuck me, I was *into* this man.

My heart thudded in my chest as we entered the small building. The ceiling was a mere two inches from the top of my head, forcing me to duck around the beams of the front room.

The entrance led into an open concept space that featured a tiny kitchen on one side with only the bare essentials, and a round table and four chairs. A threadbare couch and coffee table sat in the middle of the room, centered on the stone fireplace I had seen from the outside, and three doors stood at the back of the room, leading to what I presumed were bedrooms and a bathroom.

The entire building couldn't have been any larger than 800 square feet.

"This is your parents' place?" I asked as I glanced at the black and white photos of smiling faces on the wall.

"My grandfather's," he replied as he blew off a cloud of dust from the coffee table and slumped onto the couch. "Just as comfy as I remembered."

He wriggled his eyebrows and patted the seat beside him.

"Test it out for yourself."

I sunk into the couch, surprised by its level of support for two big men, and laughed. "Comfy. When was the last time you were here?"

Shane leaned back and looked up at the ceiling. "Ten years at least. Dad stopped coming here after Mom's accident." He grimaced. "It was too hard for her to get in and out of the road when her legs were bad. And then we just didn't come again after that."

Having watched my dad recover from his injuries in the last few months and knowing what that did to my own heart, I could only imagine what Shane would have gone through as a little kid. I instinctively reached for his hand.

"I'm sorry." I searched his eyes, seeing a rare pain flicker through them. "That must have been hard."

"It was," he said simply. Bringing my hand up to his lips, he brushed a kiss onto my knuckles. "Winter really helped me through it."

I shivered at the second kiss he placed on the back of my hand as I squeezed it tighter. "I'm glad you had her."

"I'm glad, too." He smiled lazily, his gray eyes filling with appreciation. "That woman's my everything."

"She's no longer just your friend, is she?" I blurted, my face heating at my lack of chill. "You're in love with her."

"I might be." His face turned thoughtful, and I was grateful my almost-accusation didn't offend him. "Something's ... happening, and I don't know what to make of it."

He shifted on the couch, turning his body towards me. "And something's happening with you, too."

He tugged at my hand, still clasped in his, and pulled me forward into him. I could feel the warmth of his body heat despite the layers of plaid flannel we both wore. His distinct scent of pine tickled my nose, and I wanted to bury my face into his neck to smell more of him.

To taste him.

My cock thickened to the point of pain in my jeans.

"Can I kiss you?"

The words came out like a prayer as I peered deep into the eyes of the man currently holding my dick as his captive.

"Oh, baby." He bit his bottom lip, gaze lingering on mine with hunger. "You will never need to ask my permission."

I tentatively cupped the back of his neck, running my fingers through the thick strands of his silky hair, and pressed my lips to his. I licked the seam of his mouth, coaxing him to open up for me, unleashing the pent-up longing accumulated in the two weeks since we'd shared our moment at Haven's Head.

Fuck, he felt good. So, so good.

I got lost in his kiss as he pulled me deeper into his arms. Our tongues battled for dominance as I chased the familiar Juicy Fruit flavor on his lips.

We became frenzied, desperate, as if someone could walk in on us at any moment and we'd be forced to pull apart.

Shane pushed my jacket off my shoulders, his lips not once leaving mine as he shed my outer layer. I reached to do the same for him, my hands tangling in his sleeves as I stripped off his coat and clumsily unbuttoned the long-sleeve shirt beneath.

The cabin was unheated and the air was cold, but there was nothing but fire between us. We could have been in an igloo and I wouldn't have noticed the chill.

I spread my palms along the bare skin of his taut abs, relishing their smooth, solid warmth. Winter's skin was beautifully soft and pliant. Shane was nothing but muscular, masculine strength.

He slid his hands underneath the hem of my Henley and tugged it over my torso and arms, breaking our kiss for the first time. After throwing the shirt over the other side of the couch, he attacked my mouth once again, giving me no chance to catch my breath or question what we were doing.

Oxygen was overrated anyway.

We took turns controlling the kiss, alternating between sensuous explorations and ravenous hunger, chest to chest and skin on skin.

Without warning, Shane broke away.

"Do you trust me?" he whispered; his forehead pressed against mine with the earnest request.

"I trust you," I confirmed, brushing the hair back from his face and kissing the tip of his nose. He grinned the grin only Shane knew how to do; one that lit up every pore in his face, making you question if he was a god or a man.

He grabbed my hands and led me through one of the mystery doors to a bedroom with a double bed, a simple dresser, and a nightstand.

Shane nuzzled me back onto the bed, then climbed over me to straddle my hips. The bed sunk beneath our combined weight, its creaky springs protesting under the strain. I cocked a brow at him.

"I don't think this bed can handle you fucking me right now."

His eyebrows shot up in surprise at the suggestion, but it wasn't off the table for me. Maybe not today, but someday? I didn't know what label I was, but I wanted Shane in my life as more than my best friend.

I wanted his body.

"How about we work up to that, baby?" His fingers stroked down the length of my torso before circling back to my nipples. He lowered his pillowy lips down to my right pec and nipped the tip. I shuddered beneath him as heat flooded through me.

"I know you've already topped, but you may like bottom, too."

Shane continued to lick and suck my pecs, an experience I couldn't say I'd had before, before his words finally registered.

"Wait, what? How did you—" I realized where he would have seen my one and only anal experience.

"You were there?" I asked, my words ending in a breathy moan as he trailed kisses down my abs and dipped his tongue into the sensitive skin of my belly button, making me shiver.

"Accident." He slid his fingers under the waistband of my jeans, teasing my hairline. "But let's just say I haven't been able to forget it."

The raw lust in his eyes turned my cock to steel. Before I could beg him to rip off my pants, he unbuttoned my jeans and tugged them over my hips and thighs, leaving me bare on the comforter in just my black boxers.

"I'm sure Winter's told you this, but you're one gorgeous specimen of a man, Drew Johnson. I want to lick every inch of you."

"*Every* inch of me?" I croaked out, hoping I wasn't going to suffer from this hard-on for the rest of the day.

He licked his bottom lip before biting down on it, the move so hot I was about to come with no help from him at all.

"Every. Thick. Inch."

He slid down my boxers and released my aching cock from its prison. Instead of grasping it in his large palm like I'd hoped, he lowered himself down and kissed the tip of my head. My cock jumped at the contact, the tease not nearly enough to sate my hunger.

He sucked my balls into his mouth, lightly rolling them with his tongue. His hand grasped the base of my shaft and squeezed from root to tip; my leaking pre-cum coated the tops of his fingers.

When he took me fully into his mouth, hollowing out his cheeks and swirling his tongue around my slit, I felt like I was having an out-of-body experience. I was floating on the ancient blanket and even older mattress as Shane electrified my blood and forced fireworks behind my eyes. He teased and sucked and licked until I was two seconds from coming apart in his mouth.

Then he stopped.

"Not cool, man." I groaned, my body so tense I could snap like a bowstring.

"It's okay, baby," Shane soothed as he stood and reached into his pocket. "I want to give you a new experience."

"I've never had my dick sucked by a guy before," I protested weakly. "That's a new experience."

He smirked down at me as he shucked off his jeans and tugged off his own boxers—in true Shane style, his had red Tasmanian Devils all over them—but I wasn't prepared for the enormous cock that sprang free when he stood naked before me.

The hot springs had been dark, and I hadn't had the option of jerking him off like he had me. I had not understood what this man had been packing under there.

Definitely bigger than me, and I wasn't a small man.

I was too busy staring at his not-so-mini-me I didn't notice the shiny foil packet he ripped between his teeth.

"Trust me?" he repeated. The sticky lube of the packet he'd just opened glistened on his fingers.

My heart leaped in my chest; I swallowed heavily and nodded in eager anticipation.

"Come here, baby." He beckoned me from my lying down position on the bed. I sat up and scooted down to the end closer to him.

He reached for my cock, spreading the sweet-smelling lube all over my head and shaft. My pulse hammered in my ears as his own cock bobbed in front of my face.

"Stand up."

The murmur was soft, but it was a command. I stood, our naked bodies not even an inch apart. The tip of his dick brushed mine and the contact nearly made me jump out of my skin.

Shane's eyes stared into mine as he grabbed my cock and pressed it against his, his large hand holding both of us in a vise grip. He pumped up and down our lengths, the slippery warmth of him a sharp contrast to his tight hold.

I was going to come in seconds. Micro-seconds.

"Fuck, you feel so good, baby."

His words came out between sharp pants as he took my mouth with his own. Our tongues danced as I writhed against his body, our cocks moving to the same rhythm.

"You're doing so good for me, baby. You're going to look so good when you come for me."

Fuck, this was hot. Maybe I had a praise kink, too? Winter and Shane were opening up a whole new level of sex for me, and I was here for it.

His other hand cupped my ass cheek and squeezed, forcing me to rut faster into his hand. His fingers skirted over my glutes before circling around my hole, teasing me in a way I'd never experienced.

He pressed into me, pushing through the ring of muscle and curving his finger inward. The spike of pleasure was so sharp, I was a goner.

He glided his thumb over our cockheads together, the swipe over my slit and his finger in my ass enough to make me detonate.

"Fuuuuuuuuuuuuck." I whimpered into his mouth as cum forced its way up my abdomen and covered my chest.

Shane's answering moan forced more jets of cum to coat our skin, as he exploded all over me, too.

I brought my hand up to our chests, smearing the sticky fluid all over our bodies and combining our releases into one erotic mess.

Shane swiped the cum from my pec with two fingers and pressed them to my lips.

"Open."

I complied, opening to suck on his fingers and once again tasting the salty flavor on my tongue, but this time, I was tasting him. I tasted *us*.

He kissed me with a passion I had only ever felt from one woman, then pushed me back onto the bed and collapsed over me.

The bed let out a ferocious metallic creak and broke on its hinges, falling the two inches to the floor with a resounding squeal.

Lust-drunk and almost violently happy in that moment, I laughed. I laughed so hard tears fell from my eyes and into Shane's hair, as he chuckled into my neck.

When I caught my breath, I stared into the eyes of the biggest surprise twist on my life—more surprising than learning my parents were criminals, or losing my job to Camden Lane, or falling in love with Winter and sharing her with multiple men—Shane Quicksilver was my surprise bisexual awakening, and there was no way in hell I'd ever be able to go back.

"That was incredible." I kissed the tip of his nose as the endorphins flooded through me.

"Sure was, baby." He kissed my forehead in return and stared into my eyes. "You're incredible."

He shifted off of me and was about to sit up when his gaze caught on something behind us.

Curiously, I peered over my shoulder. A beat-up metal box had been tucked underneath the dresser toward the back of the wall. Sitting any higher, neither of us would have been able to see it.

He kneeled and shimmied the box out from underneath several layers of dust and cobwebs and placed it on the bed between us.

"This was my old fishing tackle box." He wiped the grime off the cover to expose the 'Shane E. Quicksilver' engraving.

"Anything inside?"

"Dunno. I haven't seen this in over a decade." He popped the locks on either side and opened the lid. A stack of old papers sprung out. At least an inch thick, it had been tied together with old fishing wire.

"I've never seen these before." He turned them over, inspecting the worn handwriting.

"Take them with us and we can look at them together." I kissed his bare shoulder before standing to grab my clothes in the next room. I looked down at my chest, slathered in the combined mixture of our drying cum.

"We should probably rub some snow melt on us before leaving, though. No indoor plumbing here, right?"

That snapped Shane from his investigative trance. "Nope." His devious grin made my insides tingle. "I'd love to take you home covered in my cum, though."

Fuck. Me.

We washed up, back-country camping style, and made the journey home, holding hands and listening to the radio like we'd been doing this all our lives.

CHAPTER 5

LOGAN

"I think you should help Winter with her panic attacks."

Hillary didn't mince words as she barreled into the bedroom of our Cascade Falls condo like she still lived here.

She didn't. She had moved out to the Carlisle condo two days before the wedding and had been there ever since. That she was barging into *my* room at 6:25 in the fucking morning would not do her any favors. I was taking back all of her keys. *Today.*

"Hill, fuck off. I had a late night."

"Just because it's our honeymoon doesn't mean you should sleep in, Loggie-bear."

I threw a pillow at her head in the dim room; the woman had the audacity to giggle.

When she opened the curtains to flood the room with obnoxious sunlight, I shot up in bed and glared.

"Fuck you, Hill!"

"Not anymore," she sing-songed, her voice as irritating as the light burning my retinas. "As I was saying, I think you should help Winter with her panic attacks."

"And this conversation couldn't have been a phone call?" I muttered as I pulled the covers off me to go take a piss. If she wanted to act like we were still a doting married couple, she could live the life of a married couple.

Like a rabid dog, she followed in after me.

"Yeah, they're not getting better, obviously, and since you're the only one I know locally who's mastered theirs, and you've weaseled your way into her bed ..." She wriggled her eyebrows. "What a great thing you could be doing to restore your karma and balance in the universe."

I didn't bother to correct her on that last point, because that was the inevitable. I hadn't made my way into Winter Wallace's bed *yet*, but I would be. After that one little teaser of a taste, I would make sure of it.

I cocked an eyebrow as I finished up and washed my hands. "You don't think losing my access to your fortune and becoming the FBI's little bitch boy 'karma' enough?"

"That's my point!" She beamed at me. "Let's reverse that bad karma and get you back in the good books."

I couldn't roll my eyes harder if I tried.

"Since you're staying"—I gave her a pointed, sour look—"I'll make us some coffee."

I walked back into our bedroom and pulled an errant t-shirt over my head before heading out to the kitchen. Hillary had seen my scars enough times, but I wasn't willing to showcase them, regardless. Fucking Stanley would not be part of today's conversation.

I'd been forced to sit down with our fathers two days ago to review the events at our farce of a wedding. Hillary and I had convinced them it had all been an elaborate prank from one of my business enemies to tear down my reputation. Both men raged about lawsuits and pressing charges, and I'd told them to fuck off. Hillary and I would handle it in our own way, through our own channels, before we quietly divorced. Since they didn't have a leg to stand on, and Hillary was about to come into a hell of a lot more cash than the two of them combined, they'd shut up and left it in our hands.

We'd agreed to wait three months before filing the official paperwork. I didn't need any more fucking press with the amount of heat on me from Georgio *and* the FBI, especially given the due date for the money I owed Georgio was just around the corner.

I needed to talk to her about that.

Actually…

I made us two espressos in the expensive-as-fuck machine Hill had insisted on buying and sat down at the island.

"Okay, I'll attempt"—I stressed that word, since I had no doubt in my mind Winter Wallace would not take coaching from me of any kind—"to teach Winter how to manage her panic attacks. But I need something from you, too."

I laid it all out on our marble countertop. My debt to Georgio and the total amount owing—chump change in theory, but it was chump change I didn't have. I explained how I'd tied Carson into the Front Street property to stop Georgio from seizing the asset, but now I needed Carson Baker out of the picture too, given his history with Winter.

A rare look of shame crossed Hillary's face.

"I was such a self-absorbed bitch, then." She let out a long sigh. "I should have stopped that bullshit from happening when it did. Ugh. I can't believe Winter doesn't hate me for that."

"Her heart is better than ours," I said simply. I didn't fucking deserve her forgiveness, but she seemed to give it to me, anyway, in little tiny pieces. And I ate them up like the fucking starved sap I was.

"I don't need your help to exact revenge, but I need him out of the picture. I need you to look at the contracts to see if there's a loophole. And"—this was the part I'd known I'd have to do all along, but it disintegrated my pride to do it— "I'm going to need a loan from you to get Georgio off of my back."

"Fuck off, Logan, I'll just give you the money. I can sell one of Daddy's watches for that."

I held up a hand to stop her. "No. It's a loan. I need it to be no interest and open-ended, but you're getting that money back."

If I paid Georgio every red cent, he wouldn't come for the Front Street property. If Hill could find a loophole to unravel our shell corporations and get Carson off of the deed, I could get my most lucrative asset back. It was a long shot, but it would free me up to exact real revenge on Carson. The permanent kind.

I had already scoured the docs myself until two in the morning, desperate to find something that would give me the ammunition I needed. Carson had asked to meet today. I wanted to walk into that conversation knowing I had the upper hand. Right now, I didn't. And I didn't like that one bit.

She shot me an exasperated look, but shook her head. "Okay." She took a pen out of her purse on the counter and a piece of paper towel off the rack. She scribbled a few words on it and signed her name at the bottom.

"Sign here, please," she directed, and I scrawled my signature next to hers.

"That's our 'legally binding' contract for the loan, okay? I'm tucking it into my purse. If it gets lost for any reason, it's null and void."

I shook my head but refused to comment. She'd get every penny back.

"Send me the contracts later today and I'll review them. And let me know if there is anything else I can help with. I have some karma I need reversing, too." She wrinkled her nose. "Don't fuck it up with her, Loggie. I mean it."

"I won't." I fucking wouldn't either. I was getting a second chance, and Winter Wallace was going to fucking fall for me if it was the last thing I did.

I hadn't had a craving in a few days, but the raw hunger for the delicious hit of euphoria was gnawing at my insides.

Bourbon & Blues was a trigger for me, that much was obvious. I hadn't set foot inside the bar since I had the altercation with Georgio over his letter, and now, the need to take a fucking hit and sink into its bliss was killing me.

I needed a sober buddy in this joint, and all I was going to get was Carson, who was probably going to be high himself.

Fuck.

I debated calling Hill, but thought better of it. She was already taking on a huge favor after our talk this morning, and I would not be the needy addict on everyone's arm. I was Logan-fucking-Eccles, for fuck's sakes. Man up.

It was Thursday night, anyway. Winter was singing with her band, and that would be enough of a distraction to soothe my starvation. I fucking hoped.

Travis was manning the bar as I walked into the lounge.

"Hey." I'd never actually thanked him for saving my life. Though, at this point it was just a bunch of too-little, too-late. I'd give him the fucking tip of his life tonight. "Can I get a soda water with lime?"

His eyebrows shot up, but a small smile curved his lips. "Sure, man. I make one hell of a mocktail if you want to try one."

He grabbed a glass off the shelf behind him and looked at me questioningly.

"Just the soda-water, thanks," I said tightly, in no mood to be accommodated with fruity princess drinks as I desperately attempted to stay clean.

I had a thought as I waited for him to slice the limes. "Is Winter out back yet? I need to talk to her."

He looked up from his task and frowned. "Yeah, she's in the last dressing room. They go on in ten, though, man, I wouldn't—"

"Thanks," I interrupted and tossed him a twenty for the drink as he handed it to me.

She was already standing by the door when I got there, her eyes widening in surprise and then confusion. She looked fucking fuckable in her tight black sequined dress and matching stilettos. It took everything in me not to caress her curves and push her against the door for a quick and satisfying fuck.

Our first time wasn't going to be like that. I would take my princess like a fucking queen.

"I know you're about to go on. I wanted you to know that I'm meeting Carson here tonight. It's business, and I'm putting everything in place to take this man down. I don't want you thinking I'm going back on my promise."

She drew in a deep breath and let it out slowly, closing her eyes. I hated how this man affected her this way. Hated that he had wormed his way under her skin and still caused her to seize up in fear.

Her reaction decided for me. I was going to obliterate these panic attacks. For fucking good.

I cupped her cheek in my palm and her blue eyes flew open, staring through me to the rotten, damaged core.

"He's not going to hurt you anymore, Princess. Never again."

She swallowed hard with a small nod. "I trust you."

She could have told me she loved me for what those words meant to me. If she fucking trusted me, I would cherish that trust like I was going to cherish her. When I finally wore her down and she let me.

Before I knew I was doing it, I leaned down to kiss her. It was a soft promise, one I was determined to keep. She hesitated, then tentatively kissed me back, her lips warm and tender against mine.

"We're up!" A voice interrupted behind us. Winter hastily pulled away and pushed past me before turning with a small smile.

"Thanks for the heads up." She dropped her shoulders, held her head high like the queen she was and shot me a saucy wink. "Enjoy the show."

Carson was already waiting for me at a curved table at the front, drink in hand, with glassy eyes.

"Hey, man." He sneered as he eyed Winter, who'd just walked on the stage looking even better under the spotlight than she had just seconds before. "I see your girl's working the stage tonight."

His insinuation was clear; Winter was not a stripper, not a whore, not anyone Carson was going to harass any longer. I would walk a fine line to string him far enough along to get the payback deserved for everything he did to her, but he would not get away with that now. Not now or ever again.

I grabbed his wrist, squeezing until I could feel the bones shift beneath my grip. "Winter is off limits." I growled. "You don't speak about her in my presence, got it?"

I released him, knowing I didn't need a larger threat. Carson knew what I had on him, and what it would do to his reputation. Fuck, what it would do to his *life*, seeing as he was guaranteed jail time.

"Jesus," the pathetic little Mama's Boy whined as he rubbed his wrist tenderly. "Got it."

We watched the show for ten minutes; me sipping on my pathetic excuse for a drink with him sulking beside me. Oddly, I didn't seem to have a coke craving when I was in Winter's presence. Maybe I was swapping one addiction out for another.

I could live with that.

Her voice was sultry, her body sensual as she sang the words to a song I'd heard a thousand times, but she made it her own. If Winter were in Hollywood, she would have made it by now, instead of singing at a mobster's bar in the middle of butt-fuck nowhere.

It was time to break the silence and get this fucking chore over with. I turned to Carson when the song broke. "All right, what are we fucking meeting about?"

What a waste of goddamn time.

Carson wanted to meet to present an absolute shit business deal with another mob family on the other side of Carlisle, insisting it was a 'sure-thing.' It was a sure way to get fucking jailed; I'd had enough of that threat over my head to last a fucking lifetime. I told him I'd look into it.

When he invited me to the bathroom for a quick snort, it took every fiber of my weak-willed being not to say yes, but I distracted myself with Winter's long legs in those heels on stage to stay steadfast with my refusal.

When he realized the conversation was over, he left. I stayed to listen to the end of the set, hoping to speak to Winter again before she left too, but she and Travis mysteriously disappeared after their last song.

Fucker.

I reluctantly got up from the table of glasses—all delicious remnants of *water*—and glimpsed Cam in the front hallway.

"Chase!" I barked, hurrying to catch up with him.

When Hill had asked me to train Winter with her panic attacks, it had given me another idea. It involved working with a man who fucking hated me, but if it was for Winter, I was betting he'd play ball.

"What do you want, Pretty Boy?" He folded his arms across his chest and glowered at me.

A lesser man would fear Cameron Chase—his broad muscles and towering stance enough to make men cower. I wasn't scared of Chase. He was a philosopher in a body-builder's skin. He could bite me, but he was mostly all bark.

"I think you should teach Winter how to fight." I went for the direct approach, figuring I'd only get a minute of his time before he walked away.

"Excuse me?" His jaw ticked with anger. "Who the fuck do you—"

"Listen," I interrupted, my argument already on the tip of my tongue. "I'm going to work with her on her panic attacks. I have—experience—in that area. But she should know how to fight, too. We're all caught up in this shit, and I want her prepared the next time we're caught by surprise."

He continued to glare at me, not budging an inch. No surprise there. The southern oaf had the temperament of a grizzly bear and the emotional range of a carrot.

"Just think about it. You can use the gym in my building. It's private with a passcode."

I walked out to my car, the events of the day finally taking their toll on me. I had held out—no drugs—and had some help in taking care of some of the shit piling up to take me down.

I sank into the driver's seat, taking a breather before making the drive home. A crushing weight caught my windpipe from behind.

I choked against the hold, the inability to breathe darkening my vision with spots and stars.

"That was quite the display at the wedding." Georgio's voice was cool, calculated and measured. "I wonder what you told the FBI to be released so quickly, hmm? Awfully suspicious, Logan."

He tsked, and I could only gurgle out a response as the hand applied more pressure. I was going to pass out in seconds.

I was beginning to actually fear for my life when the hand suddenly released me. I sagged against the seat, coughing violently in a vain attempt to bring air into my lungs.

"What did you give them in exchange, Logan? It's best you speak honestly, or you will find yourself the unlucky victim of an overdose."

Fuck. FUCK.

My brain scrambled to find the right words—any words —to get myself out of this.

Think, Logan. You're a smooth talker, a brilliant businessman. Think.

"It was a fucking prank, all right?" I spewed angrily, mustering up as much surly indignation as possible. "Bribing an official? You know how stupid I would have to be to do that? They were false charges from an enemy that wanted to fuck up my wedding and piss Hillary off. And it fucking worked, okay?"

I took a moment to breathe. Talk too fast, they know you're lying. Talk too slow, and they know you're grasping.

"They knew I was seeing Winter and brought her into it, too, just to fuck with me. Hillary's pissed at me. Winter is pissed at me, and now I have to watch my every move with the IRS for the next ten fucking years. I'm going to bury that guy."

Silence. The pause felt like fifteen fucking years as I waited for my gamble to pay off. Finally, Georgio's voice hovered in the car.

"I hope that's the case, Logan. I really do. Stanley is a dear friend, but that doesn't mean you are exempt from retribution."

Two car doors clicked behind me, and it took a second to realize Angelo had been the one collapsing my trachea, not Georgio. Of course, the man never did his own dirty work.

The faint outline of Georgio's face came into view in the rearview mirror.

"Three weeks, Logan. Don't let me see you until then."

The doors slammed and two figures disappeared into the night while I sat there dumbly, wishing to fuck for a hit and a fuck to take off this gut-wrenching edge.

Thank fuck, I had a plan to get him that money. I wanted nothing more to do with Georgio until then.

Too bad Lady Luck would not be on my side for that wish. Time to turn my Karma around.

CHAPTER 6

TRAVIS

"So, you love her, huh?"

Cam and I were lugging barrels out of Georgio's cellar again, and I was already coated in a layer of sweat from the task. Cam didn't have a bead of moisture on him as he did most of the heavy lifting on the other end of the barrel as we hauled it up the incline of the ramp into the storage bunker.

He slowly raised his head and eyed me warily.

"Is there any hope of avoiding this conversation?"

"Nope." I cocked an eyebrow and stared at him pointedly. "Tell me your troubles, my friend, and together we'll save the world."

"So, you're a poet now," he grumbled as we moved the barrel into its final resting place.

He waited patiently as I caught my breath before we moved on to the next one in the lineup. I waited patiently for him to open up to me. When my strong and stoic friend remained silent, I tried again.

"Is it still the sharing thing? I've seen the way she is with you man, she's *into* you, she—"

"Do you not see anything weird about this conversation?" Cam interrupted, dropping his end of the barrel we had been about to move and folding his arms across his chest. "That Winter's boyfriend is trying to convince me to become her other boyfriend? Sorry, her other-*other* boyfriend. It's a little messy."

I let out a snort, because he was, in essence, right, but he was missing the point. We were building a family now. Families had people in them.

"Love is messy," I said succinctly, determined not to feed into all the reasons he was using to convince himself not to give this thing with Winter a shot. I pushed up my end of the barrel, now noticeably heavier without Cam's help. "Life is messy. Love and life are messy, Cam."

"Thanks, Aristotle." Cam muttered dryly as he moved to grab his end again. The early-onset arthritis I was surely developing eased a bit with his hold.

"Okay, tell you what." I acquiesced, knowing if I got him in a surly mood now, my bones and joints were going to suffer from his half-assed help for the rest of the afternoon. "I'm not going to spend any more time trying to convince you. I want you to marinate on this: you said, *out loud'*—I obnoxiously enunciated that part for effect, because I needed to get through to my stubborn friend somehow —"that Winter was the woman you loved. How many women have you let yourself love in your life, Cam? Are you willing to walk away from that, even if it involves some sharing?"

I refused to stop staring at the top of his shiny, shaved head until he finally looked up and back at me.

"I promise you, man, she's still all in with me, just like I am her. That part doesn't change."

He swallowed hard and managed a small head nod before shifting his weight and clearing his throat, signaling the conversation was over.

Well, okay then.

We shuffled down the concrete pad for another minute before I opened my mouth again, consequences be damned. He wasn't going to like me very much after this next conversation, but we only had four barrels left, anyway. I'd take the risk.

"I know you can't stand Logan, man, but it looks like he might be here to stay, too."

A 'harumpf' was all I got as Cam eased the barrel into the next opening.

Since it wasn't an outright curse, I continued.

"I'm not thrilled to have him permanently around, either. I don't know if you've noticed, but our girl likes to collect wounded men and nurse them back to health."

I pointed to myself.

"I'm wounded." A finger in his direction. "You're wounded.

"And he's wounded. In some ways, worse than us. Addiction is a cruel mistress."

My heart squeezed at that admission, because didn't I know it. I supposed I was lucky that I hadn't inherited Matthew Balcom's—or should I say, *Matteo Banderas'*—addiction genes, but Devon's addictions had changed the course of my life for the worse.

My brother had been home for six weeks, and so far, there were no signs of drug use to speak of. I hadn't realized how heavy the heart I was carrying around in my chest was when most of my time was spent worrying about the man. The newfound lightness was exhilarating, but I'd be lying if

I said I wasn't waiting for the other shoe to drop. I hoped that was just my bitter soul talking rather than what would become our actual reality.

My thoughts shifted to the weird exchange I had with him last night. I had invited him out to dinner with Winter and me to get to know her better, and he'd refused, saying 'he didn't think being around her was a good idea.'

Maybe his God-swayed brain thought polyamory was contagious.

"I hear what you're saying, brother."

Cam cut into my contemplative fog. I turned to catch him staring at me, those piercing blues serious and forlorn.

"Give me time. I'm not willing to lose her. I just don't know where I fit." He swallowed hard and broke his stare, turning around to pull at the last of the barrels.

Before he could lift the godforsaken knee-killer, I put a palm on his arm and squeezed.

"You fit with us, man. Our family."

He didn't say another word for the rest of the shift, and his gaze stayed lost in his own collection of doubts, resolve, and baggage.

"Travis, may I speak to you, please?"

Janet's small form barely filled out the doorway to the staff locker room as she held her familiar leather-bound notebook between her palms.

I looked around the empty space and shrugged amicably. "Sure, Janet. What's up?"

The woman ducked into the co-ed room and made a bee-line for the darkened corner in the back beside the entrance to the staff showers. She beckoned me over with her hand.

Confused, I stood from the bench and made my way over, stopping only when she held up her palm in the universal signal.

Instantly, her entire demeanor transformed from the prim, subservient assistant I knew to someone I didn't recognize. Her spine straightened, her thin lips took on a grim determination, and she removed her large round glasses to look me in the eye.

"This is one of the few spots on the inside without cameras, but we've got to be quick. I have a location for you."

She removed a ripped sheet of looseleaf from her notebook and crumpled it in her fist, handing it over to me as she continued to assess the room behind us.

"He's in Carlisle tonight. Meet him at that location at ten o'clock and bring your group. He says you'll know who."

I looked at my watch—it was already past six, and Carlisle was over an hour away.

I swallowed hard, but nodded quickly. Ever since Winter had relayed his message at our impromptu group meeting after the wedding, we'd been waiting for Kellan's call. I figured we'd have a couple of days to prepare, though, not mere *hours.*

"I'll be your point of contact between you. Never approach me; I'll approach you. You must not share my identity with anyone. Not even your friends. I've worked too long and hard to get here, and we're both dead if anyone finds out."

Her steely dark eyes glared meaningfully through me and I took the statement for what it was. It wasn't a threat; it didn't need to be. We both knew the stakes.

She stepped out of the shadows and smoothed her skirt. "Thank you for signing the last of that paperwork, Travis." Her voice was intentionally loud, for the closest camera's benefit, I was sure.

She didn't even turn around to look at me, playing her part perfectly as her kitten heels clacked down the hall towards the stairwell to Georgio's office.

Fuck me. *Janet,* quiet, unassuming Janet, was the mole.

For how long? Was she an agent, or had the FBI turned her? I'd laugh at the ridiculous phrase if I didn't feel trapped in the middle of a C-List version of a *James Bond* movie.

I scrutinized my memories, digging through the layers of brain matter in an attempt to remember the voice on the other side of the locker bank just two weeks ago. No part of me had considered it could have been Janet. Hopefully, Georgio was just as duped.

I stuffed the ball of paper still in my fist into my pocket and sent off a group text, hurrying to grab my things out of my locker and get on the road. I had questions, and it was time to get some answers.

We arrived at the abandoned warehouse on the outskirts of Carlisle at 9:45.

Cam and I had driven together since we had both been leaving our shifts for the day; Shane, Drew, and Winter drove up in Shane's truck. I spied the outline of Logan's Audi on the other side of the lot, parked discreetly beneath a broken street lamp.

No one said a word as we entered the dank relics of the processing plant. A somber feeling sat on my chest, like someone had died.

Or was about to.

The building was empty, the evidence of past uses long gone. Two fluorescent bulbs dimly hung from suspended wiring across shadows of steel beams, and the rest of the room was barren.

No one was here. No one but us and the critters skittering along the perimeter of the stained concrete.

The air held the familiar damp chill of spring, and the building felt even colder than outdoors. I shivered in the darkness and wrapped my arms around Winter from behind to keep us both warm. She let go of Drew's hand and pulled my wrists tighter around her. I breathed in the familiar lavender and vanilla scent that was my girl, and buried my nose in her hair, savoring the heat of her body against mine before this entire night turned to shit.

I hadn't had the chance to hold her since the wedding. Too many responsibilities and worries had weighed us both down since that night, and I'd been craving the chance to connect with her. Especially since she had finally uttered the magic words I'd been longing to hear.

"I love you," I whispered into her dark tresses. She turned her head to give me a brief peck on the lips and squeezed my forearms before we clumsily walked further into the cavernous room.

Each additional step tangled my stomach into deeper knots. My guts had churned the entire drive. Did Kellan know about me? Did he know where Dad was? Would he be able to protect Winter and my boys from Georgio's wrath if this all went to shit?

Georgio had financially saved me more times than I could count, and now I knew it was because I was family. In his indirect and very obscure way of showing it, Georgio had protected me and Devon, even if it had been through extortion and blackmail.

Maybe I'd be spared if we were discovered—that was a pretty huge maybe—but I actually had a card to play, though I'd never want to admit it, let alone use it.

But what about my other family?

Harsh blinding floodlights lit up the center space, nearly making me jump out of my skin. I released Winter and shielded my eyes from the glare when a booming voice echoed around us.

"Sorry for the cloak and dagger."

As my sight became accustomed to the vibrant space, I assessed the looming presence of the man making his way towards us.

When Winter had referred to him as 'The Viking', I thought she'd been exaggerating, but the title fit. Tall, broad, blond, and looking a little like Thor with shorter hair, Kellan Carlos could have stepped out of a *Vikings* Netflix commercial if he hadn't been dressed in a three-piece suit.

"Thank you all for coming on short notice."

Kellan stood directly beneath the lights. We slowly gathered around him, standing in an awkward semi-circle, with Logan standing off to one side, hands shoved into his pockets like a scolded child.

"It's hard for me to get away sometimes," the big man continued, folding his arms across his barrel chest. "But my colleague and I needed the chance to address you in person."

He gestured towards another man walking up behind him—he was tall and thin, with brown hair and beady eyes. Logan's stance stiffened, and his neutral expression shifted into disgust.

Ahhh. That must be his 'handler.' I wasn't used to having any feelings towards Logan whatsoever, but in the last few weeks, my minor discontent had turned to pity, and now, a sense of understanding.

"The tender announcement is coming tomorrow, and WAQ will be awarded the project."

Shane shifted on his feet, and Winter and Drew both reached for his hands, interlacing their fingers while not breaking their gazes from Kellan.

Interesting. Was something going on in our group I wasn't aware of?

I cocked an eyebrow at Winter, but she just shook her head, eyes locked on Kellan as he continued to speak.

"You are not agents. You are not law enforcement, and you are definitely not spies, but you have proven useful, and you are all closest to the source of these crimes.

"I will not extort you. None of you are under arrest or under threat of being arrested. Right now." He emphasized the 'right now,' as if we all had a future of crime ahead of us.

Logan snorted derisively, but said nothing.

"Georgio Carlos is a plague on your town. He has held you all against your will for many choices that didn't involve you. He is responsible for half of the addicts in this state. His operations help fund weapons procurement along the Western states. He works with my father to support sex trafficking in others. He is not a good man."

Even the rats stopped scurrying; everyone in the room was frozen in place to finally hear this version of the story.

"Georgio's been funneling money into Eccles and WAQ since both companies were formed. Your father's firms have supported these criminal activities for decades by hiding and cleaning cash. Stanley Eccles has not only funneled more than $20 million dollars through Eccles Engineering, but an additional $5 million through his retail stores. WAQ has over $10 million in false partnerships over the years, and Camden's involvement with Carlos Construction is also in the millions."

When Kellan paused, he took the time to stare at each one of us individually; dark blue eyes stared into my soul. My skin crawled under their intensity.

"This was a set-up from the beginning, a carefully crafted narrative to lay the groundwork for a major opportunity like this tender."

Winter's face was ashen, almost green, as she processed this information. When she told us she had been used to turn Darren into an informant, I'd been shocked. I couldn't believe the man who'd served us a world-class dinner and shook my hand with warmth and sincerity was a mastermind criminal.

I still struggled to believe that part, and I knew Winter did, too. There was more to this story.

"With this project, Georgio will dump millions more illegal cash and product into the market. We have evidence that he'll be doubling down on the weapons and drugs side of the business, with my father's help. This is not a small-town operation and it'll affect thousands of lives."

"I don't have any assignments for you right now. I need you to keep your ears to the ground. If you hear anything out of the ordinary, tell us. If you see anything suspicious, tell us. If Georgio threatens you from now on, we need to know about it. He's gotten very comfortable in Cascade Falls and is letting his guard down. We are going to use that to our advantage, and when it happens, we will have to act fast. That's when we will need your help."

I didn't like that ominous statement. Not one bit.

"My identity needs to remain a secret. I've played on both sides of the field for a long time, but my time is getting short."

"Are we going to be let go tonight free and clear, or will be we be blackmailed like we were by your brother?" Logan's lip curled into a sneer; the disgust clear on his face.

Before Kellan could respond, Winter blew out a long breath beside me.

"I won't be your pawn on a chessboard, Kellan." She stepped forward, jutting her chin out in strong disobedience. "Turn my dad, or not, but you don't get to use me again."

"I'm out of the diner." Drew's smooth tenor spoke out beside me. "Mom and Dad aren't laundering anymore, and I don't have any connections that will be useful. But I'm in as a support to these guys."

He nodded his head towards us and I smiled, appreciative he was still here when the only thing tethering him to Cascade Falls was Winter. Us. He could have run for the hills by now.

How far we had come.

Cam's deep voice cut through the shifting sands next. "I need to know that all of our past sins aren't going to land us in jail because of this." He tilted his head, his stare so intense he was looking through Kellan to the other side.

"Everything we did was out of desperation or coercion," he continued, not backing down from Kellan's equally impressive Viking stance. "I'm not sticking my neck out for you if you can't guarantee me we have the same courtesy."

It was like watching Muhammad Ali face off against Thor in a boxing ring. Mesmerizing.

The smaller man, who hadn't said a word until now, walked up behind the would-be Thor and angrily snapped his jaw.

"Who do you—"

Kellan up a hand in warning. The man shut his mouth as quickly as he'd opened it, but not before shooting Cam a savage look.

"You have my word," Kellan said evenly, making eye contact with every one of us before continuing, "that whatever leverage Georgio has over you will be erased when this is all over. But until he has been taken down or taken out, I can't follow through on that."

"You're asking us to help destroy our families, man." Shane's tone was laden with a melancholy I had never heard from him before. It was enough to make me reach over and squeeze his bicep in solidarity. A sad half-smile flickered across his lips in acknowledgment.

The formal expression dropped from Kellan's face and his shoulders deflated on a long breath.

"If anyone knows about fucked up families, it's me. Just know that none of this is your fault, and we'll do our best to protect the innocents in the aftermath. That's all we can do."

He gestured to the man now standing beside him with a open briefcase filled with flip-phones.

"Burners," he said succinctly, tossing one to each of us. "My number is pre-programmed in there. This is your only way of contacting me, and I expect you to use it wisely."

Great. Three phones to carry in my pocket. I'd better not get Georgio's burner and this one confused. I'd mark one with an 'X' or something, since they looked like the same phone.

He pointed toward the single warehouse door a hundred yards behind us. "Leave individually and take different routes home."

My eyes widened at the abrupt dismissal. I shoved my new hardware into my pocket and turned to leave when Kellan spoke again.

"Balcom and Chase, may I speak to you privately, please?"

I had been waiting for the inevitable bloodline conversation. My throat sunk to my stomach, but I bobbed my head and stayed in place. Cam stepped closer to me, and we stood side-by-side, heads up and shoulders back like we were about to face a firing squad.

"I'd like you to take a DNA test."

I stared back in confusion, knowing why I would need one, but why would Cam?

He looked just as perplexed as I did, his large brows furrowing like dark, knitted caterpillars over bright eyes.

"Travis, I think you're my nephew."

When I only blinked, Kellan nodded, more to himself than to me. "So, you knew."

My thoughts churned into a jumbled mess of disjointed imagery. Did he know where my father was? Could he bring me to him? Would I be able to get some closure with the man who'd destroyed our family and ruined Devon's life?

"I'd like a DNA test to confirm before I move forward with sharing any family information. I have the kits here and we can get this done tonight. We should have the results in a day or two."

If it would get me some answers, I'd do it. I was sick of living in a pseudo-state of being; I needed to know who I was and why we were abandoned all those years ago.

"Why do you need DNA from me?" Cam asked, suspicion coloring his tone.

Kellan scrubbed his hands down his face in obvious discomfort. He steepled his fingers in front of his barrel chest before letting out a steady exhale.

"Because," he intoned, his dark blue eyes assessing Cam's light ones. "I think you're my brother."

CHAPTER 7

WINTER

"It's okay to be nervous, baby girl."

My fingers gripped Basil's steering wheel tighter as I drove up through the familiar mountain road that led to Rusty's, a BBQ hole-in-the-wall that was surprisingly delicious and popular among tourists and locals alike.

We were meeting Dad and his girlfriend for lunch. The timing was perfect, truly, with everything else going on in my life. Why wouldn't I want to meet the secret woman my father had been dating for several years while also married to my mother?

I'd be a hypocrite if I said the open marriage bothered me. It didn't. I was angry my parents had kept this major relationship choice from me my entire life. They had been absentee parents, but maybe their partners wouldn't have been. Maybe I could have actually had some semblance of a real home life and a real family.

This was all in my head, naturally. Maybe Dad's girlfriend was The Good Witch, or maybe she was Cruella. My life wasn't a children's animated film, and there were plenty of children like me whose parents had no idea how to love them.

Still, I couldn't help feeling I had been robbed.

Oh, yeah, and the fact that Dad was a criminal, undoubtedly going to jail when this was all over, and I was helping the FBI put him away for said crimes.

I couldn't possibly feel like a shittier daughter than I did in this moment.

I had to have the awkward "No, I'm not a prostitute, Mom and Dad" conversation with them via text the day after I'd been released from the sheriff's office. My phone had been flooded with messages from both of them, checking in on my well-being and demanding to know who'd pressed charges against me.

Apparently, Stanley and Darren had both camped out at the jail when we were first taken, threatening legal consequences and defending our honor. I imagined Logan's father spoke more "in defense of reputation" rather than any sort of familial duty, which made me feel even more sad for the man.

Funny, Logan's family only gave a shit about him when he could tarnish their family name, and my family only paid attention when they felt I'd been wronged. Neither was preferable.

Drew leaned over and rested his large palm over my knuckles with a gentle squeeze, reminding me he was here. I managed a small smile as I kept my focus on the road, determined not to fall apart before the lunch date even happened.

I had invited Drew for comfort, not willing to experience the meet-and-greet on my own. Since he was available and needed things to do to pass the time, I wanted him by my side to enjoy this inevitable clusterfuck with me in all its glory.

Maybe we could laugh about it later.

We would have met at Johnson's had Drew not been fired three weeks ago. As it was, I'd just put in my notice that morning.

Johnson's was no longer our go-to dinner destination, and the nostalgia of childhood celebrations, my first job, and finally breaking through that sexual fourth wall with Drew flooded my memories as I mourned the reality.

The dated diner had become a home of sorts; a safe space. I was losing all of my old safe spaces, but also finding new ones in my men. That thought soothed my soul in ways greasy diner food never could.

James, Camden's newly hired manager replacement, hadn't been happy when I'd submitted my resignation formally in writing, but he couldn't dispute my reasoning.

The *very* public, highly gossiped-about arrest of a *known* sexually promiscuous woman at the biggest wedding of the century, was all people had talked about since it had happened. I couldn't serve a single person coffee without their downcast eyes, abrupt halts in conversations, or curious glances.

I wanted to laugh it off and force steel into my backbone like I'd trained myself to do after all these years, but being the center of the town's attention for the second time in my life was triggering me more than I cared to admit.

That, combined with Kellan's new involvement in my life, and my finals in two weeks, was putting me on edge. I was a month away from graduating, caught in the middle of a dangerous game of criminal cat and mouse, and struggling to wrap my head around the feelings I was juggling for four men.

Fuck the edge. I was on the precipice of a jagged cliff.

"Can you distract me from my thoughts, please?" I begged, tearing my eyes off the road for a microsecond as I searched his concerned hazel ones. "Tell me a story or something."

"Okay," Drew said slowly, removing his hand from the steering wheel and drumming his fingers across Basil's dashboard thoughtfully. "Umm, well, Shane taught me something new the other day."

That got my attention. "Oh?"

"Yeah." Drew coughed nervously and cleared his throat. "We stopped by his family cabin when I helped him with a job, and he, ummmm ..." he trailed off.

I cocked my head in his direction, knowing exactly where this conversation was headed. I was more than intrigued, and heat flooded my belly, picturing the two hot men doing dirty deeds to each other.

The lust turned to discomfort as I considered the thoughts I was having about my very best friend.

"Were you and Quick having fun without me?"

I had meant for it to come out as a tease, but in my agitated state, it came out sharp and pointed.

His rosy cheeks paled, eyes widening in panic.

"Oh, God, that's bad, isn't it? Fuck, I'm sorry, baby, I didn't think that you—you said it was okay, and now that I think about it, maybe you meant it was okay when it was three of us and not two of us and—"

I cut him off with a gentle hand to his forearm. "You did nothing wrong, Drew. I meant it when I said it was okay to explore your feelings with him. I'm sorry, I'm just so nervous, and it came out wrong."

He eyed me dubiously and stroked the stubble along his jaw. "No, I shouldn't have done that. I love you, I'm loyal to you, I—"

"I love you, too."

His head snapped up, and he stared at me so intently I was forced to take my eyes off the winding road in front of me to catch the softness filling his gaze. Softness transformed into a searing heat.

"Say it again," he rasped, his voice lowering an octave as he shifted position to get closer to me.

I giggled. My body felt a little lighter despite the burden I was carrying, having said those three little words back to one of the men who cradled my heart.

"I love you, Drew. I love you, I love you, I love you."

I wished I could capture the grin that lit up his face, like the sun itself was shining beneath his skin.

He leaned over, nuzzled his bearded jaw into my neck, and nipped the underside of my earlobe. Two fingers traced along my chest and down towards my now throbbing pussy.

"I love the sound of those words on your lips, baby girl."

When Travis took control, I expected it. When Drew took control …

My panties flooded at the most inconvenient time as I pulled into Rusty's parking lot. He removed his hand with a forlorn expression, and I couldn't help but snicker at his disappointment.

"If this is as terrible as I think it'll be, I give you permission to take me in the staff washroom."

He wrinkled his nose in disgust as we got out of the car. "Do you know how many health-code violations this place already has? Trust me, you'll come out of there with a yeast infection."

"Gross!" I shoved his shoulders as we walked towards the front door. A text from Dad had let me know they were already inside.

Drew grinned an uncharacteristic Shane-like smirk and pulled me into his side. "I'll let you take me in Basil before we drive home. How about that?"

"Won't fit." I mumbled as the server led us to a corner booth when I gave her our names. "You're too big."

He chuckled behind me the same moment Dad looked up from his menu and grinned widely. He stood for a hug, wrapping me in his arms as Drew introduced himself to the woman seated behind me.

When I unraveled myself from Dad's unusually tight hold, I glimpsed my step-mother-girlfriend; my insides felt like they were free-falling off the Swiss Alps in a wing suit when I recognized the beautiful blonde from Fight Night. Somewhat incongruously, she wore a polka-dot dress.

"Hi! I'm Marcie." She smiled brightly, and I noticed her eyes were a pretty honey-brown, not unlike Logan's. "It's nice to meet you."

Marcie and Miranda. Nice one, Dad.

She stuck out a manicured hand, and I politely accepted it in a gentle handshake before moving to sit next to my father. Drew raised his brows before moving to sit across from me, next to Marcie.

Dad's energy was restless, his body practically vibrating with excitement.

"We were awarded the tender today." He raised his glass of ale in a toast, the smile on his face practically splitting his lips from the strain.

"That's great, Dad," I replied, hoping I was infusing enough enthusiasm into my voice, so he couldn't tell I'd rehearsed it. "What an amazing opportunity."

"Emmett is beside himself," Dad crowed proudly. "Shane's going to get the chance to work on a world-class project right out of school."

"Congratulations, Darren," Drew echoed; his smile held in place by his own determination. "Shane will be thrilled, too."

We shared a brief connection of eye contact that conveyed the excruciating weight of all the secrets we were holding, sheltered behind thin protections and shoddy backstories.

"Is Shane your other boyfriend?" Marcie cut in, attempting to be a part of the conversation. Her eyes dropped into her lap in response to the incredulous look that crossed my face. "Sorry, umm, Darren had told me the reason we were meeting now was because you also had an open relationship, and I—uh, assumed that—"

"It's fine," I interrupted, really not in the mood to go down the 'open-marriage bomb' line of discussion at this dinner. "Shane is my best friend, but we're not together."

Why did my spine tingle at that admission, as if it were a lie?

"I look forward to meeting him one day." Marcie brightened with what appeared to be a genuine smile on her face.

I took the moment to *see* the woman my father had been hiding behind his skirt for five years. Five *years.* He had dated her just after everything had gone down with Carson. I had graduated high school, gotten my first car, started my college education—how much of a relationship could I have had with this woman if my own parents had sought any involvement in my life?

And how much did she know about me? Had Dad told her about my past? Did she see me as Darren's spoiled single daughter, getting arrested at weddings and having multiple boyfriends?

Did any of that matter to me?

A cyclone of emotions swirled deep in my belly that I hadn't expected, stunning me into an awkward silence.

Drew smoothly took over in my absence of speech.

"What do you do for work, Marcie?"

"I work in Tech," she gushed enthusiastically as the server came to take our orders. I requested the first thing I saw; chicken fingers.

I didn't want them, but I'd stuff them in my face if it meant I didn't have to contribute to this conversation.

I recognized my bitterness and inability to be a normal human right now would hinder my chances at any relationship with Marcie. At the moment, I wasn't sure I wanted one. Would there be anything for me to go back to when Dad was locked up for the rest of his life?

I needed to withdraw some trust fund money and start putting plans into place. I'd need to call Hillary and—

"Winter, would you mind coming to the rest-room with me?"

Marcie's feminine squeak broke into my spiraling thoughts. I nodded mutely before shuffling out of the booth and leaving the men to their own devices.

I led her to the dingy, two-stall woman's bathroom at the end of the hall, my nose wrinkling at Drew's previous yeast infection comment. I'd definitely be hovering to pee.

The click of a lock echoed behind me.

I turned to see Marcie standing at the doorway, her back pressed against the dinged metal with her arms folded across her ample chest. Her entire demeanor changed from sweet and simple to fierce and assessing.

"Honey, you're going to need to pretend better than that if we're going to keep your father out of jail."

I shook my head, dumbfounded. "I'm sorry, what—"

"I recognize you, you know." She walked slowly towards me, a panther circling prey. We were no longer two women getting to know each other.

Unwittingly, I had stepped into her lair and was about to get eaten.

"After I saw you at Georgio's Fight Night, I looked into you."

Saliva filled my mouth. I was well and truly caught. By a woman who was far more Black Widow than Daisy Duke.

All thoughts about a new woman entering my life for the potential better vanished.

"I've wanted to meet you for a long time. But Darren insisted you weren't ready. Does he know that his innocent little girl is playing tag with the FBI?"

I didn't say a word, breathing slowly through my nose to control the panic bubbling up in my chest. I would not have a panic attack; I would not have a panic attack …

"It's okay, honey." I felt her presence in front of me now. I hadn't realized I'd closed my eyes. Opening them, I found honey irises staring curiously at me. "You're not in trouble here. But you are going to make him awfully suspicious with those acting skills."

"Who are you?" I stammered, catching the scent of her cloying sweet perfume because she was so close to me.

She stepped back and plastered a wide, innocent smile on her face. "I'm Marcie."

She moved to wash her hands, even though she hadn't used the restroom. All urge to pee had left me, too. I had sweated my toxins out of my pores. I might never pee again.

She caught my gaze in the mirror.

"Your dad's been my assignment for a very long time. This town has been my assignment for a very long time. If we can do our jobs, I might have a hope in hell of getting out of here."

She turned back around to face me, leaning on the scratched ceramic counter. "There is no way that Darren will not have some blowback from this situation. But I've learned over the years that he's a good man who's made some bad choices. I'd like him to have as minimal fallout as possible when this empire finally crumbles down."

"It was you who got him out," I said out loud, understanding the truth of the words. "That's how he made it out of Fight Night unscathed."

She didn't bat an eye, choosing instead to pick some imaginary lint off her sleeve. "I've protected him from a lot over the years. More than I should have." She sighed and folded her dainty hands.

"Do you love him?" I blurted, needing to understand why she'd locked me in the cesspool washroom in the first place. Why else would she bother risking breaking her cover?

"I care about him," she corrected, although to me, it just seemed like semantics. "Darren's story is ... sad." She pushed off from the counter and walked back towards the door. "I hope he'll share it with you one day."

Before unlocking the deadbolt, she faced me once again. "So, chin up. We're meeting for the first time. Get to know me, and I'll get to know you. Be happy for your dad. Eat your chicken fingers." She smirked at me as we left the dank space reeking of toilet bowl water and chicken grease. "Give poor Drew a break from talking."

I followed her in a zombie state, processing the new bomb of information dumped over my head. New information, but I really knew nothing at all. Who did she work for? What assignment did she have? How did she know anything about me?

I looked forward to the day when I was not the last to learn something and had access to all the information the first time around. I was getting sick of being blindsided at every new encounter.

Logan had texted me yesterday, practically demanding I meet with him to work through my panic responses. I had told him I'd rather shove a pine cone in my ass, but now I was reconsidering.

Marcie had just proven that deception and duplicity were everywhere in this town, and I needed all the help I could get to shut down my triggers. Even if it came from a begrudgingly sexy twat-wad in a business suit.

I wouldn't survive this double-life as a half-assed clueless spy, otherwise.

As we walked around the corner, I squared my shoulders, filled my lungs with the fry-scented air, and pasted an enthusiastic grin on my face.

I slid back into the booth and eyed Marcie meaningfully as she sipped the Mai Tai that had been delivered in our wake. I got the message. Fake Winter was about to win an Oscar.

I pushed as much upbeat excitability into my tone as I could muster.

"Dad, you'll *never* guess what Marcie told me …"

Cringe.

CHAPTER 8

CAMERON

I punched the heavy bag with every ounce of strength behind my fist, taking the impact with my legs firmly planted in place as I jabbed the bag again and again.

My demons were out in full force tonight.

After Kellan had stunned me to silence, I had called Darlene. That's what she insisted she be called, so I didn't call her Daisy anymore. I didn't want her calling me Teddy neither. That little boy was not the man I'd become.

Not the monster I'd become.

She'd met me at the twenty-four-hour Denny's at the edge of Carlisle. I hadn't given her much choice, insisting we talked now if she wanted any presence of mine in her life. I didn't like having to give the woman an ultimatum, but the casual delivery of a life-altering truth had been about to shatter me.

She'd texted me daily since our first coffee date. A meme here or there, or a simple "how's your day?" let me know this woman was trying to warm up to me. She'd been attempting contact, at least, which is more than she'd done my entire existence.

I had longed for that contact and the little boy in me needing love didn't take it for granted. I needed answers more than her acceptance in this moment.

Travis patiently waited in the car while she and I spoke, trading his precious time and friendship with me for a simple order of waffles to go when we were done.

Darlene confirmed she'd had an affair with Antonio, so there was a possibility I was his child. She couldn't look me in the eye when she'd made the admission, leading me to believe that there was far more than a *possibility* Kellan's claim was true.

The irony I, the only adopted child to two deceased parents, was about to potentially inherit an entire family of criminals was not lost on me.

I pressed her further, so much so she was in tears for most of the story, but I couldn't relent. If I was Antonio's son, I needed to know why she'd left the way she did; what had he done to make her fear for her life? For my life?

Did her claim she abandoned me to protect me actually hold true?

My Rising Tide of Rage had an origin story. At least, that is what Darlene made me believe after revealing why she fled.

Three strippers at the club where she'd worked had been caught stealing money. Antonio had called a staff meeting with the dancers and escorts one night after hours. The three women were paraded on stage, naked and blindfolded, and shot to death in front of her very eyes. She'd been pregnant with me; about four months, she reckoned, and knew she had to leave.

I'd once read that energies in pregnancy could affect the fetus. Can't remember where a young me would have read such a thing, probably in a doctor's office magazine while waiting for a check-up. Going by that logic, I figured that one act of violence had imprinted on my growing soul, forcing me to become the man I was today.

That or, if I truly was Antonio's seed, I came by my lust for blood honestly. Given the man's capacity for evil, that thought scared the shit out of me far more than most.

I delivered Travis his waffles, and we drove home in a car quieter than a tomb while I considered Darlene's words.

If this was all true, and it was becoming harder to hold on to the hope that it wasn't, that made Travis my … nephew. Half-nephew.

I eyed my best friend in the darkness as he ate a waffle one-handed, looking lost in his own runaway thoughts. I'd always considered him to be family, a man I'd die for, but this revelation was … unexpected.

I didn't fare any better at home, losing an entire night's sleep; visions of violence and death clouded my brain until there was nothing but a dense fog of darkness.

I'd rolled out of bed needing to fight today, but I needed to fight with a purpose. I couldn't erase the demons in my head, but decided I could channel them for an act of good, if that was even possible.

I made it through a shift at Bourbon & Blues and then texted Winter to meet me at Logan's condo. I pounded into the boxing equipment in the back corner of the private space. It wasn't the gritty, well-worn set-up I was used to, but it would do for the exorcism I was currently performing.

Logan had given me the keys to the space without so much as a smirk, only asking me to drop them off in his mail slot when we were done.

I guess I could learn to work with Billionaire Boys Club after all.

A chime on my phone and a knock at the door stopped my punches dead in their tracks. I hadn't intended to teach my little violet to fight, but I couldn't argue with Logan's logic that she needed to know how to protect herself better.

I needed my little violet safe more than I needed to quell the rage inside of me.

I toweled off my sweaty shoulders, having abandoned my t-shirt long ago, and drew a long pull from my water bottle before moving to open the door.

My spitfire of a woman had one hand on her hip and a scowl on her face as she looked up from her phone; whatever she was about to say fell from her mouth as her lips popped open like a baby guppy.

"Sometimes, I forget how hot you are," she said, inhaling sharply as she pushed past me into the sterile gym. Her workout bag bobbed against her plump rear as she stalked towards the back of the room.

The caveman in me preened, while the educated man in me stood still. I'd confessed to this woman I loved her in front of a crowd of men who also loved her, but I didn't know how to move forward from that admission. Especially since I still struggled to touch her, not knowing my place in her world.

Travis's words hadn't been lost on me, but it wasn't as simple as opening my heart to let her love me. I needed to open my heart to let *them* love *her*, too, and the man who needed his own love and attention didn't know how to do that.

Winter whipped off her school sweater to reveal a black sports bra that matched her skin-tight workout leggings. My traitorous cock roused from its slumber and I fought like hell to put him back to sleep.

This would not work if I couldn't tame him into submission tonight.

What I'd give to have her tame *me* into submission.
Not helping.

"So, how does this work?" Winter asked as she moved to the mats beside the stand-alone punching bags.

When she stretched into a lunge and brought her arms over her head, the move surprised me. Winter wasn't a big woman, but she had wide hips, thick thighs, and a sizeable ass. Traits I wouldn't have considered for great flexibility. Her body was more limber than I expected, and that thought contributed to the now-solid cock in my shorts.

"We're going to take this slow," I explained patiently, moving beside her to do some of my own stretches, even though I was thoroughly warmed up. "I'll teach you some basic techniques tonight, and we'll practice them until you're comfortable. Next time, we'll build on that."

Winter smirked. A devilish glint entered her blue-green eyes. "I'm used to you taking it slow, Cam. Sounds about right to me."

Her sassiness did not rile me up. A deep sense of calm washed over me and I reached for the rolled hand wraps on the edge of the mat.

"You're in my territory now." I unwrapped the long ropes of material and motioned for her hand. Her palm soft and warm beneath my fingers, I steadily swathed her knuckles in the cotton fabric. "I'd be more careful with my words."

I reached for her second hand and wrapped it like the first. Her heat and the lavender scent of her soap overwhelmed my senses as I fought my body for control.

Her breath caught when I moved in closer and tightened my grip on her fingers with just enough pressure to exert dominance in my space. This was about her safety, and we would not make light of it.

I released her hand and walked backwards, putting distance between us.

"I want you to copy my movements."

I stood in a fighting stance, legs slightly wider than hip-width apart, dominant leg slightly forward.

"Your power in boxing comes from your legs and your core. I'm going to teach you a few boxing moves that are translatable in protecting yourself in a street fight."

She raised her eyebrows dubiously. "In a street fight?"

"When someone comes at you with no ground rules with intent to harm, yeah." I shrugged, the stickiness of the dried sweat chafing along my hand wraps. "That's why we're here, so you can protect yourself when we can't."

"There's a 'we' now, is there?" Another dubious look. Then, more softly, she asked, "Is there a 'we', Cam?"

I had walked into that one, and it was a question I still didn't have the answer to.

"Let's get through this lesson." I handed her a small set of electric blue boxing gloves I had picked up from the sporting goods store earlier that day. "Then we can talk."

Winter scrunched her eyes into little slits and bit her lip in a way that ignited the urge to sweep her up in to my arms and smooth her frown; I held back, though, determined to make it through my promise to her before diving into that pool of muck.

I taught, and she listened. Her dodges and punches became stronger as she caught on to the movements. We were only covering basic maneuvers; I wasn't willing to get her hurt by introducing techniques too advanced too soon, but she surprised me with her agility and strength.

My little violet was so much more than her beautiful face.

We stopped for a water break, the sun long since set behind the mountains. She lay flat on her back on the mat, knees spread open, revealing the patch of sweat between her thighs.

Her hair had fallen out of her messy bun, the flattened tendrils framing her chin. Her face was flushed a deep pink, and her chest rose and fell as rapid breaths filled her lungs.

Winter was temptation embodied, and I was just a lowly mortal man.

Whether another man's spirit entered my body and possessed me, or I lost all human strength to resist her anymore, I couldn't be sure. By the time I had come to my senses, I'd dropped to my knees in front of her, my body kneeled between her legs, and my lips hovered over hers.

"Kiss me, Cam."

Her whisper sent my senses into overdrive, and I was useless to resist any longer.

I molded my lips against hers, needing to claim this woman more intoxicating than any liquor I'd ever tasted. Her body arched into me, grinding against my erection with an urgency that matched mine; I pressed myself deeper into her. The resounding moan that bounced off the walls and settled deep into the head of my cock spurned me on.

I broke the kiss, yanked her sports bra over her head, and deftly secured her wrists in place with it. She wriggled on the mat beneath me and her eyes hooded with lust. Her breasts pushed out perkily as she tested my makeshift restraints.

I placed a large hand over each breast and kneaded her plump flesh as her nipples hardened against my palms. I bent over, enveloped one nipple with my mouth, sucking hard, then softly nibbled before turning my attention to its sister.

"Cam," she said breathily. The soft whimper of pleasure escaped her lips as I gave her body all of my attention. I tasted the salt of sweat on her skin and my primal need to take her then and there kicked into high gear.

I yanked down her leggings and the simple cotton thong, exposing her to my greedy eyes. She shimmied my shorts down my legs with her feet, her hands still tied up above her head and leaving her helpless to my ministrations.

I held my tip at her entrance, gaze probing her for the permission I so badly needed before entering. The teasing warmth of her wetness against my head made me shudder, my desire so strong for her I was lost to its power.

"I have an IUD. If you're clear, and willing to have all of me, and all that comes with that, fuck me, Cam," she begged.

I didn't need to say the words out loud. My admission at the lodge and my resolve to have her now were answer enough. I loved this woman. Somehow, I would figure out where I fit into her world.

I thrust into her, sinking as far as my cock could reach, before pulling out and thrusting in again. We groaned together at the connection. Her pussy clamped around me so tightly, I had to breathe through the sensation to keep from coming too quickly.

I wrapped her legs around my waist and pounded into her with a punishing pace, releasing the demons from my soul into hers. She took me and my demons insatiably, grinding against my hips with every thrust, matching my energy with her own.

My little violet surprised me when her hand came to my chest. She had found a way out of my restraints. She used my moment of shock to flip us over, straddling me with my cock still inside her.

A wicked grin traveled across her face as she held the sports bra between her fingers; her own demons wanted to play.

"Payback," she chided lightly, grabbing my wrists and tying my hands together in front of me while she continued to grind against me in a fiendish rhythm.

Shivers rippled through me as I held myself at her mercy, willing to be used and abused for her pleasure.

My cock swelled inside her, which she must have felt; her moan surrounded me in a blanket of dark desire.

"Oh, you like being tied up, do you, Big Guy?" She raked her nails along my chest so hard they pierced my skin. I hissed and bucked up my hips to pound into her harder.

"You really are a masochist, aren't you, baby?" She cooed, leaning down to brush her nipples against my pecs, and pressed a kiss on my neck. The soft touch of her lips transformed into the piercing pain of a bruising bite.

All the blood in my body drained into my cock head.

A deep growl erupted from my chest as I forced myself up and into her again, so fiercely she had to wrap her hands around my neck to hold on.

"Ooooooh, baby." She bowed her body and bit my shoulder. The indent radiated a delicious sting. Tingles rocketed up my spine as my body begged to come undone.

"Ride me hard and fast, little violet. I need you to use me until you're spent, and then I'm going to fill you with my cum."

I pulled myself up into a crunch as she obliged, rubbing her clit on my pubic bone as she bounced up and down on my cock. My bound hands nestled between her breasts as she made me a vessel for her gratification. She pressed her thumbs against my throat, increasing the pressure the more she fucked me. It slowly cut off my air supply, enhancing every sensation in my body.

She held me there—not enough to choke, but enough that my vision blurred. She cried out her release and her cum coated me as I finally had permission to fill her like I promised.

Winter released my throat, cupping my cheeks in her hands. Her glassy, sated stare honed in on me while our combined arousal seeped out of her and into my lap.

"You good, Big Guy?"

I kissed her with a ferocity I couldn't tame any longer. I was feral for this woman, an untamed animal that only needed her.

"There are cameras in here, you know."

The arrogant sound of Pretty Boy himself came from somewhere behind me. I didn't react or respond, letting Winter take the lead with her other—whatever he was.

Winter slowly rose from my lap; my primal satisfaction seeing the wetness dripping down her thighs as she stood made me grin in Logan's direction.

He was leaning against the door, a cocky grin on his face and an obvious bulge in his sweats. Whether he had come down here for a workout himself, or simply to watch the action, I couldn't be sure, but there was no doubting what we'd been up to on the mats of his gym.

"I'm the town harlot, don't you know, Logan? Might as well live up to the reputation."

She made no move to pull on her leggings, standing bared and proud twenty feet away from him. I released my hands from her sports bra—the fabric now stretched and ruined from the wear. It had never been that tight to begin with, but I'd indulged her because I enjoyed being tied up and at her mercy. Since that fact didn't scare her, I looked forward to what else she'd be willing to do.

Oddly, I didn't feel as possessive as I had imagined I'd feel with another man eyeing my violet like he was as starved for her as I was.

"I'll get them erased," he said seriously, and his arrogant smirk evaporated into a concerned frown. "I take it training went well?"

Not that I reported to him or was indebted to him for anything in this world, but I spoke up.

"She did well. She's got strength and agility. It won't take long where she'll be able to decently protect herself."

"From bad guys, or your cock?" Logan's smirk was back, an eyebrow raised at me.

"I don't need protection from his cock." Winter leveled his smirk with one of her own. "He needed protection from me."

She winked at me as I pulled my shorts back on, fully aware of the scratch and bite marks complimenting the tattoos across my torso like new artwork.

"Apparently," Logan muttered sardonically as he picked up Winter's sweatshirt from the corner of the room and tossed it to her. "If you don't cover up, I'm going to be the one biting *you*, so do us both a favor."

"You wish," Winter tossed back before pulling the sweater over her head and covering up her beautiful breasts. She tugged on her leggings next as Logan and I both watched with admiration.

"Sure do, Princess. I just hope you end our lessons the same way." He wriggled his eyebrows suggestively and left the gym before she could retort.

I wrapped my arms around her and kissed the top of her head before we went our separate ways for the night.

I'd decided to have Winter tonight, all of her, and the men that came along with it. It wasn't a decision out of lust or want, but out of the unbridled need to have this family in my life, whatever that looked like.

We weren't out of the woods yet, and to quote Travis, life was about to get messier.

But now? Now, I wouldn't have to do it alone.

CHAPTER 9

WINTER

Craaaaaaack.

The deafening rumble of bowling pins being blown to smithereens by Travis' accurate strike reverberated through me.

"Strike!" Quick crowed enthusiastically, reaching up a large palm to high-five my grinning boyfriend, who still looked sexy as hell in the ridiculous clown-like bowling shoes on his feet.

"I'm glad I called Travis for our team," Quick continued to boast gleefully, as he filled out their scores at the tiny table by the ball pick-up. "We're ahead by 50 points."

"Laugh it up, Quicksilver," Cameron called over his shoulder as he lined up for his turn. "I'm gonna channel my Pops for this one."

He wound up and threw the ball, and within seconds, all ten pins were blown to bits.

"Striiiiiiiiiiiiiiiiiiiiiike!"

It was rare to see Cam in a state of joy, and the effect was breathtaking. The man had an unnatural beauty that could stop traffic and make millions on a runway.

And now he was mine.

The surprise sex in the gym had been mind-blowingly hot. I wasn't at all shocked by his pain kink, but I had been taken aback by the way he unleashed himself for me. Cam was so hard to read sometimes, but he'd laid all his cards on that gym mat and begged me to play. The brooding man had held me at arm's length for so long, but he'd finally decided he wanted in; he wanted me.

Only a fool could resist the allure that was Cameron Chase.

The butterflies in my belly came crashing back into me like I was a thirteen-year-old with her first crush. Each of my men had that effect on me.

As I looked around our cramped lane, me, and the three men I dared to call boyfriends, and my very best friend, I couldn't remember a time when I'd felt more content.

Although, I'd be lying to myself if I said a teeny part of my heart wasn't missing the abrupt asshole who had somehow snuck into my left ventricle when I wasn't looking.

Bowling had been Quick's idea, a way for us to let off some steam. He and I had been scrambling to study for the last exams of our degrees, Drew was miserably job hunting, and both Travis and Cam had the family bomb dropped on them this past week.

I was still reeling from the information. I couldn't even imagine how Cam was feeling. Kellan had messaged them to confirm the results over our secret spy phones last night.

To discover you were the long-lost uncle of your best friend, who was also part of a criminal family; the family that had fucked you over hard, and were mostly responsible for the shitty life you were living ...

Screenwriters for *Days of Our Lives* could take a page out of our books and make a killing.

"Winter, you're up!"

Quick's smirk mimicked the devil's as I grabbed a ball and stood at the starting line. I was a shit bowler—I was actually shitty at anything involving hand-eye coordination, and he was going to milk my amateur aim for all it was worth.

Since we were a party of five, Cam was playing on both sides of the fence, while Drew and I faced off against Shane and Travis. Cam had bowled with his pop as a teenager and hadn't missed a pin yet. Travis seemed to have a natural talent for the game. Drew and Shane were decent enough to get spares and the occasional strike. I had hit one pin in five rounds.

I was most assuredly the bowling loser.

"Here, baby girl." My teammate's arms wrapped around mine as he moved my hands into a tighter position around the ball. "You want to hold it like this."

Cinnamon and the sweet undertones of clementine enveloped me as Drew adjusted my grip, his warmth hovering around me. With everything we'd gone through to get to this point, I relished it when Drew gave me his undivided attention.

"No fair," Travis joked as he came up on my other side, scrutinizing Drew's handiwork. "I'm the one who just got a strike." He winked at me and adjusted my thumb on the ball. "I should get to play instructor."

Drew ignored him and wedged his knee between my thighs from behind, adjusting my stance while squeezing my ass. Then he pulled my arm behind me in an underhand throwing motion.

"See, swing through with this kind of momentum." He mimed a pendulum with my arm before letting it go. "Give it your best shot."

He and Travis both stepped back, probably worried about getting a bowling ball to the crotch. I winced internally; my last shot had gone wide and bounced into the other lane. Harold was going to kick us out if I couldn't get my shit together, and that would just be embarrassing.

I filled up my lungs, swung the ball like Drew had shown me, and released. I closed my eyes in complete anticipation of another bowling pin failure.

When I heard the hollow echo of a pin falling, I opened them to see that pin followed by another.

"Great job, beautiful!"

Three pins had fallen to their deaths and were being herded into the metal scoop to be re-positioned.

Travis' kiwi-green eyes flashed with triumph as he spun me around and pulled me into his arms. He kissed me quickly, but thoroughly enough that prickles of tingling heat shot up my spine.

He rubbed his hands down my shoulders and grinned. "I'll recruit you to my team next round. Then I can play teacher."

"I'll role-play anytime you want, HB." I licked my lips and winked suggestively. My sexy bartender's pupils dilated; his gaze flooded with a possessive heat.

We'd definitely be exploring *that* opportunity later.

"I thought I was your Hardy Boy?" Drew questioned as he plopped himself down in the seat next to Quick.

"Hottie Bartender," I quipped, settling into Cam's lap on the adjacent bench as he pulled me down into his arms. "I have two HB's. I'm a lucky gal."

Cam placed a gentle kiss at the crook of my neck; his soft sandalwood scent tickled my nostrils, reminding me he was finally holding me as his. I snuggled into his warmth, enjoying it thoroughly and freely, and watched Travis take another shot.

Quick muttered and Drew's explosive laugh brought a smile to my own face. Despite our somber reality and shitty circumstances, this man had found happiness with us.

My best friend casually laid an arm across the back of Drew's chair. It might have looked like a 'man stretch' to the untrained eye. Or it would have, if Shane hadn't leaned over to bite the tip of Drew's earlobe, then sucked it lightly into his mouth. It was a subtle move, hidden behind his long hair and the angle of Drew's jaw, but we could see it. And the adorable flush that crept up Drew's neck.

Fuck, the two of them were cute. Seeing them like this was so … hot. I was thrilled they weren't trying to keep it a secret, owning their newfound feelings for each other.

I shifted in Cam's arms and rubbed my thighs together to stop the newfound wetness from seeping through my panties. His pillowy lips nuzzled into my neck again, as if he knew what I was doing and was determined to get me as soaked as possible.

Travis finished his turn—another friggin' strike—then watched Drew and Shane curiously as he sat next to us.

"Not to rain on this parade, but is this a thing now?" He waved his hands in Drew and Shane's direction, breaking them out of their private moment.

Shane cocked an eyebrow at Drew, clearly signaling him to take the lead. Drew adopted a shy smile and turned in his seat to face us.

"Yeah, I think so." He glanced back at Quick as if to confirm. "It was a little while in the making, and then it just kind of … happened."

Shane wrapped his arms around Drew from behind and kissed the top of his rounded cheekbone in the most precious display of man-love. "I woke up the bisexual beast in Drew." His devious smirk had me giggling when he pressed another kiss to Drew's cheek.

Drew flushed a deeper shade of scarlet, but he didn't deny the claim and his shy smile broadened into a sexy smirk of his own. "My type is 'Shane,' apparently. And Winter," he blurted, as if leaving me out of this announcement would hurt my feelings.

It didn't, and his feelings for Quick certainly didn't, but I appreciated him wanting to include me all the same. If I had to share a man with anyone in the world, I'd want it to be with the man who held the other half of my heart.

"Congratulations, brother." Another wide smile lit up Cam's face as he reached out to fist-bump Drew. "Happy for you guys."

Travis grinned and moved to do the same. "I could've called this one. You guys have had chemistry for ages. Welcome to the family, husband-brother."

He stood and attempted to give Shane the bro slap-on-the-back hug, but he should have known better with Quick. Sure enough, he pulled Travis in for a tight, intentionally long, and awkward squeeze.

Travis laughed when Shane finally let him go. "Love you too, man."

"Considering this new information, you guys can be a team next. Let's see how you fare against Winter's newfound skills." Travis reset the pins and swept his arms out in front of him, like a circus showman.

"Care to place a wager? A bet for a strike? I want to explore this role-play idea ..." He wriggled his eyebrows at me, his gaze hungry like a shark.

I put on my best sickly sweet falsetto voice and giggled girlishly.

"Why Dr. Balcom, I have no idea what you'd want to bet that for when it's time for my examination." I walked toward him with an exaggerated sway to my hips and reached for the bowling ball in his hands. The fly on his jeans expanded.

"New plan." He lifted me up into his arms, throwing me over his shoulder. "We'll see you guys back at the ranch."

I laughed all the way down the hallway. Eventually, he put me down at the concession stand and we ordered fresh drinks for everyone. We walked back hand in hand, ready to play a new round and kick their asses.

And the role-play was *definitely* still on the table.

After another hour of bowling torture, I did *not* get any better, but I got off on Travis' fingers in the private back corner of the alley during another quick snack break.

We packed up to go our separate ways. I didn't want to ruin the magic of the one night we had without the threat of our real lives over our heads, but I needed to get their thoughts on something.

We were a unit now, and we worked better together.

"I think we need to look into Dad's past more," I announced as we rounded the dark parking lot to get into our vehicles.

Four sets of eyes looked at me expectantly.

"I think that's the key to knowing how this all started," I continued, knowing in my heart that this was the right path to follow and hoping they all agreed.

"We know from Drew's mom that something happened when they were teenagers. We need to know what. I think Georgio has leverage over everyone and that's how WAQ and Eccles got involved with his criminal activities from day one. We're missing something huge here. Maybe it's the key to lessening our father's prison sentences, or at the very least, just understanding why they would ever put themselves in this position."

Marcie said Dad's story was sad. Why was it sad? What had made him get into bed with Georgio? Why did he make nice with men like Stanley and Camden, both of whom he'd obviously come to despise over the years, but by all appearances, worked with them professionally and was even invited to their children's wedding?

I also needed to know what kind of role my mother played in all of this. She'd never been mentioned in anything we'd seen, but like Emmett and Amelia, she and Dad met in university. Did she have a clue what was going on, or was she so involved in her career and her other partnerships she truly was separate from the whole mess?

The more I tried to add up the factors, the harder it was to get a whole number.

"I personally"—I swallowed the lump forming in my throat—"don't want to hate my father for the rest of my life. But I need to know more in order to do that. Right now ..."

I left that statement hanging, because despite the years of absenteeism and less than stellar parenting, I wanted to love him. I wanted the love he hadn't been able to show me.

Quick was the closest to me. He wrapped me in his arms and kissed the top of my head. "We'll put a plan together, Snow. Let's get through our exams first."

I nodded and attempted to put the theory on hold as I moved to kiss the guys goodbye. Try as I might, my mind kept running over Dad's possible history as we drove through Cascade Falls' quiet streets.

Was there any hope at all for redemption? For Dad, or for us?

Bourbon & Blues was busy tonight. I was working a serving shift, and it was a rare night where Travis and Cam weren't working. I never realized how much I relied on their presence in the building to make me feel safe under Georgio —or Georgio's cameras—watchful eye, but I was very aware of their absence tonight.

Off in five minutes, I was clearing tables and getting the last of the drink orders from my section before escaping to some semblance of safety. Safety in the form of Hillary tonight, instead of one of my men.

She was meeting me here within the hour, to take me out to her Carlisle condo for a night of 'girl time,' whatever that entailed. I imagined she had planned something well above my pay-grade, like the disgusting Beluga sperm facials Travis had been so against.

I was willing to try anything once, but I didn't know if I could throw myself off that luxury cliff tonight.

My eyes scanned the room warily, an action I'd become accustomed to since Georgio's first threat over our heads. I was getting tired with all the cloak-and-dagger our lives had become, but I hoped upon hope Kellan's new involvement in our lives would put an end to our double personas sooner rather than later.

That's if we could keep our end of the bargain—I had my doubts he'd let us off scot-free like he had implied. Although, short of seducing Georgio—not only was that an unlikely possibility, I would rather suck on Shane's rugby-sweat toes than even get close to the man—I didn't know how me 'keeping an ear to the ground' could have any value to 'Operation Georgio-Geronimo.'

I know it was another one of Quick's lame titles, but Travis had encouraged it, so we were stuck with it.

As if the devil himself heard my thoughts, the distinct timbre of Kellan's voice filled the air as I rounded the corner with my drink tray.

"You've done well here, brother. A far cry from when it opened."

The two men hovered in an elevated alcove, surveying the throng of laughing customers and the four-piece jazz ensemble on the stage; the trumpeter's solo overtook the room so I couldn't catch Georgio's response.

I was startled by Kellan's obvious comfort, fully blending in with the crowd of small-town hooligans and traveling elitists.

I averted my eyes before Georgio could catch me watching them, and brought the tray of dirty glasses back to Colin.

"Could you fill this last order for me?" I asked while my mind raced with all the reasons Kellan could be here.

I had trusted up until this point that everything he'd said was the truth. I'd seen his badge, he'd shared information, and he was obviously doing his best to keep as much of his involvement hidden.

Was tonight an act of subterfuge, meant to keep Georgio from suspecting anything? Was Kellan as on our side as he said he was? Could I truly trust anyone in this cascading waterfall of lies?

Ugh. My head hurt. I could only hope Georgio would make a false move quickly, so the rest of us could go back to our lives. Even though I could admit I had no clue what that would now look like.

I just had finals left, then I graduated next month. Presently, I had no plans other than continuing to work for Bourbon & Blues until this web of fuckery was all over. Surprisingly, I hadn't missed the diner like I thought, but my main reason for wanting to be there had been Drew, and now I got to spend time with that handsome devil as much as I wanted.

Well, as much as my schedule had allowed. Shane had spent more time with my boyfriend than I had lately, but since he was now his boyfriend, too ...

"And this is one of our servers, Winter Wallace."

I snapped to attention at the mention of my name across Georgio's lips and forced an open smile as I turned to face the two men.

"Hi," I said brightly, making eye contact with Kellan before shifting my gaze to Georgio.

"Winter is also a singer here." Georgio's face was kind yet impassive, showing no sign he knew me more than at a professional glance. He was either a sociopath or a psychopath with how quickly he could turn off his emotions. I was afraid to find out which.

Kellan nodded and smiled politely. "Nice to meet you, Winter." His face also lacked any notable emotion; I'd marvel at it, if it wasn't so disturbing.

Georgio moved on before I could say another word, requesting neat whiskeys from Colin as I blew out a slow breath of relief. The bartender handed me my finished orders, and I hightailed it toward my last table, quickly offloading the cocktails to get away from the Carlos brothers' watchful eyes.

Twenty-minutes later, I found the courage to re-enter the main lounge after Hillary messaged me to let me know she was here. My heart rate skyrocketed when I found her seated at a rear booth, chatting away with Georgio and Kellan.

"Hi, Sweets, perfect timing." She waved me over breezily. Tentatively, I walked toward them. "Georgio and I were just lamenting my botched wedding." She rolled her eyes dramatically, then slid out of the booth and adjusted her jacket as she stood tall beside me.

"Logan has more enemies than I do shoes." My Academy-award-winning actress friend laughed airily and winked at Kellan in particular. "If I wasn't smitten, I'd hang him myself."

Georgio raised an eyebrow at that, but he said nothing; Kellan's booming laugh overtook the space. He eyed Hillary with undisguised interest, which we would definitely discuss later. Hillary and I—not Kellan and I.

"I'll see you later." She latched onto my hand and pulled me toward the front alcove with a not-so-subtle grip. "It was nice to meet you, Kellan."

She wiggled her fingers in a girlish wave and continued to tug on me until we were out the front entrance and into the night.

I quirked a brow as we rounded the Jaguar and she unlocked the doors.

"Smitten? Really?" Despite the intense heart palpitations I kept experiencing in Georgio's presence, Hillary's performance had turned my fear into incredulity. Was there anything that fazed this woman?

"I know." She cackled and ducked her head as she climbed into the luxury car. "I was lucky to keep it together —what an idiot!" She sobered quickly as I shut the door behind me, the two of us now sheltered within the silence of the vehicle. "The quicker we can take Georgio down, the quicker I can move on with my life. Daddy and Stanley are way too close to him for comfort."

She shifted the car into gear before giving me some serious side-eye. "You could have told me how hot Kellan Carlos was, though. If he wasn't a baddie, I'd sit on his face." She shot me a wicked grin as I snorted.

"Well," I said slowly, a devious grin crossing my own features, "I have."

The rest of the drive to her condo, I regaled her with my one night of passion with Kellan Carlos years ago. The bitter-sweet memory was still a good story, even if I only now had eyes for his nephew ... and his brother.

CHAPTER 10

LOGAN

I walked into Bourbon & Blues like I owned the place for what I hoped was the last fucking time.

It was pay-up day, and I was ready to get the monkey that was Georgio's debt off my back and say 'fuck you and sayonara' to the man who'd held me in his chains for years.

Yeah, fucking right.

Still, the payment would be fucking sweet relief; one less thing to worry about in the filthy sea of fuckery I was currently swimming in.

Hill had delivered, as always. I had seriously underappreciated that woman, and one day, I'd return the favor. All the favors from the past few months.

Unfortunately, my lawyers were a little too good, and Hill couldn't find a technical loophole out of the contract with Carson, but she'd highlighted the morality clause my legal team had put into all of my contracts.

It was a farce really – I didn't know a single person, man or woman, who'd pass the morality clause if anyone qualified went digging into their personal life. Everyone had skeletons in the closet and bodies buried in their backyard. It was just how deep you were willing to dig for the good stuff.

I had a mountain of Carson's bodies in my back pocket— I just had to figure out how I could leak that information without it coming back to me. It was enough I could get jail time as an accomplice after the fact, and now that I had a semi-plausible out with the FBI and an actual future to plan for, I wasn't putting myself in that fucking position ever again.

I walked up the stairs to the admin offices, wrestling with the familiar craving that hit every time I entered the building. I wasn't going to let it cripple me today. Today, I'd be walking out of this fucking place a free man.

Sort of.

"Logan." A startled female voice came from behind me just before I marched into Georgio's office.

Janet Lindross, mousy librarian wanna-be and double agent detective, looked me up and down with wide eyes as she moved around me into the office space.

"What are you doing here?" she asked carefully, her face not giving a single indication that she had any other connection to me.

She was good, I'd give her that. I'd never have suspected if I hadn't heard it from Travis myself.

"It's payday, Janet." I smiled, showing teeth like the predator I was and held up the envelope in my hands. "Where's your boss?"

"Downstairs," she answered smoothly, moving to me with outstretched hands. "I can give that to him."

I moved the envelope away from her. "Hard no. I'm delivering this personally. Scurry along and let him know I'm here, would you?"

I shooed her away with a condescending smile, truly enjoying that I could treat an FBI agent like shit with no blowback.

Serves the fuckers right.

A flash of annoyance crossed her features before she turned on her heel to leave the room. I settled into a large wing-backed armchair and waited.

I was oddly at ease today. Maybe it was the thrill of knowing I was going to destroy Carson sooner than I'd hoped, or the relief that Hill had come through.

It had nothing to do with the dreams I'd been having about my little vixen of a woman and the trusting way she'd looked at me when I'd visited her in her dressing room. Or the way her naked body begged me to fuck her with another man's cum dripping down her legs.

I had that imagery on loop since I'd caught her and Chase in *my* gym.

She fucked him like they were animals rutting. I wanted to tame that panther into a submissive little kitten. But it had nothing to do with my unusual state of calm.

While I was still lying to myself, I also didn't feel the need to bury myself in a powder keg of blow right now.

Fuck. I'd call Hillary on my drive home for my daily NA call. They were getting less and less frequent, but I hated that I still needed them.

"Hello, Logan."

Georgio didn't sound irritated, but he didn't sound happy to see me either. Good.

"Hi, Georgio."

I wasted no time, not wanting to be in the man's presence, or his tempting drug den establishment, any longer. I handed him the envelope and stepped back, as if touching him would taint my skin more than it already was.

"All of it," I said, "including an additional ten thou in accrued interest."

He thumbed through the contents, and a shrewd smile took over his face. "Well done. I should have known Stanley's son would follow through. Did you have to sell a kidney to get this?"

I bristled, but bit my tongue. Now that I didn't have cocaine saturating my bloodstream, my temper was getting easier to manage. Good fucking thing, because Georgio was intentionally goading me for a reaction.

"I am a man of many means," I answered smoothly and matched his smile with one of my own. "And I pay my debts. If you need nothing else, I have another appointment to get to."

His hand snapped out, grabbing my arm. "Just one moment."

He released me and walked over to his desk, opening a top drawer. With a smug smile, he shuffled the contents around, then walked back towards me. He dropped a small clear baggie of white powder into my palm.

"A gift, to celebrate." He patted my shoulder with a knowing smirk and beckoned to Janet. The two of them left the room as I held a staring contest with my greatest nemesis.

My mouth turned drier than the desert. Blissful release sat right at my fingertips. Fuck.

Fuck.

I'd never been so tempted to dive into a corner and snort my brains out. My phone's reminder chime snapped me back to existence.

I had to get to my next appointment or Stanley would blow a gasket. I shoved the baggie into my pocket and hurried out of the building.

I'd get rid of it later, I promised myself. I fucking hoped it was a promise I could keep.

"I don't see what the fucking issue is," Stan-the-Man Eccles grumbled as Hillary walked through the paperwork one more time.

We were sitting in her office in a luxurious Carlisle high-rise. This room was very similar to our apartment in Cascade Falls. White and cream furniture, glass tables, a thick white shag rug with metal modern lamps, and a single garish pink fuzzy pillow on the sofa behind her.

Her 'Power Pillow', she called it. This woman.

We were reviewing a simple real estate sale of a piece of property just outside town she'd been holding in her back pocket for this moment.

It was her genius idea to distract Camden and Stan from all the wedding bullshit and our current cloak and dagger routines, by dangling this 30-hectare carrot in front of them.

It was worthless, by all accounts. But she'd had a guy falsify documents stating it had shown promise for mineral deposits—specifically, silver.

She was playing her cards close, acting like this was a massive sacrifice on her part to sell it to them, but she was willing to part with it as a peace-offering once she and I had finalized our divorce, which was still a point of argument for both blowhards.

"Stan, I'm not having this argument with you again," Hill snapped viciously, her blue eyes flashing with heated annoyance. "You were told long before the wedding that Logan and I would not keep up the charade. It's happening, get over it.

"The trust money will release into my account any day. And"—she fixed a withering stare on both men—"in the event of my death, or should anything happen to me that law enforcement can even find a suggestion of suspicious activity, every single penny is going to an overseas charity."

Camden sputtered in his seat. "I can't believe you're even suggesting such a thing."

"Stranger things have happened, Daddy," she replied.

She quirked an eyebrow at him. Yet, he stared back at her unflinchingly. She gestured to me.

"Since we are no longer your puppets, you'll have to settle for this generous good faith offer. I'm also considering selling all of my shares in the family's properties to pursue other opportunities. I assume you'll want first crack at those, no? Or should I go to Uncle Benson instead?"

Camden shook his head, put in his place like the old dog he was.

Fucking twat. I'd always hated the man—not nearly as much as Stanley, but I didn't hate *anyone* as much as I hated Stanley.

"Take the deal," I offered brusquely, fighting the urge to wink at Hill in triumph. "Or I will. I've had my eye on that land for ages, and if Derek says there's mining potential, I want in."

That sped things up. Nothing clamors to greed like the threat of someone taking that sweet fucking carrot away.

Once we signed the paperwork to be sent to their legal counsel, Hill changed to a more diplomatic tune.

"Thank you. I trust this offer will allow us all to move forward in peace. Logan and I are excited about our new ventures, and so should you be!"

She took out a bottle of champagne from the mini-fridge behind her and handed it to me to pop the cork. Four of the engraved crystal flutes from our wedding followed, and she had me fill them.

"A toast!" She smiled sweetly, as if we hadn't just manipulated our fathers into buying the equivalent of sheep pasture, and raised her glass as I passed one each to Camden and Stanley.

"Congratulations to Eccles on the partnership with WAQ and being awarded the tender on the largest project in our state's history. Quite a feat, gentlemen."

She tilted back her head and drained the glass in one go. I took a polite sip of mine before setting it back down. Both men looked like they'd rather drink fucking battery acid than celebratory champagne with their children, but they found it in themselves to suck it back, anyway.

"We expect you at the Gold Gala, as a couple." Stanley broke the uncomfortable silence after guzzling his second glass of champagne, his addiction bolstering his words.

"Well, yes," Hillary said impatiently, collecting his glass before he could try to pour a third. "We'll still be married in a month, Stanley, so we'll make the public appearance together."

"You can't just *make an appearance*," Stanley spoke through gritted teeth. The alcohol noticeably brought his barely buried anger to the surface. "You'll be representing both families and the businesses of this project."

"Yes, yes, and my own businesses, and Logan's businesses—what's the problem here?"

Hillary settled into the couch beside me, clearly enjoying Stanley's simmering rage. I basked in it too, even with the scars to remind me how vicious he was.

"We need to put on a united front," Camden smiled, playing good cop to Stan's bad cop.

Hillary linked her fingers through mine and winked. "We won't have a problem with that, will we, Loggie-bear?"

"Not at all, dearest," I answered dryly, but giving her one hell of a side-eye. She was enjoying this too much.

"Most of the attendees are in the top five percent, if not one-percenters," Camden said. "The Governor and Mayor will be there, and Georgio has relatives flying in. It's important our families appear to be as united as ever."

Family flying in ... I made a note to bring that up at the next Misfit Meeting. What was my life coming to?

"And they will." It was my turn to respond—Hill had been taking the weight for most of this meeting. "All we've ever done is pretend; the gala won't be any different."

I stood and slid on my suit jacket from the back of the couch, smoothing my palms over the material before buttoning it.

"I have another meeting. I hope I don't have to see you fuckers until the ball."

I nodded to Hill and tossed off a salute to the two men I'd put into a grave myself.

Logan Eccles: I need your help.
Travis Blacksheep: ... Ok?
Logan Eccles: Meet me at Kirby Park at 7.
Travis Blacksheep: I have to work at 7. I'll see you at 6:30?
Travis Blacksheep: Logan?
Travis Blacksheep: ...
Logan Eccles: 7.
Travis Blacksheep: ...
Travis Blacksheep: Fuck, okay, I'll be there for 7.

My will power took a fucking beating as I waited for Travis to show up.

I sat in my car for an hour. The packet of powder taunted me in the center console, just waiting to be inhaled and absorbed into my addicted fucking brain.

It was solely my ego that had stopped me until this point; the satisfaction in knowing the chemical didn't have its claws in me every day made me want to do better—to be more than a junkie businessman who couldn't function without a hit.

That, and the picture of a pained and disappointed Princess if she found out I relapsed. The little boy with mommy issues wanted Winter to be proud of me. A shrink could tell me all the ways I was fucked up from *that* one later.

I sat in the spring sun as it crested over the mountain. May was warm in these parts, and I cracked my windows to let in the fresh air; it didn't do a fucking thing to calm the gnawing hunger in my chest.

Travis' pathetic excuse for a car rolled up another twenty minutes later. How he could have so much swagger when he was dirt-ass poor was beyond me.

I palmed the packet and got out of my vehicle, moving to sit on the warm hood while I waited for his driver's side door to fall off.

"I'm not your lackey, you know," he fumed as he got out of his junk-drawer on wheels.

"You're still here." I folded my arms smugly.

"Yeah, and now I'm regretting it." He glared at me warily before dropping his shoulders and sitting down uninvited beside me. The hood creaked under our combined weight. "What do you want, Logan?"

I swallowed, all arrogance leaving me as I contemplated just telling him to fuck off and melting into drug-addled oblivion. I couldn't come this far and fuck it all up. But I couldn't trust myself to do it on my own.

Before I could change my mind, I shoved the baggie into his hands.

"I need you to get rid of this for me."

He looked down at his hand and his face filled with recognition. Then he looked back at me like I had three heads.

"Is this a buyer's remorse kind of thing? Have you been using again?"

"No," I barked out in annoyance. "That was Georgio's parting gift when I paid up today, the fucker. And I've been fighting myself all day."

His suspicious gaze turned to understanding, and he shoved the drugs into his pocket. "I'll get rid of it," he promised. "How close were you to giving in?"

"Close enough to text your ass," I admitted. I tossed a glance at him from the corner of my eye. "Consider this my desperate attempt at sobriety."

He surprised me with an outright laugh. "I'm glad you did." His smile disappeared. "Winter would have been upset if she knew you'd relapsed. She worries about you."

I didn't respond, but I didn't need to. They all knew how I felt about her after our jailroom friendship party, but I wasn't going to confess my adoration at every fucking turn like a sap.

Still, I felt the need to say something. After a small silence, I managed, "Yeah, I know."

"Don't do it for her, though, man. Do it for you. None of us wants to see you out of commission."

Now it was my turn to laugh. Yeah, right. They tolerated me because Winter had tolerated me. That was the extent of it.

He pushed off from my Audi and stood, then turned around to face me.

"Take care of yourself tonight. I've got to get to work."

I watched him step into the metal deathtrap before I shoved off my seat and stopped his door from slamming shut behind him.

"Thanks for saving my life."

A slow smile spread across his face. "How hard was it for you to admit that?"

Was he … teasing me? The friendly smirk morphed into the face of a concerned parent. "Stick around, Logan. There's lots to live for yet."

I lowered my chin in the ghost of a nod before shutting the door.

I slid back into my heated leather seat and turned up my music, melting into the chair and closing my eyes.

Today, I had won the battle. Next, we'd have to win the war.

CHAPTER 11

TRAVIS

"Husband-brother half-Uncle," I rolled the words over my tongue and made a face as Cam snorted beside me. "Uncle-Husband-Brother?"

"That makes us sound gay *and* incestuous," Cam mused as he moved to adjust the temperature in my car.

My decrepit Daytona chugged along as we drove through a small town just past Kensington to meet Kellan at a private shooting range. To discuss our newfound familial situation. Cam was taking the news pretty well, considering, but I was struggling to get past the fact my best friend was actually a blood relative, and a son of the biggest cartel king on this side of the world.

While I was the grandson of the same cartel king.

Life was fucked.

"We'd fit into *Game of Thrones* just fine," I joked, hoping to lighten the gray clouds sitting over my head. "Just don't think that you can start bossing me around in the bedroom with our girl because of your new title."

Another snort. Winter had been the one to let slip Cam had finally taken that step with her, and I couldn't have been more pleased for my uncle-husband-brother. Cam needed more love in his life, and Winter was the perfect puzzle piece to fit into the hole in his heart.

Before I could be on the receiving end of what was sure to be a witty comeback, I pulled onto a nondescript dirt road that should lead to the coordinates Kellan had texted.

My poor geriatric baby wasn't made for rutted roads; we couldn't hear anything above the squeaks of the struts and the rumble of the engine as it struggled to make its way up the mountain trail.

Note to self: next time borrow Shane's truck.

When we got to the top, Kellan was already waiting—by himself this time, or so it appeared. I looked around warily through my now muddy windshield, but there wasn't another human in sight.

Cam looked at me meaningfully before shifting his considerable size out of the tight space of my car. A blast of cool air hit me as I did the same. It was a beautiful May day, but the mountain breeze was chilly out here.

"Welcome."

Kellan moved to shake both of our hands; the act surprised me, but I shook it all the same. I guess we were now on more common ground than simple FBI versus small town twenty-somethings.

He motioned for us to follow him inside the small wooden building to our right. When we entered, my eyes widened at the open display of rifles, handguns, and shotguns.

"We're going to have a shooting lesson today." Kellan waved his hand over the arsenal of weapons. "Choose your weapon, and we'll go out back to teach you how to use it. Have either of you shot a gun before?"

I shook my head 'no' and swallowed roughly. The gun I carried was solely under the direction of Georgio, not because I ever wanted or needed the feel of a gun on me for protection. I could point and shoot well enough, but I'd been fortunate enough to have never needed to actually use it.

"No," Cam said simply. "My fists are weapon enough."

Kellan's expression darkened at Cam's casual delivery. "You may need this skill now more than ever. Grab a gun and follow me."

I grabbed a handgun that looked similar to the one I carried, and Cam grabbed a larger one off the end of the table as we followed behind Kellan to the rear outdoor practice field; targets had been set up at various distances.

"Before we shoot, I'm going to teach you how to properly load, unload, and clean a gun, and I want to hear your stories from the beginning."

He stopped at a table set up in front of the perimeter fence. A variety of unfamiliar tools had been meticulously laid out across its surface. Turning to face us, he folded his arms across his barrel chest and eyed us with the recognizable face of Carlos' intensity.

"I only know who you are on paper. I need to know your backstories and how Georgio came into contact with you. We need to know the whole picture if we can use your family connection to help bring him down."

He nodded in my direction. "Travis, you start."

A million emotions flooded through me as I considered which part of my story to tell. Dad? Mom? Devon?

I blew out a breath and decided on all of it. Our fates were now intertwined; we might as well all be on the same page.

I told him about our childhood; how we'd never been rich exactly, but we'd had enough to live in a small three-bedroom on the other side of Sheldonville. Dad was an alcoholic and drug user, but he'd never laid a hand on any of us; he'd storm out in blind drunk rages and drive off, leaving Mom sobbing on the kitchen floor. I admitted Dad wasn't a particularly involved father, but he'd been around enough that we had a void in our lives when he walked out on us when I was twelve.

Mom had been devastated and deteriorated quickly, and we moved into a trailer shortly after it became clear Dad wasn't coming back. Mom had been diagnosed three years later, when I was fifteen, and I became the primary breadwinner for our family within the year. Then Georgio had found me at another club where I had been working doubles almost every day as a bartender and offered me a job as head bartender at Bourbon & Blues. I wasn't even legal at the time, but my fake ID served me well. I'd worked the bar scene since I was seventeen.

I was twenty the first time Devon overdosed and I asked Georgio for a loan to pay for the first rehab stint. I'd been twenty-one when he'd put a gun and a bag of money in my hand, telling me the way to pay him back was to work off the hours in another 'branch' of his business. Angelo had then threatened Mom's life when I initially refused.

I recounted my life story as emotionlessly as possible, fighting back the rising golf ball in my throat as my shitty circumstances and shame threatened to choke me.

All the while, Kellan wordlessly showed how to take apart the individual pieces of the gun I'd chosen and the tools used to clean them. I was grateful the visual distraction allowed my sentences to flow.

When the words dried up, along with the tears at the back of my eyelids threatening to spill over, Kellan's booming voice broke through my stagnant silence.

"Matteo left so that our father wouldn't find out about you two. He'd been infiltrating another rival crime organization and working through their ranks for many years—Antonio is nothing if not a patient man. I suspect he got involved with your mother in that time, and didn't tell her his real identity. Maybe he did—we'll never know."

His brows pinched as he searched the depths of my green eyes before delivering the final blow. "Matteo died over a year ago in an FBI shootout that isn't public knowledge. I saw the body myself."

A burst of agonizing pain tore through my heart, but then dissipated into a slow burn across my chest. Matthew Balcom—Matteo Banderas—hadn't been a father to me in over a decade. His leaving—whether or not an action of mercy—had brought chaos and serious pain to our lives. He hadn't sent money or made sure we had food to eat; he'd done nothing to protect us from the raw suffering of life. Instead, he'd chosen to leave two little boys and a kind, but sheltered, woman to fend for themselves in an unforgiving world.

I wouldn't mourn the man who'd left us to rot to save his own skin.

"Thank you for letting me know," I croaked out, and the burn soothed to a soft tingle. "That's one loose end tied up."

"Make no mistake, though," Kellan said as he finished up our guns, now freshly cleaned and ready for use. "Georgio knew who you were if he sought you out. I have no idea if our father knows—I'd assume if he did, he would have you in his clutches by now. Why he kept you a secret concerns me. Georgio is cunning; you're a bargaining chip of some kind."

The tingle grew to a slow burn again, like bad indigestion overtaking my abdomen. Great.

"Did he seek you out too?" Kellan turned to Cam, who'd stayed stoically silent as I regaled my sob story.

My brute of a best friend cocked his head in thought and then nodded in confirmation.

"I've been thinking about that." He accepted the gun from Kellan's outstretched hand and eyed it warily as he continued. "I'd always thought it was my misfortune that I'd accepted Georgio's legal help after my temper got the better of me, but knowing we're blood-related makes me rethink that."

Cameron Chase laid out his own story of adoption, his normal upbringing, and his parents' deaths, which led to his wayward wandering and eventually finding his mother. Happenstance and sheer coincidence had led him to this area. One night of rage had left him indebted to Georgio indefinitely.

"If anyone is going to quietly overthrow our father, it's Georgio." Kellan leaned against the fence; his face full of fierce loathing. "The twins don't care enough to step into leadership. They do whatever our father asks, when he asks it. Matteo is dead. I've been playing the double-role for over a decade. The FBI found me in one of Antonio's training camps when I was a teen and turned me before I lost my soul. Our father thinks I'm a righteous soldier right now, playing my part in the FBI and the DEA and turning enough agents over to our side so we can grow ranks and take over North American distribution entirely.

"But Georgio is the one we need to watch. Right now, he's following every command, but he's setting his own traps. I have a feeling he found out about you a long time ago and was lying in wait for the right time. You coming to him was just the perfect set of circumstances."

I didn't miss the hatred that shadowed every facet of the passable Viking's face when he discussed his family. I'd been living a pseudo double life for a few months—to play it for a decade? It was a wonder Kellan had any semblance of who he was left in him.

His gaze caught my own. "Understand that, for the mafia, blood is everything."

"He'll be thrilled to know he has two grandsons to share the family responsibility with"—his blue eyes darted over to Cam's almost matching ones—"but he'll be rabid if he knows he has another son to step in to grow the empire. If you know where your mother is, I want to get her under our protection as soon as possible."

"And then what?"

Cam's voice was steel as it broke through the bitter fog of family trauma surrounding me.

"You protect her, and then what?" he repeated when Kellan didn't immediately respond. "We hide? We cower? We 'keep our ear to the ground?' This changes things, *brother.*"

He spat the word, not hiding his disgust for the situation whatsoever. "We're not only trapped in this scenario, but now we have targets on our backs from a family history we're just learning about today. And we're just supposed to trust you? Why aren't we being put on a plane or in Witness Protection? Instead, you're just playing us on the other side of the field."

He folded his arms and widened his stance, looking ready to haul off and punch Kellan if he made a false move. Kellan didn't bat so much as an eye as he pushed off the fence, stopping directly in front of Cam in a weird Alpha-male brother standoff.

"If you teach me how to shoot a gun right now, I'm gonna shoot you." Cam growled, his eyes narrowing to slits as he stayed as still as a statue.

The blond man's mouth split into a wide grin before a thunderous laugh escaped him. He slapped a still angry and stiff Cam on the back before grabbing the cleaned gun off the table and handing it to him. "I'd like to see you try, brother! Come on, I'll show you how to hold it."

Cam stared at the gun in his hand before his eyes met mine. Concern and leftover rage filled their depths. Reluctantly, he followed Kellan to the shooting section of the range.

An uncomfortable prickle drove its way through my skin as I assessed the man who held the fate of our futures in his hands.

DNA had proven we were family; tainted blood flowed through all our veins. Would Kellan deliver us from its evil? Or were we all destined to be damned?

"A word to the wise, Georgio's starting his fight nights up again."

Kellan's words echoed in the back of my mind as I entered the staff locker room at Bourbon & Blues for my bar shift.

I'd spent the day delivering bags of dirty cash to even dirtier businesses across this quarter of the state, and my mind and body were dead tired.

Luckily, Winter was working tonight, and I'd be spending the night at her place. It felt like forever since I'd had some quality one-on-one time with my girl.

The fight nights worried me. After a three-month reprieve, Georgio was obviously feeling self-assured enough to start them back up again, and I didn't know what that meant for us. I doubted Winter or I would get a free pass on the schedule, and Cam was his biggest money-maker. It was guaranteed that his headlining cash cow would be forced into knocking out degenerates once again.

I was more worried about my friends than I was about me. The noose had already been tied around my neck; I could only hope Kellan was my savior, not my executioner.

Winter was already at the bar, grabbing a tray of drinks from Colin.

Her smile when she saw me lit me up and pulled me out of my dark spiral, reminding me of the important things in my life; the things worth living for.

"Hey, beautiful." I leaned down, kissing her cheek, before grabbing a kitchen rag from the counter to wipe down the stools.

The evening crowd hadn't come in yet, just a few stragglers getting comfortable as the band set up their stage for the night's show. I was lost in the monotony of my routine when two figures walked past the entrance to the lounge and caught my eye.

I had a sixth sense for Georgio these days; every time he came into my periphery, the hair on the back of my neck stood on end, putting my primitive protection instincts on high alert. Thankfully, I didn't see him often, and he never appeared to be paying me any more attention than usual. It was a false sense of security—there was no question we were all most definitely under his watchful eye.

I tried to be subtle as I turned to face him more fully, playing my part with Kellan to see if I could catch anything Georgio was saying.

Nothing in this lifetime could have prepared me for the sight of my brother chatting with the mob boss as if they were old friends.

I must have frozen in place in my shock, because when Devon looked up, he caught my eye and a wide smile filled his face.

He waved me over. Shuffling forward, I was helpless to pretend I hadn't been watching them. A knot of dread formed in my belly at the thought of my naïve baby brother entering a wolf den full of ravenous predators—one predator in particular.

"Hi, Travis!" Devon pulled me into an enthusiastic hug and his smile grew as his gaze traveled between me and the man who was the biggest threat to us all. "I've just spent the afternoon getting to know our uncle! You've been holding out on me."

The debilitating feeling of dread barreled through me. I dug deep for the courage to hold Georgio's knowing gaze as Devon continued to chatter on.

Fuck, fuck, fuckity fuck.

I'd been made.

CHAPTER 12

WINTER

You'll be fine, Winter. It's just an asshole you sometimes fantasize about. No big deal.

My pep talk wasn't working, but I'd be a complete liar if I said my heart was completely in it.

Sitting outside Logan's condo, I was mentally preparing for my first 'panic-attack' training session. I wasn't prepared to spend the afternoon digging into my inner demons, but I was woman enough to admit I could benefit from some help.

That, and I was beyond curious. By now, I'd deduced Logan had been beaten as a child, the culprit his sorry excuse for a father. Hillary hadn't said as much, but she'd more than alluded that Stanley wasn't a good man, in more ways than one.

I imagined the beatings Logan had taken were brutal, if his scarring was any indication. Were they the source of his own panic attacks? Regardless of my nervousness and outright fear of how one actually mastered their panic, I needed to know how he'd done it.

Not only were they exhausting, I was tired of my body betraying me at every turn. I wasn't weak-willed, or a weak person, so I was determined my reflexes wouldn't take control anymore.

That was the hope, anyway. Logan and I hadn't spent any time alone together … ever, if you didn't count that one date in high school, and I'd also be a big fat liar if I didn't say that alone was putting me on edge.

I'd told the guys our little 'interaction' in the jail cell was a onetime deal, but I was becoming more and more drawn to the asshole. It now seemed like far more than a possibility that the man had some redeemable qualities.

That he'd had the consideration to come to me and tell me about his meeting with Carson, and actually caring about the effect it might have on me, told me more than I had expected to know; his declared feelings for me might be legitimate after all.

Not to mention the tender kiss he'd given me before he'd gone back to the lounge had left me with school-girl shivers; there was something about a man who was only soft for you that was hard to ignore.

Or maybe I was just crazy. It was too soon to tell.

I pulled up my big-girl panties and left Basil in the parking lot as I made my way to the condo entrance.

The front doors buzzed open before I even had the chance to press the call button. I groaned internally at the thought Logan had been watching for me. Had he seen my twenty-minute internal struggle as I stayed put in my car, too?

I didn't enjoy going into this lesson without the upper hand.

He swung open his door for me as soon as I stepped off the elevator. The man probably had cameras all over the building—he owned it, after all.

He probably watched Cam and I from his throne in his castle, tugging on himself as he enjoyed the show.

Despite the anxious energy coursing through my veins, that visual brought a smile to my lips. And a slight charge in my lower belly.

"What's funny?" His face held none of its usual arrogance; the open display of curiosity made him look ... kind. It was off-putting.

"Nothing." I strode into the condo like I owned the place and shucked off my jacket, hanging it off of a bar stool at the kitchen island. "Just a little nervous."

My honesty surprised me, but that was what I was here for, right? Time to face facts and beat my brain at its own game. It was going to require some vulnerability on my part; an emotion I was probably as used to showing as Logan was, but it was time to put away the games.

For today, at least.

Logan's genuine smile gave me serious *Twilight Zone* vibes.

"I'm nervous, too," he admitted, spinning the bar stool around and plunking himself down on it, gesturing for me to do the same in the one beside him. "I've never had to teach somebody to do this before." He ran a hand through his hair and cleared his throat. "It's not something I've shared with anyone before."

Vulnerability overload. This man was seriously attractive when he shut his mouth and opened up his heart.

After a moment of silence, since I had no idea what to say to that, I broke it.

"So, what do I do? Do we listen to Zen music and meditate or something?"

His amused chuckle sounded wrong, as it lacked any sort of bite or irony. "Something, sure. Let's sit in the living room."

He clicked a button on a remote on the counter and the space filled with soft classical music. I cocked my head at him as if to say 'really?' but he ignored my gaze.

I moved to the buttery-soft white leather sectional I once had the luxury of sleeping on—ironically, post-panic attack. Logan sat beside me, turning his body to face mine.

"One of the first considerations when working through panic attacks is understanding what triggers you." His liquid honey-brown eyes stared right into my soul as he said the words; I was transfixed by the subtle flecks of milk chocolate around the irises. "Do you know what those are?"

"Umm, I think so." I scrunched my nose as I considered the most recent ones I'd had. "At first, they resulted from the bullying, but if I look deeper, it's not so much a lack of control, but when I'm fully blindsided by something."

I'd had a panic attack when I'd seen Dad at the fighting ring, when I'd been shopping with Hillary, when I was taken at the wedding—all instances of feeling overwhelmingly vulnerable. My men had been showing me vulnerability wasn't as scary as I'd always thought, but that didn't mean I'd had a lobotomy in the time we'd started dating.

Nope, my brain was still as damaged as ever. Winning?

Logan nodded slowly, his gaze contemplative. "Okay, I can work with that."

"What's your trigger?" I blurted out the words before considering them, as if I needed us to play a game of vulnerability Tic Tac Toe. My X for his O.

To his credit, he didn't hesitate. "Feeling trapped."

A memory niggled at the back of my mind. "You said you hated tight spaces. Is that a part of it?"

Another nod and a rough swallow. The overconfident businessman suddenly didn't look so confident.

"Stanley used to lock me in a closet as punishment."

I just blinked at him, surprised and saddened all at once. Despite all of my own parents' failings, I'd never once felt unsafe in their presence.

I reached for his hand and gently stroked the smooth skin across his knuckles. I softened my expression, giving him permission to go on. After a tense moment, he did.

"Mom died when I was five. Something Hillary and I have in common. Hers died in childbirth, mine died from cancer. Stanley had all the money in the world, but he couldn't save her, and he liked to take it out on me."

We wouldn't be able to go back from this conversation; I was hearing his truths, the reality and rawness of his life, and I was surprised to know that I *wanted* to. I wanted to know the enigma that was Logan Eccles. Maybe I'd always had.

"Stanley is an alcoholic; he hides it well, though. He'd get drunk every night and scream a lot, but the actual beatings didn't start until I was around ten; he established fear through confinement, mostly. On the nights he was feeling generous, he'd lock me in my bedroom. When he was feeling evil, he'd lock me in the laundry closet. I once spent two days in there after saying the wrong thing at a cocktail party and making him look bad."

His tone turned murderous at that admission, a sinister promise of retribution lacing the words.

Ice crystallized in my bloodstream as I envisioned a lonely little boy locked in a closet for days because of his father's fragile ego.

Logan lifted the hand I was holding and brought it to his lower back, hovering just above the outline of the belt-shaped scar I shouldn't have seen in the cellar all those months ago.

"I got that one after our date." His words were as soft as a prayer.

All feeling leached from my body as I considered the implications of that one admission.

"Why?" I whispered numbly, afraid of the answer.

"I was supposed to be Hillary's. If I didn't play ball, it would fuck up his deal with Camden. And he hated your father. Dual lessons learned."

I couldn't control my movements—I was a marionette of heartache and compassion as I shifted on the couch and straddled Logan's lap. I cupped his cheeks between my palms, staring into the unbridled pain locked within the windows of his soul.

"I'm sorry."

Words were not enough, but they were all I had. The sincerest image of this broken man stared back at me; regret, sorrow, and confusion rolled off of him in waves, hitting me like a Mack truck as I held onto all of it.

He reached up to tuck a lock of my hair behind my ear, the touch a whisper of a caress as he let me see every facet of the man he was. Before I could consider my actions, I leaned in and brushed my lips against his.

Logan's lips weren't puffy like Cam's or pouty like Drew's, or sensual like Travis and his piercing, but they were warm and supple, and so uniquely made for mine.

The kiss was tentative, the two of us truly exploring each other's bodies as if we had all the time in the world. We were two entwined strangers, getting to know each other through our mutual pain and passion. He licked the seam of my mouth and flicked his tongue between my lips, exploring and tasting every part of me as he wound both hands in my hair, lightly tugging at the nape of my neck and holding me in place.

The soft bulge in his pants hardened to stone as I relaxed into him; my hips rocked over him more insistently as each pass of his tongue on mine made my panties damper.

The sexy, manly groan emanating from his chest spurred me on until he broke off the kiss and pushed me back. Putting a few inches between us, we panted for air.

"As much as I'm going to hate myself for this later, I really need you to get better at dealing with your shit, Princess."

Irritation coiled through me as his entire demeanor changed. The cocky, aristocratic smirk was back in place, as if it had never left at all.

"Fuck you, Logan," I grumbled, sliding off of his lap onto the seat beside him.

The soft notes of his scent, amber and frankincense, lingered on my skin as I shook out the dirty thoughts in my head to get down to business.

If that was how he wanted to play it, fine. I would not beg him to keep kissing me, if that's what he was after.

He tilted up my chin with the pad of his thumb and the intensity of his gaze caught my heart in my throat. "One day, Princess, one day. Make no mistake that I want you. All of you."

He kissed my temple with a reverence I was unprepared for, stirring a deep ache in my chest and between my thighs.

"The first thing to stop a panic attack is to first realize you're having one."

Well, duh. I bit back my reply as he sat on the other side of the couch, as far away as he could be from me while remaining in the room.

"I want you to get comfortable with some grounding techniques. Ways to stop yourself from spiraling when you're triggered. Focus on your five senses, and try to identify five different things you can hear, see, taste, touch, and smell."

"How the hell can I taste five things?"

The glare he shot me would have put Medusa to shame.

"Five things you can see, four you can touch, three you can hear, two you can smell, *one* you can taste. Close your eyes and try it."

I rolled my eyes but did as he requested, closing my eyes and taking a deep breath to relax into the couch.

"Picture somewhere you've been recently where there is a lot going on around you."

I immediately envisioned the bowling alley where we'd had our group date the other night, and settled into the vision.

"Where are you?"

"Harold's," I answered, lost in the imagery behind my eyelids.

"Okay; focus on five things you can see. What are they?"

"Cam is bowling. Drew and Quick are sitting at the table. The bowling lane is to my left and Travis is sitting beside me."

"What can you touch? Four things."

I immersed myself in the pseudo-world of Harold's in my mind.

"Travis' hand in mine, the hard bench beneath me, the scratchy wool of my sweater, and the hot air from the heater above us."

"Three things. What can you hear?"

"Pins falling, kids behind us shrieking, and the roll of bowling balls."

"Two things you can smell."

His voice was closer now, but I wasn't willing to open my eyes and break my concentration.

I shifted in the seat, deepening my focus. "Ummm, wood varnish and Travis' body wash."

"One thing you can taste."

I gave myself an internal high-five that I didn't have five tastes to figure out—who the hell could taste five things at a time was beyond me.

"My mint Chapstick."

I could sense his heat hovering above me when he whispered. "Good."

My eyes flew open; Logan's brown eyes took up all the space in front of me.

"How do you feel right now?"

I ignored the staring that was making me decidedly giddy and assessed my body. A controlled calm had washed over me. I felt more relaxed in my skin than I had in months; maybe years.

"Good." I smiled reluctantly and met his searing gaze. "Really relaxed, actually."

The genuine satisfied grin that filled his features was breathtaking; it was if I was seeing the true heart of Logan Eccles for the first time.

We did the exercise again, using three different scenarios, before he taught me a few different breathing techniques to use based on how out of control I felt. It was surprisingly easy to spend this time with him, and strangely far more intimate than my fighting session with Cam.

"Practice this exercise before bed. You need to condition your body to reach for this tool when you're in a panic state —like muscle memory. You won't be able to do that if you're not used to using it."

He moved to sit beside me on the couch, the heat of his thigh searing against mine.

"You can also redirect your focus to a single thing."

He motioned to his right hand, where a chunky gold ring with Harvard insignia I hadn't really noticed before sat on his ring finger.

"This is my tether when I struggle to keep it under control. I focus on every micro detail—the color, the shape, the size, how it feels on my skin, how smooth the metal is …"

His voice trailed off as he continued to stare at the jewelry, sinking into the memories of the staved-off panic of his past.

"Hey."

I reached for his hand and interlaced our fingers, rubbing my thumb over the indented crest of his ring.

"Stanley's going to get his, Logan. We're going to make sure of it."

He tugged on my hand so sharply, I fell into his lap, my face shunted into the crook of his elbow. He let go of my hand to adjust me into a seated position and intertwined our fingers again.

"Carson will, too." He kissed the top of my head as I settled into the rare comfort that was Logan Eccles, enveloped by his expensive cologne and powerful arms.

I can't honestly say how long we sat there, still and silent, as he held me tightly to his chest. The beat of his heart, strong and steady, thrummed through me like a Tibetan meditation bell.

Before I could get lost in his hold for the rest of the day, I stood from our protective cocoon and moved to grab my coat from the bar stool.

The peaceful moment couldn't last forever. I had to work a shift at Bourbon & Blues, and Logan had his own life to tend.

"I have to work tonight," I explained as he followed me to the door. "But thank you. This was really ... helpful."

He crowded my space in the doorway, tilting my head to look up at him. He brushed the hair back from my forehead and placed a tender kiss in its place.

"We'll do it again soon," he said seriously, before that obnoxious smirk stitched back into place. "You don't have your shit together yet, Princess Peach."

A flush heated my cheeks at his insinuation, the not-so-distant memory of him tasting me on his fingers heating my core.

Instead of giving him the satisfaction, I scoffed and playfully pushed him out of the way, reaching for the doorknob to leave.

"If you guys do all go out again ..." After a long silence, Logan finished. "Let me know."

A small smile traced his lips before he closed the door behind me. Our afternoon of mutual trauma and solidarity put a fresh spring in my step as I traipsed down the hall.

CHAPTER 13

SHANE

All my love,

Brenda.

I stared at the words that had all but shattered my faith in my father.

Love letters, about twenty of them, laid scattered across my coffee table, their forbidden words taunting me with a pain I'd never felt before.

Unless there were multiple Brendas in Dad's life, the woman who had hit Mom in the car accident—losing her life and ruining Mom's in the process—was my father's secret lover.

The letters spanned across years—as far back as when Shiloh had been a baby. If I hadn't had known who'd written them, they would have captured a beautiful love story.

Instead, the pretty words on paper were tainted by the ink of betrayal.

I wondered if Mom knew. If the sadness and pain she had been carrying all these years wasn't the result of a shattered femur, but from the infidelity of my father.

My heart felt like it was being blendered in my chest, and I fought the urge to throw up and cry, not necessarily in that order.

I didn't know whether to burn the letters in a massive bonfire at the cabin, or to have them copied and framed and leave them in Dad's office to expose his poor choices.

I had been in the middle of studying for my finals when curiosity got the better of me and I took out the box I had left in my truck a few weeks before. At first glance, I had thought they were letters between my parents; they met in university and had been in a long-distance relationship for a few years before Mom moved to Cascade Falls.

I nearly fainted when I read the signature at the bottom.

My father, the man I'd looked up to as a guide my whole life, was a cheating son of a bitch.

I felt a newfound empathy for Winter. Her parents disappointed her constantly; mine never had. If this is what it felt like regularly, I would have left that family long ago.

Hope was something I usually had in spades, but I was losing it. Graduation was less than a month away, and my primary job prospect was a company sure to burn to the ground in the next couple of months, if Kellan and his team had anything to do with it. The secure suburban family existence I had always known was now just another foundation built on nothing but lies.

My feelings for Winter were getting stronger by the day, and I couldn't find a way to take that step with her; not without the fear my only constant tether in this fucked-up world could be snipped. Snow was getting better with being vulnerable, but would she be that way with me?

Did she even feel the same way about me?

Drew's solitary presence brought some peace to my world, at least. I'd call him the Batman to my Robin, but he was so much more than a sidekick. Winter, Drew, and I could be a trio, like the *Three Musketeers,* but as … more.

I needed them both right now. I wasn't ready to face this pain and deal with my feelings.

I sent Winter a text before remembering she was studying with Raven tonight. Not wanting to disturb her, I sent her another message telling her to forget it and called Drew. He answered on the second ring.

"Hey man, want to come over?"

He arrived within a half hour, showing up on my doorstep with a frozen pizza and a case of beer. Bless this man.

"What's going on?" Drew cracked a beer as we both settled into the couch with the hockey game on in the background.

I wasn't able to get the words out; I'd share them with Drew eventually, but tonight, they were still too raw and painful, like the first breeze of air across bad road rash. I knew the scabs would heal, but it would be a bitch to get there as they faded into dull scars across the skin.

With WAQ's embezzlement, Dad and Georgio's history, and now this marital infidelity, I didn't know how these wounds would ever heal. But right now, I didn't need healing. I needed a distraction—in the form of Drew's hot body.

My gaze wandered over the gorgeous man's bulging frame in his navy-blue standard Henley. The stubble on his jaw was at least three days old, framing his kissable lips in the perfect way; his hazel eyes beckoned me into their depths as the shifting colors of the game on the TV flickered behind us.

I bit my lip, desperate for the feel of him against me. I hoped he was ready for the next step tonight, because I needed to fuck him so badly, my balls hurt.

"I just needed to see you."

I plucked the beer out of his hand and set it on the coffee table before sliding over into the seat next to him and eliminating the space between us.

Leaning in, I placed light kisses along the column of his neck, nipping at his Adam's apple as he swallowed hard against my teeth.

"I just needed to taste you."

I kissed those pouty lips hungrily, forcing him to open up to me and let me in. I explored the heat of his mouth with my tongue, tasting the first few sips of his beer and something minty, as I deepened the kiss until we both needed to come up for air.

Slowly, I slid my hands over the bulge in his jeans, loving the effect I had on his body. I pushed my palm over his restricted shaft with light pressure, and he shuddered beneath my touch.

"I just needed to feel you," I whispered reverently, shifting to straddle him completely and kiss him again, our layers of clothing the only thing between us.

He groaned deep in his chest, the sound so fucking sexy I could come to it on the spot. I ground my hips into his erection, relishing the feel of his cock on mine, sharp tingles of pleasure rocketing up my spine.

He grabbed the hem of my t-shirt, whipping it over my head in a flurry as I moved to do the same to him.

Shirtless, breathless, and hard as fuck, I took my shot. My gray eyes sought his as I stated my intentions.

"I just need to be inside you."

Those innocent eyes widened in surprise, but then flared with the heat of a thousand suns. He hauled my face to his, kissing me with such ferocity my full weight fell into him.

He unbuckled my belt and slid it off me, throwing it somewhere in the corner of the room before he shoved my jeans and boxers over my ass. The heat of his palms squeezed my ass cheeks, gripping me even harder as I ground against his still-covered cock.

I pushed off the couch, yanked my pants down and off, and reached for his belt to do the same. Pulling him to stand, I stripped him naked faster than I'd ever taken clothes off anyone, man or woman.

What a fucking specimen; his cock stood stiff and proud in front of me. I stroked the underside of his length, my finger following along the thick vein to his tip, enjoying the twitches that followed my every touch.

"Are we really doing this?" Drew's question came out on a shiver. I grasped his balls and gently squeezed them between my fingers.

I leaned in, licking along his jaw. Stopping at the soft flesh under his ear, I sucked so hard it would leave a mark.

"I want to." I brought his earlobe into my mouth, nibbling the tip between my teeth. "Are you ready for that?"

He needed to say yes to move forward. I not only wanted his permission, I needed him to *want* this; I needed to know I wasn't just an experiment for him, this was the real deal. He was going to break my heart and rip my soul in two, if it wasn't.

I had it bad for Drew Johnson and I was in too deep already, regardless of what his answer was.

"Yes."

My chest lifted like a hot-air balloon and I crashed my lips into his for the kiss of my lifetime. I barely heard the lock turning over the clash of our lips and shallow pants.

"Oh, shit!" Winter's startled cry froze me in place faster than Mr. Freeze. "Oh, God, I'm sorry guys, I—I'll go."

Drew whipped around to face his girlfriend, his toned ass pressing into my hard dick and making me groan. The two of us stood skin-to-skin in the middle of my living room, eyes locked on the beautiful woman we both loved with our whole hearts.

"H-Hi, Winter." Drew's neck reddened, but he made no move to go to her or to cover himself, his drool-worthy birthday suit on full display.

A smirk traced her lips. "Hi, Hardy Boy."

Her cheeks were flushed with embarrassment, but there was no mistaking the lust in her eyes. Was a tiny part of that lust for me?

I dared to hope.

She must have seen my message and came over, anyway. I should have known my Snow would always come when I called. There was nothing in the world like the bond I shared with this woman.

"Wait."

I hadn't meant for it to come out like a command, but it was—sort of. What if I could test the boundaries of this situation? What if I could have everything I truly wanted— with Drew, and with Winter?

I searched her familiar blue-green eyes while I slowly ran my hands down Drew's sides. Reaching around, I palmed his cock in my fist. I leisurely stroked upward, savoring his groan that reverberated through both of our bodies,

"Would you like to join us?" I continued to tug on Drew as I assessed Winter's reaction. There was a hesitance, but no disguising the outright want in them as she fixated on the relaxed hand job I was giving her boyfriend.

Our boyfriend.

"Ahh, fuck." Drew's curse of pleasure snapped her out of her state, and she moved to stand in front of her naked lover.

"What do you want, Drew?"

His answer was to cup her cheeks in his palms and kiss the ever-loving shit out of her, while I continued to work my hand between them both.

"I want you—both of you," he croaked out, when he finally let her lips go.

Fuck. Yes.

I cocked an eyebrow at Winter with the silent question. Was this an actual go? Was she willing for this?

It's not like I hadn't seen her naked before—other than my living wet dream when I accidentally saw her and Drew together. We'd had actual sex before. Granted, it was both of our first times and not the greatest sexual experience, but it was with her, and so it would always go down as one of my best.

I was starting to see I'd had actual feelings for Winter Wallace for far longer than I'd realized. Maybe the entire time I knew her.

I knew she wasn't there yet. I could only hope she'd get there someday soon, and we could share a moment like this without Drew in between us as the buffer. When that moment finally came, it would just be about her and about me.

But tonight, I'd settled for this. Fuck me, I'd sacrifice my body to these two like an Aztec on an altar.

Winter didn't answer me in words; she leaned into Drew's chest and kissed a delicate trail up to the skin beneath his ear. Skin I'd just marked as mine.

"Take my clothes off," she demanded in a whisper as she kept sucking on his neck, hardening both his cock in my hand and my own to fucking steel.

Drew wasted no time pulling her sweater over her head. Two perfect tits nestled in a blue lace bra. He quickly unclasped the bra and stripped her of her leggings, tugging her panties along with them. Within seconds, my beautiful best friend was the sexiest wet dream I'd ever laid eyes on.

"My bed, now," I growled, so desperate to be in Drew's ass and fucking him senseless while he fucked Winter, I was going to blow my load at the mere thought of it.

Winter grabbed Drew's hand and led us over. The view of her perfectly rounded cheeks churned thoughts of what it would be like to take her ass like Drew had—how good she'd feel around my cock.

How I could fuck both their asses in a night, giving them as much pleasure as I could wring out of them.

Another time. Tonight, I'd enjoy every inch of Drew's tight hole; I was going to make this so good for him, he'd be dreaming of this moment for a week.

Winter laid down at the end of the bed and opened her legs wide, revealing her glistening pussy and arousal dripping down her thighs.

What I wouldn't give for a taste.

Not tonight. But Drew could taste her, and I could taste her on him. Fuck, yes.

"Drew." I nodded towards her open thighs. "Lick her clean."

He kneeled in front of her, enthusiastically burying his face between her legs. He ran his tongue up and down her slit, around her clit, licking every drop of juice from her skin. Her moans were the very definition of sin.

I grabbed him by the neck and hauled him to his feet before he could make her come. Forcefully kissing him, I tasted every remnant of her wetness on his mouth.

Fuck me, she tasted sweet. I could only imagine the flavor of her cum. The thought brought the most delicious wave of pleasure through my shaft.

I was all for delayed gratification and foreplay, but I couldn't wait a second longer to fuck this man senseless.

"Are you going to fuck her while I fuck you?"

I bit his bottom lip and massaged his cock in my hand again, stroking him hard and fast until his breath caught in his throat.

"Yeeeessss." Drew moaned into my mouth. I spun him around, leaning him over the bed to line up with Winter's pussy.

"Fuck her nice and slow," I directed, while I moved to the nightstand to grab the tube of lube.

He thrust into her slowly, her body convulsing around him. She arched her back and tilted her hips to match him stroke for stroke. Drew palmed her breasts and placed kisses all along her collarbones; I lubed up my cock behind him.

The sexiest man in our state paused only when I squeezed some lube onto his ass, softly pushing it into his hole with two fingers. I scissored him until he buckled beneath me, stuttering his thrusts.

"You like that, baby?"

He balled his fists in the sheets as I pushed another finger into him, curving upwards to stroke his G spot.

"Fuck!"

His back arched off the bed as he pushed back, forcing my fingers deeper inside of him. Winter chased his body, rising on her elbows and kissing him like her life depended on it. He shuddered inside her.

"Keep giving Winter what she needs, baby. I'm going to take your ass now. Deep breaths, okay, baby? You're doing so well for me."

I gripped his hips and brought the head of my cock to his entrance, slowly sliding in and meeting the resistance of his virgin hole. His heat wrapped around me like a tight mitt—so tight my vision blurred and stars dotted behind my eyelids.

When he finally relaxed against Winter's body, I could make it all the way in, burying my cock inside him to the hilt. Ever so slowly, I moved.

My thrusts pushed him deeper into Winter's pussy; her mewls of bliss got higher and higher as I ramped up my pace; our bodies writhed to the same rhythm as we gave in to our basest needs.

I couldn't stop the lust burning through my veins and the insatiable need to possess these two from taking over; soon, I was slamming so deeply inside of Drew I was going to combust any second.

Winter fell over the cliff first. Her body bent into Drew's and a ragged cry escaped from her throat. The dirty sound pushed Drew to come; his body tensed beneath me as his cum exploded inside of her.

"Can I come in you?" I panted, reining in the very last lines of my control as I waited for his response.

"Yes." Drew groaned as he shifted his weight and pushed into me harder. "Fuck, Shane, make me yours."

Jets of hot cum burst from my cock at his permission; I filled him so thoroughly I knew I'd be seeping out of him for hours.

I pulled out as he collapsed on my bed next to Winter. He held her tightly to him as they both gasped for air. I grabbed a warm washcloth from the bathroom and handed it to Winter to clean herself up.

I'd do the cleaning one day—but today wasn't that day.

I snuggled in behind Drew, and the three of us laid on my bed, naked and blissed out, for a few stopped moments in time.

I'd tell them both about my discovery ... tomorrow.

I peeked over Drew's shoulder to glimpse my satisfied best friend; her perky nipples, her relaxed body, the soft lines of a sated smile.

She caught my eyes, and despite the gleam in hers, I could read the message, loud and clear. Fifteen years of friendship meant we had our own language, and I knew what she was saying.

Despite how right everything just felt, that moment we'd just shared had been for Drew.

But I couldn't shake the feeling we'd done it for us, too.

CHAPTER 14

DREW

I anxiously drummed my fingers across the hardwood table as the kind librarian looked up the selection I'd requested.

The Sequoia County library was a massive Grecian-style structure in the middle of the city center, and I couldn't remember the last time I'd been here.

It had been over a month since my last shift at the diner, and the feeling of being useless while everyone else continued on with their lives was making me feel extra shitty.

With all the new revelations with Travis and Cam and their family ties, Winter's father's shady agent girlfriend, and now Shane's dad's affair evidence, I had volunteered to do some research today while everyone else was tied up with work and final exams.

Last night, I had stayed the night at Shane's for the first time; Winter headed home to finish prepping for her exam this afternoon, so the two of us threw on our boxers and settled in to watch the next hockey game on TV cuddling on the couch until we moved to the bed to pass out.

It was different waking up in the firm hold of a man's arms, instead of cradling a woman in my own, but I couldn't have chosen a better option.

Sleeping with a man was not something I had considered until I'd gotten to know Shane, and now, now, I didn't know how I could ever *not* want him. Did that make me bisexual, or more sexually fluid? I had no idea, but it didn't matter what the label was.

I was into Shane; I loved Winter. That I could have both of them in my life the way they were was some incredible twist of fate.

And last night ... My sex life was currently a roaring blaze compared to the dumpster fire it had been before those two came into my life, but ... fuck. Every time I replayed the scene of Winter beneath me and Shane behind me, I got an instant hard-on.

I was going to chase that feeling between them until the day I died. Given our current set of circumstances, I really hoped that wouldn't be soon.

The librarian led me to a dark room at the back filled with rows of cabinets of microfilm reels. She stopped at the cabinet with the dates I'd asked for, and left me to my own devices.

My conversation with Mom months ago had been reactivated by Shane's discovery. There were too many coincidences; each answer brought up four new questions, and it all seemed to stem from their shared past.

The pain in Shane's voice when he shared his father's betrayal, and witnessing how torn Winter had been over the past few months over her father's life choices, was enough to spur me into action. I wanted to help. And I could—by figuring out what bound their fathers to Georgio all those years ago.

A person didn't just start doing illegal shit out of some act of friendship or loyalty, unless something cataclysmic was on the line. I could be pushed to do a lot of things out of the love I had for my family, but to risk absolutely everything meant I would have to lose absolutely everything in return.

Why would Darren and Emmett, two otherwise upstanding citizens with a very successful business, hitch their wagon to the likes of Georgio? Stanley and Camden were far easier to believe; Winter had shared little, but I knew both Hillary and Logan had divulged horror stories about their fathers.

And bad guys rarely started out as 'bad' guys. I couldn't believe Georgio was an evil teenage boy; my mom had her faults, but she wasn't the type to fall in love with the villain.

It was only a theory, but I had a feeling whatever happened to the Shambala Society in high school was the catalyst for the mess everyone seemed in today.

So, with all of my free time on my hands, I was out to prove it. Or at least find enough evidence to know I was on the right track.

It was why I used that year as a benchmark; I'd confirmed the exact time period with Mom on my drive to the library. Now, I was standing in front of hundreds of newspaper articles on tiny little film disks, hoping one of them had one lick of an answer.

It was hours before I got my first clue: an obituary and attached story about the accidental drowning of a teenage girl, Cheryl Simpson. The article said Cheryl's body had been found at the bottom of the Cascade Falls River basin, so badly beat up it took three days to identify her.

I looked up the obituary of Brenda Simpson on my phone as my mind raced with the new information. There weren't many Simpsons in these parts, and I couldn't believe that this was a coincidence.

It wasn't. Brenda was 'predeceased by her loving little sister,' Cheryl Simpson.

Shit.

I double-checked the dates; Cheryl's death was within the week of Georgio breaking up with Mom.

Double shit.

I tried to find more information about Cheryl, but the only other mention of her was the announcement of a closed casket funeral in the back of the Cascade Falls Chronicle.

My heart ached for that poor family. If Rosie or Dawn were ever found that way… my throat tightened at the mere thought of it, let alone the devastation of it being real. I'd hug them a little tighter at family dinner this weekend.

In the same year of archives, I came across a front-page feature on all the scholarship winners in Cascade Falls—Darren Wallace and Emmett Quicksilver were awarded a full ride for engineering—no real surprise there; but the family name on the scholarship fund caught my eye most of all; The Baker Family Fund.

Our town was small—it was virtually impossible this Baker family wasn't one and the same as Carson and Wyatt.

Another thing to look into later.

I searched the archives for another hour, but could find nothing else of value, other than a few 'Business Profile' articles featuring Antonio Carlos' business interests in Sequoia County. He was welcomed into our little communities with open arms, no one the wiser that he would slowly poison them all.

I packed up and thanked the librarian on my way out. Back in the privacy of my car, I called Mom again.

"Can you tell me more about Brenda?" I asked as I pulled out of the parking lot.

"Drew, I don't want you looking into this, I—"

"Mom, I say this with all the love in my heart. I'm in this mess because of you and Dad. And I'm going to get to the bottom of it. So, you can help me get there faster, or I'm going to do it myself, but it's happening, regardless."

Her resignation was evident in the silence that followed. I was about to prompt her again when she let out a deep sigh and said, "What do you want to know?"

"You said she was 'troubled' before. What did you mean?"

Another pause.

"Brenda wasn't ... mentally stable. I think she would have been diagnosed with bipolar disorder, if there was as much information about it back then as there is now. Maybe she was, and we just didn't know it. She self-medicated a lot. Usually just weed or alcohol, but sometimes pills. She used sex as a distraction, too. She fluttered between most of the guys in our friend group, but she was hyper-fixated on Emmett."

That wasn't surprising. At least the affair with Shane's dad was making a little more sense.

"Were they a couple?" I asked bluntly, not willing to betray Shane's confidence, but needing answers for him as much as for myself.

"Sometimes. I think Emmett really cared about her, but she couldn't commit to just him."

I thrummed my fingers against the dashboard in thought.

"Did anything change after Cheryl died?"

"How did you—"

"I'm investigating, Mom. What happened?"

Cue third lengthy pause.

"Brenda was a wreck, and our friendship collapsed. In hindsight, I probably could have been a better friend to her, but I didn't know how. She had all sorts of conspiracy theories and would accuse random people of pushing Cheryl into the river, and her parents sent her away for treatment at one point. When she came back, it was after we'd all moved on to university, and I didn't end up connecting with her again."

I couldn't think of anything else to ask her in that moment, so I thanked her and hung up, but not before getting a mother-fueled lecture about 'being careful' and to 'stay safe.'

If only she knew.

I suddenly had a very ballsy, potentially terrible idea. Before I could overthink it, I drove to the WAQ Engineering building and made my way up to their main office on the tenth floor.

I had never been here before. Feeling like a fish out of water, I stood at the reception desk and requested an impromptu meeting with my girlfriend's father, but I would not lose my new courage. Not until I had my say.

"Drew?" Darren's confused face popped into view as he rounded the corner. "Is everything all right?"

I reached to shake his hand out of habit. "Do you have five minutes to chat? It's about Winter."

I was about to overstep here in a way I'd never overstepped before, and Kellan and the boys, hell, probably even Winter was going to kick my ass, but we needed real answers, and I was tired of living my life with this anvil hanging over my head.

"What's this about Winter?" Darren questioned as he settled into a large office chair at the head of an intimidating board room table.

Nervous energy rocketed through me as I threw myself off the cliff.

"First of all, I love your daughter, which is why I'm coming to you like this."

Darren nodded, the unsettled look still all over his face.

I had to be careful here—Kellan had made it clear they were monitoring WAQ, so I couldn't risk hidden microphones catching anything they shouldn't.

What a weird life I was living.

"Winter knows that you grew up in Cascade Falls. We were going through old yearbooks recently, and we saw the picture of the Shambala Society. Mom was in the picture, so I asked her what it was about. She told us about your friend group, and how you were in foster care and usually crashed at Emmett's place."

The words came out in a rush, but I managed to say them all without given away anything else incriminating.

Darren's face molded into a mask of calm, the confusion melting away into a carefully crafted neutral expression. What I wouldn't give to hide myself from the world like that.

"The reason I'm telling you this is that Winter is really hurt and is struggling to come to you herself. I'm definitely overstepping here; I'm going to have to meet the consequences for that later, but for the sake of your relationship with your daughter, I think you should talk to her about it."

"I see."

Gone was the friendly man who had made us supper in his home, replaced by the stoic presence of a protective father. His sharp eyes, almost identical to the woman I loved, assessed me critically as he leaned back in the imposing chair.

Good; Winter's weird, dissociative relationship with her parents made it impossible to predict how Darren would react to my random ambush, but I was pleased that he was showing some sort of fatherly care.

Might as well push the envelope even further.

"Did you know Carson Baker is back in town?"

Darren's eyebrows shot up. Apparently not.

I didn't remember seeing Carson or Wyatt at the wedding, but that meant nothing. With hundreds of people there and my focus mostly on our own group, I could have missed their presence easily.

"It's bringing up a lot for Winter, and she's having to work through it all over again. We know about your history with Wyatt, and that's probably a good conversation to have with her, too."

I was bluffing here. Other than Logan's cryptic comment and a newspaper clipping about a scholarship, I had no idea what Darren's history was. But since I was a gambling man today, I might as well go all in on red.

Darren leaned over in his chair and scrubbed his palms over his jaw, his usually bright and youthful face looking far older in the time we'd been talking.

Well, I'd been talking.

He straightened suddenly, stood from the chair, and stuck out his hand.

"Thanks for dropping by, Drew. I'm afraid that's all the time I have for today."

I shook his hand, searching his eyes for any sign of resolution, but found nothing but a cool, emotionless blue.

"Thank you—sir." I tacked on the respect, hoping my attempt would soften the blow of my unannounced semi-demanding visit.

I left the building dutifully dismissed, but with a lightness I hadn't felt in weeks. I knew Darren loved his daughter; it wouldn't give us all the answers, but maybe enough to find a few more leads elsewhere.

It was a risk, but I could only hope it would pay off. Could we fall much farther down the rabbit hole than we already were?

I didn't actually want to know the answer to that question.

Another surprise hit me as I walked through the parking lot; Logan's Audi was parked beside my Corolla. He was sitting in the driver's seat, talking into the air and gesturing, obviously on a phone call.

Fuck it. I was going to be three-for-three today.

I opened his passenger door and slid into the soft leather seat.

"What the f—" Logan sputtered angrily. "Beth, I'm going to have to call you back."

He ended the call and glared at me, although it was lacking its usual venom.

"What do you want, Johnson?"

"To thank you, actually," I replied smoothly. Used to Logan and his moodiness by now, I was seeing his pretty-rich-boy act as comical instead of annoying.

He stared at me blankly. "For?"

"Winter said her first panic attack session with you went really well. Thank you for taking care of her."

His eyebrows rose in surprise and he was at a loss for words for a few seconds.

I had a feeling Logan wasn't thanked often.

"It was Hillary's idea," he mumbled, reaching into the backseat to grab his briefcase before turning to stare at me again.

"Was there something else?" he prompted, in an attempt to get rid of me as quickly as possible.

"You here on Eccles business?" I ignored him and nodded towards the massive building looming in front of us, the huge WAQ sign taking up the whole top of the building's real estate.

The man must have realized I was in no hurry to go anywhere. He huffed a breath of irritation and tucked his briefcase into his lap. He reached into the center console for a pack of gum and settled back into his own cushy seat.

"Yeah, I'm Stanley's bitch-boy today." He popped a stick of gum into his mouth and hesitated before handing the pack to me.

A peace-offering in the form of chewing gum. I'd take it.

"I know what that's like, you know." I grabbed my piece of gum and tossed him back the pack like we were old friends.

"Joe isn't Stanley, but my dad's shitty decisions fucked me over, too. Camden thought he was being a dick to fire me, but he was doing me a favor."

"Difference being you have a father you like." Logan's gaze caught on something in the distance. "Stanley could die tomorrow and I'd dance on his grave."

He said it so matter-of-factly, I knew it was true. Logan was his own sort of asshole, but his father had to be an evil son of a bitch to garner that sort of hatred from his only son.

He was right; I had a family I still loved and wanted to spend time with, and I'd inherited a new family, too. He could have that, too, if he could get over himself.

"When all this is over, he'll get his. You'll get out from underneath his bullshit, and you might even get the girl."

It was a really weird day in the universe when I was comforting Logan Eccles, especially with the carrot of my girlfriend, but here we were.

I was Bold Drew today, and I kind of liked that guy.

Logan snorted and fixed me with a scrutinizing stare.

"You can't really mean that. How are you just *okay* with sharing her?"

I shrugged, finally having a genuine answer to this question. "She's not mine to own. I haven't lost any of her heart to Cam or Travis—I still get everything she has—and it's worth it."

I bit my lip as I considered my next few words.

"She cares about you, and she's been willing to invite you into her world—that's a huge deal, so don't waste the opportunity. Regardless of you being the town's biggest dick most of our lives, if she thinks you have some redeemable qualities, I'm going to believe you do, too."

He shook his head in disbelief, but didn't respond. I took the silence as my chance to put the final nail into the proverbial coffin.

"Have you ever had a family you *wanted* to be a part of? There's one dangling right in front of you. This shitshow is going to be over someday soon. I wouldn't want to be alone when the dust settles."

I opened the passenger door and left his luxury vehicle for my little-old-man car, determined to leave him with something to think about.

That, and I seldom had the last word. Since I was Bold Drew today, I was going to have the last word.

Now, here's hoping all my bullshit gambles paid off.

CHAPTER 15

CAMERON

Thwack. Thwack. Thwack, thwack, thwack.

I pounded my fists against the unforgiving surface of the focus mitts, letting the sweet music of contact ring in my ears.

To his credit, Logan held the mitts tight and secure; a man who not only knew how to use them, he knew how to stand his ground. It should have surprised me, but it didn't. Billionaire Boys Club had his own current of anger roiling beneath the surface of his skin—a caged animal could recognize its equal.

I *was* surprised when he'd invited me back to his gym to spar with him, instead of my little violet. Curiosity got the better of me—that, and with Georgio reviving his fight nights and me being his primary punching bag, I could use the practice.

Logan had proven to be a worthy opponent. He couldn't hit as hard, and his footwork was less agile, but he was light on his toes and seldom did what I expected. We'd been sparring for the better part of two hours, but I could go all night.

A better man than me might even admit he was having fun.

I held up my fists in a 'break' gesture and reached for my bottle of water on the mat. My bloodied bare knuckles left streaks of crimson against the leather pads; the biological artwork a sure sign of pain to come.

"When'd you start fighting?" I sat down on the rigid vinyl and grabbed my towel to mop the sweat from my chest; I'd long ago abandoned my shirt.

The smaller man paused for a beat; his brown eyes seemed to stare through me as he considered his answer.

"I started lessons at seventeen," he finally said, reaching for his own bottle of water and taking a seat across from me. "Stanley had beaten the crap out of me for the last time, and I was making sure he wouldn't get another chance."

"He the one who scarred you?" I nodded to the hem of his t-shirt, stained with rings of sweat clinging to his body. I had glimpsed the raw, ragged patches of damaged skin when his shirt rode up, but despite the heat and the soaked material, he hadn't taken it off.

Logan's face morphed into a murderous glare. "Yeah. And one of these days, I'll pay the bastard back by killing him."

I dipped my head at his conviction. You could always tell when a man meant something with his whole heart—like the very fabric of his being depended on that one truth.

"I'll help you." I tossed him the fresh towel beside me to clean up. "Men who beat innocents deserve to die."

His eyes widened, but he caught himself before giving anything else away. He shifted to standing from his seat on the floor; after a moment's hesitation, he offered a hand to pull me up.

I took the offer for what it was—a gesture of peace.

I understood the man more than he knew. We both held our cards close, refusing to trust those around us with our lives. Every person in our circle had earned their place. Logan wore his arrogance like a shield; I wore my silence. We weren't so different.

This round, I held the pads, letting him focus his ire into the center of my protected palms. He unleashed his rage with an acute accuracy, and I wondered if he'd ever consider getting into the ring professionally. I dismissed the thought as soon as it had come.

Picture-perfect Pretty Boy wouldn't want anyone knowing he was anything but presentable.

We moved from practicing jabs to grapples—more MMA style fighting than boxing, but the release in aggression soothed my restless soul for the time being. I could feel his own demons dissolve as our bodies tired and our muscles knotted from use.

At the next water break, I glanced up at the wall clock on the other side of the room.

"I'm going to have to get going." After another beat, I gave him a brief explanation—not that he was owed one. "We're moving Darlene tonight."

I had taken Kellan seriously when he said my biological mother wasn't safe. She may have lived under an alias in a dumpy-ass apartment on the outskirts of Carlisle, but after having found her after months of searching, I wasn't willing to take the risk of Georgio, or worse, Antonio, finding her because of her connection to me.

It had taken a full week of pleading. While I wouldn't say she had become anything near motherly, we'd spent the last few months tentatively forming a relationship. She might never be anything more than Darlene, but she wanted to be in my life.

Right now, that meant messages and occasional chats over coffee, but she was starting to mean more to me than just the woman who birthed me. Under her prickly persona, she had a kindness deep-rooted in Southern hospitality, and a sense of humor that caught me off guard more often than not. She had chosen not to be bitter, even though life had not been kind to Darlene Knightly. I wanted her safe.

I was about to kidnap her myself, not caring about her consent if she was only going to get herself killed, when she'd suddenly agreed to let us get her away from Carlisle for a few weeks. I could guess that a convincing violet had something to do with it, but I wouldn't question the gift horse.

Kellan agreed to provide a safe house on the other side of Kensington; I was supposed to drive her there tonight in Drew's Corolla—the least conspicuous vehicle of all our cars. Because Pop's Chevelle stood out like the beauty she was, we couldn't take the risk of someone noticing anything out of the ordinary.

It might be a misplaced sense of paranoia, but I was going to trust my—brother—on this one.

Logan sneered, his arrogance back on full display. "What a good little brother. Kellan having you do his bitch-work again?"

I stiffened as all the somewhat pleasant thoughts of my opponent disintegrated under his ingratiating tone.

"That depends. The Feds still making you their little bitch-boy?"

His jaw ticked and his glare could have melted another man to syrup. I let my ire dissolve as soon as it had come.

Logan wasn't my enemy, as much as he had the tendency to get under my skin.

"I'm choosing to trust him right now," I said matter-of-factly. "Just like I'm choosing to trust your prickly ass."

Logan's gaze was calculating as he assessed me. He blew out a noisy breath and threw his towel in the laundry bin across the mat.

"Do you need help?"

My brows melted into the evenly shaved fade of my hairline. The only time I had ever seen or heard Logan offer his help was in protecting our auburn-haired beauty. I briefly wondered if he was on the drugs again, or as desperate for the feeling of a family that I realized was in my own heart.

"It could be dangerous." I shrugged, tossing my towel in the laundry in acknowledgement that we were done for the day. My muscles were aching the longer we sat, anyway.

I shifted my body into a stretch, working out some of the lactic acid before I stiffened up. After a moment's hesitation, Logan dropped beside me to do the same.

"Seems to be the theme of our lives these days," he muttered darkly. For a few minutes, we remained silent, working our muscles out in a familiar line-up of poses.

When he said nothing else as we left the building, I sighed in acquiescence. We were both too filled with pride to seek help or extend it. I would also be foolish to turn the blind faith offer away.

"I'm going to shower and then I'm headed to Drew's to pick up his car. If you want to join me, it's probably better to have someone who knows how to fight with me."

The comment hadn't been an attack on Drew. I had come to like and respect him and he gave Winter the world. To my knowledge, he couldn't shoot a gun, and while I was sure he could throw a punch with his sheer size alone, he wasn't a trained fighter.

Logan's cruel smirk lit up his face. I also hadn't meant to stroke the man's already inflated ego, but if that's what it took to get him to do some good in the world, I'd play that card tonight.

"You can shower in my spare bathroom." He gestured to the elevator as he strode toward it. "Come on."

Dumbly, I followed him. We stood like sentinels in the gold-painted box as it skyrocketed to his penthouse. The last time I'd been here was when Winter was drugged and unconscious. My fists clenched at the memory. I never wanted to see my little violet vulnerable like that ever again.

I watched my unlikely companion for the evening from the corner of my eye. He had proven he would take care of our girl as well. Protect her when I couldn't. His demons held him hostage like my own, but Winter lightened their burden—only a blind man wouldn't see the changes she was making to his darkened heart.

The changes she was making to all of our stained souls.

He unlocked the door with his fancy keypad and left me in the foyer. Okay, then. I made my way to the bathroom on the other side of the condo and cleaned up. In twenty minutes, we were washed, dressed, and making our way down to his parking garage.

He'd insisted on taking his car, arguing mine was too conspicuous. Instead of the silver Audi he usually drove, he unlocked a shiny black Land Rover parked in a hidden slot at the back of the underground concrete compound.

I climbed in, overtaken by the new car smell and the sheer luxury of the vehicle. Logan and I may have similar dark spirits, but our lives couldn't be any more different.

The drive to Drew's was quiet, but not unpleasant. My body was still buzzing from the endorphins of our sparring session, and adrenaline had seeped into my veins by the time we arrived at his garage apartment.

I had never been here before, but Drew wasn't here much, anyway. Shane's apartment, as cramped as it was, was more the home base for our group of misfits.

Logan stayed in the car while I walked up the steps to Drew's door. It was fully dark now, and the cool June evening air calmed the building inferno of my skin.

Shane opened the door with a grin. "'Bout time you showed up!"

His smile was wide, but his eyes had dark shadows under them, like he was being haunted from the inside out. Maybe he was. The events of the last few months had taken their toll. Shane probably had the best heart of us all, so I wouldn't be surprised if his had cracked the hardest.

Winter and Travis were working at Bourbon & Blues tonight; I should have expected Shane would be with Drew. The two were a packaged deal these days.

I couldn't begrudge their happiness. If Winter accepted this change in their relationship, so could I. There was nothing ordinary about any of our connections, and I was quickly admitting this was the way it was. I loved the woman, so I had to love her men, too.

My thoughts shifted to the man in the car one level below us. I would at least tolerate them.

I heard keys jangling when Drew's head popped up behind Shane's. "Ready to go?"

I startled. "You're coming?"

We hadn't discussed him coming. I was to pick Mom up and deliver her to Maverick, Kellan's second-in-command, and he would take her to the safe house. I didn't like this arrangement, but it was an opportunity to stop anyone from following us, and Kellan had convinced me he trusted Maverick with his life.

The only men I trusted with my life were here—Travis notwithstanding—but I had to have some faith he'd come through.

The subterfuge and secrets were giving me one hell of a headache.

"Hell yeah, I'm coming. I wouldn't have you do this alone."

"I'm coming too." Shane piped up. "Three's better than two, yeah?"

I rubbed the back of my neck awkwardly. "Um, Logan's here too."

Both pairs of eyebrows shot up as the two men ambled out of the doorway and brushed past me to get down the stairs—to see for themselves, I guessed. I followed them, anticipating a hostile interaction.

Instead, Shane opened the driver's side door with a beaming smile. Logan appeared startled as he looked up from scrolling through his phone.

"Hey, brother!" he boomed, rubbing his large palm over Logan's hair and mussing it up. "Glad you could join us!"

"Fuck off." Logan growled and shoved Shane away before running a hand over his head to flatten the tangled nest Shane had made. "What are you doing here, anyway? Chase never mentioned the puppy was coming."

"Drew and I are fucking now, didn't you hear?" Shane quipped as Drew's cheeks bloomed into a purple shade of cooked beets.

Still, he didn't speak up to deny it.

Logan's gaze shifted between the two men and rolled his eyes. "Figures. Whoever said 'nice guys finished last' was a fucking twat."

He nodded to Drew with a look of disgust. "Of course, Preppy Boy's getting the most action of all of us. Or have you finally made your move with your sexpot of a best friend yet, Quicksilver? Are you getting in on the two-holes action, too?"

He didn't wait for an answer before he turned in his seat to look back at his phone, but I didn't miss the loaded look Drew and Shane shared. That was a story for another time.

I waited for the rage to roll through me at Logan's words against our girl, but it never came. Irksome prickles bled through my chest, but that was the extent of my emotional turmoil. Logan had proven himself to be an ally, not a threat, so his words no longer held the same cutting weight that begged me to cut off his head.

Mostly.

Shane smirked, also not swayed by Logan's antics. "Definitely getting more holes than you're getting."

Drew aggressively cleared his throat, obviously eager to shift the conversation to anything but his—holes.

"We're not all going to fit in my car, guys."

Logan looked up from his screen and huffed dramatically. "We'll take the Rover. I'm not getting in the backseat of that thing,"—he gestured to Drew's car sitting innocently in the driveway—"and I don't trust any of you fuckers to drive."

"Who died and made you boss?" Shane said cheerfully as he opened up the back of the Rover and slid into the seat behind Logan.

Drew and I looked at each other and shrugged. This wasn't the night we had planned, but I could admit I felt better having the backup.

We climbed into the passenger seats and buckled up. Logan finally put down his phone and backed down the long driveway.

The cab grew unsettlingly quiet. Outside, the streetlights faded away along the mountain highway to Carlisle. Logan turned the knob on the expensive stereo system and a light, classical melody filled the empty space between us.

"Should have known you would be a classical man." Shane's head poked in between the seats and he clapped his hands on Logan's shoulders. "You're high brow, bro."

Logan shrugged Shane off of him with a jerk of his body. "Don't touch me, Quicksilver. Listen to the music or give Johnson a blowjob or something."

Drew choked on air in the backseat. "That won't be necessary," he sputtered. I couldn't see his face in the rearview mirror, but I didn't imagine it had lost its purple hue.

Shane brightened. "Voyeurism is your thing, huh? Cool. We'll explore that one later." He mussed up Logan's hair again and Logan growled.

"Touch me again, and I'll leave you out here to hitchhike."

Shane put up his palms in a signal for peace. "Just getting a little bonding in with you, brother. You know I'm touchy-feely."

Logan didn't respond, and the cab fell quiet again, the swirling notes of a talented pianist blanketing us with their song.

Within minutes, the roiling tension between us dissipated. My mind went still as I disappeared into the darkened landscape of shadowed, jutted rocks and spruce trees. Before I knew it, the lit-up sky of Carlisle could be seen in the distance.

I gave Logan the address to Darlene's place, and we arrived in fifteen minutes. This wasn't a good neighborhood; many of the buildings had bars on the windows, and graffiti and garbage smothered every surface of the city street.

I had texted her ten minutes before to let her know to be ready. When we pulled up to her complex, she'd rushed from the shadows to the car.

"Oh!" Her mouth dropped open when she pulled the passenger side door open to find Drew.

"Hi, Ms. Knightly," Drew said politely, getting out of his seat and holding the door open for her. "Let me take that."

He took the bag out of her hands and gently placed it behind him in the back. It didn't look like much, but then again, I didn't know how much she owned to pack.

I turned around to smile at the woman, knowing this was not the welcome wagon she'd been expecting.

"It's okay," I crooned soothingly, needing to comfort this woman who'd lived a life full of fear. "They're here to help."

"Hurry up," Logan barked from the front as Drew helped Darlene into the center seat of the car. "I don't want to get carjacked."

"Fuck off," Shane, Drew, and I all said in unison. Darlene's gaze snapped curiously between the four of us, but she said nothing.

Once we'd cleared the sketchy area by taking multiple detours—I didn't know if this was intelligent or paranoia, but we weren't taking the chance—Logan pulled back onto the highway and picked up speed, eager to make up some lost ground. It was approaching midnight, and Kellan had already messaged my burner that Maverick was already at the meeting site.

"So, you're all friends?" Darlene spoke up after ten minutes of weighted silence.

I looked at her in the rearview. I was about to answer when Shane's bright teeth flashed in the dark cabin, using the smile that could put anyone at ease.

"Sure are, Mrs. K! All friends, banded together by blood and brotherhood. Isn't that right, Loggie?"

"Don't call me that," Logan barked. He shot Shane an evil eye in the mirror I was still looking through.

Darlene's brows rose, but she asked no more questions.

I owed her an explanation, at the very least. She'd been running for years and had put her trust in me. I valued that trust, even if she was still earning mine.

"We're all tied to the same—issue." I tried to be as tactful as I could, given the situation. "My friends here"—I speared a look at Logan, but he ignored me—"wanted to help get you to safety."

The air shifted in the vehicle and I should have known Logan couldn't resist stirring up trouble.

"What he's not saying is that they're all into his girlfriend."

His shit-eating grin needed to be smacked off his face. I supposed I should be grateful he didn't bring up the 'holes' conversation again.

I wouldn't give him the satisfaction, even as my fists clenched in my lap.

"Including you," I deadpanned. "Difference being, they have a chance."

I knew it was a lie. One I wanted to be true, but I was resigned to the fact Winter had obvious feelings for Logan. But I wouldn't give him a leg up on anything today.

"Oh, look! We're almost there," Drew muttered hurriedly, shifting the focus back to the real topic at hand.

Logan pulled off onto a quiet rest stop without security lights and tucked the vehicle into a secluded copse of trees. We sat quietly for thirty seconds at the most, before the shape of a tall, thin man materialized from the other side of the parking lot.

"That's our cue." I climbed out of the car; Drew, Shane and Logan did the same; Drew grabbed Darlene's bag and helped her down the high step like the gentleman he was.

"Whole gangbang crew is here, I see." Maverick's pretentious sneer was held in place by years of righteousness and capturing bad guys.

Could he hear the stories of the people he was so desperate to put behind bars? Could he taste their pain, along with their poor decisions? Did he see his place of privilege to have never been put in a decision where he chose survival over morality?

I had my doubts.

"Fuck off, Maverick." Logan spit the name like it offended him. Given his history, it probably did. "Do your fucking job and get Cam's mother to safety. Then do more of your job and get us to fucking safety."

They had their macho stare-down while I guided Darlene gently toward Maverick's vehicle. I opened the rear door of the sedan and gave her time to get situated before dropping to my haunches in front of her.

I palmed her cheeks and kissed her forehead. It was more intimate than I'd ever been with the woman who'd given me life, but it felt appropriate. If we made it out of this mess, perhaps even symbolic of the relationship to come.

"Text me when you get there and you feel safe, okay?"

She clutched my hands tightly, squeezing the life out of my fingers before releasing me and clasping them in her lap.

"You stay safe," she murmured apprehensively. I gave her my most reassuring smile and closed the door. Walking back, I witnessed four men staring each other down in a silent pissing contest.

"Let's go." I grabbed Logan by the elbow to bring him back to his car, but he wrenched out of my grasp.

"Stop fucking touching me."

Still, he followed, and we piled into our seats as Maverick stalked back to his own car. I shot off a quick text to Kellan, letting him know we'd made the drop.

The drive home was uneventful; a somber stiffness filled my limbs as I succumbed to my own thoughts in the dead of night. The others were just as quiet. Shane and Drew fell asleep against each other in the backseat, only waking groggily when Logan dropped them back off at Drew's place with little fanfare. Finally, we arrived back at his parking garage in one piece.

Logan looked even more tired than I was. I felt the need to thank him for his help, but all I had were my words.

"Why'd you do it?" I asked instead, needing an honest answer to his unexpected altruism.

His heavy eyes appraised me before he blew out a breath. "I never had a mother to save."

With that cryptic response, he stepped into the elevator and disappeared into the tower of his castle.

It took me twenty minutes to get home—I rolled all the windows down to keep me awake. Stumbling up the apartment steps to my humid abode, I stopped dead still when I found two people fast asleep in my bed.

Travis and Winter had waited up for me. He was the only one with a key to my place, and by the looks of things, they had come here straight from work, their black uniforms shucked in a pile by the door.

Travis was curled around my little violet's body wearing only his boxers, and Winter wore a pair of my boxers with one of my boxing tanks. The apartment was hotter than hell, so they had abandoned the blanket and thrown it on the floor.

My heart stuttered at the sight. A less exhausted man would be aroused. Instead, wispy tendrils of contentment filled me; a feeling I only experienced in my violet's presence.

I pulled off my own clothes and crawled into bed on the other side of them, careful not to disturb their slumber.

Within seconds I was asleep, my heart whole with the two people I cared most about in this world tucked safely in my arms.

CHAPTER 16

WINTER

I floated in the in-between state of unconsciousness and waking, my body molded into the comfort of my cotton sheets and nestled into my downy feather pillows. When I was about to drift back into the unconscious side for a little while longer, a hot, wet tongue lazily flicked against my clit in the most delicious way.

As I moaned, the tongue gently circled around me before a soft set of lips latched onto it, sucking and nuzzling until my entire core was a gushing geyser of need.

My hands reached around in the dark, landing on Travis' bobbing head as he flattened his tongue to lick me fully; his fingers traced the outline of my pussy before opening me up to spear me with his talented tongue.

I couldn't tell you how long he'd been pleasuring me—I didn't even know somnophilia was his thing—I just knew I was seconds from coming all over his chin.

He spread my thighs wider, went back to sucking on my clit, and thrust two fingers inside of me, curling them into my favorite spot. My back bowed off the bed in response, but he held me down, forcing me to accept his ministrations, unable to get away from the building sensation in my lower belly.

Maybe it was because I was already so relaxed, or maybe it was because Travis really was a seasoned pro at making me come, but the uncomfortable burn of needing to pee rocketed through me before a literal dam broke, soaking his face and my sheets. The orgasm ripped a scream from my throat and unbridled pleasure swept through my entire body. My ears rung and my heart pounded like it wanted out of my chest.

"Fuck, that's hot," Travis said breathily as he lapped up what he could of my cum. "You've never squirted for me before, beautiful. But fuck me if that's not going to be my mission from now on."

A euphoric smirk overtook my face in the dark, and with what little strength I had left, I pulled him up over my body and kissed him, tasting myself all over his lips.

He groaned into my mouth, and his erection dug into my belly. I continued to kiss him while sliding my hand down between us. I guided his hard cock into my swollen pussy. He stilled when he was all the way in. When he cupped my cheek in his palm, his eyes, visible through the dim light, were soft and bright, full of warmth.

"I've missed you," I whispered into his hand.

He kissed my forehead tenderly before pulling out and slowly thrusting back into me. I arched into him, eager to feel him everywhere. He continued the tortuous languid strokes, kissing me so deeply that I had no breath in my lungs, but I refused to come up for air. There wasn't an atom of space between us. Our bodies fused together, so many words passing through without a single one being spoken.

The sex took a desperate turn; his thrusts became ruts and his pace quickened to the point of frantic. I matched his every move and writhed on his dick like the world was about to end. Like it was our last chance to make each other come.

I bit and nipped his neck and his chest, my hands gripping his biceps so hard I knew I'd leave a mark as he pounded a permanent imprint into my mattress. My body was tight as a bowstring, the pressure building to the point of no return.

The tension broke like a popped balloon; I cried out his name while my body deflated until all that was left was a pile of Jell-O bones and blood cells. Travis stuttered out his release and moaned my name into my hair.

I should have gotten up to pee; I should have moved him off of me, or at the very least, move out of the growing wet spot underneath my ass, but I was too sated to care.

Sunshine streaming through my windows woke me hours later. Travis was still curled around me.

Despite the burning need to pee—curse past me's decisions—I stayed still, tracking the flutter of his eyelids as he remained lost in his dreams. The dark fan of eyelashes across his angular cheeks, the flop of his wavy dark hair over one side of his face, his long masculine fingers splayed across my belly in a possessive and protective way... Tingling warmth spread across my chest as I watched him.

I loved this man with my whole heart.

My chest constricted, and I worried my lip between my teeth. He was holding it all together, despite another unwanted shift in his relationship with his uncle.

As if he sensed my eyes on him, his lips curled into a sleepy smile. "Good morning, beautiful." His raspy, croaky man voice did funny things to my insides. "Ready for today?"

My tingles turned to riotous butterflies.

"No." I groaned and shifted Travis off of me to escape to the bathroom. From the open door, I complained, "I was having perfectly good thoughts, and you ruined them."

"I'm sorry," he called out from the bed. His sleepy voice indeed sounded chagrined. "Let's start over. How about I make you come again and we can forget your meeting with your parents today?"

I washed my hands and walked back into the bedroom. "Way to help me forget, HB." I dubiously cocked an eyebrow at him. "And"—I looked at the time on the nightstand —"Shit! I'm supposed to be there in an hour. I've got to shower!"

Racing back into the bathroom, I threw myself into the cold-water spray, using soap to wash away the evidence of our pleasure. I didn't enjoy cold showers, but today was going to be all sorts of uncomfortable, so I might as well make it a theme.

My hot boyfriend had the good sense to join me in the shower after the water heated up. He didn't make a move, knowing how stressed I already was about the day, but he ran his fingers through my hair, helped me soap up, and relaxed me enough to halt my internal hyperventilating.

Dad had invited me to the house today for a family chat. *"Things we need to discuss,"* he'd said.

Given all the secrets I was hoarding like a dragon, the very thought of this discussion was giving me heart palpitations. I hoped he'd be the one doing the discussing, and I'd just listen long enough to get out of there intact.

Travis had offered to go with me, but he needed to work and even though I didn't know exactly what the topics of conversation were going to be, I figured they wouldn't be appropriate for an audience.

Although, it was my parents who'd announced they'd been in a long-term open marriage in front of four men, three of whom they didn't really know, so perhaps my judgment was way off on that one.

I kissed Travis goodbye as we left my apartment together.

"Call you later," he promised, leaving me to drown in my overwhelming apprehension.

I was being dramatic; after all the truly dangerous things we had hanging over our heads in the last eight months, here I was, terrified to have an adult conversation with my father.

The drive to my parents' house whizzed by on autopilot. I swallowed every angry bee buzzing in my gut and steeled myself for whatever would be said in the next hour. Good or bad—most likely bad—I could handle it.

I used one of the breathing techniques Logan had taught me. Basil and I sat in the circular driveway, my limbs too heavy to move on their own. It was more effective than I'd hoped; a contented calm crept into my veins and stopped in the recesses of my heart—enough for my legs to carry me into the cavernous foyer of my childhood without an accompanying panic attack.

"Hi, honey." Dad's voice came from somewhere beyond the kitchen at the same time I closed the heavy wooden door behind me. "We're in your mother's office."

My mother's office was on the opposite side of the house. Nestled behind the garage, it had an expansive view of an exposed ravine on one side of the property. Normally a beautiful sight, this morning's dense fog obscured the lush forest. I took that for the ominous sign it was.

Mom and Dad were chatting quietly on the gold velvet couch centered in the room and got to their feet when I walked in. I submitted awkwardly to their hugs before I vacated to the overstuffed slipper chair across from them. I rested my feet on the wicker coffee table that acted as a buffer between us.

"You're alone?" Mom questioned after they had both settled again. "I assumed you'd bring one of your boyfriends with you."

Bemused, my brows rose quizzically. "This seemed like a Wallace family matter, so here I am."

Dad cleared his throat. At the clear sign of his discomfort, I took the moment to appraise my usually handsome father. His hair seemed to be graying a lot faster at his temples, and puffy bags of skin hung below his eyelids. He looked like he hadn't slept in days and he'd rather be anywhere but here.

That makes two of us.

Mom looked unflappable as always, but then again, she was always the hardest to read. I seldom knew what to expect from my mother—I just knew she never responded in the way I needed or hoped for.

Wah, wah, poor me.

"Why don't we get this over with?" The words came out bitchier than intended, but I was so damn tired of the lies, the half-truths, and excuses of protecting me. "What did you want to discuss?"

Dad didn't look surprised at my outburst. Instead, he released a long breath and scrubbed his face with his palms.

"It's come to my attention that you're aware of some ... things, and I'm embarrassed that you had to find out from someone else."

Aware of some things ... That statement was a loaded machine gun with a heavy hand on the trigger.

I remained silent, not trusting that any break in his concentration wouldn't stop the conversation from happening all together. I willed my face to maintain a neutral, open mask, hoping to hell my strong lack of filter wouldn't betray me.

Sure enough, a few time-expanding seconds later, Dad told his story. The true version of it.

"I grew up in Cascade Falls. Just outside of it, actually, on the old Thompson Road. I bounced from foster home to foster home from the time I was nine. My father was a deadbeat, and my mother was an addict, and child services removed me four times before deciding to get me out of there permanently. My foster homes weren't much better—I had my fair share of abuse, so I stayed with Emmett mostly, when his mother would let me. Native American families didn't have the same rights in the system, and they weren't legally allowed to foster me, let alone adopt me, so I'd just run away and escape there whenever I could. It was because of them I stayed on the straight and narrow to even hope to go to university. They probably saved my life."

My heart hurt, thinking of any child in that situation. My parents were absent, but they weren't bad people. A chink appeared in my long-time frustration with them. Maybe Dad just didn't know how to be a good parent.

"We should have told you we had a history here. I thought because we had the freedom of no family ties, and with my dark cloud of an upbringing, that it would be better for you to think this place was a fresh start for all of us."

Like a five-year-old would have cared about whether Daddy grew up down the street. I could understand the foster system was a complicated machine to explain to a small child, but we could have had this conversation light years before now.

"When you were a teenager, I had hoped to come clean." Dad continued, as if reading my mind. "And then everything happened between you and the Baker boy, and it wasn't the right time or place. And I was feeling guilty enough about what that boy did to you as it was. I didn't want to admit that we had lied to you on top of it."

My brain stuttered. "Why would you feel guilty? It wasn't your fault."

I could have said Mom could have toned down her sexual rights vendetta and kept me out of national newspapers—that *had* been her fault—but that wasn't the point of today's talk. It would only fall on deaf ears, anyway.

Oddly, my older look-alike kept quiet. Her hand lightly stroked Dad's arm as he regaled his tale. Her lips were flat and her eyes were tight, as if this was painful for her, too.

"Wyatt Baker was a dick, just like his son." The venom in Dad's tone took me aback.

"He bullied Emmett for years, and then when Emmett got his growth spurt, he moved on to terrorize his sisters. Emmett couldn't retaliate without severe consequences, but I could. When Wyatt went too far and forced himself on Aidie, I beat the shit out of him. There were no witnesses, so he couldn't prove it was me, but he never forgot."

My mouth filled with saliva and I shivered at the burning image of an innocent Aidie pinned under Wyatt. Dad's fists clenched and his eyes filled with a heated anger so palpable its waves washed over me.

"When Carson came after you, I knew. Like father, like son. It was why your mother and I tried to bury him alive. I know it didn't seem like it, but we wanted that family to pay. I wanted to break their assault cycle once and for all. Wyatt was a menace who hid behind his father's money, and then Carson did the same."

Hot tears pricked the back of my eyelids as the first few tendrils of understanding collected h my consciousness.

"But you paid the price, honey, and I'm so, so sorry for that."

A sob escaping, I buried my face in my hands, hiding behind my hair, a privacy screen between me and the truths of my parents.

"I wanted to tell you about the open marriage years ago."

Mom spoke for the first time in what seemed like hours, her smoky voice breaking through my tears. "I was a coward and didn't think you would be open to the idea—I guess I was worried that Carson's actions would traumatize you, and you wouldn't have been comfortable with this aspect of our lives. I should have trusted you."

You could have knocked me out with a feather. It was like we were on Dr. Phil's couch with the bald man himself in the corner directing the dialogue of our forgiveness journey—or whatever the hell this was.

"I know we've never been great parents." Mom smiled weakly, another red-hot acknowledgment spoken into the confines of her office. "We tried to make you strong and independent, but I know we missed the mark sometimes."

Mom wasn't good at being vulnerable. Dad wasn't great at admitting anything was ever wrong. I had woken up in an alternate universe, I was sure of it.

"Why now?" I croaked out, so caught off-guard by the deluge of confessions that I needed to divert the conversation enough to get my bearings again. "Why bring all of this up now?"

Dad stroked his jaw, avoiding my scrutinizing stare. He squared his shoulders before matching my stare with one of his own.

"Drew came to me and put me in my place about a few things. You've got a good man there."

I didn't expect that. My Hardy Boy was bearing the weight of the world on his shoulders and trying to come to my rescue besides? The feminist in me wanted to be indignant; the woman, though, she felt unbelievably loved by a man willing to face her father and wanted to kiss the shit out of him.

The revelation also explained why this conversation had not one mention of the FBI, or ties to Georgio, or WAQ. Drew must have made the focus on me.

Guilt filled my pores as I realized my parents were trying to pass me an olive branch—whether solicited by

Drew or not—and my actions may end up putting Dad in jail for the rest of his life.

His actions. *His* actions were going to put him in jail. Now, more than ever, I really needed to know why. Why would my father, who defended innocent women's honor, who had worked so hard to get out of this town that wasn't kind to him, come back and set up roots here with illegal start-up cash? I couldn't push the topic today, but I needed to know the answer before he paid the ultimate price for his decisions.

A clammy film seeped out of my skin and covered me; a cold sweat battling with hot flashes of panic. I clamped down hard on my go-to reaction. Hell, no.

Taking a fortifying breath, I stood. "Thank you for telling me." I stiffly moved to the door of the office before I turned around. Not meeting either of their stares, I said, "I need some time to process. I'll call you when I'm ready."

Tears blurred my vision most of the drive, but I knew the mountain roads like the back of my hand. My mind was empty, like I'd opened up my head and scooped out every thought. I was grateful for the mild reprieve, even if disassociation was most assuredly *not* a sound coping technique.

I soon sat in the parking lot of Shane's apartment complex. I should have known this was where my heart would take me when my entire world was too heavy for me to carry.

We were blurring the lines of our friendship in a way I didn't understand, but hadn't pushed back against. The night we'd shared with Drew between us was one of the sexiest, sinful moments of my life, but I couldn't bring myself to regret it.

The way Quick's gaze had worshipped my body; the way his hands had worshipped Drew's ... There was a *rightness* to all of it I couldn't ignore. But the thought of taking our soul-bond to a higher level was, at best, a terrifying consideration.

He wasn't expecting me, but I was too bone-tired to take out my phone and give him a heads up. I made my way up the three floors and let myself in with my trusty key.

My handsome best friend looked up from his position on the couch. His tall frame was sprawled out, his head on the armrest, and his feet dangled over the other side. One of his sci-fi thriller books lay on his chest.

He was wearing a baseball cap backward, with his dark hair tucked behind his ears, a white t-shirt, and black joggers. His gray eyes searched mine. Whatever he saw there was enough for him to leap off the couch like the panther he was and wrap his arms around me in three seconds flat.

"Hey, Snow," he murmured, rubbing his large hands in soothing circles along my spine. "What's wrong?"

Through my soul-weary haze, I vaguely made out that his usually neat and tidy space was trashed. Three pizza boxes lay in a haphazard pile on his tiny breakfast table, and from the smells lingering in the air, they still had remnants of day-old pizza in them. Piles of dirty clothes littered the floor, and food wrappers and stubbed out joints lined the coffee table. The room didn't reek of an ashtray, but the mild, sweet smell of pot smoke clung to the small space.

Now wasn't the time to question him, though. We'd all been under a lot of stress, and he'd only finished his final exams last week. My apartment was pretty gross-looking too—although that was more my norm.

I buried my nose in the soft cotton of his t-shirt, and his calming scent of pine trees and new leather enveloped me.

"Just had a talk with my parents." I spoke into his chest, the muffled sounds sounding more tragic than intended. "I'm just a little overwhelmed with life right now."

He grunted an acknowledgment and held me tighter to him. His body heat and heartbeat quelled all feelings of distress for the time being.

Quick had the most beautiful gift of being able to bring me peace under any set of circumstances. I wouldn't need panic attack lessons from Logan if Quick could be permanently attached to my side like a Siamese twin.

The imagery of that thought made me giggle through my tears; Shane thumbed my chin and tilted my face up.

With an inquisitive look, he asked, "What made you go from 0 to 30 on the giggle scale?" His gaze continued searching my eyes—for signs of insanity, no doubt.

"I pictured you as my Siamese twin," I answered honestly, my giggles nearing hysteria. His responding look assured me he did indeed think I was going crazy.

My giggles dissipated into full-body wracking sobs. My brain finally cracking under the weight of our world; even the super-glue that was Shane's comfort couldn't put me back together.

"Hey, hey, hey."

His soothing tenor covered me like a well-worn blanket. He pulled me onto the couch and arranged me in his lap to drape over him like his own cover. My deluge of waterworks drenched his shirt while he clutched me against his chest, his arms banded across me like a soothing straight jacket.

When my blubbering finally ebbed into staggered sniffles, Quick took my face between his hands and kissed the trail of dried drops on my cheeks before peering into the depths of the distressed soul.

"Snow, what do you need right now? How can I take away your pain?"

The silver in his irises called to me, pulling me in to their crystallized warmth. My Quick; my savior, my calm in every storm. I licked the salty remnants of teardrops from my lips as my eyes landed on his; their pouty pink outlines beckoned against his deeply tanned skin.

I hesitantly flicked my tongue against those lips; tentatively testing the proverbial waters. He stiffened, every muscle of his torso locking in place like iron bars. Keeping me held to him, he drew in a sharp breath when I explored further, called by a force I was helpless to fight against.

I pressed my lips to his with a gentle pressure, feeling the heat of his skin sweeping through me. His mouth parted in surprise; I swept my tongue against his, tasting the combination of flavors that could only be my best friend; my Quick.

Before it could register, I was hoisted in the air. My arms and legs latched around Quick's like a spider monkey clinging to its mother. He laid me down against the worn cracking leather of his couch, pressed his weight on top of me, and kissed me fiercely.

I don't know where his body ended, and mine began. The ferocity of his kiss was feral; he consumed every part of me, delved into my mouth with such an animalistic hunger I didn't dare to breathe for fear he would stop. The heavy weight of his erection pressed against my belly as he ate me alive, so thoroughly did he fuck my mouth with his tongue. Need for more engulfed me all the way down to the tips of my toes.

I dug my fingers into the firm muscles of his shoulders and he shoved his hands under the hem of my t-shirt. His warm, calloused palms caressed the soft flesh of my belly.

Groaning at the contact, my head spun from the potency of my hormones and the comfort his touch stirred in my soul.

This kiss. This man. This—fuck. This was my best friend, and this was a bad idea.

I froze in place; Quick got the message immediately and shifted his weight, sitting up on his knees. His face filled with concern as he offered a hand to pull me up.

"Too fast?" He asked as he pulled me back into his lap—sideways this time, not in the dangerous position of straddling him again.

I swallowed hard and nodded; I couldn't confirm in my heart if it was simply too fast or treacherous territory we should never explore again. Of everything I was willing to lose in my life, Quick was number one on my 'Must Keep at All Costs' list.

I would never, *ever*, risk losing him. It was too high a price to pay.

A deep sigh emanated from his chest, but he said nothing else. He kissed the top of my head, tucked me under his chin, and reached for the remote hidden underneath the pile of garbage on the coffee table.

We settled into a sitcom on Netflix, not breathing another word about our intimate moment for the remainder of the night, even when he tucked me into his bed and snuggled in beside me.

I fell asleep in my best friend's arms. With the ghosts of his kisses still on my lips,

I knew I was in trouble.

CHAPTER 17

TRAVIS

"*What the fuck, man?*"

"*I have every right to get to know my uncle, Travis. This isn't just about you.*"

"*It's not about me at all! Do you have any idea how many people you're hurting? How many people that man is hurting? Fuck, Devon, get over your daddy issues and give your head a shake. That was stupid, even for you.*"

"*Fuck you, Travis. I'm practicing forgiveness Wind getting closer to salvation while you're working at a bar and sharing a woman with God knows how many men. It's not me who needs to get my life together.*"

"Christ, Devon. I guess me being dead is the better option, huh? Because you probably just dug my grave with that stunt."

The heated exchange with my biological little brother three days ago continued on loop in my mind as I trudged up the steps to Bourbon & Blues in the morning, long before my scheduled shift was to start.

I'd been waiting for this call—dreading it—and it had finally come. Georgio wanted to meet, to discuss the revelation of our family ties, no doubt. I cursed myself for ever believing Devon could be trusted with such information.

The bitter irony, of course, was everything I'd done for Georgio—every sin I'd committed, every felony I'd perpetrated—had been to protect Devon. To pay for his recovery, to get him out of town and away from the shit show that was our existence. Yet here I was, about to dig an even deeper hole because of my gullible, brain-dead, self-loathing little brother.

I wanted to rip him a new asshole while bringing him into my arms for a soul-soothing hug. Brotherhood was its own branch of insanity.

Janet met me at the door with a loaded glance and silently led me up to Georgio's office without a backward look.

Yeah, I know, Janet. I fucked up, okay?

I steeled myself for whatever was to come as I walked into the familiar, intimidating office.

"Welcome, *nephew.*" Georgio's friendly invitation mimicked the smooth, enticing tones of a snake-oil salesman. "Take a seat."

It was a command, not a request.

He was leaning against his monstrosity of a desk, arms folded across his chest in a relaxed manner. Like this was just a casual meeting and not a soul-crushing acknowledgment.

I sat in one of the stiff chairs in front of his desk, unsure how to play this. I'd given Kellan a head's up, and he'd cursed Devon to high heaven, but what else could he do? At least I hadn't shared any of the new developments with my dim-witted brother, so he had no idea about Kellan's involvement, or that Cam was actually a part of our family.

Still, he knew enough to cause serious damage, and my main goal was coming out of this conversation alive and unmaimed.

I hadn't wanted to tell Winter, but I wasn't willing to keep any secrets from her after it nearly destroyed our relationship the first time. She took the news better than I thought, but not without a couple of breath exercises and extracting promises from me to call her as soon as I was done.

"Travis, in light of your new discovery, I'd like to officially welcome you into the family business."

Okay, we were diving right into the good stuff. Awesome.

I swallowed hard as my saliva, like gritty sand, threatened to choke me.

He looked at me expectantly, and I realized he wanted me to say ... something. I forced the sand down my throat and stuttered out the words he wanted to hear. "Thank you."

It came out more of a strained question than an affirmation, but my acting skills weren't enough to give him any more than that.

Frustration ravaged me; I was scared for my family, and I was so frigging pissed with Devon, I could hurl him off a cliff.

"I'll keep this short and sweet." Georgio circled his desk and sat down like a king on a throne. He steepled his fingers and watched me through them.

"You are too good a bartender to lose, but I'm moving you from your financing position to my personal security."

Financing position. What an elegant description of running drug money to be laundered.

The personal security title threw me, though.

"Um." I summoned my inner calm, whatever was left after Georgio's call had smashed it into tiny shards, and cautiously tried again. "I'm not a big man, Georgio. And I have no fighting experience. Hell, I'm not even very good with a gun. I'll—"

Georgio cut me off with a dismissive wave of his hand.

"Angelo can teach you these things. For now, I want you with me. I have no sons, and now that you know your true heritage, I will groom you to be my successor." His lips twitched into a dangerous grin. "Should you succeed in your initiation, of course."

Of course. The sand was back, filling my mouth one grain at a time until I could barely breathe.

Georgio tilted his head, clearly watching me wrestle with my inner panic; I used every molecule of energy in my body to keep my face passive and emotionless.

Resisting was futile, though, and would only put those I loved in danger. Against all odds, maybe Devon's fuck-up would give us the opportunity we needed to take Georgio out once and for all.

I just hoped *I* wasn't taken out in the process.

"When would you like me to start?" I asked in a flat tone, not bothering to hide that I was resigned to my fate. Resignation was better than showing fear, at least, and I couldn't pretend to be thrilled by the offer.

The delight that filled his eyes made my stomach curdle.

"Tomorrow." He beamed at me, as if I'd just given him my soul on a platter. "I am resuming our gentlemen's fighting evenings, and there are many details to get sorted so that we don't experience any interference."

Okay, I could handle that. I'd worked them before—I knew what to expect. I couldn't deny the prick of nervousness at the thought of getting trapped again, but Plan B had worked once. It could work again—right?

"There is also an important event in Carlisle in two weeks. I expect you to attend. You may bring a guest—in fact, I insist. I assume you will take Winter?"

He didn't wait for my response. Instead, he shared a pointed look with Janet, who, to my surprise, had stayed present by the closed door.

"Janet, please ensure Travis and Winter are both off of the schedule here so that they may attend the Gold Gala."

"I'd prefer to leave Winter out of my business here—sir," I tacked on, hoping my deference was enough to change his mind. I didn't want Winter anywhere near Georgio's criminal activities; at least, not nearer than she already was.

Georgio's eyes hardened, reflecting the true villain he was. "I insist, Travis. Please do not insult my kindness. The seats to the dinner are over a thousand dollars a plate. Consider it a nice date night. For which you will be at my personal disposal."

A shiver swept up my spine, but I nodded my agreement all the same. There was no benefit in pissing off Georgio today.

Georgio finally leaned across his desk, his face stern and serious.

"Travis, I know I don't need to say this, but a reminder is always prudent. Your life, your choices, are in your hands. But make no mistake: you will have to live with the consequences of those choices. Your mother, your brother ... no one is immune to those consequences. And certainly not little Winter. Do we understand each other?"

An icicle dug into my heart. "Yes, sir."

He clapped his hands together like an excited child and smiled widely. Shiny teeth and laugh lines did nothing to hide his quiet menace.

"You may go. Please report here tomorrow at nine, rather than to the warehouse. You will attend a few meetings with me before your shift tomorrow evening."

Once again, appearing the unassuming mafia boss, Georgio shuffled a few papers on his desk and turned his attention to his computer, as if I was no longer in the room.

I stood and shifted out of the office as quickly as I could. Janet allowed me to pass while avoiding my gaze, and she closed the door behind me.

Now what?

I was an FBI-lackey, a mobster's nephew, a brother, a son, a boyfriend, a friend. I was wearing too many conflicting hats. At some point, it was probably going to get me killed.

I looked at the time on my phone. I had a few hours to kill before my shift tonight, and I wasn't in the mood to stick around here.

I didn't want to go back home—Mom had been doing relatively well these past few weeks. I didn't want to risk seeing Devon; I was too furious with him, and I wasn't going to put myself in the position to say something I'd regret.

I shot off a text to Drew, our one friend who had a flexible schedule today.

Travis Balcom: Hey man, what are you up to?

Drew J: Doing some research. Wanna help?

Travis Balcom: Sure. Where are you?

Drew J: Home. Come on over.

Within half an hour, I was knocking on Drew's door for the first time. We'd never spent any time at his place, and I had never been invited. Granted, we usually got together at Shane's.

"Come in," a voice called from inside.

I opened the door to see Drew seated at his small kitchen table, laptop open, with a notebook on his knee. He was scribbling something furiously on its pages.

I peeked at the computer screen. Colorful pages of houses upstate stared back at me. I shot him a curious look. Real estate?

He looked up at me and must have noticed my confused expression. "I'm looking for places to live when this all blows over."

Ummm ... what?

"You're leaving?" I asked dumbly, surprised, and a little taken aback. Winter loved Drew, Shane loved Drew, whether he'd admitted that yet, and I liked the man—we were our own fucked up version of a chosen family. And he was planning on leaving?

"We're leaving," he said matter-of-factly. "I had Logan send me some listings of places that might fit our criteria. Six bedrooms, a few bathrooms, well outside of Cascade Falls area, but close enough that we could visit our families on weekends if there is anything left of them by then."

His expression soured, but he didn't elaborate. He didn't need to. We had no idea what the next steps were. But by the looks of things, half of our parents were going to end up in jail. Life was fucked.

Six bedrooms. Was he proposing the six of us—Logan included—share a home together like a cuddly bunch of romantic roommates? Was that even a thing?

"We're leaving ..." I echoed, still shocked. Could I leave? Mom and Devon, despite the pain in my ass that he was, were my responsibility. I had never had the option of living my life for myself. I couldn't even picture what that looked like.

Then I snapped to reality. I barely had two nickels to rub together outside of living and support expenses—I wouldn't be able to afford a house, especially ones as nice as the one on the screen. Trust Logan to send Drew luxury mansions instead of bare-bones homes we could actually pay for.

"Drew ..." I hesitated. I didn't want to insult him, but I needed to splash a dose of realism onto this plan before he got ahead of himself. "There's no way I'm able to afford any of these—even on a six-way split."

"Winter wants to use her settlement money." Drew set his notebook on the table and crossed his arms over his chest, stretching out his long legs beneath the table. "And I think it's a great idea. What better way to say 'fuck you' to the Baker family than to buy a house to share with her boyfriends?"

His grin was uncharacteristically sadistic, and I couldn't help but snort at the scenario. That was a big 'fuck you' all right.

"Let's face it." He eyed me carefully. "I have no job prospects here; no real ones, anyway. And I don't want to be here anymore. Winter won't have anything here once this all goes down and her parents are locked away. Same with Shane—he doesn't want to work for WAQ anymore. If it's even a viable company after Kellan takes it down. Cam is a wayward wanderer, and Logan ... well, I'm not sure what his deal is, but he told me in no uncertain terms was Winter going anywhere without him. So, I guess we're stuck with that guy." His words were joking, but his face was serious.

"And you've been stuck more than the rest of us." His tone was softer, kinder, even. "Don't you want to escape this hell when the time comes? Build a life you'll be proud of?"

I mulled over the idea. Our own home, a chance to go to school, waking up with my beautiful woman every day. Not to mention a band of brothers I could create a life with. It was an enticing offer.

But I'd have to abandon my mother and brother to do it.

I'd have to weigh this on my heart for a little while. But I wouldn't dismiss it altogether.

I asked another question, instead of answering. "Does Winter even have enough to cover a house? That's an enormous investment."

Drew quirked a blond brow at me. "Man, her settlement was three million."

I let out a low whistle. Three million, just sitting in a bank account for years. She worked two jobs and paid her own way, with three million available at her disposal? Fuck.

My girl had scruples. I loved and respected the woman, but that little tidbit of information was impressive. I didn't know if I would have had the same willpower.

"She insists that if she's going to touch the money, it has to be used for *us*." He shrugged and reached for his notepad again. "If that's what she wants, and it's going to help her move past that douchebag, I'm happy to give it to her."

"How does Shane feel about this?" I was confident Cam hadn't heard of this plan yet, or he would have mentioned it to me. But there was no way our boisterous friend was out of the loop.

"He's on board. After he found his father's love letters, he's been a bit of a wreck, to be honest. I'm not sure what to do about it. I'm hoping this is enough of a distraction to get him out of his funk."

Huh. I had seen little of Shane other than bowling recently. I knew just how badly the sting of family betrayal bore into a man's soul. I'd send him a text to check in later.

"Want to see some options?"

He turned the computer screen toward me and I leaned forward to see what our rich, pretentious pain-in-the-ass had sent over.

Each place was more stunning than the next. High ceilings, marble tile, bathrooms fit for kings … The houses were the kind of opulence I could only dream of. My heart twinged at the very thought. I wasn't an elegant man, not by any means. But I couldn't deny the pull toward this possibility of a future.

We both agreed on one in particular. It had a closed in backyard with a huge pool and hot-tub, and a kitchen made for a true cook.

Shane and Winter were useless at cooking. I had no idea if Logan could cook, but all I had ever seen him eat were salads and high-protein healthy meals—the man had once inhaled cocaine like it was oxygen, but he didn't eat bacon.

Where one was willing to draw the line was a psychotherapist's wet dream.

Cam knew his way around a grill—his Southern cooking was to die for, and Drew and I had been living the independent bachelor life for years. A real kitchen to cook in with the time to do it was an appealing feature.

Butterflies flapped their wings in my stomach. I wanted this life so badly; but could I leave Mom and Devon to do it?

Once the houses were thoroughly vetted, I filled Drew in on my morning. He scrubbed his palms down his bearded jaw and grimaced.

"Fuck, man, that's shitty. How are you holding up?"

"Surviving." I released a long breath and allowed every ounce of exhaustion to show on my face. "I'm drained to hell, but I'll make it through. We're all in the same boat here."

A long silence sat between us before Drew straightened and clapped me on the shoulder, changing the depressing topic before I melted into the floor with the weight of it all.

"I've got another question for you." He flipped the pages of his notebook to an earlier page.

"Think you could find out what Kellan's initiation into the Carlos Cartel was? I have a theory that Georgio's initiation led to all our parents making bad decisions. But I couldn't even guess what it was."

Kellan sent me messages semi-regularly; at least every few days. I had to bring him up to speed with Georgio's power display this morning—I should have let him know right away, but I'd needed the temporary reprieve from all the double-agent subterfuge for a few hours. It was exhausting being everyone's piece on this chessboard.

I would feel better if I knew which piece I was.

"I'll ask him tonight." I stood to leave.

My shift started in two hours and all this talk of our potential futures made me want to check in on Mom, Devon's presence be damned.

"Sounds good. Thanks for coming over, man."

Drew's smile was genuine and full of warmth. The origin of our friendship was definitely unorthodox, but I couldn't deny the man had grown on me.

I returned his smile. "Keep me posted, okay?"

I made it to my personal hell hole with ten minutes to spare and jumped onto the bar to relieve Colin for the night.

I'd play this game, and put my limited optimism into a future beyond Georgio, Kellan, and the fuckery that was this town and everyone in it.

I'd make a life with my girl and her band of men. My band of men.

And hopefully that dream wouldn't break my heart.

CHAPTER 18

WINTER

"Do you think Kellan was a child soldier?" Hillary's voice emerged from her enormous closet. I sat on her ridiculously soft bed, browsing the six takeout menus in front of me.

Her bedroom at the Carlisle condo was a contrast of six different shades of gray and white, but it felt warm and inviting. Large floor to ceiling windows looked out into the bustling town below, its lights twinkling as the dark blue sky transitioned to navy.

My bougie friend had wanted to 'take me out on the town' tonight, but I'd begged her to let us stay in, eat enough salt and MSG until we felt extremely bloated, and watch shitty television until we passed out on her couch.

She had looked at me like I had three heads, but relented when I told her she could take me out for breakfast and choose what we watched tonight. I had a feeling I was going to regret that.

"It's possible," I murmured thoughtfully as I scanned the paper menu for my favorite dishes. "Travis said he'd joined the FBI when he was 16—something about being in one of Antonio's training camps."

"That's what I thought." Hillary appeared in the doorway wearing the most luxurious silk pjs I had ever seen. She had gifted me with my own set upon arrival; a light blue t-shirt and short set that perfectly matched my eyes. Her set was similar, in a light peach, with a monogrammed breast pocket.

I was convinced she was secretly attempting to *Princess Diaries* me. She was going to be sorely disappointed, but I liked the pajamas all the same.

"I've been doing a little digging." She reached for the hairbrush on her dresser and ran the bristles through her shiny blonde hair. "Antonio's initiations are said to be brutal, and no one is spared from the guts and glory. You know the incident Cam mentioned with his mom at the club when she was pregnant? I guess that was the twin's initiation. They had to kill in cold blood—they weren't even 18."

The limited contents of my stomach curdled, and I wasn't so hungry anymore.

"I don't even want to know how you found that out." I threw her a pointed look and tucked my arms into my armpits, my body freezing cold suddenly despite the lush feather duvet beneath me. "Please tell me you're being safe."

"Always, Sweets," she said airily, breezing through the room as if we were talking about the weather. "What do you think Georgio's initiation was?"

My mind immediately went to the gruesome photos of Cheryl Simpson's body in the police files Shane got his hands on from his aunt. I didn't know how legal that was, but I wasn't complaining. I felt like we were on the cusp of an answer—a big one. We just had to fit in those final few missing pieces.

How it would actually help us get out of this mess, I didn't know. But knowledge was power, right?

"Something to do with Cheryl's disappearance. I'm sure of it." I considered my next words. "And somehow, all our fathers were involved. I have no idea what a sixteen-year-old girl would do to get the Carlos' family's attention though—unless she saw something she shouldn't? Or maybe she and Georgio had a thing on the side? It's weird to think Drew's mom was his girlfriend."

"I'll do some more digging to see what I can find. And there's no accounting for taste, I guess." Hillary shrugged her shoulders flippantly as she plopped down on the bed beside me.

I pursed my lips to hold in my laughter. "You're one to talk, Mrs. Eccles. No accounting for taste, I guess." I mocked her in a sing-song and she grinned back, unrepentant as always.

"I made quite a lot of money on that transaction." She flipped me the finger and snorted when my mouth dropped open. "And considering you'll be next in his bed, you're one to talk."

Her dry tone did nothing to hide her amusement. I didn't dignify that with a response.

"Chow mein?" I asked instead and tossed a menu at her for Bao Phu's. "I've got a wicked craving for ginger beef, too."

"Get what you want," she said while she perused the crinkled paper copy in her hands. "I'll order some extra egg-rolls too. They're the best. Aaron and I had some the other night."

I perked up at this juicy morsel of gossip. "Who's Aaron?"

She shrugged dismissively. "An old friend. He owns a lot of property in the area and we hang out sometimes."

I tossed the menu at her with a wide grin. "You're sleeping with him, aren't you!?"

She wiggled her delicate eyebrows at me suggestively. "Sometimes. He's got a great ass."

"Scandalous!" I eyed the who-knows-how-high-of-a-thread-count sheets I was sitting on. "Have you washed these since? I need to know what I'm getting into here."

"Excuse me, Miss Harem." Hillary's signature haughty expression melted into a naughty grin. "You've got four swinging dicks waiting for you at home. How often do you clean *your* sheets?"

I bit my lip—my three official men—and now, including whatever was brewing with Logan, had somehow turned into four and a half. I wasn't ready or willing to face my in-the-moment decision to kiss Quick, or admit out loud how many times I had thought about that kiss since.

I could feel a rolling heat creep up my cheeks as the image of him on top of me materialized unbidden in my mind's eye.

"You dirty dog!" Hillary exclaimed as she shoved me back into the softest blanket I'd ever laid on. "Who crept into your thoughts just now? Was it that cutie, Travis? Or Cam's buff bod? Was it all of them?"

I swept those feelings under the rug and laughed, imitating her airy tone. "All of them, of course. I can't choose just one."

My longing for Quick's kisses shifted to pain for Travis' predicament. So far, he was just assigned to Georgio's personal security during some sleazy business dealings, and he'd told me that under no circumstances would he allow himself to commit murder. I didn't know how he'd have the power to stop it, short of getting harmed himself.

Hillary nodded thoughtfully. "You've got me curious about that possibility." She picked at an errant stitch on her duvet. "When the divorce is final, maybe I'll start developing my harem of sexy men. One blonde Viking man, one handsome businessman, and one … roguish stranger."

I snickered, picturing that fictional band of men, knowing full-well she was into the elusive Viking that was Kellan Carlos. "I highly recommend it," I teased, before turning serious. "When is the divorce completed?"

"In about a month. We've signed all the paperwork; we just need to submit it. Technically, we're seeking an annulment since we never consummated the marriage."

She rolled her eyes dramatically. "Good old religious values keeping our virtues in check. You gonna consummate it on my behalf?"

I never got the chance to answer—not that I had one. She shot me a wicked grin before rolling off the bed to grab her phone.

"I'll order our food." She tossed me a remote from her nightstand and gestured toward the windows. "The screen comes down over there. Pick your top five cheesy reality show options."

I pressed the top button on the remote and a massive screen, larger than the king-size bed where I sat, lowered from the ceiling, blocking out the view of the dark city streets. I could pretend I was used to this woman's life of luxury, but I absolutely wasn't.

I did as she asked and chose five of the most brain-melting, cringe-worthy shows I could—secretly relishing our trashy TV date. This was girl bonding at its finest.

That Chinese food had better be the best I'd ever tasted.

Thoughts of Travis popped into my mind as I loaded an episode of *Love is Blind* while I waited for Hillary to return. My closet romantic not-so-secretly loved this show. I took a picture of the screen and sent it to him. He was working tonight, but I knew I'd get a cheeky response when he got back to his phone.

Of all my men, I was currently most worried about Travis. Devon's meddling had gotten Travis more entrenched in Georgio's illegal affairs, and my stomach churned every time I pictured what he could be up to on Georgio's behalf.

I couldn't lose Travis. Not now, not ever.

Whatever we were building for ourselves, I knew it had a sense of permanency. I wasn't in this group relationship—our family, as everyone continued to call it—on a whim. Whatever we wanted to call ourselves, it wasn't just the result of a trauma bond; we were cementing a foundation of love and trust, with the goal of creating a real future. I didn't know how all the moving parts would come together just yet, but I knew it was what I wanted. What we all wanted.

I still had to figure out where Logan and Quick fit into the mix, though. Those details were still ... unclear.

Speak of the devil—Logan's indignant tone echoed down the hall.

I strained to hear the hushed voices in the main living area before giving up and padding out of the bedroom to see what was going on.

Logan and Hillary were whisper-arguing, their heads bowed over the kitchen island in frantic discussion. As if sensing my presence, his brunette head popped up, his honey eyes roving over me with interest.

"Hey Princess, nice pjs." Logan winked. When he reached me, he enveloped me in a tight hug.

I stiffened, not used to this level of intimacy with him, but the reaction only lasted two seconds before I felt compelled to wrap my arms around his waist and reciprocate. I could admit I liked the feeling of being in his arms. His annoying self-confidence held a safety and security only he could offer.

I buried my face in his tailored dress shirt and breathed him in—amber and frankincense with an undertone of clean man smell; my Logan.

My Logan? Oh god. Who had served me the Kool-Aid?

"This is cute."

I looked over to see Hillary standing with her head cocked to the side, amused curiosity filling her gaze.

Logan ran his fingers through my hair and kissed the top of my head before letting me go. His tenderness continued to surprise me.

"Winter won't mind if I stay—will you, Winter?"

"Wait, what?" I looked back and forth between them as I tried to catch up. "Who's staying?"

"I was just explaining to Hill that I have an early meeting tomorrow, and I'm not booking a hotel when my name is also on the deed of this condo. I'll just stay in the spare room. She doesn't want me crashing your girl's party."

He scrunched up his face in obvious distaste.

"I won't be crashing your girl's party," he reiterated. "I have work to do, and I'll do it in the office while you gossip and braid each other's hair."

"She can't sleep with me, Logan." Hillary's tone was sharp, and I turned to face her; now I was the one who was curious. I'd always slept in the spare room until now, and I'd never questioned it. Hillary *couldn't* sleep with me? That was a story for another time.

"She can sleep with me," Logan responded smoothly, reaching for me again and pulling my back to his front, grasping my hips possessively.

"Not an option." Hillary picked up her phone from the quartz countertop and started dialing a number. "I'll book you a room at the Hilton."

"Hill—it's fine." I pushed out of Logan's arms and forced a smile. "I'll just put a pillow between us or something. That bed is huge, anyway."

My pulse raced at the thought of spending the night next to this enigma of a man who was getting deeper under my skin by the day. We were adults. It would be fine.

Hillary looked between us discerningly before placing her phone back on the counter.

"Alright, if you say so," she said dubiously. "Chinese will be here in fifteen. You"—she pointed a manicured finger at Logan—"go do your work and leave us alone. Winter promised me all the trash TV we can fit into a night, and I'm not wasting the opportunity."

I stifled a laugh and followed her back to the bedroom, ignoring the intense holes Logan's stare was drilling into my back.

We settled into the California King bed of pillows; Hill only left to grab our food from the delivery guy. She came back with the cardboard containers carefully laid out on a long wooden tray and set it between us. We gorged on food that would surely kill a few blood cells and feasted on television that would surely kill a few brain cells.

Still, the evening was nice, and the distraction made me stop ruminating on all our woes for a little while.

When the last episode of the season finished, Hillary turned to me with an apologetic smile.

"Sorry to kick you out." She fluffed a pillow behind her head and opened her nightstand, retrieving a bottle of pills, a fluffy pink eye-mask, and a pair of expensive-looking earphones.

I scrutinized her sleep aids. "You need all of this to sleep?"

She wrinkled her nose in a rare admission of weakness. "Yes. It's a story I'll share at another time, I promise. Right now, I'm beat, and you"—her pointed stare was loaded with innuendo— "have to go share a bed with my husband for the night."

Right. This was a fucked-up scenario if there ever was one.

Her gaze softened. "Hey—I can make him sleep on the couch if that makes you feel better—not that it would stop him from crawling into bed with you if he really wanted to."

Another scrunch of her dainty nose. "I need to teach you some Krav Maga moves so you can kick his ass when he gets out of line.

I laughed loudly at that imagery and threw a pillow at her head.

"I can handle Logan Eccles." I shrugged and hauled myself off the bed. My tiredness seeping into the crevices of my bones, I left her to her consortium of sleep aids. "Goodnight."

Down the hall to the opposite end of the condo, I tiptoed to where the spare bedroom, office, and bathroom were situated on the other side of the open living space.

To my surprise, the lamp was still on, but Logan was already asleep; his bare Ken-like buff chest on delicious display. The sheets draped across his lower abdomen. I was relieved to see a tiny strip of black boxer elastic peeking out of the covers. My poor heart couldn't handle a naked, sleeping Logan right now.

The Pretty Boy sure was pretty in sleep, though. His normally scowling face held a tranquility I'd never seen before—he almost looked boyish in the soft glow of the reading light beside him. A pair of black-rimmed glasses rested on the nightstand beside him, on top of a ... was that a comicbook?

I swallowed a giggle and shuffled over to the light, taking one last look at Logan's thick eyelashes fluttering across his cheeks in sleep. Clicking off the lamp, I slowly fumbled to the other side of the bed; luckily, I knew the layout of this room or I'd have broken a toe on the modern settee at the foot of the bed.

As I scooted between the cool, soft sheets, my previously sluggish body lit up with nervous energy, acutely aware of the sexy demon less than twelve inches away from me.

I focused on one of the breathing exercises he'd taught me—finding all kinds of scenarios to use those regularly these days—and felt my limbs sink into the memory-foam coils and drift off to dreamland.

It could have been minutes or hours; my internal alarm must have been chiming when my eyes flew open to see Logan's heated stare watching me intently.

He'd shuffled closer. Our bodies had curled inward to each other; only a hand's width lay between us. His hot breath fanned across my cheeks, smelling of muted toothpaste.

His eyes were liquid lust, gleaming wickedly in the dim light of the moon sneaking between the gaps in the curtains.

He shifted his position on the pillow-soft mattress; I looked down to see the bobbing motion of his fist on his lower abdomen, and it didn't take a genius to know what he was doing.

It should have creeped me out—I should run for the hills from this man touching himself next to my unconscious body.

Yet ... my body didn't lie; my pussy gushed at the knowledge Logan *needed* to relieve the tension and pressure in his body. The same tension and pressure was steadily building its way through me.

"Is that a rocket in your pocket or ..." I licked my lips. The buzzing adrenaline of anticipation tickled up my spine as a patch of wetness spread across my silk shorts.

Logan's trademarked arrogant smirk was laced with a raw hunger; his fist stopped bobbing, and he rolled his body over to hover on top of me.

"It's a rocket, all right, Princess." His low murmur filled the barely there space between us and his body heat and layered scent overtook my senses.

He yanked at the waist of my shorts and panties, pulling them down my legs in a meticulously slow movement that forced another gush. Soft lips kissed a light trail up my thighs, across my lower belly, but he avoided the one place I needed his mouth, intentionally teasing me with his ministrations.

Long fingers nimbly unbuttoned my pajama top, pushing it open to reveal my naked breasts. He kissed each one, swirling his tongue around each nipple with far too much control.

I was going to combust with his teasing, but I was so turned on by him taking what was his, with only my lack of protest as his permission.

An unrelenting need swept through me as he pulled the shirt off of me all together; the move forced him to sit up. When the covers fell away from his naked body, even in the dark gray light, I could see how truly gorgeous Logan Eccles was.

He was lean, the leanest of all my men—his body built like a swimmer; lithe, toned muscles and none of the bulk. His abs weren't shredded, his arms weren't corded, but he exuded a powerful sense of self; he could hold his own, and his confidence, while annoying, was a result of hard work and determination. He owned his body.

And now, I needed to be owned by him.

He seemed to sense the change in me as I squirmed under him. An unforgiving ache welled up, but when his lips found mine, he kissed me so passionately, I could taste his desperate desire for me on his tongue.

"Do you need me, Princess? Do you want me to stuff my cock deep inside your tight cunt?"

I whimpered. The need to feel him, to cross this invisible line after all these years, finally crested its inevitable summit.

All I gave him was a single, solitary nod of my head when his eyes searched mine for consent.

He kissed me languidly like we had all the time in the world. Then he flipped me over in one fell swoop. His hands trailed over my cheeks, and then guided his cock to my entrance. He teased me with its light pressure before slowly pressing his naked shaft into me.

I closed my eyes to revel in every inch of his girth filling me. I was about to fuck Logan Eccles. After one taste of him, I'd never be able to take it back.

CHAPTER 19

LOGAN

Fuck me.

I looked down in time to watch her greedy pussy swallow my cock whole. Her lips stretched around to grip me so tightly, I was going to fill her with my cum in less than a minute.

I couldn't have that. My princess was going to feel me everywhere tomorrow. There would be no mistaking who kept her up all night to make her scream when she went home to her boyfriends in the morning. I was going to mark her. Scar her. Christen her slick cunt with my seed and then stuff it back inside her when it dripped out onto Hillary's sheets.

The vision of my cum dripping out of her tight hole made my cock twitch with pain, despite the fucking bliss that surrounded me. I had dreamed of this moment for literally years. Now that she lay beneath me like a delicious candy desperate to be sucked and fucked, I needed to savor every debauched second.

I bit down on her shoulder, sinking my teeth into her tender flesh enough to bruise as I pulled out and slammed back into her welcoming cunt. Her back arched in response, her ass grinding into my balls as her body begged me for more.

Fuck yes, little Princess. I'll give you everything I have.

I rocked into her again, no mercy or care for how deep I was entering her body or how hard I was pushing her. I used her hot, tight pussy like it was mine to own.

She was mine to own. At least in this moment.

One hand gripping her hip, I wrapped the other around her throat, squeezing gently. She shuddered beneath me as I continued to apply pressure and slammed back into her again and again, reveling in her slickness coating my cock and the hair on the tops of my thighs.

I wanted to bathe in her arousal. I didn't want anyone confusing the fact that this woman owned me. I'd walk to the ends of the earth for her; for her sweet smile and her snarky comebacks and for this precious, incredible cunt.

My cunt.

A growl forced its way from my chest as I released her throat and flipped her over to face me.

Her eyes were glassy in the dim light, her cheeks flushed, and her lips swollen and puffy from my kisses. Fuck any porn I'd tugged my dick to until this moment; nothing compared to this woman's body beneath me.

I claimed her breasts, holding each weighted mound of delicate flesh in my palms and kneading them as I fucked into her harder. A demon possessed me, forging my anger, frustration, passion and pain into a rage-fueled fuck machine. She bit her lip so hard to keep from crying out, she was going to draw blood.

I hoped she did. I would suck it clean from her body like I was going to suck her cum.

My little princess was submitting to me, and doing so well. I'd reward her for it later.

Her hands raked over the damaged flesh of my back, digging her nails into the skin the harder I fucked her. Good. I wanted—needed—her to mark me, too. I needed the marks to bleed; no one in this world was going to confuse who I belonged to.

The woman I had always belonged to.

I slipped my hand between our pounding bodies—hers meeting mine desperately with every stroke, every thrust—and circled my thumb against her soaking clit. I increased the pressure with every pass. Covering her mouth with my own, I swallowed her gasps with my tongue.

She stiffened beneath me and I knew I'd met my mark as she shuddered her release and sagged into the mattress, her hands still holding on to my back as she gasped.

I could spend the entire night giving her orgasm after orgasm, but I didn't want to. There would be time for that later—I needed my pent-up release more desperately than I needed to breathe. I sat up on my quads and brought her body up to sit flush against me. Then I drove my cock so deep into her channel, I didn't know where she ended and I began.

My balls drew up without warning, and sharp pleasure rocketed up my spine as I finally loaded her pussy with every drop of cum I could give her.

I hadn't had bareback sex with anyone in my life. I'd be burning every condom I owned to feel her cunt on my cock until the end of time.

I gently laid her on the bed. She rolled over, her smile sated and spent, as she looked up at me behind heavy lashes.

I slid down to the foot of the bed and tenderly kissed each hip bone before latching my mouth over her filled pussy.

She let out a strangled cry as my tongue forced its way between her swollen walls, lapping up our combined releases. I held the sweet and salty mixture in my mouth, crawling back up her body to kiss her. I forced her lips open and pushed our cum between them, making her taste the unmistakable flavor of us.

"Taste what you do to me, Princess."

She swallowed the mixture with a sexy hum. My cock stiffened to half-mast just at the sound.

Now I knew what she felt like, how her body responded to mine, I wouldn't be able to let her go. The only fucking downside was I'd have to share her with four other fuckwits.

I never cared about that side of things. I didn't need her to be mine and only mine, like some fucking caveman. But if I was going to be hers, she needed to take all of me—every asshole piece, and fit them into her puzzle—or whatever poetic bullshit someone like Chase would say.

I pressed light kisses to her jaw, her neck, and trailed them along her collarbone before tucking her into my side and pulling the blankets back over us.

She settled into my arms and the powerful scent of her shampoo filled my nostrils. It would now be the smell of the best fuck of my life.

Within a minute, her breathing evened out, and she fell asleep against me. As I felt myself doing the same, the last thought in my head was that Winter fucking Wallace was finally fucking mine.

And I'd tear apart any man who tried to take her away from me.

I woke to the sun streaming through the windows, giving me an instant fucking headache. I had blackout automatic blinds at my condo; this bullshit was for poor people.

I rolled over, expecting to feel my princess beside me, but the bed was cold.

After pulling on my t-shirt and boxers from the floor, I brushed my teeth in the ensuite. As much as I'd love the taste of her cum on my tongue as a permanent tattoo, I needed fresh breath to kiss her good morning.

Because I was definitely fucking kissing her this morning.

I didn't bother putting in my contacts. I grabbed my glasses from the nightstand and padded into the open kitchen, now fully awake and ready for Hillary's fancy-ass coffee.

The devil herself sat at the island in a fuzzy pink bathrobe, sipping her own espresso and reading the newspaper like an old fucking grandma.

She cocked a brow at me as she looked over her paper in question. "Did you have a pleasant evening, *husband?*"

I scoffed at the term. One more month and we'd be free of this farce of a life we'd been putting on, and I'd be able to show off Winter as the woman who belonged on my arm.

I ignored her and made my own espresso, working the gears of her expensive-as-hell machine and crafting the coffee just the way I liked it; strong and bitter.

I sat across from her and took a throat-burning swallow.

"The accommodations were fine, thanks," I deadpanned, not interested whatsoever in talking about my sex life with my *wife*.

Our lives were fucking weird.

"Where's Winter?" I asked, diverting the conversation to the real reason I had gotten out of bed.

"She's showering in my room," Hillary responded cheerfully. "She didn't want to wake you."

Cute. It was tempting to climb in with her, but I thought better of it.

"I'm glad you finally made your move, Loggie-bear," Hill teased, winking at me over her coffee. Her grin turned stony, though, in a second flat. It was almost scary how she could do that. "Don't you fucking hurt her, Logan. Or I'll kill you myself."

"She's not a fucking toy, Hill," I shot back, annoyed by her warning. "I'm not going to fucking hurt her." I crossed my arms over my chest. "Unless she asks for it," I tossed out smugly.

"Ask for what?"

Winter came down the hall in a college sweater and leggings, with a towel around her head and no makeup.

She never looked fucking sexier.

"Nothing," I said dismissively. I pulled her into my arms as she walked past my seat at the island. I settled her between my legs and wrapped my arms around her waist. "Good morning, Princess."

She wrinkled her nose at the nickname but didn't protest. *That's my girl.*

A shy smile filled out her lips and her gorgeous blue eyes peered into mine under her dark lashes.

"Hey." She reached up and poked the bridge of my glasses. "I like these; they're cute. Are you secretly a nerd, Logan Eccles?"

I snorted. "Hardly. This body's close to perfect, but I have some flaws."

Hillary choked on her coffee behind me, but I pretended not to hear her.

A wicked grin crossed Winter's face. "I'm not sure that's true. I saw your comic book last night. Quick's going to have a field day when he knows you have something in common."

I rolled my eyes in real irritation. "It's Manga." I growled, not wanting a thing in ten lifetimes in common with Shane Quicksilver, other than the woman we were fucking. "It's *art*, not a comic. But forget that."

I lowered my mouth to hers and pressed a deep, longing kiss to her lips. She tasted like citrus and mint, and something so uniquely *her*. I wanted to devour her.

"As cute as this is," Hillary interrupted sharply to my right, "I am not letting you two fuck in my kitchen. How about we order breakfast?"

I spun Winter around in my arms and nestled my head on her shoulder, keeping my hands locked around her waist. I sought out the time on the microwave clock and blew a long breath into Winter's hair.

"I only have time to shower and then I have a meeting." I squeezed Winter tighter to me. "You should have waited for me, Princess. We could have showered together." I bit the tip of her earlobe and then released her, getting up from the counter to get moving with my day.

The meeting I had was important and necessary to move things forward with our web of fuckery. The band of fuckwits were counting on me, and I wouldn't be the one to let them down.

Not something I ever thought I'd say, but here we fucking were.

I showered and dressed in twenty minutes, choosing my navy suit and pale pink tie for the special occasion.

Before I could leave, I needed another taste of my girl. I tucked my hands in her hair and cradled her to me, kissing her until we were both breathless and wanting.

I dropped a light kiss to the tip of her nose and soaked in the look of pure joy on her face. My princess was my most precious possession, and I'd be kissing those lips every fucking morning from now on.

"Don't forget, you have a tux fitting at nine tomorrow!" Hill called after me just as I swung open the door.

"You don't control my schedule anymore, Hill!" I barked back in annoyance before shutting it behind me; even though I'd fucking forgot about that stupid appointment and actually needed the reminder.

Like I needed more stupid suits in my closet. Camden and Stanley were on us more than ever to be the Golden Couple at the Golden Gala. The last fucking thing I wanted was to be paraded around like Stanley's fucking show pony, but it would be the last time—the very last miserable time.

Maybe I'd get lucky and Georgio could kill him for me. I'd put a bug in Travis' ear, since he was the next coming of the Carlos family. Poor fucker almost had a family worse than mine.

Almost.

I sped out of the parking lot and made my way to Doug Fraser's office, just outside of the city. I needed a discreet PI with no previous ties to me for this job, and Chase had given me his number. The guy had found his mother, so he was fucking competent, at least.

The building was a generic strip mall with seedy underpinnings, and I grimaced internally. Of course, Boxer Boy wouldn't have recommended someone in a nice corner office with a high retainer. This looked more like something out of *Better Call Saul.*

The investigator's appearance did nothing to sway me from my initial judgments. Cheap suit, greasy hair, and stained teeth. A slime-ball.

"Take a seat." Douglas motioned to a battered metal office chair in front of his worn wooden desk. His computer looked like it still ran on DOS.

Unbuttoning my suit jacket, I obliged.

"What brings a rich, trust fund baby here to see me?"

Douglas pulled a pack of cigarettes out of his pocket and lit one with a match. He blew blue smoke into the air like we were all happy to die of fucking cancer and cocked a bushy eyebrow at me.

Ignoring him, I threw the brown file folder on his desk.

"I need you to dig up some dirt on this man. I need recent dirt, but I'll take everything you can find."

Doug opened the file and scrutinized the photos of Carson Baker on his desk. They were newspaper printouts from the Business Profile pages, highlighting the insufferable twit's success since he'd moved home.

I had made my success because I worked hard and made savvy business decisions. Carson's success came from a combination of fear and his daddy's money.

The seedy detective leaned back in his chair and rested his hands atop his burgeoning pot belly.

"What's my motive? Did he do something to you? A spurned lover, perhaps?"

The question caught me by surprise and I barked out a chuckle. The balls on this guy. A spurned lover …

"He's a rapist, a sexual predator, and a thug who hides behind his father's influence."

Doug's eyes darkened. He sneered and spit a wad of phlegm into the garbage can beside his desk.

Charming.

"How soon do you need the information?"

"Yesterday," I confirmed and stood to leave, ready for this conversation in the disgusting office to be over. "I'll pay double your rate for your speed and discretion."

Doug stood as well. I was grateful he didn't stick his hand out to shake. Gross.

"All right." He tugged at his waistline to pull his pants up before adding, "I'll call you at the end of the week to update you on my progress."

I bobbed my head in acknowledgment and quickly made my escape to my clean car. This visit served two purposes:

enough dirt to get him off the deed of my property, and the evidence needed to get the psychopath sent to prison once and for all.

Out of habit, I reached for my glove compartment to pull out my old vice of choice, but it was empty. I sighed, wishing I could snort some of the delicious cocaine that had been my companion for so long without the side effects. I had come this far, though, and I would not fuck it up.

For me, or for my girl. She didn't deserve a drug-addled asshole for a boyfriend.

Whether she'd confirm that, I didn't care. She was mine now.

I pulled out a pack of mint gum instead and chewed the shit out of it; the spearmint flavor did fuck-all to tame my coke craving, but it would have to do.

I glanced at my watch. I had three more meetings to get to before I met with Chase again for a good sparring session. The muscled oaf was growing on me, and he was the best fighting partner I'd ever had—even if he sucker punched me in the kidney last week.

I liked it when he fought dirty.

I drove out of the parking lot to get on with my day, content for the first time in years. Carson was going to be taken out for good, and Winter had finally let me in.

For the first time in a long time, I had something to live for.

CHAPTER 20

SHANE

"*W*e should probably talk about last night."

I quirked an eyebrow at Winter, surprised at her unusual willingness to talk about shit.

"You used him, Quick. You used him and used me to avoid your feelings."

Heat flushed the back of my neck.

"I didn't use him, Snow. I escaped into his hot body for an hour, so that I wouldn't have to feel the pain in my heart. I escaped into yours for comfort. But I didn't use him."

I shook my head vehemently. "I-I think I love him."

Her expression immediately softened at the admission that had put a boulder-sized lump in my throat to say the words out loud.

I loved with abandon—not recklessly, at least, I didn't see it that way—but to give my heart willingly to my two best friends... Well, to say it hadn't already happened would be an outright lie.

I loved Drew. I'd known it for a while now, even if I couldn't say the words.

And I loved Snow. And the pseudo threesome we'd had gave me some degree of hope they'd love me back. Or, more specifically, she could love me back like that.

Fully, completely. A completeness we'd never shared.

"I know I love him," I corrected, liberated by those three words.

I took a deep breath, saying a silent prayer I hadn't misread our sexual chemistry last night, and said the other words written on my heart.

"There's something going on between us, too, Snow. Can't you feel it? I just... You complete me down to my core, and I can't help believing we could be ... more."

My insides twisted as the many emotions flashed across her face like the characters in the opening credits to a Marvel movie.

"Quick, I"—she swallowed roughly and shut her eyes so tightly I thought her eyeballs might pop. "I don't know."

That moment had been on repeat in my mind for two weeks, drilling every word into my brain like a Hell Diver from Mars.

It ran through my mind now, as I paced the floor of my father's office, ready to tear out my fucking hair.

I was trying to distract myself from the anger, the betrayal, and the outright disgust that had boiled the blood in my veins when I had read those damn letters.

I couldn't stand it anymore. The anger was eating me up inside, chewing me into micro-pieces of fish food and then spitting out the ragged bits on repeat.

I hadn't showered in days. I didn't smell like ass, but the sheen of grease that coated my skin was getting gross, even for me. Despite that knowledge, I couldn't bring myself to get clean. It was too much effort, and I was just too. Damn. Tired.

I'd brushed my teeth at least.

I'd barely slept, and my eyeballs were raw and gritty. Anxious energy buzzed in my veins from my frontal lobe to my toenails. I was in a bit of a manic state, and I knew it, but there was no going back now.

The Spartans were going against the Persians. Unlike in the battle in *300*, I didn't know who was the winner here.

I had worked a few days at WAQ since my final exam and avoided Dad and Darren as much as possible, as if my secret spy activities were written all over my face. Graduation was in a few weeks, and I'd have to play my part as a dutiful son until this was all over.

I woke this morning with a pounding drumbeat inside my skull, and I knew I couldn't hold on to this pain any longer. I had to let it out, and Dad was going to be the unwilling recipient.

He had been out on the job site today with most of WAQ's underling team. Construction was well underway on the bridge project, and they were starting with the abandoned mine in the middle of the mountain, designed to become a pivotal tunnel. Demolition would happen within the next few weeks.

It was early evening now, so Mom said Dad would be home any minute. I had given her an extra-long hug, holding her tightly to me to convey how much I admired her strength and mourned for her pain.

My mom, this incredible woman, who raised Shiloh and me with her whole heart and brought Winter into the family like it was her purpose in life, hadn't deserved my father's disloyalty.

I had strode a decent tread in Dad's thick blue carpet by the time I heard the thick wooden door to the office creak behind me.

"Son?" My father's puzzled voice filled the stagnant air as he looked at me in bewilderment.

"Dad, we need to talk."

I wasn't mixing messages with this conversation. I wasn't his young son speaking to him with deference or respect. I was a man who had also suffered from his betrayal. My father had drilled morals and respect for women—respect for *all* life—into me from a young age, and here he was; an embezzler, a white-collar criminal, and an unfaithful husband.

My skin crawled with disgust.

"Okay." My father moved to one of the wingback chairs in the center of the room and sat, motioning for me to do the same. "What's on your mind?"

After a stiff minute, I sat my ass down on the chair next to him.

"Drew and I stopped by at the cabin the last time I was out checking GPS markers for the project." I wasn't easing into this, not by a long shot. "I showed him Grandpa's cabin while we were out, and I found a tackle box—my old tackle box, filled with letters. Your letters."

I let that declaration hang in the air and observed his reaction. A tight gulp, a slight eyelid droop, a brief clench of a hand in his lap. But he said nothing.

Okay, I had to spell it out for him. Fine.

"In those letters," I continued, "I found an interesting story of love and betrayal. Care to explain to me how the woman who destroyed Mom's life was your lover?"

The rich pink color of shame painted Emmett Quicksilver's face as he cast his gaze down into his now-clasped hands.

"Shane," he began, opening his mouth to provide what was sure to be an excuse or a line of reasoning, "you have to know that—"

"You're right," I interrupted, "I do have to know. Why the fuck would you risk everything like that, Dad?"

His head snapped back like I had hit him. I never swore at my father—ever. Typically, I was nothing but respectful to my greatest mentor and guide. That ended today. Between Brenda Simpson's love trysts, WAQ and Georgio's involvement, and learning my father wasn't the man I had grown up believing him to be—he didn't deserve my undying loyalty. Not anymore.

"I had ended it." Dad's voice was barely above a whisper, a sharp contrast to his usual booming tenor, similar to my own. "I had ended it, and she took it badly."

His eyes filled with unshed tears; drops of sin clinging to his lashes. "Your mother and I had switched vehicles that day. She thought it was me in the car. She was angry and tried to make me pay. But Amelia was the one who paid the price."

A teardrop fell, sliding down the weathered tan of his cheeks.

"Every time I look at your mother, I'm crushed by that guilt. Brenda got to escape her consequences, but I'll live with regret until the day I die."

Good.

I folded my arms across my chest and stared him down, my face a stone mask. If I raged, he would shut down. My father had a heart. I could still believe that, but he'd only take insubordination for so long.

Respecting your elders was a big part of our culture. I would only get so much leniency.

"When did this start? The Shambala Society?" I asked softly, aiming to keep him talking. I was sidestepping through any discussions about WAQ and his criminal status, but I wanted the total story here. Every deplorable detail.

Dad's eyes widened in surprise. "How did you..." he shook his head as if to clear it. "It doesn't matter. That was in several places. You could have found it anywhere."

He muttered under his breath, as if I wasn't in the room. He took a few long breaths before staring into my matching gray eyes.

"In high school, Brenda and I were together more often than not, but she didn't enjoy sticking with one boyfriend. And then her sister died. I felt responsible for her. And that responsibility never seemed to lift, even after I met your mother."

Responsible *for* her, or responsible *to* her?

We'd all suspected the ties that bound the Shambala Society into the underworld life after high school. Hillary's discovery of Georgio's twin brothers' initiation, and Travis' probing of Kellan's initiation—to kill a competitor's son in cold-blood—which, Kellan admitted to actually doing, meant Georgio's initiation had to do with murdering someone. We just didn't know who.

A fifteen-year-old girl from a middle-class family didn't seem to fit the bill. But maybe Brenda's sister saw something she shouldn't have? Or maybe Dad himself saw something he shouldn't have? Or did she actually just die from natural causes, drinking by the river and falling in?

These cyclical thoughts plagued me daily—sometimes hourly—and I was getting another headache.

"Does Mom know?"

If he was still keeping this secret, I was going to blow it wide open. Ignorance was *not* bliss, and I would not let my parents live a lie. If Mom worked through it, that was her prerogative, but I wouldn't be my father's secret keeper.

Dad pursed his lips and dipped his head. "Yes. I confessed everything after she was hurt. I was wracked with guilt and couldn't live with the shame. She took the time needed to recover, and I did everything in my power to show her it would never happen again. She stayed."

A part of me was relieved Mom was indeed here of her own free will, knowing all the facts. Did Mom know about WAQ, too? My heart sat in my throat at that thought. I had always assumed she was completely in the dark about Dad's activities, but what if she had known everything all along?

I stood from the armchair and shot him a hard stare.

"Mom may have forgiven you, but I don't. You're not the man I thought you were."

I marched to the door and turned back before I lost my nerve. "I won't be coming to work this week. Fire me if you want, I don't care. But this"—I motioned between him and me—"will never be the same."

I gave Mom a kiss on the cheek on the way out, knowing she could read me like a flashing neon sign, but I couldn't breathe a word without falling apart. I climbed into my trusty truck and made it all the way to my apartment before the dam burst.

Salty tears fell onto the steering wheel as I leaned my head against it. My chest was an agonizing dumpster fire, and the gasoline Dad had just poured on it burned worse than the risk of Georgio coming for all of us like fish in a barrel.

There was something about your parents letting you down that drove a screwdriver into your heart. I was fortunate enough to grow up in a world believing my parents were my protectors, my spirit guides, and my brightest inspirations.

That illusion now lay shattered, leaving me with nothing but shards.

I needed a joint, I needed my best friend, and I needed a fuck.

I shot off a text to Winter and made my way inside, trudging up to my apartment like my world was ablaze.

Nope, just my rosy family reality.

The joint I rolled at my coffee table was the biggest I'd ever made. I inhaled the sweet smoke and sat back on the couch, shifting all the garbage that had accumulated there this week. I wasn't usually Winter's caliber of a slob, but I couldn't bring myself to care.

Winter hadn't responded to my texts yet, and Drew was spending the afternoon with his siblings; I didn't have it in me to interrupt his family time. I took another toke of the joint and let the warm haze of being high wash over me.

Everything was fucked, and now, as I felt the languid laziness of the weed take over my body, so was I.

I woke with a start; groggy and with a serious case of the pasties as I rolled my fuzzy tongue over in my mouth.

Yuck.

The dank taste of ash and the scent of my body finally overpowered me. I rolled off the couch with a groan and walked to the bathroom; the hot shower and toothpaste felt as good as an orgasm.

I checked my phone after I pulled on some clean clothes. I was at the limits of my wardrobe; I'd needed to do laundry weeks ago, and now I only had two white t-shirts and a pair of gray sweatpants without sweat or stains on them.

Winter had sent me a bunch of texts, threatening to come get me if I didn't respond in the next fifteen minutes. That had been an hour ago. I sent her a quick message I'd be there in twenty minutes. She responded within seconds, telling me she'd throw a pizza in the oven.

Perfect. Now that I had my wits about me, I was starving. I told her to put in two and tucked my phone in my pocket.

Winter had a washer and dryer in her apartment—I'd pack up a bag and do my laundry there.

Things hadn't been strained between us since she'd let me kiss her. A fucking phenomenal kiss that had forced its way between the gray matter creases in my mind. I couldn't *stop* thinking about it. Instead, life had continued on as normal—whatever the hell *that* was for us right now, with our daily messages and moving forward with Operation Guantanamo Georgio.

If I didn't still feel the ghosts of her kisses on my lips, I'd swear nothing had happened between us.

But it had—first the threesome and then the life-changing kiss. I couldn't undo it. I didn't want to—I needed Winter Wallace to be my everything. My *actual* everything. Mind, spirit, *and* body.

But where did we go from here? Did we talk about it? Did we just let our bodies lead the way? All I fucking did these days was *talk* about things—I was sick of talking. But Winter, as free-spirited as she was, would make me talk about it. If not now, then eventually.

I was sweating bullets when I arrived at her apartment. Not just because of the unusual June evening heat, but because I didn't know how this encounter was going to go down. We could just eat pizza and watch a movie—or we could talk about our feelings and then fall asleep watching reruns of Seinfeld—or we could give in to what I was positive was brewing between us, and have the most blissful fuck of our lives.

I was desperate for the third option.

She was just taking the pizza out of the oven when I walked in. The apartment was surprisingly clean—way cleaner than mine at the moment—and I took that for the warning sign it was.

Winter's apartment was only clean when she was stressed. Or doing some major procrastinating.

Was she stressed about me? Was I so big-headed to think I could cause a scrubbing frenzy?

I shook my head, knowing her stress could be from any of a thousand things in our lives right now. Her parents, my parents, the town falling down around us—take your pick. I secretly wanted it to be about me—I needed to know she was as torn up about this recent development as I was.

I wanted her to need me as badly as I needed her.

I dropped my laundry bag on the floor and wrapped my arms around her waist, burying my nose into her lavender-scented hair while she cut the pizza.

She dropped the blade and held my hands tighter to snuggle into my hug before turning around and nuzzling me.

"Have you been taking your meds?"

What? Fuck, that wasn't what I wanted to talk about. By the determined glint in her eyes, I wouldn't get away with stone-walling.

Fuck.

I tucked my freshly washed hair behind my ears and rubbed the back of my neck with both hands, grabbing onto my shoulders and looking up at her retro popcorn ceiling.

If she was asking, she knew I wasn't. But fuck me if I wanted to have this conversation.

"You know the answer to that question, Snow."

Her fingers brushed my chin as she pulled me down to look at her. I stared into the beautiful eyes of the woman I'd give my life for in a heartbeat.

"Why, Quick? Why would you torture yourself like that?"

I brought my hands up to wrap around her wrists. I turned my head to kiss her palm and leaned into the security of her warmth.

"I don't *need* the antidepressants, Snowflake."

"You do, Quick." Her tone was gentle, but her expression was firm. "You know every time you stop taking them, you spiral. This is a bad time to decide to go medication-free, don't you think?"

I closed my eyes and held her tight as I admitted that fact in silence.

I *did* need the antidepressants. She knew it, and I knew it. I'd been taking them ever since my early teenage years, when I struggled to get over Mom's accident and the hormonal changes of puberty. My brain just wasn't wired properly, and the chemical imbalance could only be tempered with the help of some handy synthetic drugs.

I didn't hide it, but it wasn't how I wanted to start a conversation, either. Depression was an experience I had to mitigate, not the definition of who I was. Sometimes, people who hadn't suffered from the illness couldn't separate the two, and I didn't like feeling like I was a victim of some terrible disease. I wasn't.

There was no difference between me and a diabetic needing insulin, or a person with a heart condition who needed their life-saving meds. We were all just playing poker with the hand we were dealt, getting a little help from modern medicine.

I'd missed a dose a few weeks ago. And then, I'd missed another dose—and two more. It wasn't intentional, but once I was feeling shitty, I struggled to force myself to take the meds to feel better.

It was hard to explain, but with Winter, no explanation was necessary. She'd seen me through every relapse I'd had since I was fourteen.

I should have come to her before now, but avoidance was my favorite vice, and I excelled at it. A-plus, Michelin Star-level avoidance talent, at your service.

I opened my eyes to see she still awaited my answer. She hadn't stopped gaping at me, or staring through me, it would seem. I loved and hated that she could see the very thoughts streaming through my head, like my mind was a made-for-TV movie.

I steeled myself for her rejection, but I had to go for it. It was time. We'd waited years for this moment, and I wasn't letting it slip away.

"I need two things right now, Snow. And neither of them are my pills."

I tried to convey every twinge in my heart and the need slowly hardening in my sweats. "I need you, and I need your beautiful body. I need you to give me everything—everything *we've* ever needed. Are you ready? Can you give that to me?"

Fuck it—if I was going to do this, I was going all the way.

I dropped her wrists and pulled her into me by her hips, rubbing her against my rock-hard erection. I dipped my head and dropped a light kiss to the side of her neck.

She shivered beneath me, but didn't push me away.

"Let me own you tonight, Snow. In the morning, I'll take my pills and life will go back to whatever-the-fuck our normal is. But tonight—let's pretend nothing exists but you and me."

CHAPTER 21

WINTER

Quick's declaration sped my heart rate to a thousand. Maybe a million. Is this what drug users feel like after a hit? Blistering heat swept up my body as I stared into the probing eyes of my panty-melting best friend.

My panty-melting best friend who wanted me. Who *needed* me.

I couldn't deny the chemistry between us. Our love and care for each other was genuine and perfect, and Quick was asking me to take an irrevocable step.

Not asking. Begging. *Needing.*

Was I able to risk everything we had by going for it? Would I end up losing him if I didn't?

Indecision warred within me as his erection pulsed between us. Quick's naked body was no mystery to me; I'd seen it a handful of times—most recently during two boiling, sexy sessions.

My panties were soaked, and I cursed my body's treachery. My pussy wanted him, my heart wanted him, but my damn head kept getting in the way.

He pulled me closer, his lips trailing little kisses from the sensitive skin beneath my ear to the corner of my lips and back again.

"This is good for us, Snow," his supple lips whispered into my ear, the soft skin nuzzling me and sending tingles down to my toes. "The only thing still between us. I want all of you. Every square inch of it."

Fuck, I loved him. I always had. We said it every day, but now ... now it meant something else. It meant ... more. He meant more. If that was even possible.

If I pushed him away tonight, I'd live with the regret until the day I died. I wouldn't do that to myself, or to him —my brain be damned. But I needed to be sure.

"I can't do this if this is your distraction, Quick. I can't take this step if this is your lack of meds talking, or if you'll only live to regret this later. I won't be able to come back from it."

"Snow." His tone was firm. He forced up my chin until I could stare into his captivating gray eyes. "I've loved you my entire life. It took me years to see what you truly were to me, and this isn't a distraction. I'll take my meds tomorrow, and get back on the mental health train, but tonight, I want to love you like I've always loved you. I can't watch my friends share in your love when I'm so desperate for it, too."

My chest exploded with affection for this boisterous, beautiful man who had the brightest mind and the kindest heart.

I pushed up on my tiptoes and caught his lips with mine. The action caused him to gasp a little before he leaned into the kiss, capturing my mouth and claiming it. His tongue swept between my lips and his hand cupped my jaw, holding me in place while he sucked, nipped, and kissed every part of me.

I held on for dear life; I loved his control over me and my body. I could have fought out of his hold; instead—I surrendered. Quick was going to have his way with me tonight, and I was going to finally give him everything. Every square inch of me, just like he asked.

This wasn't like our high school experience; two awkward teenagers sharing in an intimate act to rip off the Band-Aid before college. This was our reckoning.

He swept me up into his arms and, never letting my mouth go, he tucked his hands under my ass and held me to him. I wrapped my legs around his waist and pressed into his body so forcefully he fell back against the fridge behind us.

His mouth still didn't break free. I couldn't think, much less breathe, and melted into the bliss of submission.

Quick stood upright and his long legs took us to my bedroom. He leaned over the bed and cradled my body on the blankets beneath us, cocooning his gigantic frame over mine. His solid cock nestled at the apex of my thighs in the most excruciating, teasing way.

It was the longest, deepest, most exhilarating kiss of my life, and an emptiness overtook me when he finally pulled away.

"I've fantasized about fucking you in this bed ever since I found you and Drew in here."

My eyes widened momentarily out of their hooded, lustful haze. "What? You saw that?"

He ignored me and sat up to pull his shirt off in a one-handed tug, revealing the bronzed muscles beneath. Any way you sliced it, Quick was model-worthy attractive. It really was a miracle I hadn't felt the urge to jump on his body sooner—aside from my other men, he had to be the hottest guy in town.

And he wanted me. He wanted to be mine.

His fingers trailed the hemline of my t-shirt. He yanked it firmly, pulling me toward him before sliding the shirt off over my head. He unclasped my bra and sucked a breath through his teeth as his gaze roamed over my exposed breasts.

Shane had been discreet during our threesome, but I'd felt the searing heat of his gaze on me through most of it. Honest me would admit I had basked in his attention.

Just like I basked in it now. His large palms held my hot, heavy breasts in his hands. Massaging the flesh, he used his thumbs to stimulate my nipples into spikes. His impressive cock twitched behind the cotton layer of his sweats.

Those sweats needed to disappear. Now. I tugged at the waistband and Quick rose on his knees, allowing me to bring them down over his ass to the bridge of his calves. He shucked them off with a kick, his usual comic-character boxers nowhere to be found.

My mouth watered at the naked specimen in all his glory, kneeling over top of me. Shane Quicksilver had a huge cock. Thick and long, with a slight curve at the end, the satisfying mushroom head was going to hit all the right places.

Overtaken by the need to have him, a moan escaped, blocking all of my other senses. Quick's devilish grin brought more sparks to my pussy as he wasted no time pulling my shorts and panties down to my ankles.

He didn't hesitate. Now we were both naked, he wouldn't give me time to change my mind. I knew he would stop the second I asked him, but it wasn't going to happen. We were too far gone. It was time.

He palmed my pussy, his hand cupping me and collecting my wetness as he brushed his thumb over my clit.

My body bucked off the bed at the light, tight circles; I was so wound up; I knew it would take nothing to make me come. By the look of satisfaction on Quick's gorgeous face, he was counting on it.

He leaned over the bed and reached into my nightstand, fumbling around until he brought out my vibrating egg. With a knowing smirk, he held up the pink silicon toy and wiggled it in his hand.

"Is this what you use to get yourself off, Snow?"

He sucked the egg into his mouth, and I nearly came on the spot at the dirty gesture. It was clean, but the move had the desired effect. His other hand still held my cunt, and a fresh wave of sticky arousal coated his palm.

Quick popped the egg out of his mouth and smacked his lips appreciatively.

"Have you ever gotten yourself off thinking of me?" His raised brow and dark expression were wicked.

I swallowed hard, as his hungry eyes never wavered from mine.

"Yes," I whispered, finally admitting my true desires. Yes, I had thought of him fucking me in this bed while touching myself. More than once. But they had been forbidden thoughts.

His storm-gray eyes lit up in triumph. "Dirty girl."

He turned on the egg, letting it vibrate against his fingers for a second before placing it delicately on my clit.

Fuck, that felt good. He released my pussy and slowly thrust two coated fingers into me while he rolled the egg against my clit over and over, causing a heady rush of sensation.

I moaned and writhed on the bed beneath him, so close to blissful release. He continued to fuck me with his fingers before sliding a well-lubricated pinkie into my ass.

I pressed into all of his fingers, every one of them forcing pleasure into me as the egg never left my clit.

"That's a good girl." At the praise in his deep voice, I lost myself to every thrust and pulse and vibration. "You're going to look so pretty taking my cock."

His filthy words pulled the orgasm right out of me—my walls clenched and I gushed my release all over his slowing hand.

He pulled his fingers free and brought them to his lips, taking his time to savor my flavor as I came down from my high.

"That was so fucking hot, Snow. I love watching you come apart for me."

He dropped his body on top of mine and kissed me with such feral desire. He was every bit of the panther I always teased him to be.

"Your cum is so fucking sweet, Snow. I'm going to clean you up before I own your body with mine."

He slid down me until his mouth covered my pussy; his tongue licked me like a delicious popsicle until every drop of my arousal was gone.

I was quivering for more. For all of him. I needed him to stuff his cock so deep inside me he would become a part of me forever.

He sat up again. With his eyes closed and his head tipped to the ceiling, he smacked his lips.

When they opened, his gaze locked on mine and he shifted his weight over me. Lining up his cock with my entrance, he notched himself within me. The light pressure of him made me lightheaded in anticipation.

"Eyes on me, Snow. I need to see your soul when I make this pussy mine."

I couldn't even blink, too afraid to miss a detail as he sunk into me, one solid inch at a time.

He was large, and I was swollen from my first orgasm, but the faint sting as I stretched around him was a welcome pain.

His forearms settled on either side of my head, and for one stopped moment in time, we peered into each other's souls, connecting, finally, at an atomic level.

Just like that, the moment broke, and he pulled back and thrust inside me so deeply, it was as if he had read my thoughts.

He wanted to own me, and he did. He held my hips in place and pulled me up to seated. When I wrapped my legs around his waist, he moved to standing.

He held his stance as he ground my body back and forth on his cock. His pubic bone rubbed my clit so perfectly, I knew I'd have no stamina for this round.

Sweat beaded down his temples as he used all of those well-honed muscles to keep our balance while pounding the shit out of me. When I couldn't hold back any more, I screamed his name in exultation and convulsed in ecstasy around him.

It was a domino effect of orgasms. Quick pumped twice more in aggressive bursts before stuttering to a halt and coming inside me. He held me so tightly to him; I felt my bones might break.

He carried me back over to my bed, but didn't release me. He flopped down on the mattress and pressed me deeper into his chest. We caught our breaths; our hearts beat in sync as he softened inside me.

This was it. The pivotal, defining point of our relationship. Our hearts, our souls, our bodies—fully fused together like they'd fulfilled their destiny.

"I love you," he murmured into my neck as he pulled out of me and shifted our bodies to cradle me in his arms. "I love you so much, Winter Wallace."

I let out a contented sigh and cuddled deeper into his hold. "I love you too, Shane Quicksilver."

I had to be the luckiest girl in the world. I hadn't won the parent lottery, or even the town lottery, but somehow, I had won the boyfriend lottery. Five men—five incredible men—had slotted their way into my life and into my heart. I knew then and there I wouldn't need anyone else to fill in the gaps. I had them, and they had me.

I had never felt so complete.

I stared at the long lineup of glass jars and scrunched up my nose at the selection.

When had the brand options for strawberry jam exploded? I was looking at seventeen different varieties of mashed berries with sugar. Talk about decision overload.

I'd had a craving for sweet strawberries ever since the turn of seasons with the June heat. But fresh berries weren't ready yet, so strawberry jam would just have to do the trick.

Grocery shopping felt like a pretty mundane task with everything else going on in my life. Laughable, even.

I finally settled on the cheapest one—because, really, what difference did it make to my amateur palate—and moved on to the cereal. Quick loved Coco Pops, and I always kept a box in the cupboard just for him.

Quick. Last night had been ... there were no words, really. Exhilarating? Mind-blowing? Life-altering?

My muscles were still sore from holding on to him for all he was worth, and I had tender bruises where his hands gripped my hips and ass while he pounded into me.

When we woke this morning, we had sex two more times, like it was the most natural thing in the world. The heat of his body still lingered across my skin in a way it never had, and along with the strawberry jam, I craved his closeness.

Maybe we could play with the jam ... I knew without a doubt Quick would have no issues with me slathering his cock in sticky sweetness and licking it all off like a dirty Dairy Dip.

Huh. That was a delicious thought for my bedroom and my egg, not surrounded by breakfast options.

I was about to head to the checkout line when a familiar face came into view.

"Hi, Devon!" I smiled brightly, trying to push as much warmth into the gesture as I could.

I didn't know Devon well, practically not at all, but he was important to Travis, so he was important to me. I never knew firsthand the connection siblings could have, other than my chosen bond with Quick, and Travis' brother had been his entire world before I met him. I wanted us to become friends, or, at the very least, friendly.

"Oh, umm - hi." Devon frowned and awkwardly shoved a hand in his pocket as he cradled his shopping basket tightly to his side.

Okay, so not the warm welcome I'd have appreciated. Maybe he didn't remember me? We'd only met twice under less-than-stellar circumstances.

"I'm Winter." I tried to smile wider, showing all of my teeth. Non-threatening, pleasant. "You may not remember me, but I'm—"

"Yeah, I remember you." Devon's lips curled into a disgusted sneer. "You're the whore Travis is throwing his life away for."

I stepped back like I had been backhanded across the face.

What the hell?

"Excuse me?" I gritted out once my brain caught up to the shock of his words. "I'm Travis' girlfriend, yes. But to call me a whore is just—"

"But you are, aren't you?" His matter-of-fact tone interrupted me, and he stepped farther away as if I were a contagious disease. "A modern Jezebel. Sleeping around and killing my brother's mind with your poison pussy."

If my eyebrows got any higher, they would disappear into my skull. The mouth on this man—some saint he was.

"Aren't you supposed to be a man of God now?" I shot back, done with his unwarranted attack on my character.

This man didn't know me, yet he was going to judge me? Didn't he love his own brother enough to try?

"What happened to 'Love thy neighbor?' 'Love thy brother?' 'Casting the first stone to judge' and all that?"

I was paraphrasing. I wasn't religious and my knowledge of the Bible wasn't great, but the God I'd been told about was one of love and acceptance, not this scathing vitriol.

"Don't pretend you know anything about the Bible," Devon spat, his eyes now full of hate. "You're a stain on my brother's soul, and he'd be better off without you."

"I'm a stain!? Are you kidding me!?" I almost dropped my basket. "Do you know how much trouble Travis has gotten in because of your choices? How much his love for *you* has almost gotten him killed? Fuck you, buddy. If you truly loved him, you'd stop taking advantage of him."

I stormed past the ungrateful idiot, done with the bitter exchange. I didn't even know if I could tell Travis. It would break his heart, and my man had had his heart broken by Devon enough to last ten lifetimes.

I was almost out of earshot when I caught his vicious parting words.

"I'm glad I reported you, you nasty slut."

My limbs shook with raging energy. It took every ounce of self-control to not drop every grocery and scratch the pompous, pious man's eyes out.

Fuck him. Fuck *him*.

Everyone had a story, and most of them had an element of tragedy. That's what life was. It wasn't kind or evil; it was ambivalent to the plight of us mere mortals. But every one of us had the power of choice—the power to make the best of our shitty situations. Our tragedy could define us or just be another element to our tale.

Devon had let it define him. He'd chosen to let it *destroy* him. And I'd be damned if he took Travis down in the process any more than he already had.

I abandoned my basket at the checkout, grateful I didn't have a melting tub of ice cream in there, and seethed all the way to Basil.

I wouldn't come between Travis and his brother, but we had agreed to a relationship without lies.

I forced a breath through my nose before picking up my phone.

I dialed my Hottie Bartender with a heavy heart. This was not the call I wanted to be making today.

The line rang a few times before his husky voice answered.

"Hey beautiful, what are you up to?"

I took a deep breath, closed my eyes, and rested my forehead on Basil's steering wheel. "Hey baby, I'm sorry to drop this on you, but there is something you should know..."

CHAPTER 22

DREW

"Cowabunga!"

Shane launched himself off the cliff edge above my head and tucked his lithe body into a tight ball. He hit the water with a loud splash; fat droplets of water hit my forehead from my position on the rocks beside the old swimming hole, just a few miles down from the actual Cascade Falls.

I hadn't been here in years. The last time was probably when I was a senior in high school. Scenic beauty surrounded me, just as I had remembered it—large smooth rocks stacked on either side of the slow part of the river, and a few jagged cliffs on either side of a small waterfall.

The water was chilly and a welcome reprieve from the scorching sun.

We had to hike a little way in to get in here, but the natural beauty of the spot was worth it. Despite it being a hot July day, we were the only ones here.

We, as in, our consolidated group of misfit boys and one girl.

Winter's beautiful body lounged on a towel next to me, her red bikini distracting me every few minutes when she shifted in the sun. I'd willingly slathered her in sunscreen earlier, and now she was tanning herself to a rosy crisp.

Cam and Travis lounged in the shallow pool just a few feet down, seated on the natural stone benches just beneath the water's surface, where they chatted quietly.

Today, Logan had also joined us. He was treading water on the deeper side of the pool, grimacing with annoyance at my boyfriend's actions.

My boyfriend. I loved the sound of that.

"Cannonball contest!" Shane announced when he spluttered to the surface. "Come on, Cam—I want to see those muscles in action!"

Cam looked up mid-sentence and a rare, full-teeth grin filled his face. "You're on. Are you a bettin' man, Shane?"

"What are you laying on the line, Big Man? I'll consider it." He wriggled his eyebrows suggestively and Cam laughed.

"I want a snowboard lesson." He said it so matter-of-factly, I had a feeling he'd been holding on to this request for a while.

Shane's face lit up like he'd been given a million dollars.

"Really!? Hell, yeah, man, I'll give you a snowboard lesson anytime. You can thank me for that generous offer later when you lose today."

His obnoxious laughter echoed around us as he pulled himself out of the water and made his way over to climb up the cliff face again.

"Fuck, you're on." Travis and Cam left their nook and followed him. I squeezed Winter's plump ass cheek and got up to do the same.

"I want to borrow your truck!" I called after them as I heaved myself up the familiar handholds to the ledge above.

The four of us stood in a staggered line, surveying the ten feet below.

"Logan, fuck off and be a team player. Come on up, you chicken-shit," Shane taunted.

Logan spun in the water and gave Shane the middle finger. "Fuck you, Quicksilver."

Shane rolled his eyes and called out to Winter instead. "Snow! You're the official judge. Get off your lazy ass and tell me when I win!"

I could hear her snort from here. She pushed up from her beach towel and rolled over, exposing her sexy body for all of us to gawk at. I didn't need to look at my brothers to know I wasn't the only one checking out our girl.

The floppy hat she wore had drooped over her face in the way of the pin-up girls in the 1940s. My Audrey Hepburn.

"Alright, gents!" she called out. "Let's see your splashes!"

Cam went first, leaping outward to avoid the sharp rocks at the base below.

"9!" Winter exclaimed with a laugh as Cam swam toward her, tilting his head up for a kiss. She gave him a quick peck on the lips and pushed him away.

"Next contestant!" she called out. I loved hearing the smile in her voice. I looked forward to when I would hear it every day.

Travis dove off next. The man may be charming, but his cannonball was nothing close to graceful, and he landed with an awkward belly-flop.

"Ouch!" Winter waited for him to swim over to her for his own kiss. "6.5! Sorry babe, that wasn't the greatest."

Travis shook his head in defeat, but did not hide the grin on his face. We were all having fun today.

"Next!" Winter called, and I took my chance, flying like a deranged chimpanzee before tucking in the last minute. The cool water embraced me, and I pushed off from the sandy bottom, welcoming the warm air on my face as I broke the surface.

"8!" Winter yelled, smiling down at me as I swam towards her. "Nice job, Hardy Boy," she praised, and I received my own quick congratulatory peck.

I followed Cam and Travis and climbed out of the water to warm up on the hot stones.

She turned her attention upward. "Come on, Quick!"

"Just a second," he yelled back. "Logan, get your ass up here before I make Cam carry you up!"

"To be clear, you can't *make* me." Cam said dryly. "But I'll gladly volunteer." A devilish smirk crossed his normally stoic features. "Don't make me volunteer, Pretty Boy."

Logan watched us all from the opposite side of the swimming hole and rolled his eyes.

"Fuckers," he muttered, probably thinking none of us could hear, but he indulged us and pulled out of the water, anyway.

Despite the heat, Logan still wore a fitted black tee along with his swim shorts. He climbed up the cliff face with an athletic swiftness and stood a good five feet away from Shane at the top.

"You can go first." Logan crossed his arms and nodded his chin towards the water below.

"No can do, brother! Can't have you chickening out on me." Shane's glee wasn't subtle. He loved pushing Logan out of his comfort zone.

I couldn't say for sure who was the biggest shit disturber in our group, but Logan and Shane would probably tie for first place.

They had a miniature stare-off, neither of them blinking for several seconds. Then, without another word, Logan launched himself off the cliff.

His splash was decent, but definitely not Cam's.

"8!" Winter exclaimed as Logan swam toward our group of sunbathing penguins.

She cradled Logan's cheeks in her palms when he swam up to her side and gave him a brief kiss before ducking her head to whisper something in his ear. I couldn't hear what it was, but his irritated expression immediately softened.

He pulled himself out and sat beside her in my spot. I hoped he realized I'd be taking my prime perch back.

"Alright, Quick! Strut your stuff, you show off!"

"Wahoooooooo!"

Shane dove off and held himself in the hedgehog position long before he hit the water. He splashed all of us on the sidelines; I had to wonder if he lined his pockets with rocks when we weren't looking.

"10!" Winter yelled. Her cheers dissolved into giggles as Shane swam up to her and dragged her into the water by her ankles.

She shouted in surprise and wrapped her arms around Shane's neck so tightly she looked like she was going to choke him out.

"Quick!" Her screeches halted when Shane closed his mouth over hers in a deep, more-than-friendly kiss.

"Fucking finally," Logan barked out at the same time Travis crowed, "I knew it!"

I had known about this latest development. Shane and Winter had both told me separately, given the nature of our now-triad relationship. By their reaction, the guys hadn't been brought up to speed yet.

Winter slowly turned her head to face the four men on shore. Her cheeks were tinged pink—from the heat or Shane's kiss, I didn't know. A shy smile crept across her face as she looked at us.

"Ummm, yeah," she admitted with an embarrassed laugh. "So, we're all...in a fully formed harem now. Probably a little late to have this conversation, but ... is everybody in?"

She scrunched up her brows and bit her lip as her gaze hesitantly landed on each of us individually.

Cam, Travis and I didn't need to confirm with each other. We'd known what we were getting into. We all bobbed our heads in agreement. Shane still held her in his arms and nuzzled his lips into her hair. "I'm in, Snowflake."

Her gaze fixed on Logan. He held her stare for a moment before sighing out a breath. "Princess, of course I'm fucking in. I'm the one trying to find this annoying bunch of twits a house, aren't I? I'm in."

He reluctantly turned to us. "I'm in."

What an impassioned, heart-wrenching speech.

I couldn't take my eyes off of Winter's relieved smile. Of course, we were all in. We had fallen for her and gained a band of brothers—and, in my case, a boyfriend—in return. There was no turning away from the life we were building, one small plan at a time.

The rest of the afternoon was reminiscent of lazy summer afternoons as a teenager, with few cares to speak of. More contests, more bets. Logan even surprised us all with a catered picnic basket of some of the tastiest cheeses I had ever eaten. He warmed up as the day progressed; he almost seemed like he was enjoying himself.

In late afternoon, it was time to leave. Travis, Cam, and Winter all had Bourbon & Blues shifts to get to, and it was family dinner at the Johnsons' tonight.

"Loggie-bear," Shane said seriously before we took to the water one last time. "Take off your shirt, man."

"Fuck off, Quicksilver." Logan retorted, making no move to do so. "It's none of your business."

"Okay, but hear me out." Shane's voice was actually kind as he continued his train of thought. "We're in this, right? A fucked-up family, yeah? We're going to get a house with a pool one day, and swim and play and have naked fucking orgies every Sunday?"

His face morphed into a salacious grin, and he winked at me before turning back to Logan. His tone softened and his eyes held an earnest sincerity.

"If we're brothers, don't be afraid to show us your shit. We all have shit. I-I'm on antidepressants and can't go a day without them. That's my shit. Oh yeah, and my father's a lying, cheating bastard."

Birds chirped in the background, but no other sound was heard as Shane's announcement filled the air between us. It was news to me; it didn't change how I felt about him, but it seemed like a significant secret he'd held tight to his chest.

Travis spoke up beside me. "I'm going to have to cut my little brother out of my life," he declared sadly. "He's damaged, but he's toxic, and I can't throw my life away for him anymore. That's my shit."

Wow. Heavy. I hadn't known that either.

"I'm the long-lost brother to mobsters, and if they find out, I'll have to go into hiding or take on the family business." Cam's words were dark and bitter. "That's my shit."

My turn for a confession.

"I don't know who I am," I admitted for probably the first time. "My whole life has been living for others, and I don't have a sweet fucking clue who I am without that expectation. But I know I'd like to figure it out with you guys along for the ride."

Logan stared at us. His mask conveying nothing, he took us all in for what we were. Broken men with baggage in spades, but with hope for something beyond our shit.

Winter came up beside him and gripped his hand in solidarity, offering silent support.

Finally, he nodded his head in some sort of acknowledgment before wrenching the soaked t-shirt over his head. He turned around, exposing a gnarled webbing of red, battered flesh. The imprints of belt buckles were actually visible in the mottled, raised skin. I couldn't imagine the agony he'd gone through to survive the beatings that had caused them.

Winter stroked the scars with gentle hands and said nothing. Clearly, she had seen them before.

"Shit," Travis muttered. Cam was his usually soundless self, but he clenched his fists.

Shane placed his hands on Logan's shoulders and turned him back around.

"We're going to bury that fucker," he swore, a true promise of retribution.

Cam came up to stand in front of him too. "Don't hide them anymore," he commanded with the true authority of a Carlos son. "He doesn't deserve that power over you. Only little men beat their children. Show him what a pathetic little man he is."

Logan was uncharacteristically speechless; he swallowed hard at Cam's words, but he didn't move to put the shirt back on.

"Last contest." Shane's declaration cut through the somber air that had settled over us. "Who has the best jackknife? Annnnnnnnnd go!"

He and Travis raced up the cliff, with Cam following close behind.

"Come on," I wiggled my eyebrows at Logan. "Let's see if we can cut that cocky fucker down to size."

I didn't wait for his response, but a snort sounded behind me. As I raced up the rocks to make a name for myself, I had a new bet in mind ...

One I was going to win.

"You're sure about this, baby?"

I had won my bet, although I really didn't think it would have taken much convincing either way. Ever since Shane and I had fucked for the first time, I had fantasized about taking his ass like I had Winter's. The vise grip she'd held me in still made me see stars in my dreams, and I needed to feel the same from Shane.

My gorgeous man was spread out in front of me, his bare ass at the ready for me to try my hand being a top. His ass was so biteable; two muscular chunks of tanned flesh just waiting to be squeezed and covered in teeth marks. Another day.

"I want to fuck you raw, baby," I replied, finishing the final coat of lube over my rock-solid shaft.

I dripped lube all down his hole, worked it inside with my fingers, and scissored him in rhythmic strokes. He shuddered beneath me with a deep, cock-stiffening groan. "That's right, baby, take my fingers like you fucking own them. Do you like that?"

"Fuck, I like it when you talk dirty to me," Shane whimpered; I reached around with my other hand and grasped his steel erection.

"Yes, baby." He groaned and bucked into my hand as I pumped him hard. "Fuck, yes."

I was taking a page out of his book. He loved dominating me, and I learned I liked to do the same. I loved it when Winter took the reins with me, but with Shane—we could be two fuck-buddies on a football field, trying to outdo each other with our passes—except with our cocks and our words.

I removed my fingers from his ass and pulled him up on his knees in front of me, lining my cock up with his entrance and notching the head just inside his tight hole. The way he gripped me was euphoric, and I slowly pushed my way in.

Sweat beaded my brow as I forced my way into his intense heat. I didn't want this to be a fast and dirty fuck.

His ass flexed, and his grip on me shifted, sending lightning up my spine.

Screw it. I didn't need to savor this moment. I'd savor cuddling and his sweet words after. I needed to come inside him and feel his cum coat my palms.

I banded my arm around his ribs and thrust into him deep and hard, pushing us both up the bed with the force of each pulse of my hips. I held his cock tight in my fist, jerking him off to the same rhythm. The sustained pumping of my cock flooded me with a type of pleasure I had never known before Shane.

"Fuck, baby. Do you feel how deep my cock is in you right now? Do you need me to fuck you harder? Tell me what you want, baby."

Shane's body was tensing, his movements against my palm frantic. He was so close to dissolving into a puddle at my feet.

"Rip me a new fucking asshole; destroy me, baby. Fuck me so deep, your cum won't be able to come out of me."

I didn't respond. I just did as he begged; fucking him roughly as my balls slapped against his and my hand developed callouses, I pumped him so hard.

We exploded at the same time—hot cum coated my fingers as jets of my own burst into him. Our bodies sagged onto his mattress in completely spent exhilaration.

"If that's what happens to me when you win a bet, I'm always fucking losing." Shane snickered into my arm with a satisfied sigh.

"As long as I'm with you, I'm always fucking winning," I answered, resting my head on the crook of his shoulder. "I love you, Shane."

Despite his Jell-O body from an earth-shattering orgasm, he shot up from the bed and whipped around to face me. His long dark hair framed his gorgeous face—the gorgeous face contorted into a massive grin, like a dopey Golden Retriever.

"Really!?" He beamed down at me with an energy only Shane possessed. It could penetrate through you and give you the same boost in mood, no matter what had happened to you that day.

"I love you too, Drew."

He kissed me sweetly, then lay back down and cradled me between his strong biceps. After one more round of orgasms, we fell asleep in each other's arms, like proper lovers do.

CHAPTER 23

WINTER

No part of my psyche could have predicted my plans for the day.

It was a rare day where I wasn't on Bourbon & Blues schedule, and my exams were over. I had planned to curl up with a new dark romance on my Kindle and veg out.

That beautiful picture-perfect day had washed away when I got a phone call from Mom. We hadn't spoken since I'd left the house a few weeks ago.

'To check in,' she'd said. She'd been 'worried about me.'

I was confused, and feeling slightly guilty, for whatever reason, and downright dumbfounded when she'd asked me to spend the day with her.

I could have said no, but the little girl in me had always wanted attention from her mother. Adult me wasn't so far removed that I didn't crave the same, even if it was deep down and semi-buried under a collection of hurts.

"I'm excited to shop with you, honey. I feel like we haven't spent time together in ages."

When Mom had found out I was going to the Gold Gala —an event she and Dad were apparently playing some kind of role in, she'd decided our day of spending time together was to take me shopping for a gown.

She was taking me *shopping.* Mom and Dad didn't financially support my education or living expenses, and we'd never even exchanged gifts once I became an adult. Mom didn't take me shopping.

My mother's actions confused me on the best of days, so I'd decided to just go along with it. When she asked if any of my handsome men could come along as chaperons, I stifled a groan and made a litany of excuses for their regrettable absence.

That was probably Mom's agenda. To take me shopping, maybe, but I'd bet the 'spending time' had more to do with the tasty eye-candy she couldn't seem to keep her hands off of.

Gross, Mom.

She looked at me expectantly, and I realized I hadn't answered.

"Er—yeah, Mom." I attempted a weak smile. "This is nice."

She'd shocked me when she parked at Riches Row and led me to a small shop next to Stanley's; the last time I'd been in this area, I'd had a panic attack in Hillary's arms.

Thanks to Logan, I was stopping that nonsense.

The inevitable had happened between Logan and me, and I wasn't sad about it. Memories of our midnight rendezvous still made my cheeks flush, and seeing the man in Clark Kent glasses made for some sexy fantasies. Logan was like an ogre—so many layers.

He'd kill me if he heard me say that out loud. Or maybe punish me...

"Try this one on." Mom shoved a satin emerald green dress into my arms, poking me with the hanger. "The green will look beautiful with your hair."

The delicate fabric was a soft caress across my fingers. It was beautiful, and elegant, and ... *expensive.*

I held the tag up for her to see.

"Holy hell, Mom! You're not going to spend $600 on a dress for one night."

Mom's eyes tightened and the ghost of a sad smile traced her lips. "I haven't bought you much, Winter. Let's call this a step in the right direction."

Who was this woman and where was Miranda Wallace?

My protests fell on deaf ears, so I tried it on, along with a blue silk mermaid dress, and a champagne A-line that was far too *Cinderella* for my liking.

Mom had been right on the money with her first choice. The delicate dress had a plunging neckline with teases of dainty eyelet lace. Backless, it hugged my hips and thighs like it was a second skin. It could rival any of Hillary's dresses in her closet, though I knew for a fact hers cost far more than this one—to my continued chagrin.

Travis and Logan's jaws were going to drop to the floor when they saw me in it.

"Definitely that one," Mom agreed, as I did an awkward turn on the raised platform in front of a triangulation of mirrors. Then, more softly, she added, "You look stunning, honey."

I really didn't know how to take this version of my mother. I felt like I was on the receiving end of some television show practical joke series, but the smile in her eyes was genuine.

"Thank you."

I returned her smile, stepped off the dais, and changed back into my jeans and sleeveless blouse. By the time I made it out of the changing room, Mom was waiting by the front door, having already paid for the gown.

"Do you need to be anywhere this afternoon? I'd like to go to Madegan's."

"Ummm, sure." I cocked my head as I studied her, eager to get any sort of clue why she was so interested in out-of-the-blue 'hanging out'. "Don't you have some book stuff or research to do?"

"Not today, sweetie. I'm all yours."

Huh. Okay. Twilight Zone vibes.

I remained contemplative as we deposited the dress back into her black Lexus and walked down the cobblestone street to the up-scale coffee shop at the end.

She ordered us croissants and lattes while I grabbed us a cozy booth tucked away in the corner. The entire space was dressed in varying shades of teal, silvers, and crisp white; it felt like a magical adult *Frozen*-themed haven.

We sipped our lattes in a relatively comfortable silence, listening to the dull roar of a filled restaurant, jazzy pop in the background and the clinking of dishware as people enjoyed their meals.

This day was too contrived, too out-of-the-ordinary. Mom wanted something from me, but I wasn't sure what.

I licked the last of the milk foam from the rim of the pretty handcrafted mug and decided I was going to find out.

"Care to tell me what all of this is *really* about, Mom?" I flattened my lips into a thin line and stared her down.

They'd lied to me about not having a history in Cascade Falls, they'd withheld information about Carson coming after me, they'd been in an open-marriage for *years* without my knowledge and Dad's entire childhood had been a bedtime story as fictional as *The Three Billy Goats Gruff.*

What else could she possibly want to talk about today?

It took four minutes for her shell to crack.

Finally peering back at me, her lips creased into a grimace.

"Since the wedding, I've had lots of time for reflection. The FBI took my daughter. My innocent daughter, who I *know* did nothing to warrant it. Your reason for being taken was a weak one, honey. Your father believed it because it was convenient, but I didn't."

She closed her eyes and drew in a deep breath, as if the coffee-scented oxygen around us would give her strength. Maybe it could. Logan's exercises had done wonders for me.

My heartbeat picked up as she found her calm. Did Mom know anything? Anything useful? While Mom breathed, I held every molecule of air in my lungs as I waited for her to continue.

When she finally opened them, a determined glint shone there.

"Your father and I have known you've been working at Bourbon & Blues for years. Georgio mentioned it when you first started working there at a cocktail party. I had waited for you to come home and tell me about your new singing career, but you never did. I thought maybe you were hiding it for a reason, so I never pushed."

Huh. News to me. But it was nothing particularly revealing.

"We raised a smart girl. I knew you wouldn't be oblivious to Georgio's other businesses for long."

Mom fiddled with her napkin. It was a eulogy of sorts— the truth recounted in a final summary before our day of reckoning. What a depressing thought.

"Your father had committed to Georgio long before I met him. When we knew we were serious about each other, he admitted he would have to move back to Cascade Falls with Emmett as a part of a previously negotiated business arrangement. I loved him and with my career, I could work from anywhere, so I agreed."

Her throat bobbed, and she crushed the last piece of her croissant between her fingers. "My history wasn't a lie. My parents died when I was a teenager, and I had no relatives either. It was something your father and I shared. A new town was a welcomed change.

"What he never told me was what that business arrangement actually was. But over time, I came to suspect. Darren did not want you near any of the money from WAQ. That was my first clue. And then bits and pieces of his actual business came to light. And, once I was fully aware of the situation, I agreed; I didn't want his tainted decisions affecting you, either.

"When you received the settlement from the Baker fiasco, we breathed a sigh of relief. It was your money, and you wouldn't need to rely on the dirty cash for school or for your first apartment. We were shocked when you wouldn't touch a penny of it."

So, their rationale to leave me to my own devices was to … protect me? That was a twist I hadn't been expecting. And a really warped way to justify it.

"But I had no idea that you knew anything at all about that side of our lives. Until the wedding."

"How?" The simple word tore at the deepening wound inside me.

"Because, Winter, the FBI approached me to turn on Darren, just like I know they approached you."

The icy claws of realization dug into me as I froze in place. Mom knew everything. She knew everything and yet she was here, in front of me, saying these things casually, as if our world couldn't burn down in front of us to brittle ashes at any moment.

"Why didn't you?" I whispered, not daring to ask any louder, despite the noisy din of the surrounding restaurant.

Mom's eyes held a deep sorrow, but her gaze never left mine. Instead of responding, she asked her own question.

"What would it take for you to turn on the men you love?"

My heart sunk from my chest into my stomach. Nothing. Short of cold-blooded murder, and maybe even that, there was nothing my men could do to make me turn them in, regardless of the consequences.

Suddenly, I understood my mother, just a bit more. The position she had been put in with Dad's omissions of truth, the risk she'd taken to move to an entirely new place, and the loneliness she might have tried to fill with no other family to rely on.

I had only wished she had filled that loneliness with me, instead of her career and the weight of her secrets.

The server cleared our table long before we moved to leave. We sat beneath the dense fog of our own choices in a pensive silence.

I only spoke up once we were walking out to Mom's car.

"Thanks for telling me this side of the story, Mom. It's … clarified a few things."

Her mouth molded into a melancholy frown. "I'm sorry it has come to this, baby girl. I hope there will be redemption some day for your father and I. But you, you have a whole life ahead of you."

Following those ambiguous words, she drove me home with a beautiful new dress and a heart full of woe.

"I have a home in Brenton that I want you to run away to for a little while."

Hillary made this statement casually as she flipped through a magazine while sitting on my couch.

It was laughable, really, her elegant posture sitting among my colorful bohemian pillows and my macrame hanging potted plants; but she hadn't stuck her nose up to complain about my meager apartment.

Still, I was pretty sure her outfit cost more than all of my furniture combined.

"Run away to? I have a life here, Hill. And a job, and—"

"Yes, yes, I know, Winter." Hillary waved her hand dismissively without taking her eyes off the page. "But you need to have an escape plan. And I'm providing one for you."

"In the form of an empty house?"

I raised my eyebrows and plopped down on the cushion beside her, finally diverting her attention from *Cosmo's* educational piece on 'How to Make a Good Boy Turn Bad.'

"No, it's furnished," she stated matter-of-factly, not taking my bait. "And far out of Georgio's sight line. You and your harem keep getting more roped into this situation, and I don't like it."

"You and me both." I sighed, overwhelmed by the many revelations we'd uncovered over the last several weeks. "Kellan keeps reassuring us it'll all be over soon, but I have a hard time believing it."

She perked up at the mention of the particularly hot, blond Viking god.

"That man is a woman's walking wet dream." She bit her lip and waggled her eyebrows suggestively. Then she shrugged, her attention moving back to the riveting and informative piece of literature that was *Cosmopolitan*. "I'd spin on his cock if he let me."

I choked on my laughter. "Yeah," I sputtered, "he's worth the whirl."

"So, back to the house idea." Hillary was nothing if not a relentless, perky pit-bull. "I'm going to give you the address and a passcode, okay?"

"Sure, Hill. Give me the address and the passcode." I wouldn't argue the point further. She would win anyway, so it was better just to roll over and play dead.

Her gaze snapped up to mine, and the veil of seriousness that covered her icy blues surprised me. "I mean it, Winter. Please take your safety seriously. I may not be there to protect you when the time comes."

This powerhouse of a woman had a fierce love, and she protected her own even more fiercely. I wasn't good at showing her how grateful I was to have her in my life, and I was going to change that.

Pushing aside the God-awful magazine Quick had bought me at the gas station as a joke, I took her hands in mine.

She quirked a brow in confusion.

"Hill, I appreciate everything you've done for me. I'm sorry if I don't show it enough."

She squirmed awkwardly under my sincere stare, but she didn't pull away.

"Friends don't need to thank each other, Winter. I enjoy being there for you." Then, as if this level of vulnerability was too much for her, she cleared her throat and shot me a cheeky grin. "But you should absolutely always listen to my advice, and accept that in almost every instance, I'm right."

I dropped her hands in mock disgust and rolled my eyes. "I take it back. You're the worst."

"You love me," she said cheerily, standing from the couch and walking to my fridge, frowning at the dregs of the leftovers rotting inside.

"Put on some pants. We're not eating here."

I looked to the ceiling for strength from whichever deity in the universe who would take pity on me and my choice in friends.

I came out of the living room and peeked into the fridge. I could admit she had a point.

"All right," I called after her as I did, indeed, search my room for a clean pair of pants. "But we're not going to that gross Mongolian place again."

"Nope!" she yelled back, her voice way too chipper to be kind. "We're expanding your palate! There's a new Somalian place I want to try!"

So much for my favorite standbys of french fries and pizza. Today I'd been gifted a house and a probable stomach ache.

Wooo.

CHAPTER 24

CAMERON

"I want you to wear a tracker."

My brother's authoritative voice crackled over the speaker of my burner phone as Travis and I sat in the safety of Pop's Chevelle.

He had woken me up this morning with the shrill beeping of a message demanding an impromptu conference call to go over the details of the Gold Gala tomorrow night.

Both Carlos brothers were attending, and Kellan wanted Travis and me on high alert.

For what, I hadn't known. I wasn't going—men like me didn't get invited to black-tie dinners that cost more than my rent. Kellan wanted me to linger around City Hall the night of the event, a dark spirit waiting in the wings in case I was 'needed.'

His cryptic responses when I'd asked questions made me grind my teeth, but to spare us both the pain of putting my well-worn fist through his jaw, I had opted to keep quiet.

Until now.

Travis's voice filled the cabin of my car before I could beat him to it. "We all need trackers. I want Winter and Logan to have the same safety that we'll have."

"What are you expecting, dear brother?" I intoned. "I thought this was a simple meet-and-greet for the rich, *upstanding citizens* of Sequoia County? Why the sudden need for ankle monitors?"

The silence on the other line hung over our shoulders like the heavy weight it was.

"Fine," Kellan snapped, as if asking to protect our people was an inconvenience. "I'll provide you all with trackers. You'll have to meet me tomorrow morning to get them. I won't have time tomorrow night."

"You sound worried, Kell." Travis' voice held thick concern.

Apparently, my brother was on a nickname basis with the Viking spawn who had taken over our lives like a raging tsunami. I wouldn't be making such an effort.

A burst of blown air blasted over the tinny line. "Georgio's planned a big supply drop while most of the higher-ups are preoccupied with the event. My team is ready for the sting operation, but my double-life is going to be a challenge."

Another brief silence.

He broke it again, his tone exuding careful control. "And Janet may be compromised. I'm working on an extraction plan, but I won't be able to get her out until tomorrow."

"Anything we can do?" Travis asked, naturally sliding into his savior auto-pilot. It was going to get him killed one day.

"Stay alert. Do what Georgio asks, so he doesn't get suspicious. I'll have eyes on you throughout the evening."

A litany of chattering voices rose in the background.

"Gotta go." Kellan hung up abruptly, leaving Travis and me to pick up the pieces of his puzzling words once again.

I watched the delicate dance of two bluebirds in an oak tree across the parking lot as I gathered my thoughts.

"I don't like this," I muttered. To myself or to him, I wasn't sure.

"I don't either, but we don't have a choice." Travis' shoulders slumped. "I never have a fucking choice."

My friend's dejected face and tired eyes pulled at my heartstrings. I turned to face him and reached out, taking him by his shoulders so he was forced to look at me.

"We have to have faith this will be over soon. And then we can start our lives as a family of lost souls in a ridiculously over-priced house Billionaire Boys Club picks out for us. Don't lose your hope now, brother."

His eyes slightly brightened with that mirage, and I let him go to start the car up again. We had the rest of our day ahead of us. I wouldn't waste it when our world could end tomorrow.

Perhaps I needed to hold on to my own hope, too.

Billionaire Boys Club had asked me to spar with him again tonight. His monster had connected with mine through the splitting of knuckles and swapping of sweat.

I was grateful for the distraction to pound out the clinging, anxious thoughts clouding my judgment.

I had two fight nights under my belt over the past few weeks. We were playing to a much smaller crowd, and my competition had been weak. Georgio had given me the directive to pound them to sand, and I had, but it gave me little satisfaction.

If Kellan was right, and I had to believe he was, then Georgio knew my origins and was biding his time. My criminal half-brother in blood gave no indication he had any knowledge of my past or my lineage—I was a trinket of his to use, like a well-trained show-pony. His ability to hide his true motivations was spell-binding. And terrifying.

My sparring partner today was also a confusing man. He'd given me the passcode to his building and to his apartment, telling me to 'come over when I was ready.'

I couldn't say we were true friends. We were *friendlier* thanks to the binding force that was the threat of our own lives being taken, and the tether that was my little violet. We had become chosen brothers to survive this scenario and work toward futures we'd always wanted; always needed.

But friends?

I stepped from the golden elevator more glamorous than any home I had ever lived in and stiffly walked down the corridor to his condo in the sky.

I hesitated in the doorway, unsure of what to do. Did I walk in? Knock?

I settled on a quick three-beat knock. I shouldn't be walking into his apartment unannounced like I had any right to be there.

"Come in, Chase," a muffled voice gruffly called from the other side of the metal frame.

I punched in the door code and slowly ambled inside.

Not even a vision from God himself could have prepared me for the sight before me.

My beautiful woman was laid out on Logan's marble island top like a hedonistic buffet on a golden platter. Her hair splayed around her shoulders and she had her eyes closed. Her soft pink dress draped around her waist. Logan's head was between her creamy thick thighs and his ministrations were coaxing the most tempting moans from her delicate lips.

I would murder a man to be in his place.

"If you're busy, I can come back at another time," I said, as his mouth latched onto her clit with the air of a man well-practiced in such things.

Winter's eyes flew open and caught mine in a sensuous stare-off; her body shuddered with Logan's pleasure, but her gaze never dropped from my face.

Logan's head popped up, and his wicked grin confirmed my suspicions. The timing of this alluring charade was an intentional ploy to bait me.

Suckling tit of a piglet. He would not get the luxury of my attention.

"Glad you could make it, Boxer Boy." He stood from his prime location and strode towards me. The smirk on his face rivaled Shane's whenever he'd won a game, or Travis' when he'd outdone Drew in any contest.

When he stepped close enough, I caught the sweet musk of her arousal clinging to his chin in a shiny mask.

"Our girl is dripping all over my countertop. Help me clean it up."

My brows rose skyward at the suggestion. Instead of taunting me with his position of pleasure, he was offering to … share?

I eyed him with open suspicion. "You want me to help … clean her up?"

"Unless you'd just rather watch like a fucking virgin."

Logan's sneer would have been infuriating if his offer wasn't so intriguing. The possessive man in me wanted to lock Winter in a room and have her ride me hard until we blacked out from coming apart more times than we could count.

But hearing her moans while Logan feasted on her sweet pussy had had an effect. My cock had hardened to granite in my gym shorts; I now needed to bury it between her thighs until my cum marked her as mine.

My feet betrayed me, bringing me closer to my little violet's display. Her hooded blue eyes and glistening pink pussy brought me to my knees. My mouth hovered over her; Logan's presence behind me no longer mattered—I couldn't deny such a delicious meal.

I licked down the seam of her lips, relishing her taste. She bucked into me as I closed my mouth around her fully to spear her with my tongue. The vibration of her moan rippled through me, spurring me to suck harder. I gripped her hips and pulled her across the cold surface more tightly to me, and the heat and suppleness of her skin overtook my senses.

The muscles of her thighs tightened around my head. I pinned her beneath me, unwilling to let her escape until the sweetness of her coated my tongue.

I didn't have long to wait. Her body tensed, and the ragged cry that left her lips was the sweetest symphony to my ears. I lapped up every drop before standing to pull her off the island and into my arms for a lingering kiss.

She melted into me. Her cum on my lips wasn't enough for me. Desire forced its way through my body like a speeding freight train, and my cock twitched with an urgency to plunge into her.

"That wasn't so bad, now, was it?"

Logan's smug tone broke through our moment, and I was tempted to maim him for it.

He stepped up behind her, latching his mouth onto her earlobe as I held her flushed skin against me. I captured her shivers as he nipped and sucked a trail down to her shoulders. He paid no attention to me—his undivided attention directed solely to the woman between us. He sandwiched her—pushing her more deeply into my arms and her belly into my throbbing shaft.

I resumed my exploration of her lips as her hands held my t-shirt in a death grip.

"Yeeeeeeeeeees," Winter moaned into my mouth, wriggling against me. I could feel beads of pre-cum cover the tip of my cock as it anticipated its release.

Logan chose that moment to look up and wink at me.

"Why don't we take this to the bedroom?" the calculating deviant purred into our woman's ear.

Her eyes popped open and lingered on mine with uncertainty.

"Cam?" Her whisper was a question—or a plea; I couldn't discern the difference in my lust-filled haze.

I wanted this. Needed this. I had held out for my little violet long enough. If I wanted her, I needed to accept these other men. We could try this once, but if it was too much, I would simply take my moments with her alone.

"I'll try, Little Violet. I need to feel you around me tonight."

When I released her from my arms, Logan led us to his bedroom; the last time I had seen these walls, Winter had been drugged. We needed better memories to saturate this space.

Logan wasted no time, tugging Winter's dress over her head and unclasping her bra, exposing her nakedness to my eager eyes. Her body held luscious curves and a softness I loved on a woman.

She was a feminine goddess, and I was just a simple man.

Logan had removed his own clothes in the time I had taken to admire her form. I had never wanted to see Logan Eccles in all of his pompous glory, but here we were. Without overthinking it, I shucked my t-shirt into the corner and pulled down my shorts and boxers in one go; my heavy cock bobbed against my abdomen, impatient to fill her up.

I sat on the edge of the bed and tucked her naked body between my legs. I palmed her perky breasts and squeezed, savoring her breathy responses as I tweaked her nipples.

Logan left, grabbing something from his bedside table, but was back in seconds. He pushed us forward until I was laying down with Winter fully on top of me.

"Have you ever been fucked by two cocks before, Princess?"

Her glossy eyes looked back at him as she held her weight above me. "Yes."

Logan's smirk took on a darker hue. "How about two cocks in your pussy?"

Her breath quickened and her eyes grew wide. I had never done such a thing. I had seen it in a porn once, but would never have dreamed I'd be part of one.

"Logan, I don't think—"

A bottle of lube appeared in his hand and he squirted the clear gel all over his jutting cock.

"Shut up, Chase. I want to feel her cum drench my cock, and I know you do, too. I'm not into your dick—you don't do it for me. I want to make Princess forget her own name when we stuff our cocks in her tight cunt."

His quirked brow taunted me, as if I was too moral of a man to take part in this debauchery.

I wasn't. Winter Wallace was made for the beautiful sins of the flesh, and tonight, I'd be partaking.

I shifted my weight and wriggled up the luxurious duvet, holding Winter in my arms as I settled into place.

She sat up and straddled me, grabbing my cock between her small hands and stroking hard. I trembled beneath her touch, and before long, I hauled her hips up and plunged her down on my aching shaft.

"Fuck." We groaned together as her walls clenched around me. I grabbed her plump cheeks and thrust into her from below, overcome by the pleasurable zings of heat licking up my spine.

"Stay still," Logan commanded. Winter immediately leaned over my body, kissing me deeply as Logan got into his own position.

I felt him before I could see him, the tip of his cock sliding wetly against the bottom of my shaft. He spread sticky lube all over the back of Winter's entrance and onto the base of my cock. I had never felt the hands of another man on my cock before, and I didn't love the experience.

Those thoughts disappeared as soon as he eased his way into Winter's tight pussy; the friction of him against my shaft felt far better than I expected.

"Don't move, either of you." He was all the way in; I was held in such a tight vise and the feeling was just short of euphoric.

I held still as he thrust against me; I could now understand why straight men chose the feel of another man's cock in these situations. Whether this was heaven or hell, it didn't matter. I never wanted the moment to end.

Winter lost herself to the sensation and writhed between us with abandon. I held her up as Logan picked up speed, rocketing unfamiliar pleasure through my body.

I was going to come any second, and I wasn't going to be able to stop it.

Winter's final cries as she came gave me the permission I needed to explode into her. Her pussy walls wrapped around us both so tightly she milked every ounce of cum from me. Logan too; his groans matched mine as we flooded her body with our combined release.

Logan pulled out first. He headed into the bathroom while Winter climbed awkwardly off of me like a drunken baby deer. I shifted over to one side of the massive king bed and tucked her body against mine in an endorphin-fueled cuddle.

I'd never felt so high from an orgasm.

Logan came out with a warm washcloth and cleaned her thighs. He shocked me when he dipped his head into her swollen lips and swept up our combined cum with his tongue; he held it in his mouth a moment before depositing it into Winter's mouth with a deep, leisurely kiss.

"Taste what you do to us, Princess. We taste so fucking good, don't we?"

Winter swallowed and smacked her lips. "So good," she agreed with a sleepy mumble. Then she snuggled into my body and closed her eyes. In mere seconds, her soft snores filled the space between us.

I was so sated, I didn't bother questioning that unexpected display. I sunk into the feather-soft mattress as Logan climbed in on the other side and covered the three of us with the duvet from the floor.

I closed my eyes just for a second, and before I knew it, I was asleep too.

Several hours later, I awoke to the light of the moon filling the room with soft silver beams. Winter was still tucked in the crook of my arm, but Logan was missing.

"He's gone to the gym, Big Guy. You're welcome to join him if you like."

I wrapped my arms around her still-naked body in a tight hug. "Why would I choose that when I could be here with you? Only fools leave beautiful women in bed alone."

Her lips broke into a smile against my pec. "You make a fair point."

We laid in the room's darkness, content in each other's quiet company. Her heart beat steadily against my ribs, and the puffs of her breath were warm against my collarbone. I clung to the tranquility of the moment, desperate for this peace in our world of uncertainty.

"Cam?"

"Yes, Little Violet?"

She interlaced our fingers under the warm blanket and lightly squeezed.

"I love you."

My heart stuttered at the three words; I had uttered them in a public declaration months ago, but had never uttered them again. This woman loved me. She loved me, despite so many other good men showering her with affection and care.

I was included in the group of men who held her heart. My chest expanded so much; my ribs felt like they might break under my elation.

"I love you too, Winter."

I gripped her chin with my thumb and tilted her head up to meet mine. I kissed her slowly, pressing all of my love and devotion into it; I needed this woman to be mine more than I'd needed anything or anyone in my life. More than the pull to find Darlene, or the need to quash my violent soul, or the desire to build a future Momma and Pop would be proud of.

Maybe I could have everything; maybe it could all be possible with her and her men—my brothers—at our sides.

When we broke apart, Winter flashed a wide smile in the moonlight.

"Let's piss Logan off by making popcorn and having sex on his couch while he's gone."

She leaped out of bed and scampered out the bedroom door to the living room with a high-pitched giggle. I chuckled and followed her; I would forever take advantage of an opportunity to piss off the arrogant part of our forever-family.

I shook my head as a sense of purpose and contentment flooded my soul. Our forever-family. I really liked the sound of that.

CHAPTER 25

WINTER

The Gold Gala was a night of exorbitant wealth and extravagance. I'd had the audacity to think Hillary's wedding was opulent, but this – this dinner for Sequoia County's elite was the congregation of our tiny corner of the world's one percent.

I hadn't realized so many rich people lived in our fair state. It wasn't just the uber-wealthy business magnates, although they made up most of the guest list. In attendance were politicians, the children of founding families, university deans, and the named partners of several professional firms, including WAQ and Eccles Engineering.

Every guest was dressed in finery and drinking champagne from flutes even more ornate than Hillary's wedding favors.

Travis stood beside me in a fitted black suit, one Georgio had tailored for him, and it hugged his shoulders and trim waist in the way only expensive suits could. He looked so handsome; the dark waves of his hair fell over his bright green eyes in a sexy styled bed-head tousle. Only the plugs in his ears and enticing lip ring separated him from the very conservative crowd.

We were both on edge, not knowing our place among a group so far removed from our lives and lifestyles. Georgio had made Travis bring a gun, and that demand on its own made the acid in my stomach burn its way up to my throat every few minutes. Even if we made it through tonight with just a belly filled with caviar and a light buzz from expensive bubbles, the anxiety of not knowing the purpose of our inclusion was enough to kill the whole evening.

We were surrounded by people in the main ballroom and had been making polite conversation with a tech mogul and his husband. Mom and Dad were over by the front entrance, speaking to a man and a woman I didn't recognize, although I could only see their backs. Emmett and Amelia had been invited as well, but I hadn't come across them in the sea of talking heads.

I had glimpsed Kellan when we'd come in, but he'd been absent ever since. Georgio was busy charming the group that surrounded him. My mouth dropped seeing Janet Lindross by his side in a beautiful fire-engine red dress that fell to the floor in flowy waves. She looked stunning, but her appearance here wasn't a good sign.

Travis had brought me up to speed that her double-agent status might be compromised when he'd fitted me with our trackers this morning. Mine was in a tiny silver pendant that hung from a long silver chain—the perfect accompaniment to my dress's neckline.

His hand lingered at the base of my spine and his thumb gently stroked the exposed skin of my back in a tender gesture of possession.

"There's Logan and Hillary," he murmured quietly into my ear. He lightly pushed me in their direction as we excused ourselves from a particularly dry discussion.

"You look gorgeous, Sweets."

Hillary wrapped her arms around me, bathing me in the scent of her floral perfume. Her mermaid-style shimmery gold dress with rhinestone spaghetti straps complimented the décor beautifully, as if she herself were throwing this party.

"So do you." She was radiant, embodying every bit of her heiress title. All that was missing was a diamond tiara, and I was pretty sure she owned one.

Logan drew me into his arms in a friendly but professional hug. His lips hovered over my ear. "I can't wait to take this off you later, Princess. But I'll enjoy watching you from afar tonight."

He pulled back with a subtle wink and released me from his hold.

He wore a suit similar to the one from his wedding, only it was a lighter shade of navy that brought out the gold in his eyes. His thick brown hair was swept back from his face, aristocratic features on display. His air of power and dominance—the same air that had made me want to poke his eyeballs out in the past—was now fast becoming my ultimate weakness.

All of my men were my ultimate weakness.

Cam was somewhere close by—again, for what purpose, I didn't know. Kellan was moving his ignorant pawns around the FBI chessboard tonight. I had to hope he knew what he was doing. If he played chess at my skill level, we were all fucked.

Drew and Shane had stayed at Hill's condo, where we were all supposed to meet up after the event. Both men had hugged and kissed me roughly a thousand times before we left the building, but I couldn't fault them. If we had to trade places tonight, I would climb the walls until they were back in my arms, safe and sound.

The four of us stood off to the side, observing the masses from the safety of the wings. Hillary and Logan took turns respectfully answering questions from family friends and business associates while Travis and I hung back, nursing our champagne and keeping a watchful eye on Georgio.

A pair of identical men entered the room to our left and their long and easy strides took them to Georgio's side. These must be Kellan and Georgio—and Cam's—brothers. I discreetly assessed them; dark short hair and chiseled cheekbones. They had the stunning features of South American models. Whereas Georgio wielded his unassuming charms and Kellan used his size and presence, these men exuded a masculinity that intimidated through hard edges and dark scowls. Their molded bodies and imposing stature couldn't hide the dangerous energy, like a testosterone-infused Venus Fly Trap.

Where was Kellan? Did he know they were coming tonight? My nervous energy was gesticulating with unadulterated dread.

Georgio greeted them with a wide smile and introduced them to Janet through a round of handshaking and forced pleasantries. At least, that's what a little lip reading and limited body language knowledge was telling me.

Georgio looked up and made direct eye contact with us, as if he knew we were there the entire time. He beckoned us over with a slight hand gesture.

Travis squeezed my hand and pulled me toward them; we didn't have a choice but to play Georgio's social games tonight. I could only hope it would be enough to appease him while Kellan kept up his end of the bargain.

Janet slipped away before we said hello and I crossed my fingers that was a good thing. Perhaps Kellan was waiting to get her out of the ballroom at this very moment.

This night was exhausting. How Kellan had played this double life for sixteen years was unthinkable.

"Travis, nephew!" Georgio's smile looked every bit the genuine warmth of a doting uncle. "I thought you might want to meet your uncles. Kellan is around here somewhere, but allow me to introduce you to the Carlos twins." He turned to the imposing men standing in front of us, their dangerous air far more potent at close range. "Jonah, Mical—Matteo's son has finally come home."

I forced my neutral mask to stay in place as the three brothers crossed their hearts in that 'Hail Mary' Catholic cross thing in what I could only guess was in recognition of their deceased brother. I wondered how a murderous family justified their actions for weekly confession?

A thought experiment for another time.

The men gruffly shook hands with the mafia version of a bro nod. Travis switched on his trademark charm and acted as if meeting them was truly an honor. He even threw in another thank you to Georgio for inviting us to this event—stroking the don's ego just a little more.

"One day, this will be yours." Georgio leaned in with a wink, the slightest hint of his true nature peeking through his well-honed facade. "And I have a surprise for you later."

Fuck me. No more surprises. I was going to need an entire tub of Tums to make it through the rest of the night.

Georgio tugged Travis away from me by his elbow and forced him to move in the opposite direction. "Come, I have people for you to meet."

Travis gave me a quick kiss on the cheek and shot me a look of apology as his demon uncle hauled him away. I took one look at the twins, who eyed me with amused disinterest and, to my utter embarrassment, a terrified squeak escaped. Before I could do anything else to attract their attention, I muttered out a weak excuse and darted away to find Logan and Hillary again.

"Winter!" Mom waved me over as I pressed my way through the Chanel-scented throng.

Eager for a familiar face at the Great Gatsby party, I made my way over to their corner. Dad turned around; his face contorted into a pained grimace before smoothly covering it with a welcoming grin.

He could try to hide it like he had my whole life, but Dad knew I shouldn't be here, and was upset that I was.

Yeah, you and me both, Daddy-O.

Still, I was relieved to see the pair of them, dressed to impress and with what I believed were genuine smiles. Mom was wearing a beautiful royal blue gown that made her look at least ten years younger, and Dad held the same youthful glow in his black suit with a tie to match Mom's dress. The couple they had been speaking to looked up, and I was surprised to recognize Marcie.

Duh, Winter. We're in the middle of an FBI sting operation.

Of course, she was here. Where the fuck was that bottle of Tums?

A round of hugs was shared while everyone gushed about each other's wardrobe choices.

"Winter, this is my husband, Oliver," Marcie simpered.

The tall and reed-thin bespectacled man looked like he belonged in a NASA testing department with a pocket protector and sensible shoes. Was he another lover in the open square my parents had going on? Was he an FBI agent, too?

It didn't matter. I couldn't keep killing my brain-cells trying to figure out everyone's secret identity. Oliver was just going to be Oliver. Cool.

I made small talk with them for a few minutes, though I scanned the room every thirty seconds, hoping Travis,

Logan, or Hillary would come around the corner at any minute and relieve me of a fraction of my building anxiety.

Guests were now being led into the adjacent dining room for dinner, and I caught sight of Hillary's golden dress in the fray.

"Thank you for keeping me company." I gave Mom and Dad a peck on the cheek and quickly weaved between the hungry partiers to catch Hillary before she disappeared beyond the double doors.

Travis was still nowhere to be seen.

A large hand clamped around my bicep in the chaos, and I was pushed through the crowd into a dimly lit corridor just off to the side of the ballroom. My assailant held me in an iron grip bordering on painful; with each step, they squeezed me harder.

I couldn't wrench around to see their face, but the familiar scent of sea air and amber flooded my nostrils, causing my pulse to skyrocket.

The sound of the large wooden door slamming shut behind us was the final nail in the coffin. Carson Baker spun me around and pressed me into the wall.

The hallway was silent, save for my ragged breaths. My tormentor loomed over me, his face mimicking a hungry jungle cat who'd just cornered his prey.

I wouldn't cower in front of him and give him the satisfaction, though I was sure my jugular was pulsating, my heart was hammering so hard.

I willed myself to control my frantic lungs while Carson hungrily appraised me. His build was like Logan's, tall and thin, but enough to fully lock me in.

Where Logan wore his arrogance like a protective shield, Carson wore his like a sharpened sword.

"You look stunning this evening, Winter," he purred, lowering his head to brush his lips over the shell of my ear. "I've been just waiting for the chance to *snap you up*."

His words were dripping with dark intent, and I wasn't strong enough to mask the shiver of fear that swept through me. Why wouldn't this man leave me the fuck alone?

"What do you want, Carson?" I asked; my voice far steadier than the chaos of my insides. "Haven't you learned not to fuck with me yet?"

He forcefully yanked up my chin. As I stared into his blown pupils, his gloating smile morphed into a hateful sneer.

"You don't have anyone here to protect you now, you dirty slut. Did you really think you'd be the one who got away?"

So, I was a trophy to him. There were few things more repulsive than a man who believed he had a right to a woman's body. I was terrified, and disgusted, and filled with shame. I was simply a name on a list—a twisted list of innocent women who'd gotten caught up in Carson's charms.

Before I could knee him in the balls, which my brain clamored to do, my body betrayed me by remaining frozen. Carson spun me around and slammed me into the decorative wainscoting.

His body heat threatened to smother me as his swollen erection ground into my back. He dropped his hands to my hips and grazed my thighs with his palms.

Fuck, fuck, fuck. *Think,* Winter.

Carson was a sociopath; a serial rapist. I had been lucky to get away the first time; if I didn't fight harder, I wouldn't have the same outcome tonight.

I ignored Carson's revolting touch for a microsecond, scouring my mind for something I could use.

Cam's lessons. He had taught me how to get out of a hold from behind. This wasn't the same thing, but it was all I could think of as Carson's fingers tried to cup my pussy from the outside of my dress.

I relaxed my body, going limp in his arms. When he struggled to hold up my dead weight, he stepped back just enough to give me an inch or two. Dropping to the floor, I turned, which put my face at crotch level, but it was the perfect height. I bucked up and headbutted him in the nuts.

It was the closest I would get to his private jewels ever again.

"Fuck!" Carson swore and dropped to his knees. I scrambled out of the way with an awkward crab walk. "Bitch!"

He clawed at the train of my dress, tearing the fabric but managing a strong enough hold to keep me in place. I army-crawled along the carpeted floor on my elbows as the train completely ripped in two. My relief was short-lived. His long fingers wrapped around my ankle and pulled me backward.

The carpet burned my knees, but that slight pain was the least of my worries.

My scalp caught fire when Carson fisted my French braid and hauled me back hard against his chest. I tried in vain to elbow him, but his other arm came around me like a steel band.

"You're not going anywhere until I'm done with you."

I fought back the sob forming in my throat. Silent tears laced with grief and shame dropped to my cheeks as he kissed a trail down my neck.

It would have been a fitting time for a panic attack, but it never came. Overwhelming futility crashed over me instead; I was ashamed I couldn't get away. Ashamed I had let this entitled monster win.

He pawed at my taped breasts beneath the bodice and wrenched my nipples into painful twists. I desperately bucked my torso, but my body barely budged.

"That's it, you dirty slut. Just lay down and take it like the easy fuck you are."

I willed myself to go numb; I could disassociate. This would be over soon, and I would get the therapy I needed, just like last time. Carson could take my body, but he wouldn't take my soul.

Humiliation spread through my limbs. I wasn't prepared to fight off a rapist. I had failed by not knowing how to protect myself.

It was probably what I was wearing. Isn't that what all women are told? Even as I untied my mind from my body, feminist rage heated my insides.

My mind snapped to reason. As if what I was wearing could eliminate my rights as a human being. I was learning to fight off rapists. I had smashed my head into his balls, I

—

A stifled sob threatened to choke me as, despite my attempt to recover, Carson's body slammed against mine and numbness started to take over my mind.

The booming resonance of a heavy door slamming behind us disrupted my disjointed thoughts. The resounding crack of bone on bone echoed behind me.

My eyes flew open as Carson dropped me to the floor in a muddled heap. I kicked my brain back into gear. Wasting no time, I crawled to the wall a few feet away before spinning around to see my savior.

Logan's face was mottled with wrathful hate as he held Carson in a choke hold. "I had other plans for you, but I think we're going to have to take out the trash another way, you fucking neanderthal."

Within seconds, Carson's face shifted from pink to red to purple, a kaleidoscope of color, before he stilled, unconscious. Logan released him and he fell unceremoniously to the floor.

Logan immediately stepped in front of me, his angry mask shifting to careful concern. "Can I touch you?"

I nodded mutely. He sat down beside me and gently pulled me into his lap, wrapping his arms around me in a light but firm hold.

"It's okay, Princess. He won't hurt you, or anyone else, any more."

He rocked me and untied my hair ribbon, running his fingers soothingly through my ruined braid. My scalp stung at the roots, and a few chunks of my hair fell out when Logan worked his hands through it.

"That fucker." He growled and flicked my dead strands onto the floor. He whipped out his phone from his pocket and typed a quick one-handed email; the 'sent' sound filled the surrounding space.

He tucked away his phone and pulled me tighter into his chest. He kissed the top of my head reverently before explaining.

"I was going to handle this another way, but I just sent Doug's file of evidence to Carlisle's Chief of Police, and a copy to both my legal team and the Baker family directly. There's enough in there to get him sent to prison for at least ten years, if not life."

I nodded mutely and snuggled into his embrace. We sat in silence for another few moments, and I allowed Logan's soothing touch to bring me down to earth. I was traumatized, but we would have to deal with it later. The altercation with Carson had not been in our plan for tonight.

We had to find Travis and contact Kellan. Georgio and his dangerous family had an agenda tonight, though I highly doubted it had anything to do with the wealthy rapists of the Baker family.

When I finally looked up into Logan's honey-brown eyes, they held their usual determined and conceited glint. But there was a newfound tenderness and care reserved for me and only me.

He brought his hands up to cup my cheeks and peered into the abyss of my damage.

"I'm a broken man, but I won't let anyone break you. I've got baggage, but I won't weigh you down. I won't coddle you, but I'll cherish you. You are my princess, and you're also my queen."

His declaration made my heart stutter; of course, the asshole of our group would be the most poetic. Perhaps he was just trying to erase the pain of the minutes before, but it was working. His words meant the world to me.

"I think I love you too," I whispered with a wan smile. This was not a suitable moment for confessions of feelings, but sometimes life didn't work like the movies.

He scoffed then, and the arrogance that could only be Logan came back into full view. "Love isn't close to covering it." He kissed me quickly but fiercely, as if trying to convey that very sentiment through our lips and tangle of tongues.

Too soon, he pulled back; our gazes fell on Carson's still form.

"We need to hide him and get you out of here," he announced resolutely. Pushing me off of him, he stood. I took his outstretched hand, and he pulled me up too.

I was about to protest until I looked down at what remained of my gown. The bottom half was shredded and by the tightness of my eyes and cheeks, my face probably matched its battered appearance.

Fuck. Tonight wasn't going to plan at all. Whatever the 'plan' was.

I forced a steadying breath through my nose and prepared myself to regroup.

"All right." I acquiesced, squeezing his hand and letting go to grab one of Carson's limp limbs. "Where are we putting him?"

CHAPTER 26

LOGAN

We stuffed that miserable fuck into an unlocked broom closet down the hall. I'd call in a favor to get access to the building's camera footage later, but it would be pretty obvious to anyone who watched the tapes Carson had been about to rape a woman in the private hallway.

Not just any woman. Our woman. I was fucking seething at the cunt of a man who had the balls to force himself on her again. He would never touch another woman; I was going to make sure he learned the valuable lesson of consent in prison.

Carson would make a beautiful bride.

Winter was holding up better than expected, but we were getting her to a psychologist as soon as this shitstorm was over. I knew full well the damage recurring trauma created, and I'd be damned if Carson continued to have any sort of fucking power over her.

Her mental state was better than her physical. Her makeup was streaked across her cheeks and her dress looked like she had been put through a blender. I'd have to sneak her out a side door and have Cam pick her up.

I herded Winter down the hall toward another unmarked door. I didn't know the layout of this place; I was leaning on instinct and, hopefully, some luck.

I turned the knob and listened for any activity on the other side.

Tugging her hand, we crept through another dark hallway. It wasn't like this was cloak and dagger shit, but Hillary was probably wondering where the fuck I was, and hopefully Travis had found Kellan somewhere in this fucking mess.

My queen also didn't need any additional eyes on her tonight. The world wouldn't be seeing her as a fucking victim; she was the winner of this battle.

I stopped short at voices up ahead.

"Angelo, I have no idea what this is about. Now can we please—"

Janet 'secret agent' Lindross' voice was calm, but any idiot could hear she was in trouble. If she was with Georgio's second-in-command, she was in real trouble, even if Angelo was just a gorilla in a suit on the best of days.

Fuck. Turn back, or check in on the situation? I couldn't give two shits about Janet, but if she was compromised, we'd probably be next. I cocked a quizzical brow to Winter, who, naturally, the do-gooder, motioned me forward.

Alright then, we were fucking Boy Scouts today. Yay.

I kept us out of the light streaming out of the barren office, but I had a decent view of the inside from where I stood. Janet had been backed into the corner behind an old desk, holding her hands up in a non-threatening gesture and speaking calmly to a gun-wielding Angelo.

Fuck me, this night was getting complicated. I could probably get the gun away from Angelo if I caught him by surprise. I knew how to use it, even if it had been years since I'd trained.

Winter let out a small squeak beside me when the room came fully into view. She clapped her hands over her mouth, but it was too late. Angelo swung around at the sound; his gun pointed at us, but he didn't shoot.

His face lit up with a menacing grin. "Welcome to the party, Mr. Eccles."

He waved us into the room with the gun. After a moment's hesitation, I walked in with my head held high, keeping Winter squarely behind me, protected by my body.

Now wasn't the time to show weakness. Fuck this brainless thug—he wouldn't kill me unless Georgio gave the go ahead, and since Stanley was his bestie, I was going to bank on that protection for now.

Stanley wouldn't care if I was maimed, but his fucking pride wouldn't tolerate his only son, the Eccles heir, being killed by Georgio's Gorilla Man.

"What's this about?" I barked, not interested in playing nice. Innocent Logan wouldn't play nice. "What's Janet done to piss you off? Misfiled your psych exam? Swapped out your idiot meds? She's a mousy little secretary, for Christ's sake. Let the poor girl go."

Angelo let out an annoyed huff, but he didn't make any moves to threaten me. He knew the score too. Smarter than he looked, ol' Gorilla Man.

"She ain't innocent." He gritted out, his gun back to pointing at her chest. "I'm keeping her here until Georgio decides what to do with her."

The devil himself appeared in the doorway, as if summoned for a soul swap. His eyes roamed the room. When he saw us, his eyes lit up with evil glee.

Fuck. That wasn't good.

"New plan, Angelo. These two will make a perfect addition to our test." He clapped his hands together and subtly nodded toward the black case I hadn't noticed on the desk.

"There are more than enough supplies in there. Jonah and Mical will help you out."

The identical Latino men with severe frowns walked into the room and the first real traces of fear trickled through me.

One of them opened the case and took out three hypodermic needles in their packaging, along with a bottle of a cloudy liquid. I reached around to hold Winter tightly to me, knowing we wouldn't escape this fate. I hoped to fuck whatever they were about to shoot us up with wouldn't hurt Winter or derail my treatment.

We wouldn't have a choice in the matter, though. I was an egotistical bastard, but I wasn't stupid enough to think we'd make it through a wall of armed criminals.

"We're going to be okay," I whispered to Winter, squeezing her hand one last time before the needle pricked my skin and all I saw was black.

My skull felt like some fucker had hit a home run using my head as the ball. My cheek pressed into a rough surface and when I breathed in, I got a nose full of dirt.

Fucking gross.

My hands were bound behind me, but my feet were still free. I shifted awkwardly into an upright position. Winter lay beside me, curled up in the same position and out cold. I'd shake her awake in a second, but first I needed to see where the fuck we were.

At first glance, I thought we were in the cellar, but once my vision fully cleared, I could see we were in a tunnel of some sort. Dim light came from a pneumatic lamp buried into the wall above our heads.

Janet lay on the other side of the tunnel. A deep gash at her hairline was bleeding down her face, and her lip was split in two.

We were in trouble. *Real* trouble. Where in the fuck was Kellan?

Winter moaned beside me, and I shuffled my ass over to give her the comfort of my touch. I had no other fucking options with my hands tied.

"Hey, Queenie." I tried to be soothing, but what the fuck did that look like in this massively fucked up scenario? "How are you feeling?"

"Fuck off, Logan, and tell me how bad it is."

Her rebuke was slow and slurred, but it made me smile. Winter was a fucking fighter, and I loved her for it.

Fine, I wouldn't sugarcoat this for her. That wasn't my style, anyway. Let Drew or Travis be the White Knight.

"Pretty fucking bad," I admitted. "I think we're in a mine shaft or something."

How long had we been fucking out? The closest mine was twenty-five minutes outside of Carlisle.

I no longer had my phone on me and my watch had been removed. I looked down to see my tie clip still in place—the tie clip with the tracker in it. Thank fuck. At least someone could find us, sooner or later.

Hopefully fucking sooner.

Where *in the fuck* was Kellan? FBI leader or not, I was going to *murder* the fucker.

Winter fumbled her way to a seated position and surveyed our earthy jail cell with her own eyes. She gasped when she saw Janet.

"What can we do to help her?"

I scoffed in irritation. "We're fucking tied up, Winter. What do you think we can do?"

I could appreciate her heart of gold, but it was a pretty useless trait right now. More softly, I added, "Can you walk? The best thing we can do is find a way out of here to get her some help."

Winter wiggled her legs and nodded. Her sexy yet impractical heels wouldn't last long in here, but they'd have to do. At least with the bottom half of her dress gone, she'd be able to move.

We never got the fucking chance to move. Voices carried down the shaft, and there were many of them.

I sidled up to the wall again and Winter maneuvered herself into my side before the four Carlos brothers appeared around the corner.

Finally, Kellan made his fucking appearance.

I froze when Travis came into view behind them. His body language was calm, but his eyes were frantic. I focused on him until his gaze landed on mine. I gave a minuscule nod and hoped he could grasp my meaning.

Stay calm. Play the game. Trust in his bastard uncle.

Georgio paid us no attention. He walked up to Janet and kicked her in the ribs, hard enough to make me wince. She cried out, spitting up a stream of blood. Georgio yanked her upward by her hair.

"Traitorous bitch," he hissed before violently dropping her back to the ground.

Turning to the group of Carlos' men, he held out his hands and smiled.

"Welcome to shaft 19, everyone." He smiled politely, as if he were a circus master and he was introducing the next lineup.

"This abandoned gold mine is the start of one of the largest engineering projects in the world. This government-funded *gold mine*"—he paused with an amused chuckle at his own joke—"will be the first financial shelter for most Carlos' operations on the Western seaboard. Antonio is very excited about this opportunity. We'll be setting up the channels over the next several months. I am offering you the opportunity to shelter your assets with me for a small percentage of your profits. Trust me, your investment will be worth your while."

The Carlos men looked on with feigned interest, probably used to Georgio's massive fucking ego-stroking diatribes and shady deals. Travis leaned against the dirt wall with his arms crossed in an attempt to look bored, but he just looked like a twitchy addict in need of a fix.

I knew that look well.

"All of this could have been shared among modern comforts, G."

Kellan folded his arms across his barrel chest and stood toe to toe with his smaller brother. "I know you love your shows, but why the theatrics? I have a beautiful woman's hot pussy I could bury my face in this evening."

The Viking hadn't even glanced in our direction, and it was making me nervous. Ever since he had taken us from my wedding, I wanted to believe he could at least take us out of Georgio's clutches, but watching them now, I had my doubts.

Georgio's face lit up with a vicious grin. "I have a surprise, little Carlos. You met our nephew this evening, and I've recently become aware of another brother in our midst. Antonio's seed knows no bounds."

His lips curled into a sneer and it was very apparent Georgio hated his father as much as I hated mine. As soon as it had crossed his face, it was gone.

"But that's a story for another time. I will properly vet him before introducing him to you, in case he is not fit for this life."

He walked back over to Janet and wrenched up her head by her hair again, holding her at an angle that had to hurt. She stared blankly back at him, as if she wasn't even here. Maybe they'd given her something stronger than what we had.

Fuck, this was bad. And it was all going to go to shit, fast.

"Brothers, I invited you here tonight to witness Travis' initiation."

Mother-fucking *fuck*. I hated being right sometimes.

CHAPTER 27

TRAVIS

Of all the shit I'd done in my life to protect the people I loved, this had to be the dumbest.

Georgio's promise of a surprise was the first clue to my demise this evening. After I was paraded around like Georgio's ventriloquist dummy for an hour, I'd escaped to the bathroom to text Kellan on the burner.

Georgio hadn't questioned the phone when he had Angelo pat me down earlier. I'd taken the risk, but the two phones were identical in every way and the gamble had paid off. Or, I thought it had, except Kellan hadn't messaged me back or given me any sign he knew what was going on.

I hadn't even had the chance to speak to him until Georgio rounded us all up two hours later to head to another location.

I kept searching for Winter or Logan in the dining room throughout the evening, but I hadn't seen them anywhere. I held onto the possibility they were off somewhere safe together. Georgio hadn't let me out of his range long enough to check in with Hillary to see if she knew where either of them was, so I buried my anxiety and smiled and nodded wherever appropriate.

Kellan finally joined us at dinner time with a tiny brunette clinging to his waist. No one commented when both Georgio and my dates were missing during the meal. Another bad sign, but still, I kept the need to melt down tucked tightly away. Years of running money for Georgio and constantly being on high alert allowed me to turn down my emotional turmoil, even just a little bit. I wouldn't have gotten through the night without it.

Only when I was seated between my newfound uncles in a blacked-out SUV did I let out the panic; it coated my skin like the thick film of guilt-laden grime it was.

Walking down the mine tunnel was akin to the scared blonde chick in any horror movie walking right into the mutant bad guy's lair. I could almost hear the crescendoing notes of the ominous soundtrack with each step; every hair on my body stood on end like I was experiencing a miniature electrocution.

Georgio chatted with his brothers like we were out for an evening stroll instead of deep underground surrounded by dirt. Jonah and Mical looked straight ahead, their strides unhurried and their faces permanently creased into matching frowns. Kellan had barely glanced at me since he'd met us at the front doors of City Hall, muttering about 'an errand for Father.' The twins and Georgio had just nodded knowingly before shoving me into the car with them.

When we rounded the corner, the foreboding melody in my head hit its jarring high note. Janet looked half-dead in her heap on one side of the tunnel, and huddled together on the other side were Logan and Winter.

Terror thickened my blood to cement; I was held in place as it lazily oozed through my veins.

Were we found out? Was Georgio going to kill us all and bury us down here?

Logan's suit had ripped and his face was streaked with dirt, but it was Winter who looked far worse for wear. Her pouty lips were split open, and the shadows of fresh bruising dappled her arms. Fury blanketed my fear for a brief instant. Who hurt her?

My newest husband-brother looked at me with an almost imperceptible nod. Okay, they were okay. We just had to play the game, and maybe we could make it out of this alive.

Stay calm, Travis.

As Georgio addressed his brothers, I kept my focus on our girl. She was scared, but stable, and I was proud of her for fighting her own panic, given this situation was far more distressing than being trapped in the Bourbon & Blues cellar all those months ago.

I brought my focus back to my uncle's words when he'd offered a hint about Cam. I would fucking die before I let my brother become another casualty in the dysfunctional Carlos family.

"Brothers, I invited you here tonight to witness Travis' initiation."

My heart came to a literal stop. Georgio's grin was cold and calculated; the true mask of a madman. He motioned me to come forward. My feet betraying me, I shuffled ahead; terror fogged my brain and slowed my limbs.

Georgio bent down to Janet's semi-conscious form and slapped her hard across the face. A strangled moan halted my movements.

"Janet," he announced to his entranced crowd, "is a traitor. An undercover agent working for the FBI." His gaze fell back on me. "The Carlos Cartel does not give second chances to traitors." He spat on the ground beside him and fired out something in rapid Spanish.

"It is a tradition in our family that when a Carlos man comes of age, he must complete his initiation. Travis, you are fulfilling this requirement far later than any of your uncles. My initiation was when I was seventeen."

The twins nodded solemnly. I'm not even sure Kellan blinked. Then again, how could I tell with the terror clouding my vision?

"The cartel life is a hard life. To lead it is to control it with a firm fist. Discipline is paramount. To initiate is to prove you can do what must be done. That you can take care of your people and your business by whatever means necessary. You must kill."

My heart had gone from stock still to pounding faster than a hummingbird's wings in a less than a minute.

"Who did you kill, Georgio?" Winter asked, her voice tentative but strong. "And how did my father get involved?"

Smart girl. Keep him talking. Stall him while I get my ever-loving shit together.

Georgio tsked in amusement. "He was of no consequence. Someone causing trouble for my father." He waved a hand at both of them. "Your fathers came to intervene, worried for me. They shouldn't have—I'd long since accepted this would be my life. But when the girl followed them because of some wayward crush on *your* father,"—he shot an irritated scowl at Winter— "I had to improvise. And then, they were all accomplices."

"So, you went to murder someone, and your friends—our fathers—went to stop you out of the goodness of their hearts, and instead, you killed an innocent tagalong and roped them into accepting the blame for it?" Logan summarized; his lips curled in unadulterated contempt.

Georgio shrugged, as if tying his group of friends to the murder of a blameless girl simply couldn't be helped. "This is a dangerous business. And I was a useful friend to have, wasn't I? I supplied start up cash for a piece of their pie. I kept all evidence locked up in a safe location so they would never have to face the consequences for their part of that crime."

"You mean you blackmailed them." Winter's acidic tone burned through the tunnel as she glared daggers at the man who'd plunged our lives down the toilet.

"I encouraged them to live their dreams and supplied the means to do it. Honestly, Winter. Do you think I allow anyone to speak to me like this? You are here right now because your fathers are dear friends. Otherwise, I would kill you."

My beautiful woman was undeterred. "Is that what you said to them? Were they to be killed if they stepped out of line or shared your dirty little secrets?"

Georgio let out a surprising bellow. Its sound pierced me like a million shards of broken glass.

"What dirty secrets, dear girl? The only people in town not aware of my businesses are knitting grannies and small children. The Carlos Cartel provides for its communities, and Cascade Falls has become a tourist destination solely from the cash infusions my businesses have allowed."

His grin widened with unbridled amusement, but the calculating darkness didn't recede from his eyes.

"Your college? The university? Partially owned by the Carlos Cartel and its associates. Sheldonville's new water-treatment facility? Built and financed through Carlos Cartel's generosity. Kensington's hospital? All upgrades were made through a generous donation from one of my subsidiary companies."

The mafia leader's smug smile morphed into a sinister smirk as he leaned down to eye level to taunt her . "We own this town, dear Winter. We own *all* these towns. And right now, I own *you*. I'd be careful with what you choose to say next."

Winter blanched and shrunk back into Logan. Her gaze caught mine for a brief second, and the miserable resignation in her eyes nearly brought me to my knees.

His pleasant threats must have been the segue to his original train of thought, because Georgio stood and his attention immediately fixated back to me.

"Travis, a choice must be made. You can open your arms to your bloodline and accept the responsibility that is being a Carlos leader, or you may decide that this life it not for you by ending your own."

I froze at his simplistic explanation of this task. The law of the jungle—eat or be eaten; kill or be killed. I wasn't an animal, but this was about survival.

He turned to the mafia men lined up at his back, who watched the scene unfold with apparent casual interest.

"Should Travis decide to end his life today, we will pursue our newfound brother to join the ranks. I will need a successor, and he is close to Travis' age, so he is a suitable replacement. He has a moral compass that will need to be broken, but he has skills that will prove useful."

Georgio spun to face me once again and reached out to press a warm, smooth palm against my cheek. I withered under his touch, but my feet wouldn't stir. His words had glued me to the earth, and I was an immovable pillar in his hand.

He patted my cheek in a condescending caress. "Besides," he added with a sadistic wink, "we are very good at breaking men, no?"

The acid in my stomach boiled up to meet the back of my throat, and I nearly gagged with gut-destroying nausea. I had to kill or Cam would be Georgio's next pet project. It was me, or the brother I'd always said I would give my life for.

I had meant it.

Georgio's burst of irritated breath skated over me, and he whipped out his gun from the holster beneath his tailored suit jacket.

Apparently, I was taking too long.

"I can see some added incentive is involved." He cocked the metal weapon and pointed it at Winter's head.

He was five feet—maybe seven feet away from her. Close enough range for serious damage. Life-threatening damage.

"I will not kill your girl." He delivered his promise in a soothing tone. "Darren wouldn't forgive me for that. But I *can* make her a paraplegic. Or destroy her ability to conceive. Or maybe ..."

He let his warnings consume the air between us.

I swore and took out the gun Georgio insisted I carry tonight. It felt heavier now, a weapon weighted down by savage guilt and bad intentions.

His grin mimicked the Chesire Cat as I moved to comply with his sadistic demands.

"Kellan, place Janet on her feet, please." Georgio calmly directed our so-called FBI protector, and I heard the shuffling of feet behind me. The men had been so quiet, I had almost forgotten they were there.

Kellan supported Janet by her elbows and brought her up to standing. She wavered on her feet, but didn't crumple back to the floor like I'd hoped, which would have given me more time to come to terms with the task in front of me.

I would never risk Winter. She was my morning star, my guiding light, the dream for a future I could never have. I had found the woman I wanted to spend the rest of my days with. If her days were numbered, I'd cash in all of mine to face that end date together.

I knew Georgio would follow through. The bastard had never given me an actual choice, not since the day he'd convinced me to come work for him all those years ago. I'd been fucked when I walked through the doors of Bourbon &

Blues, and now—now I was going to have to sleep in the bed I'd made.

Tears flowed down Winter's cheeks in little rivers, and Logan's eyes had their own mist clouding them. I loved her, and I loved them, and all the men in our makeshift family. They'd take care of each other; I knew they would. My fate did not have to be theirs.

The ominous click of Georgio unlocking the safety finalized my decision. He was forcing my hand, but he would not harm a hair on my woman's head.

I filled my lungs with dank air and blew out every atom while I brought the gun up to aim and shoot. The barrel shook in my hands; I fought to steady myself, to accept this new stain on my soul.

My double-agent uncle made no moves to intervene; he stepped out of the line of fire and avoided making eye contact. I was truly and utterly alone in this.

It was a familiar feeling; one I'd experienced most of my life.

I muted all sounds around me. I dulled the hums of Winter's soft whimpers, Logan's harsh breathing, and Janet's pained moans. I'd have to block a lot more to live with this decision, but I wouldn't regret saving Winter from Georgio's torture. Her life would always be worth more than mine.

I cocked the gun, determined to channel Kellan's lessons and make this quick and painless.

At least my double-crossing uncle had been good for one thing.

Before committing cold-blooded murder, I closed my eyes.

I pictured my mother when she'd been young and healthy, her radiant smile showering Devon and me with love.

I pictured Devon before he'd let his abandonment carve out his center, when he had allowed light and laughter into his heart.

I pictured the last year, when I collected new parts of my soul with Winter, Cam, Shane, Drew, and Logan—like a backward horcrux; except now I was going to shatter those pieces apart. Maybe I'd find them again one day, like Harry did.

It took only a moment—three seconds, at most, but it centered me. My eyes flew open, and I aimed for my victim's heart with pinpoint accuracy. The resounding cracks of two gunshots echoed through the passageway.

They weren't mine.

Georgio dropped to the dirt floor with a grunt, his gun skittering to the other side of the earth. He clutched at his chest where blood flowed through his fingers and down the woven fabric of his cream suit.

The surrounding earth trembled with the blast and dust crusted my eyes as my mind tried to sort through what had just happened.

"Jonah! Mical!" Kellan commanded with authority. He scooped Janet up into his barrel chest. "Drop him off to the nearest emergency room. I'll have his file sent up the FBI chain and get his charges expedited immediately."

The twin soldiers responded in Spanish and did as he asked. Kellan shot back a few more orders in the same language. My Spanish wasn't great, but it sounded like "remember our deal."

He turned his attention to me.

"Travis—get them to safety. Get to Hillary's place. You need to lie low for the next few days until I get this sorted. Cam is nearby, waiting for you."

Following that confusing set of instructions, he took off on a jog behind my uncles, carefully cradling Janet in his arms.

"Wait!" I called after him, needing far more answers than he had given. "What's going to happen now?"

He didn't turn around and continued down the earthen shaft as if I'd said nothing. I let out a scream of frustration, my anguished cry absorbed into the dirt walls with little effect.

My muscles burned; the tension of the last twenty-minutes still clung to my body like an aggressive koala. My mind shuffled through a dense mist, unseeing or feeling as the adrenaline dissipated like vapor through my limbs.

"What deal, Kellan?" My voice was hoarse; hollow, with a tinge of hysteria. "What fucking deal?"

He paused in his tracks and reluctantly turned to face me. He was fifty feet ahead—maybe more—and it was hard to make him out in the dim light. But he had paused, at least.

I breathlessly forced my blendered body to jog down to meet him as he stood stock still, Janet hanging limply in his arms.

"Georgio will no longer be a problem for Cascade Falls," he spat gruffly. This close, his blue eyes were frigidly cold. "My brothers will take over his operations on this side of the country, and set a new standard for the Carlos Cartel."

My numb mind struggled to keep up. "But—how? Aren't you FBI? What—"

"This plan is bigger than me. Bigger than all of us. To cut off the head, you need to work from the inside."

The head. Antonio? They were taking out Antonio?

"She needs medical treatment," Kellan barked, shifting his weight to resume his jog down the hallway. "You'll get more answers when the dust settles," he called over his shoulder as I stood mutely in place, watching his form recede into the shadows beyond.

His evacuation kicked my ass in gear. I needed to get my family out of this forsaken place.

Winter and Logan had managed to stand, but their hands were still bound. I quickly untied them both and held them as tight as my trembling muscles would allow, crying relieved tears and thanking every god in the universe I hadn't become a killer tonight.

"I love you," I whispered against Winter's lips, delicately holding her against me as salty tears poured into both of our mouths. "Fuck, I love you."

"I love you too." She forced a watery smile and sidled out of my arms. "We're okay. We're all okay."

She was repeating the words to herself, but I needed the reassurance too.

"Let's get out of here." Logan grabbed both our hands and dragged us down the long tunnel to the surface.

I had never been so happy to see the night sky.

CHAPTER 28

CAMERON

It would have been a tranquil summer night in July; the dark navy sky played canvas to an ocean of stars floating within its depthless waters. Crickets chirped from tree to tree, singing their song in search of their mates. The distant gush of the falls echoed off the stone faces of the mountain, absorbed only by the feathering of evergreens that thinned out at the mine's edge.

It would have been tranquil, but the frenzied air within Shane's truck cabin mirrored a New Orleans Street party without the festivities.

His was the only one of our vehicles that could fit all six of us semi-comfortably, and Kellan's directions had been evasive enough to make me wary. After we'd been trapped in the cellar for over a day, a quick getaway seemed prudent.

The borrowed truck came with two distraught boyfriends; each vibrating at such a high frequency, I felt the resonance deep in my bones.

An equivalent dread took up space in my body, but not in vibrations. My familiar companion unfurled its ugly head deep in my gut and released heady shots of uncut rage into my bloodstream.

Yet, I remained still. My demons would get their comeuppance. I couldn't match the tranquility of the night, but I acted as a counterweight to Shane and Drew's lack of calm.

Shane stared out the passenger side window, frantically searching for any sign of movement. His knee bounced aggressively—a detached limb with epilepsy; he was going to force a hole into the floor.

He turned his beseeching stare back to me. "Man, if you clench your jaw any harder, you're going to lose your teeth."

Immediately, I relaxed my facial muscles and felt the tight pang of pain from lactic acid build-up.

Perhaps I wasn't so calm.

Kellan had messaged me a few hours into the evening. Shane and Drew weren't with me then; I'd been in a side lot a few streets over from City Hall, playing my part in my brother's secret plan as we waited for the events of the night to unfold.

His text was brief. A set of coordinates about forty minutes outside of town, an address to a safe location six hours north in Brenton, and the troubling description of *'3 for pickup. Stay out of sight.'*

It was only a three-minute detour to pick up Shane and Drew. We all had an emergency bag packed as a 'just-in-case' stashed at Hillary's condo. They'd brought theirs with them, tossed them in the extended cab, and I'd made the trip to the cryptic location in under thirty.

Shane was familiar with the place—an abandoned gold mine primed as a central tunnel for their massive bridge project. The truck was now parked in a gravel pit close by within the shroud of a copse of trees. We couldn't see the mine entrance, but we could see the rough gravel road that led directly to the highway.

None of us voiced our questions of how they'd gotten here and why. They were too scary to say out loud, and we had no answers to assuage our fears.

"I see something!"

Drew's exclamation shot me up with adrenaline. Shane and I peered out of the rear window; two shadowed figures raced down the rocky path with a limp body between them. Pain pierced my chest, which was briefly smothered by confusion when another larger figure, carrying its own lifeless form, came into view.

Shane swore behind me. "What in the ever-loving *fuck* is going on?"

"Those aren't ours."

Whether I said that to soothe him or to soothe myself, I wasn't sure. But the shadows didn't match the outlines of our friends, and it was a bright enough night to make that distinction with some certainty.

"There! Cam—that's them!" Drew's voice was quickly approaching mania.

It *was* them. If I hadn't known their gait or outlines, I'd know it from the way they held hands, as if they were one human protective chain.

I turned the key in the ignition; the headlights flooded the space in front of us, and the three bodies froze like trapped baby deer.

Drew and Shane opened their doors and stepped out, shuffling everyone in. Shane latched onto Winter and wouldn't let her go, carrying her into the front seat between us. Logan and Travis climbed into the back, their grim, dirty faces set in matching worried scowls.

My little violet's hair was matted in dirty clumps, and her beautiful gown had ripped in several places. When she turned her head, the insatiable need to maim rippled through me. Her face was bloody, her body was bruised, and her eyes were troubled by whatever had happened in there.

Now wasn't the time to push. As if she sensed my warring consciousness, she slipped her hand in mine and squeezed.

"I'm okay, Big Guy." She shuddered, but didn't shrink away from my assessing stare. "We're okay. Get us out of here and we'll fill you in later. Please?"

Her muted plea spurred me into action. I drove one-handed, not willing to release her touch. Shane held her tightly to his chest, and every few minutes, one of the men in the back reached out to feel her.

No one slept, but the cab remained a silent tomb. I imagined we were all reflecting on the past several months of our lives.

Tonight had been too dangerous—too close to real damage for comfort. We'd never be able to go back to our lives as they were, but we'd known this; for most of us, there wasn't much of a life to return to.

We were driving toward our new lives. A man could only pray this version had the good fortune of being better than our last one.

Several hours later, we stopped at a gas station three hundred miles north of Carlisle just as dawn broke up the night sky.

Winter cleaned herself up in the woman's bathroom and everyone else changed into fresh clothes. Shane stocked up on breakfast snacks and I double-checked the coordinates on my GPS.

Luckily, the single bored teenager working the cash register that morning had no interest in the six fugitives using their facility.

I stopped Travis in his tracks before we both reentered the truck.

"I'm really glad you're alive, brother."

My throat tightened at the thought of losing him. My closest friend, my blood relation, and now—something short of a life-partnership in a group setting. This man knew parts of me I hadn't shared with anyone. He knew the sins that marred my soul and the scars that adorned my body.

His eyes held the haunted gaze of a man who walked with ghosts, but he managed a tired smile. "Me too, man."

I clasped his shoulders and drew him in for a tight hug. My words would not be enough, but my hold would convey my worries, my relief, and the friendship I held for him in my heart.

He knew. He squeezed me back with the same vigor before pulling away to help Winter back into the cab.

When Shane took over the driving, we slowly came to life as the sun rose. We couldn't continue on the journey in silence. We were hungry for answers and the reassurance we were heading toward peace.

With some coaxing, Winter explained Carson's attack and how close he had come to raping her. Unadulterated wrath detonated through the cab from five live grenades; despite the need to get to Hillary's, we stopped the vehicle to downgrade its destroying power.

I paced the length of the truck several times, my love for Shane the only reason I didn't put my fist through the hood. If Logan hadn't gotten there in time...

Logan. I had never been so grateful for the preppy asshat who'd entrenched himself into our lives.

I opened the rear truck door and yanked him out of the cab onto the pavement beside me.

"What the fuck, Chase!" Logan exclaimed in surprised irritation. "What do you—"

I crushed the smaller man to my chest and held him tight, inhaling his ridiculously expensive cologne as I conceded the damage that disturbed man would have inflicted without intervention.

"Thank you for rescuing her."

Logan's forceful shoving to get out of my grasp immediately faltered, and he relaxed slightly in my grip.

"Uh—you're welcome," he answered as if he were asking a question and wrenched out of my assaulting hug.

Logan straightened his sweater. "It's our job to keep her safe." Then he climbed back into the truck, though not before shooting me an acknowledging nod of solidarity.

Yes, it was. For as long as she would have me, I would keep this woman safe at all costs.

Another hit of rage flooded my bloodstream; I craved the feeling of Carson's blood dripping down my fists. Our calculating brother's plan would destroy Carson's future, but I wanted the man dead.

We would explore that option later.

We each took turns holding Winter in our arms, convincing ourselves she was safe and unharmed. My little violet would not be leaving my sight for the foreseeable future, and I'd bet the men surrounding me felt the same.

She hated the smothering, but it wasn't a choice—it was a necessity to protect the one person we cherished above all else.

Travis filled us in during the remainder of the drive. I was relieved that our Carlos 'friend' had followed through in the end, but the involvement of the twins—my *other* brothers—troubled me. Kellan was swapping out one cockroach for two more. Surely, that wasn't a viable solution.

Georgio threatening Winter's life to force Travis to commit murder infuriated me on two fronts. My best friend would have killed himself or killed Janet before he would ever accept harm to our woman, and the crushing weight of that decision would have killed his soul if he hadn't done the deed himself.

His layered trauma would require therapy, reflection, and time.

I would make sure this man did not fall apart before he had the chance to live the life he'd never allowed himself the luxury of dreaming of.

Solemn silence fell as the drive dragged on, commiserating our miseries in an old Dodge truck.

CHAPTER 29

DREW

Hillary's home was probably the nicest I'd ever seen, aside from Winter's parent's place. And it wasn't even where she lived. I'd never be able to truly comprehend the level of wealth some people had.

We'd been here for almost a week, lying low, and attempting to make the best of our circumstances. Winter had slept for almost two days; we all took our turns holding her as she moved through the various phases of exhaustion that came from facing your abuser and having a gun pointed at your head.

Travis hadn't fared much better, but some light reentered his eyes by day three or four. He checked in with his mom's nurse every few hours, but there was no word from his brother. Logan had hired a security guard to watch their trailer as a safety measure, and he'd already been looking into care homes—not that he told Travis that.

Logan was an asshole, but he was *our* asshole—and he was insufferably protective of his people. Or in this case— his people's people. Since he and Travis had escaped that tunnel with Winter between them, they'd developed a bond I hadn't thought Logan capable of. It was kind of cute, to be honest.

Darlene was safe and said she would come up to see us soon—turns out, Kellan's safe house was only an hour's drive from here. Cam hadn't said much, not that he ever did, but his sparring with Logan over the last few days had been particularly violent.

I'd checked in on Mom and Dad earlier in the week. They were reassured to hear we were okay, but I kept most of the details out of our conversation. While Darren and Emmett's fate seemed pretty set in stone, I had no idea how the FBI would treat my parent's crimes, even if they were no longer involved. I held on to hope there would be leniency, but I was resigned to the fact that they'd made their own decisions and would have to live with the consequences.

Despite our scars and anxieties, we tried to live our lives as normal—or whatever normal could be for six people learning to be around each other 24/7.

Shane set up movie nights in the media room. We enjoyed the enormous pool in the backyard and shared the mundane tasks of cleaning and cooking.

Hillary had ordered a grocery delivery, and Travis and Cam took over dinner-time duties; The Carlos bloodline of our family were decent cooks, so we were all well-fed as we hid in our castle waiting for Kellan to let us know the coast was clear.

Shane had his ear glued to the Carlisle news station, regaling us with the daily play-by-play every evening.

A journalist reported that WAQ and Eccles Engineering were currently under investigation for several white-collar crimes, and all activities on the Sequoia County Bridge project were suspended until the authorities could determine the extent of the criminal behavior.

Emmett, Darren, Stanley, and Camden had been arrested, but were currently out on bail, with a compliance order to not leave the county. Winter and Shane had spoken with their parents briefly, but they were keeping their distance as the dominoes fell. This was the inevitable outcome, and we had done all we could do—*more* than we could do as a group of twenty-something small-town average Joes with no special skills.

It was amazing we were still alive.

Brendan Anderson, the mysterious partner of WAQ who Winter had never met, turned out to be a pseudonym for Georgio. My memory niggled at the mention of that name in the news, and I looked back through my notes from the library. A Brendan Anderson was reported missing the same week Cheryl Simpson showed up dead at the bottom of the falls. We'd need Darren or Emmett to confirm it, but my guess was Brendan was Georgio's initiation kill, and he'd forced the naming issue to drive the blackmail knife in a little further.

What a psychopathic bastard.

Kellan finally called another week later. We were getting stir-crazy and the tension within the house was at an all-time high. Logan barked orders to his poor secretary, Beth, hourly, and not even a surprise visit from Hillary had cheered Winter up.

Travis put our Viking extension of family on speaker as we crowded around the coffee table in the living room.

Kellan gruffly apologized for the delay and explained he'd been negotiating with his brothers to set up the 'new-

and-improved' Carlos Cartel branch in our former part of the county. A 'lesser evil,' he called it; one he could monitor from afar. When he'd found out Georgio had cornered a group of 'kids', he hadn't wanted us getting involved any more than we'd needed to, especially when he discovered two of the men in our group were his actual family.

"What about Marcie?" Winter asked from the cradle of my arms. "Why was she involved?"

"Your father's girlfriend wasn't a priority," Kellan responded dismissively.

"You mean ... she wasn't your agent?" My Audrey Hepburn bit her lip in confusion at Kellan's pause over the line.

"No," he drawled. "Why did you think she was?"

"No reason," Winter squeaked out, her brows knitted into a deep frown. Marcie had told Winter Darren was her assignment, didn't she? Did she *say* she was the FBI?

I was troubled by this discovery too, but it really was the least of our worries. Marcie's mysterious purpose didn't even make the list.

"You don't need to stay in hiding anymore." Kellan's parting words flooded us with relief. "I've kept your gang out of any reports, and I'll do my best to submit your statements with no need for additional follow up. You will not be charged or implicated in any of Georgio's activities. Live your lives. I'll be in touch."

The grumpy giant hung up without awaiting a response, and we stared at the phone in stunned silence. The dark clouds above us were breaking up, and good weather was finally on the horizon.

"Whelp," Shane declared as he stood from his seat on the cushion beside me. "I don't know about you, but I'm going into town. Who's coming?"

"I'll go." Travis shot up from the couch.

"Me too." Logan still glared at the phone like it had offended him, but stood all the same. "I need to pick up some better shampoo. And you"—he shoved Shane as he moved past him—"need some mouthwash."

"Fuck you too, Pretty Boy." Shane said cheerily. "Road trip! You guys staying here?"

I settled into my corner of the couch and hugged Winter tighter to my chest. Cam flopped onto his side and sprawled out on the opposite end.

"Yeah, we'll stay here, man. Bring me back something nice." I winked and blew him a kiss. Shane caught it in the air and grinned.

"You got it, baby." He blew his own kiss at Winter and turned to leave.

"All right, fuckers!" he shouted out the door. "Who's going to hold my purse?"

CHAPTER 30

WINTER

Two firm, masculine bodies boxed me into the middle of the bed; their soft snores ruffled my hair and every few minutes, one of them would let out a contented sigh and hold me tighter.

It would be a marvelous den of comfort if Shane and Travis weren't so damn *hot*. I'd kicked off the covers, but it had only brought a brief reprieve.

We came upstairs to take a nap hours ago. The lightening sensation of pure relief had caused an adrenaline crash later in the day, and the two men laying beside me were the winners of whatever method they'd used—did anyone 'draw straws' anymore?—to have the honor of napping with me.

We were going to need to get a bigger bed. And I was going to need an air-conditioner.

Slowly, I uncurled my limbs from each of their holds and awkwardly shimmied down the mattress, eager for a cool shower. A large hand clasped my elbow.

"Where do you think you're going, Snow?"

Quick hauled me back up to his chest and kissed the shell of my ear.

"You guys are a jillion degrees," I complained, pushing against him with little luck. "I need space. And a popsicle."

Travis groaned at the sudden intrusion of movement and sound. "'S happening?" he mumbled, and he reached out, blindly wrapping an arm around my middle. "Where you goin', boo'ful?"

He swiftly fell back to sleep, his child-like face in slumber glowing with serenity. The man was beyond adorable in this state.

"I'll give you a popsicle." Shane stroked his steel erection against my ass and kissed my exposed shoulder. His fingers caressed my arm in feather-light touches, and a shiver of desire unfurled in my belly.

"Mmmmm." I murmured approval as his hand glided down my abdomen and stopped at the waistband of my shorts. "Tell me more."

I loved this playful, sexual side of Quick. To think we could have shared this part of ourselves years before now. Though, if we had, I probably wouldn't have found the rest of my men.

I didn't believe in woulda-shoulda-coulda. We were here now, as we were always meant to be.

"Think you can be quiet, Snow? Think I can fuck your tight pussy from behind with Travis right beside you?"

My nipples hardened to stone at his dirty words. Fuck yes.

I pressed my ass harder against his cock and he took that for the permission it was. Tucking his hand inside my shorts, he slid his fingers through my wetness.

"Fuck, baby, I love how wet you get for me. I'm not going to play with you right now. I need your pussy for a deep, hot, and dirty fuck. Can you handle that?"

"Mhmmm." My whimper was barely above a whisper, but I could feel my best friend's smile against my skin.

"Good girl."

He removed his hand and tugged my shorts down to my knees. He shifted his weight on the bed, slowly and carefully slid his own boxers down, and I soon felt the velvet head of his cock notched at my entrance from behind.

Quick was big, but I was gushing; his controlled movements slowly eased his length into me, and I basked in the feeling of being stuffed full.

For a moment, we just lay there, a lock and key finally put in their rightful places.

Without pulling out, he rocked into me; my walls clenched around him in pleasure. I closed my eyes, losing myself to the sensation of his subtle thrusts. Travis' arm still loosely draped around my chest as I swallowed each pant and gasp Quick's touch was pulling out of me. My arousal coated his cock and dripped between my thighs as he worked me toward a delicious release.

My eyes flew open when fingers circled my clit. I stared into the kiwi-green irises of my half-lidded boyfriend, whose forearm had settled over my pelvis, his thumb moving in slow, tortuous movements.

"So, this is what happens when I take a nap, huh, beautiful? You let another man fuck you without me?"

His sexy, playful half-asleep smirk as he watched me from beneath dark lashes set my insides on fire, and my walls clenched again.

"Oh, she likes that, Trav. She's holding me in a vise grip right now."

Quick let out a pained groan and adjusted his position, pulling out to thrust harder into me now that Travis was awake. His movements pressed me against Travis' body, and there was no hiding the hard tent in his pants.

"How do I join in, beautiful? Do I get a taste of your sweet pussy, too?"

Cue gushing and clenching. This unexpected wake up was going far better than a cool shower and a popsicle.

"Fuck, if she keeps responding that way, I'm going to come way too soon."

Quick thrust deeper and his labored breaths filled the room while I wriggled and moaned against him. Travis didn't take his eyes off me and strummed my clit like a symphony orchestra.

That was all it took. Their ministrations threw me off the cliff so fast, I was floating and weightless as I came back down to the earth below.

"Fuck, that was gorgeous, beautiful. I love watching Shane make you scream." Travis bit the shell of his lip ring, his eyes full of ravenous need; I felt the desperate pull to satiate his hunger.

My best friend abruptly pulled out of me and I mourned the loss. Travis shared a look with him over my shoulder. Then he gripped my hips and hauled my lower half toward him. He shoved down his pants and wasted no time thrusting hard into my eager, dripping cunt.

"Yes!" I cried out. He pulled my leg up over his hip to hit a deeper angle, his Prince Albert rubbing deliciously all along my walls to enhance my pleasure.

I gripped his shoulders and held on for dear life while he pounded into me like a voracious animal. His grunts and growls were nearly rabid as he worked me toward another toe-curling orgasm. My ass cheeks ground against Shane's still hard shaft as he held me steady for Travis' plundering of my pussy.

I writhed and squirmed and the familiar warmth in my lower belly grew into an atomic inferno. I was just about to detonate—then Travis stopped his thrusts altogether, his cock perfectly positioned, but doing nothing about it.

"What the–" My irritated growl halted in my throat when the cool glide of lube dripped onto my tight hole.

"Wanna be the filling in our sandwich, Snow?" Quick asked lazily as he massaged two fingers into my ass. "We're going to fuck you so thoroughly; we'll have to carry you downstairs."

He didn't give me any time for a comeback. He notched himself at my other entrance from behind, then pushed his cock past the tight ring of muscle until he was fully seated inside me.

"Fuck, that feels good." Travis buried his face in my hair as I adjusted to the most complete feeling of fullness. "Jesus, you're so tight."

"A fast and dirty fuck, Snow," Quick reminded me, then he pulled out, only to fill me once again. "Just remember to scream both names, or our feelings might get hurt."

Travis snorted and started moving inside me again; the two men thrust into me with an almost practiced rhythm, and the roiling ball of pleasure started expanding once more.

Their thrusts got harder, faster, more urgent as our grunts and groans and whimpers and whispered fucks became frantic. They controlled my body; used me for their own release. I was a vessel for their pleasure, and I was here for it.

I came first—the blissful high blacked my vision and muted all sounds as every muscle in my body contracted and turned to jelly in their arms.

Jets of Travis' hot cum filled me and Quick's release was only seconds behind. Their sated, sexy growls extended my orgasm until we all collapsed in a gooey pile.

A slow clapping of hands echoed from the doorway, and I picked up my heavy head to see Logan propped against the doorframe.

"Now that was a fucking show, Princess."

He sauntered into the room and sat on the edge of the bed, his eyes glimmering with aroused mischief.

"I just sent a picture to Cam and Drew, so you can bet they'll be up here in..."

A clambering of heavy feet on wooden stairs echoed down the hall.

"Now." Logan's grin was all smug satisfaction when Drew and Cam peered into the room, their lusting gazes equally starving.

I sunk back into the comfort of my two sexed-up men and grinned. What an afternoon this was turning out to be, indeed.

"Too late, boys." Quick's retort was muffled as he spoke into my hair. "All the fun's been had. Maybe next time."

"Like fuck." Logan grabbed my ankle and yanked me down the bed until I was a cradled ball in his arms.

"What do you say, Princess? Is there anything left in the tank for me? How about Cam and Drew?"

I wanted to say no; my body was just put through a wringer, spun out, and now hanging to dry—but the new wetness coating my thighs—along with Travis' cum, betrayed me.

"Drew," Logan ordered as he caught the new need blooming in my eyes. "You want a piece of this action? Get over here."

My bossy businessman positioned me on the end of the bed and spread my legs to expose my dripping pussy to the audience in the doorway.

Drew hesitantly walked forward, his eyes searching mine for permission. When he saw my nod and smile, he settled between my thighs and pulled down his swim trunks.

"Looking good, baby," Shane called from his position behind me.

Drew's ears turned pink, but he looked up and shot a sexy grin back at his boyfriend—our boyfriend; his devious little smile made me impossibly wetter.

He hovered at my entrance; his thick cock stood to attention and leaked beads of pre-cum as his gaze roved over my body.

"Take me, baby," I pleaded, widening my thighs even further. My coaxing snapped him out of his hesitation—he fisted himself and plunged into me so deep I let out an anguished cry.

Logan moved onto the bed, sitting on his knees right beside my head. He had removed his jeans and his stiff erection hovered above my lips.

"Can you take me like this, Princess?" His words were more like a taunt, a challenge instead of a plea.

Bastard.

Someone behind me scooted forward and held me upright against their chest, banding colorful arms around me. Travis. He held me at eye-level to Logan's cock. A pearl of pre-cum glistened on its head.

I grasped his shaft and stuck my tongue out, licking the salty drop from his tip and stroking over his slit. His shoulders trembled at the sensation. I sucked the head into my mouth and swirled my tongue around him in the way I knew he liked best. His groan was dark and sweet, and I relished giving him this kind of pleasure.

Drew continued pumping his hips into me, alternating between short, hard thrusts and long, drawn-out glides; each technique successfully built me higher, my tender walls and swollen lips eager to have him stuff me full, like the insatiable bitch I was.

Travis' hands had loosened, and he kneaded my breasts as I slurped and swallowed another man's cock.

"How does it feel to fuck in another man's cum?" Logan's snarky question didn't stop him from jutting his hips against my chin.

I didn't need to see Drew's face to know the shade of coral it turned.

"Really... good. Fuck, so good." As if to punctuate his admission, he let out a long, sexy groan and my walls fluttered against him.

The bed dipped. Shane appeared in my periphery at the end of the bed behind Drew.

"I'm going to take your ass, baby." He caressed Drew's muscular cheeks and lined his newly shiny cock up; Drew leaned over to give him better access. He stilled, and I stopped sucking Logan to give them the time they needed.

Drew shuddered when Shane entered his tight hole, his face slack-jawed at being so full. Shane gripped his shoulder and his thrust pushed Drew's body so deeply into mine, I would feel him for the rest of the week.

I had only done this once before. It had felt incredible then, but now that we were *all* 'all in', it felt even more amazing. Who could go back to boring missionary sex with one man now?

Not this girl.

Unperturbed by the newly formed sex-chain, Logan pressed himself back against my lips, and I opened wide to take him in. He fisted my hair in one hand and drove into my mouth, causing tears to form in the corners of my eyes. The orgy party *he* created was turning him on so badly, he was desperate to cum.

I let him use me, relaxing my throat so he could bottom out; tears continued to leak down my cheeks, and I lost myself in the sea of sensuous sex. Shane's thrusts into Drew that pushed him deep into me and the sound of their breathy groans and sexy-as fuck grunts. Logan's breathy pants as his thrusts become frenzied. Travis' thickening cock against my back.

Where was Cam?

Another large body settled into my other side—there he was. My sexy boxer's naked form cuddled into mine. His fingers trailed along my hips and brushed my clit between Drew's movements. The fresh sensation snapped firecrackers off behind my eyes; my orgasm hit so hard and fast I wasn't prepared for the blast of euphoria that rocketed through my chakras.

I arched out of Travis' hold and cried out around Logan's cock as he swelled against my tongue; bursts of hot, salty cum filled my throat, and I guzzled them greedily.

Shane's rhythm faltered and his frantic thrusts stuttered as he exploded with his release. Drew instantly followed him with his own ragged cry.

The room went quiet, save for the sounds of hoarse breathing and blissful sighs. Logan climbed off the bed and Drew gently pulled out of me, his cum leaking onto the sheets.

I sagged against Travis. My body was a pure puddle of orgasmic ecstasy, but I couldn't ignore the sword sticking into my backside.

And Cam—I wanted Cam to share in this moment with us. An impromptu bonding experience that would set the course for the rest of our sexual chemistry. I wanted them all to share in it.

I wanted them all to share *me*.

Drew and Shane moved to the armchairs on the other side of the room, and watched me with sated, half-lidded gazes. Logan leaned against the wall, his stare not breaking for a single moment.

They were waiting to see the finale. They were in this too.

Sorry, my tired, broken body. We had to do this. For science.

"I need you, Big Guy." I begged; the words barely coherent in my goopy pile of bliss. "Take me."

My gorgeous blue-eyed GQ model pursed his puffy lips and palmed his glistening erection. His stare darkened into one of a hunting predator.

"I'll take you, Little Violet."

I turned my head to Travis, drinking in his mussed-up sex hair and dancing eyes. "You too."

His face held surprise, but he quickly shifted me out of his arms and pushed me up.

"Hands and knees," he ordered, motioning Cam to lie down on the bed beneath me.

His taut boxer body did as Travis directed, and I wasted no time sinking down on Cam's solid length when he moved into the perfect position. His groan resonated through me when I rose and sunk back down, rocking my hips into his pubic bone.

I was so sensitive; we wouldn't be able to have another group-sex session for a little while, but I wasn't stopping until we'd all connected bodies, hearts, and souls.

Travis' hand pushed at my spine, bending me over, and lined up behind me. His lubed piercing forced its way through the ring of muscle before penetrating deep inside, taking my tender ass for the second time today.

Fuck me, he felt good. *They* felt good. I was on Cloud 9, over the moon, in seventh heaven ... and whatever other cliché could fit this feeling of completeness.

I didn't know if it was possible to come again, but I needed my men to walk away with pep in their step. I knew Cam liked to be tied up ... but would he enjoy being choked?

Tentatively, I wrapped my hands around my dark protector's throat and squeezed lightly. His eyes widened, but then fluttered closed in pleasure. I pressed a little harder; in response, he bucked his hips upward, driving into me with such force, I would have toppled off if Travis wasn't holding me steady from behind.

Choking was a 'yes,' then. We were going to explore all the possibilities with that little tidbit later.

I kept up the light pressure across his neck as Travis started a consistent rhythm from behind. Cam matched it from below, his thrusts pushing into me each time Travis pulled out. Once again, I was a vessel for my men's pleasure as they worked themselves to orgasm.

I couldn't tell you who came first; I had become an astral projection, floating above my body as the last crash of oxytocin and uncut bliss detonated around us like some hippy Viagra love bomb.

Cam and Travis stilled inside me, lavishing me in sweet kisses from all sides.

I was lifted off Cam and laid down on the bed like a delicate doll. Travis left the room and returned with a warm washcloth, taking the task of cleaning up the copious amounts of cum from every part of me seriously.

I whimpered when he brushed against my clit, the nub so raw I was truly going to need sexual bed rest for the foreseeable future.

Worth it.

I opened my eyes at the sound of Quick's boisterous laughter. His gaze had caught on Travis' naked body, the metal dick adornment on full display.

"Nice piercing, bro. Could poke an eye out with that thing."

Travis looked down at his penis jewelry and back up at him with a slow, scandalous smile.

"Nah, man. I just poke out orgasms."

His errant comment caused me to erupt into a fit of choked giggles. Within seconds, all six of us dissolved into peals of uninhibited laughter.

That lightness carried us through the evening and into the next day. We were here, we were whole, and while our future remained unknown, we would see it through together.

That was more than enough for me.

"What do you mean, 'it's our house'?"

Hillary casually lounged on the teak wooden daybed beside me as we watched the boys play volleyball in her pool.

Or apparently, they were playing in *our* pool, since this was *our* house.

"It's pretty straightforward, Winter," my beautiful blond best friend said airily as she shifted her floppy sun hat to cover more of her face. "Logan said you were looking at houses in this general area. I found a house that met all of your criteria, and I bought it. For you."

I let her words sink in. This beautiful home did meet all our criteria; the large detached garage would fit all the boys' toys; the private enclosed pool for Shane's proposed orgy parties; six large bedrooms all on one level, all with their own attached baths; a huge open kitchen and living area for us to spend real time together, and a home office space for Logan.

In fact, now that I thought about it, I truly was an idiot. Why would Hillary own a home in Brenton, of all places? My bestie was random, and richer than God, but even that was a stretch.

"Hill, there's no way in hell that we c—"

"Before you protest," she interrupted me with a perfectly manicured pointer finger in the air, "I'm going to put something into context for you." She turned to face me, moving her hat to peer over at me with one exposed eye.

"Because of dear old Granny's will, Logan lost out on a little over 300 million in assets."

I choked on my martini with an astonished gasp. There's no way Hillary had *that* much money. Did she?

No, that was beyond richer than God. That was Richard Branson kind of money.

As if hearing my thoughts, she removed her hat completely and stared me down. "Yes, I have that much money. The least I can do is buy you and Logan and your hottie harem a house. If you don't like it, we'll sell it and find you a new one."

She turned back to the pool again and delicately placed the straw—or was it spun gold?—hat back over her face. "Don't insult me, Winter. It's a gift. Just name your first-born child after me or something."

I blew out a pained breath and shook my head, knowing that resisting anything Hillary had her mind set on was a futile endeavor. Even if I was still completely floored she had bought us a *house*.

What the fuck do I get her for her birthday now?

"Any word from Kellan?" I asked instead, eager to hear more news about her tryst with the big man.

I had more than enough boyfriends, but Hillary deserved her fresh shot at happiness now that she wasn't saddled with the weight of her 'daddy's' expectations and back-corner marriage deals with a man she didn't love. She'd filed their divorce papers yesterday and was on the fast track to becoming a free agent. Apparently, that had included a micro-minute sexcapade with Kellan.

"No, and I don't expect to." She shrugged dismissively. "I'll find another blond Viking man to join my imagined harem."

Hmmm. Wasn't that an intriguing thought?

"Come on in, babe!" Drew interrupted, his voice barely audible over the cacophony of whoops and splashes.

"Yeah, Snow!" Quick piped up. "Come on in and we'll play a different game." His suggestive smile left no illusions as to the games he wanted to play.

"Shane!" Hillary snatched the hat off her face and glowered with the heat of a thousand suns. "Don't you dare.

There will be no orgies or fuck-fests within my view plane while I'm here. I will gut you."

My sexy, tanned drink of water enjoyed playing with fire, and today he was going to get a sunburn.

"Awww, is Hilly Willy not getting any action?" Shane tied his hair up into a ponytail and stuck out his tongue. "Lighten up, Hill! I was going to suggest water polo."

"Naked water polo." Logan's grin was all teeth in a rare show of solidarity with my exuberant boyfriend. "Strip for us, Princess."

"That's it, I'm out." Hillary snatched her phone and cover-up from the side table and stalked into the house, muttering about my 'insufferable assholes' under her breath.

"We're waiting, beautiful." Travis leaned against the pool's edge, his back to the concrete and his arms spread wide. His gaze wandered lazily over my royal blue bikini with blatant interest.

"Let's play some water polo, baby girl." Drew tossed the volleyball up in the air and caught it one-handed. "I'd like the chance to win another bet."

Shane shot him a scheming little grin and blew a kiss at him.

Cam swam to the edge closest to me and held out a hand. "Come on in, Little Violet. Play with us."

I took in the view before me—five beautiful souls who'd found it in their hearts to love me.

Shane—my Quick—my brilliant best friend; the man who already had my heart but could never have my body was finally mine—mind, body, and soul. I cherished his zest for life and impenetrable optimism.

Travis—my hottie bartender; the sexier than sin liar who'd made it his mission to keep me—and he did. I admired his selflessness and willingness to do whatever it took to protect those he loved. We would smother him with the love he'd never received from his own blood.

Drew—my innocent boy-next-door who I'd crushed on for years. The all-American football star was finally discovering who he was, and I loved the man he was becoming. His openness and ability to take things in stride kept me in check.

Cam—my sweet, southern gentlemen whose darkness couldn't be tamed; his darkness was his bloodline, but the calm, centered man before me had found his home with us. He instilled in me a sense of comfort and peace from his stoic stillness and quiet grace.

Logan—my bastard pretty-boy millionaire who had once wanted to destroy me. Turned out, he instead vanquished my enemy with a fierce vengeance. There was nothing he wouldn't do to guard the sanctity of the beautiful family we'd chosen in each other. I accepted his past, and would celebrate his future as a healthier, happier man.

They each held my heart in their grasp; my soul in their grip; my essence in their blood.

I rose from my seat and shed my towel. Padding over to Cam's outstretched hand, I squeezed it in my own.

Our days and nights alone had come to an end.

I couldn't wait for our new beginnings.

EPILOGUE

WINTER

6 Years Later

"Fuck off, Logan."

I shot him an exasperated glare from the loveseat on one side of our living room.

Logan just smirked at me, his eyes dancing with amusement behind his sexy Clark Kent glasses.

"To love me is to love all of me, Princess. And Johnson knows he's a pansy with his romance books."

"He's a very generous lover, actually. Maybe *you* should read some romance books." I tossed a pen at him from my side table, but he caught it gracefully in the air.

"Oh, Princess, you know I'm nothing if not generous." He spun the pen around in his fingers. "Should I prove it to you? I've got"—he glanced at his watch— "twenty minutes. Nothing but time."

He waggled his eyebrows tauntingly, but I wouldn't take the bait. I had places to be today too.

"There's some romance in our Manga collection," Shane quipped from the couch. "Don't be shy, Loggie-bear. I saw some dried tears on the pages of my latest *Yona of the Dawn*."

"Don't call me that." Logan glowered, shooting daggers in Shane's direction.

But he didn't deny it.

Cam was perched on the overstuffed armchair in the corner by our stone fireplace, his nose stuck in his own book. "I just finished *War and Peace*," he mused thoughtfully, peeking up at us behind the pages before concentrating on *Of Mice and Men* again. "Does that count as a romance?"

Drew's face was a mask of mock horror. "*That's* your idea of romance? How did you snag Winter again?"

"I'm a Southern boy, Drew," he said dryly as he turned the page. "Romance is a school subject where I'm from. I don't need your books."

Drew's ears turned pink, but he stood tall and puffed out his chest. "I don't *need* them either. I *like* them. And Winter likes them too."

He winked at me and settled into the other cushion next to Shane, pecking him on the lips before handing him a steaming mug of coffee.

"Cam listens to opera too," Quick added, with a mock-solemn nod. "Opera is the music of heartbreak, isn't it, Big Guy?"

"No," Cam intoned passively, not even glancing up from his reading. "It's not."

"I read one of Winter's polyamory books recently." Travis walked in with two steaming mugs of his own and handed one to me with my own tender kiss.

I smiled at him appreciatively and took a long swallow.

"Really?" Shane perked up, eager to hear all the gossip, as usual.

"Yeah." Travis shrugged and settled into the space beside me. "I mean, it's our life, isn't it? I was curious."

"And?" My best friend-turned-lover leaned forward in his seat. "What's the verdict? Some good boinkage? Everybody getting their boink on?"

Drew snorted beside him and Cam shook his head with a thinly veiled grin. Only Quick would say the word 'boink' with the utmost seriousness.

"Lots of group sex, yeah. One scene even had TVP, and I gotta tell you, I don't think it's possible." He wrinkled his nose and grimaced, and I grimaced along with him.

Three dicks in one hole. Ouch.

"Oh, it's possible," Logan chimed in. "But I think you'd need something to hang from to really get in there."

As the five guys debated the logistics of how a TVP situation could work, I sat back and watched the beautiful men who made up our family.

Shane had let his hair grow long, and it hung down his back in a beautiful herring bone braid today. When WAQ was restructured under new ownership and management, he officially left the company to pursue his master's and then immediately after, his Ph.D. He was now a professor working toward tenure at Sequoia State University. I had never seen my handsome best friend so exuberant as when he was talking about his lessons or his students. He was made to teach, and his students were lucky to have him.

Cam had started his own carpentry business. Despite his master's degree in poli sci, he'd decided he got more satisfaction from working with his hands. Chase Carpentry now had six employees. The firm specialized in custom trim work and design. He came home from work in a good mood almost every night, and it soothed my soul to see my brooding boy so calm.

He still fought to keep his anger out of his daily life, though. Logan had a circuit set up in the basement, and they sparred together at least once a week. When they were feeling brave, the other three would have a go, but it wasn't often. They enjoyed keeping their teeth intact.

Travis had enrolled in college as soon as we had settled in to our new lives. He'd taken business courses and graduated top of his class. His mother lived long enough to watch him cross the graduation stage, and he told me afterward it was the proudest moment of his life. She passed away a few months later from disease complications. Travis had mourned her loss, but I think secretly, he found relief in the fact she wasn't suffering anymore. Scleroderma was a terrible illness.

Devon disappeared once Georgio was imprisoned. Travis thought he might have gone on a bender and either lived on the streets or had died from an overdose. He occasionally went out to the darker parts of Carlisle to search for him with Cam or Logan at his side. But so far, he hadn't turned up. It wasn't something we spoke about—the regrets were still too raw for Travis to face, and it might always be that way.

Drew, Logan, Travis, and I had combined our business skills and natural talents and opened up a series of clubs all over Sequoia County. Drew headed up the dining aspect, Travis managed the bars, I oversaw the entertainment, and Logan was Chief of Operations. We'd opened one club at a time, tweaking and experimenting as we built. Now we had four locations, and plans to open three more over the next five years.

My favorite was Club Quintessence. It was the epitome of elegance. We took all the things we loved about Bourbon & Blues and made them our own. Royal blue and gold were our club colors, each building ornately decorated to create a roaring twenties vibe. Hillary had her hand in designing each space, and I wasn't disappointed.

Logan kept his head in the books and was our wheeler-and-dealer, building business relationships, and keeping our operations running smoothly. He'd stayed clean but kept his distance when the clubs were in full swing; the pull to use would never completely go away, and we all did what we could to support him.

Occasionally, I made an appearance to sing with our regular bands when I was in the area, but that was a rarity these days. I had other things on my plate.

I looked down at my swelling belly and shifted uncomfortably in my seat.

Children weren't something I'd ever considered. Not that I *didn't* want them. I just hadn't thought about it. I hadn't aspired to be a mother, and seeing how all of us had been betrayed by at least one of our parents, I hadn't expected the guys to want children, either.

It came up in conversation one night while watching a movie. I can't remember how, but it was Drew who'd said he looked forward to seeing me pregnant.

The statement had shocked me so much, I'd nearly choked to death on my popcorn. It brought up a pretty raucous debate. Drew and Shane wanted children, Travis was a hesitant neutral, and Cam and Logan were firmly on the 'no' fence.

I couldn't blame them—both men didn't want their DNA polluting our unborn child, even though they were incredible men who hadn't let their unfortunate parentage define their own lives. Still, they wouldn't budge.

Other than their adulthood discoveries, Shane and Drew both had good upbringings with siblings and family meals, and all the scenarios that would be featured on a Christian family pamphlet. They were both excited at the prospect of being fathers, and I knew in my heart, they'd be amazing dads, but it hadn't been enough to sway me to their side.

I was with Travis. At that point, we had just started our business. Shane and Travis were still in school, and we had no idea what the future held, other than we wanted it to be together.

So, we tabled our family planning talk to get our lives in order. Then, when we finally did, life didn't give us a choice, anyway. Some defect in my birth-control had gotten me pregnant.

I was sure the five shots of strong sperm I was getting on a regular basis had nothing to do with it.

It took a little while for everyone to be accustomed to the surprise, but my men had warmed up more quickly to it than I'd thought; more quickly than me, even. Once we were all on board, we'd agreed we wouldn't get a DNA test and would let it all play out naturally.

These men were all fathers, regardless of genetics. Given how different my men looked, I was pretty sure we'd be able to tell without a test, anyway.

It had taken a little while to establish a true family dynamic, but we'd gotten there. It was hard to navigate six relationships among six people, but through continuous communication and the willingness to be vulnerable, we'd made it through. We still had our fair share of fights and gripes that any family had, but in the end, our commitment to each other never wavered.

We couldn't legally marry on this side of the world, so Logan had surprised us with a trip two years ago to Nepal, where polyamory was a legally recognized relationship. We'd exchanged commitment rings on a stunning cliff edge overlooking a Nepalese valley, confessing our vows to two villagers and the tree-tops from hundreds of feet above.

Drew and Shane professed their own oaths to each other and exchanged rings they wear on their right hands.

It was the most magical moment of my life.

Travis kissed the side of my head and pulled me from my reminiscing. "I'm going with you this morning." He eyed the clock on the wall behind me. "We'll have to leave in the next half hour. You ready?"

Today was my twenty-week ultrasound. Shane had championed an arm-wrestle battle to determine who was going with me; I had told them in no uncertain terms was I bringing five men into a gynecologist's office. To everyone's disbelief, Travis won. He'd confessed to me later that he and Devon used to arm-wrestle all the time, so he was well practiced. The sadness never left his eyes when he spoke of his brother.

After a round of kisses goodbye and two pee breaks, we entered the four-door garage.

I'd kept Basil in tip-top shape, and drove him whenever I could. I bought Travis an upgrade as soon as he'd graduated—it would have been years sooner, but his pride wouldn't let me get him a new car until I practically threatened divorce if he didn't accept one as a graduation present. His shiny black Jeep Cherokee beeped in the driveway.

"We're taking my car," he joked, as we made our way to his vehicle. "We're going to go broke if you get any more speeding tickets."

I gave him the finger and stuck out my tongue, but said nothing. I *had* racked up quite a few recently. I paid them, at least.

"Have you called your parents yet?" he asked as I buckled up.

"Not yet. I'll call them after we get the results."

Dad and Emmett had gotten reduced sentences and early parole for good behavior. Mom and I had gotten closer while Dad served his time. She now had a very regular presence in my life. Once we could see past our detached history, I even discovered I *liked* Miranda Wallace. She had a wicked sense of humor and could give some really sound advice when the poly dynamic felt too challenging to navigate.

Amelia had spoken to Shane at length about his father and his transgressions. Over time, she'd convinced him to give his father another chance. Their relationship was still strained, but he could understand the guilt Emmett had harbored over Brenda's death. I was secretly hoping their new grandchild would be the key to bringing them back to the father-son duo they'd always been.

Drew's parents didn't understand our lifestyle, and it took a while for them to accept their son coming out as bisexual with both a male and female partner. They were happy for him though, and his sisters were ecstatic about the prospect of being 'aunties'.

I had forgiven Dad a long time ago. He'd paid the price for his choices, and after I had compromised my own ethics in Georgio's web, I could see that slippery slope for what it was. I wouldn't punish my father or myself for the rest of my life. We'd all suffered enough.

When my parents heard they were having a grandchild, Mom screamed with excitement and Dad's grin was the widest I had ever seen. Tears streamed down both their faces and they immediately started throwing out baby names. I was going to have to set some boundaries; I had a feeling we'd be getting lots of unannounced visits.

Darlene had also been ecstatic, or as we called her these days, Momma D. We'd set her up in an apartment close by, and she'd gotten a job at a new insurance company, working her way up to manager in three years. She'd changed her name again since Antonio was alive and still very much doing business in our part of the world, but with Kellan monitoring things for us, we didn't live with a target on our backs.

The Viking Spy was pretty much radio silent, though he checked in with Cam or Travis every few months, and we were now far enough removed from Cascade Falls we had no interaction at all with the twins. I only heard about Kellan through Hillary—they had continued their 'on-again, off-again' *thing*. As much as she was totally willing to discuss his dick size, she was very tight-lipped about anything else. I already knew how big his dick was, so there was nothing to talk about.

Stanley Eccles had been missing since the FBI ransacked his home and found it empty. Camden made a mysterious plea deal that wasn't public knowledge, and even Hillary couldn't dig up that dirt on her father. She'd bought out all of his companies since he could no longer own the assets, and kicked him off of all the governing boards. She sat on her throne of billions, but I knew she was battling her own demons. I didn't get to see my friend nearly as much as I wanted to, and I missed her.

She'd shipped me thousands of dollars' worth of baby stuff already; so much so, we had to store it all in the basement. I was going to have to put a moratorium on baby gifts, or we were going to need a new house. And she had gifted us the house!

Georgio had met his demise in the showers at the maximum-security prison he was sentenced to. I didn't know which Carlos' brother arranged the hit, but I'd bet my spleen it was an inside job. I was grateful Travis and Cam had nothing to do with that side of the family. The Carlos clan were toxic, twisted creatures who caused nightmares and ate children in bedtime stories.

Speaking of toxic, twisted creatures; Carson Baker was attacked by his cellmate at the jailhouse in Carlisle before he could even be sentenced. He suffered a bad brain bleed from blunt force trauma, and no longer controlled his mental or physical faculties. He was a vegetable and I couldn't bring myself to be sad about it. He had earned his end, and Karma was a feisty bitch.

Travis held my hand as we drove, stroking my fingers lightly and humming a light tune.

I loved seeing him happy, the most tragic hero of our motley bunch. He, Logan, and I had enrolled in counseling once everything died down with Georgio's arrest. Carson had reopened my wounds. The almost-murder had reopened Travis'. And Logan never got the closure he'd needed from Stanley's abuse. The cascade of lies in our small town brought us together and forged a love more fortified than any castle or kingdom, but Georgio had branded himself on our souls.

Luckily, therapy works, and today most of what we went through was a distant memory. But Travis held onto those scars the most.

"Ready?" he asked as he helped me climb out of the vehicle.

"Ready." I smiled and gazed into his kiwi-green eyes, basking in their hope and joy and wonder.

I hadn't just found one love to last a lifetime, I'd found five. It was time for this next chapter in our lives to share that incredible love with someone new.

And I was ready for it.

About the author

One day, Cora Flynn decided to sit down and write a book – for funzies.

What started as a fun project on maternity leave became an entirely new adventure between the pages of her created worlds; complete with characters who've become her best friends, an abundance of book boyfriends, beautiful bromances, and story plots that keep her up at night.

When she's not writing, Cora attempts to manage the chaos of a two-toddler household with her extremely patient husband, while maintaining a job in the 'real world.' She loves reading as many books as she can fit on her Kindle, her bookshelves, and her nightstand, and doesn't discriminate against any genre, although reverse harem will always be her favorite.

Come on and join the fun on Instagram and TikTok by following @coraflynnauthor.

www.ingramcontent.com/pod-product-compliance
Lightning Source LLC
Chambersburg PA
CBHW020230010826
48973CB00006B/1444